* * * * * * * * * * *

Follow and "LIKE" Isles End on Facebook

http://www.facebook.com/IslesEndThriller

* * *

Purchase Additional Copies at amazon.com

* * * * * * * * * * *

Isles End

A Spiritual Thriller

By J. H. F. White

BHB
*** Bome-Biv Harbor Books ***

ISBN-13: 978-1463519315

* *

The town of Isles End is where Harry starts over, but a woman, a human cloning operation, and an old chest, create complications.

* *

* *

Dedicated to:
Benjamin
Joseph
Reuben
Olivia
&
Yoho

"I have another story for you . . . are you ready?"

"Oh Ho!"

* * * * * * * * * * * * * * * * *

A special thanks to Patricia,
whose support, input and patience
helped me complete this project.

* * * * * * * * * * * * * * * * * * *

This novel is a work of fiction. The characters, incidents, names, dialogue, and plot, are the products of the author's imagination and are entirely fictitious. Any resemblance to actual persons, places, companies, or events is purely coincidental. The story is metaphorical and not to be taken literally.

* * * * * * * * * * *

EDITING
Arlyn Lawrence
Olivia White
Ivan Amberlake

* * * * * * * * * * *

Cover Design By Graphic Artist: Michelle Varma
services@mavtechnologies.com

CHAPTERS

1
Harry Turner

There were rumors about whether the fire on Ivory Lane had been an accident. No one in the small rural town of Isles End really knew, but it did seem suspicious that the old place had burned down just after it was sold. It was sad, too. The home had been a lovely dwelling with steep pitched gables, gingerbread siding, and a small turret on the front corner facing the street. Nearly a hundred years old, its unique architecture had been well-maintained by the old woman who had lived there for so many years.

Now the new owner would collect the insurance money, demolish what was left of the place, and build something contemporary to blend in with the rest of the neighborhood. A local insurance agent referred him to one of the more reliable small builders he knew: Harry Turner, of H.T. Construction.

Having lived in Isles End for only a year, Harry already went about his routines like an established local. He had stumbled into the town entirely by accident and found himself drawn to it immediately. The truth was, he had been ready to settle for almost anything anywhere that could help him put the past behind him and move on with his life. To move on—*that* would be a most welcome beginning.

"Hey, Harry! Cup o' coffee?"

Harry looked up from the driver's seat of his old red pick-up. An older, rustier version of his truck had just pulled up beside him, a Styrofoam cup dangling from the open window.

"Yeah, great," Harry answered. He remained seated and casually observed two men step out in front of what was left of the Ivory Lane home.

"Thanks for thinking of me," he greeted them from his cab.

Ed Cromwell was a self-employed jack of all trades and master of none. He was always interested in taking on side work and jumped at the chance to help Harry with this project. Harry hadn't met the other fellow yet, but the guy looked strong.

Ed sauntered over to Harry's truck with the coffee. "Looks like we got the extra-large dumpster," he gestured toward the heavy looking container that had recently been deposited in front of the site. "Here ya go, Harry."

"Yeah," Harry said, accepting the cup. "I guess an empty dumpster in front of the job site makes it official."

In the background, the other man was busy adjusting his cap and fidgeting with his tool belt.

"Why don't you guys go ahead and get started—I'll join you in a minute."

Ed nodded and turned back toward the daylight side of the old foundation.

Harry activated his cell phone and clipped it onto his belt. He took a moment to study himself in the visor mirror. The image reflected his dark brown eyes and broad forehead, divided by his strong, angular nose. He'd always thought his nose was too big, but Jenny had said it was one of the very things that had drawn her to him. With this thought, he smiled. His dark hair and unshaven face gave him a rugged appearance. His smile faded as he attempted to comb his hair with his fingers. *You'll never get a date looking like this, pal.* Not that he had any prospects, but maybe he was ready to consider the idea.

Harry sipped his coffee and realized he'd allowed himself to think about Jennifer. He needed to stop doing that, but letting go of her was still hard. Staying home had become the easy thing to do, but just because he was slightly introverted didn't mean he was a hermit. It might take some effort but he committed himself again to the task of meeting new people, women in particular. Self-confidence had not always been a concern when it came to the opposite sex, but oftentimes he either felt awkward or just didn't have a lot to say.

With Jennifer it had been different. She had always been easy to talk to, and seemed to know just what it took to draw him out. Aside from Jenny, he felt clumsy around most women one-on-one. And what only added to the problem, after the accident, were his old friends who kept trying to set him up with prospects long before he was ready. Fortunately, he *was* confident in himself and his work and was quite content to focus on that. He didn't feel the need to hurry into any relationship.

When he flipped the visor back up, two photos slid out and landed on his lap. One was of Jennifer and the other, his

11

sister, Gwen. They were his two girls. He'd forgotten they were up there. The picture of Gwen went back under the visor and the one of Jennifer in the glove box. Gwen had been a good older sister to Harry, even though she fussed over him too much. She would call and remind him that it was over a year now and time to move on with life. He assured her regularly that if the right opportunity came along, he would know it. He explained that he still had some things to work through. She would say, "There are other girls out there like Jenny. You just need to find someone else like her."

No sis, sorry . . . but there will never be anyone like Jennifer.

The sound of an air compressor forced Harry's attention back to the job. He could see that Ed and the other fellow had extension cords and tools all laid out next to the freshly deposited dumpster. It was a huge thing: sixteen feet long, eight feet wide, and taking up most of the driveway. With all the rubbish, he knew they would haul away several loads. He stepped out of his truck and pulled on his work gloves.

"Harry, I'd like you to meet Butch," Ed called out, patting the other man roughly on the back. "The second guy I had lined up didn't show, but Butch here, he can do the work of two men, no problem!"

"Thanks, Ed! Thanks a lot!" Butch frowned. Then a big smile formed on his coarse face as he shook Harry's hand.

Harry couldn't help but notice Butch's one heavy

12

eyebrow, which grew widely across his large forehead and looked like it could be combed. His face was like a bulldog, big and round, with the possibility of becoming mean-looking if necessary.

Harry smiled back at the hardy fellow. "Nice to meet you, Butch. I'm glad you're here—as you can see, we have a lot of work ahead of us." Harry glanced at what was left of the building and back at the two men. "So, you guys ready to tear into this?"

"Only if we have to," Ed responded, laughing a little too hard and then gaining control.

"Great," Harry continued, "Let's start down here at the basement—see if we can get the bulk of it loaded into the bin before the day is over."

The dumpster had been backed up close to the daylight side of the basement where the three men quickly knocked out a worn pair of French doors and a section of the wall. Now, they had plenty of room to move the material from the basement out to the dumpster. They worked vigorously. Starting near the opening, they began hauling out pieces of damaged furniture, old mattresses and box springs, curtains and raggedy rugs, all soaked and covered with ashes and bits of insulation and plaster. There were remnants of bookcases and books all around, burnt and saturated with water—most of which had come crashing through the ceiling when the floor burned through, piled in heaps over the rest of the rubble. Further in, a baby grand piano lay crippled on its back, a gaping hole in what was left of the ceiling above.

Behind it, an old sea chest—bound with leather straps and adorned with fancy brass hinges, corners, and latches—sat seemingly unscathed. The more they hauled out, the more Harry wondered whether there might be something of value to be discovered amongst all the junk.

The three men worked well together. By noon, the trash bin was nearly full and Harry figured they'd be ready for another one soon. He called in the order on his cell phone and decided to break for lunch. They quickly devoured their meals and were back to work, filling the remainder of the dumpster just in time to have it hauled away and an empty one left in its place.

The rest of the day went slower. As they cleared a path deeper into the back rooms of the basement, they found areas where the contents of the entire upper floor had come crashing down to literally fill the rooms to the ceilings. Whatever hadn't burned was locked into a compressed and tangled mess.

As five o'clock approached, Ed and Butch decided they would get the piano out of the house and then call it a day. Now that they had cleared a path to the baby grand, it was a simple matter of getting the thing onto a wheeled platform and rolling it out.

As the three men gathered around, Butch nodded toward the chest. "Check that out—looks like an old pirate chest."

Ed stepped over to it. "Let's move it over just a bit—get a little more room around this piano." He moved his small wiry body into position, then lifted his leg up, rested his foot against the side of the chest, and gave it a shove. It barely moved. He recoiled and nearly fell over.

"Shiver me timbers," he said in his best pirate voice. "That thing's heavy!"

"Let me give it a try," Butch said pushing his way past the others. He grabbed hold of it with his well-muscled arms and heaved. He managed to force it out of the way just far enough to make more room for the piano, then let out a loud groan as he nearly lost his balance.

Harry smiled at Butch and then gave Ed a wink. "You guys read the small print in the contract, right?" he said in a mock serious tone.

Butch bought the line. "What contract?" He looked back and forth from Ed to Harry with a curious expression on his face.

"I guess I forgot to show it to you, Butch," Ed frowned, playing along with whatever Harry was concocting.

Harry continued. "Well, I'm talking about the part where you forfeit your share of *any* pirate treasure. That includes any gold or silver, doubloons or pieces of eight that are found on any jobsite."

Butch scowled immediately. "Okay . . . yeah, right! Let's just get this thing outta here so I can go home, that is, if it's okay with you two mates?"

The other two chuckled as they positioned themselves around the piano and lifted it up while Butch slid the platform underneath. Soon they had it up and outside, next to the dumpster.

"On that note," Butch said, brushing himself off, "I'm ready to hit the road. Are we done?" He looked at Ed with a hopeful expression.

"You guys don't want to bust that chest open?" Ed coaxed.

"I don't have time to play explorer in a basement full of junk," Butch scowled. "I gotta be someplace."

"It's not going anywhere," Harry intervened.

"Alright, I think we're good for the day," Ed answered, and then turned to Harry. "What's the plan for tomorrow, boss?"

"Tomorrow's Saturday, Ed! Take the weekend off and I'll see you guys here on Monday, bright and early."

"Oh, yeah," Ed grinned, climbing into his truck where Butch was already waiting. Looking back, Ed added, "Hey, Boss, don't work too late now, ya hear? There's a whole *five* days in the next week."

"I'll see you guys," Harry said as Butch waved. He watched the rusty truck cruise to the top of Ivory Lane, and disappear. Turning back toward the basement, he let out a sigh.

Alone again, dark thoughts came creeping in. He was still having trouble at times just getting the headline from the news story out of his mind. It had been over a year now since the accident and there were still many nights when all he could see when he closed his eyes was "Plane Goes Down—Three Perish in Tragedy." Over time, it had become like a song in his head, a cruel nursery rhyme playing over and over again. They had been the three people he'd loved most; now they were gone forever. He'd never had the chance to say good-bye, at least not a final good-bye to their faces. *Good-bye, Mom and Dad. I love you! Have a great time. Good-bye Jennifer, my love! My beautiful fiancée! See you when you get back . . .*

When you get back!

But they would never be coming back.

The sad thing was that the accident had been just a simple malfunction of the instrument panel, nothing wrong with the pilot or the plane. The gas gauge had read "full." They had simply run out of fuel and had nowhere to land.

Plane Goes Down—Three Perish in Tragedy.

The pain that Harry couldn't seem to escape reminded him regularly that life was not fair. There were dark times when Harry wished he'd been up there with them. Many nights he had spent lying in bed fantasizing through the whole scenario, even down to the final words they might have spoken as they saw the ground rush up to meet them during their last moments. Sometimes he wished the headlines had read: *Plane Goes Down—*Four *Perish in Tragedy.*

The first several months had not been easy. Harry worked for a large construction company and returned to work soon after the accident, pretending he was okay. Each day he would carefully step around the gaping well of his grief, and every night he would fall into it. His motions were mechanical—a routine of

17

repetitive work and tasteless meals, quietly receiving the well-intended wishes of friends and co-workers by day, and dropping exhausted onto the couch by night with the television on until he drifted off into a restless sleep. Each day forced itself into his life like an unwelcome stranger, as he quietly wrestled through the anguish and emptiness of each moment alone.

The first few months passed by slowly, but Harry was determined to stay focused and make the best of his circumstances. He was used to keeping busy and, when he wasn't, he got used to being alone. He kept in touch with his sister, Gwen, who checked in with him regularly.

After moving to Isles End, he bought a small home with a portion of the inheritance money, secured a contracting license, and soon had a list of reliable contacts. He met Bob Moore, the insurance agent overseeing the Ivory Lane project, and before long the agency was referring him to clients on a regular basis.

Now, Harry stood in front of the burned-down home. There was little to salvage. He realized he had underestimated the clean-up. Much of the damage had been from the fire and smoke—the rest was from the water it had taken to put the fire out. The old woman must have traveled around the world collecting things like she was attending a giant garage sale. Now her collection was just a mess to be hauled away before rebuilding could begin.

Except for the chest. I wonder what's in that thing . . .
Harry decided to take Ed's advice and call it a day. On his final

walk-through, Harry went back into the basement to where the baby grand had been. Off to the side sat the chest, now looking rather conspicuous. He whispered to himself under his breath. "Nothing valuable so far, except maybe that—" Stepping closer, he leaned over and quietly spoke, "Pieces of eight." He repeated it again a couple of times, the way a parrot might sound. Feeling a bit silly, he looked around self-consciously as though someone could be listening. Then, putting his foot up on the edge of the chest like Ed had done, he gave it a shove. Again, it hardly budged.

There's no way this thing's going into the dumpster until I know what's in it.

He hurried out to his truck and quickly returned with a hammer and a crow bar.

This can't be too difficult!

With one end of the crow bar and the claw end of the hammer, Harry began working the padlock, twisting it to the left and to the right, and then pulling it out away from the lid and back toward the chest. It started to loosen a bit, but was not going to snap apart like he'd hoped. He didn't want to ruin the latch. The whole thing was in great shape and someone might like to keep it.

He had another idea. He went back out to his truck and returned with a reciprocating saw which he plugged into a nearby extension cord. Placing a scrap of wood under the lock, Harry bore down with the metal blade. This was working! With a steady hand, he continued to press into the lock bolt. The sharp steel blade slowly carved a clean path straight through the metal until it finally snapped apart.

"Okay, let's see what we've got in here," Harry said aloud. The lock swiveled open easily in his hand as he turned it and slid it through the latch. He paused and looked around nervously again.

What am I worried about?

It was the mystery of not knowing what he would find that was getting under his skin. There was probably nothing unusual inside the old crate. It was getting dark outside and he was suddenly aware of the unfamiliar surroundings. His mind began to wander. What if the trunk *was* full of gold or riches? Or maybe a body stuffed inside, old and decayed, or worse— a fresh body! Now his thoughts raced.

He dropped the lock. It made a dull thud on the concrete floor. He packed up the saw and the extension cord and carried them outside to the back of his pick-up. Looking around, he could see lights flickering on from nearby homes. The properties were large and private, with alders, firs, and hemlock keeping most of the homes well-hidden. Someone had been careful not to take too many trees out when they did the clearing, and now they were giants.

Feeling less tense now, Harry walked back into the basement and over to the chest. He heard something and stiffened. It was only a car passing by, but he still waited. Had someone pulled into the driveway? Now it was quiet. Ignoring his apprehension, Harry knelt down next to the chest, placed both hands on the front of the lid, and lifted it up. It opened easily. He tipped it back until the leather straps on each side became tight and held the lid in place. He peered down into the dark cavity of the box.

"Hello there!" came a voice.

2
The Chest

A strange sensation moved through Harry, like a strong breeze accompanied by an unusual scent. He dropped the lid down and turned around straining to find the source of the voice. In the darkness where the French doors had been, there stood the figure of a man wearing a full-length overcoat and a brown fedora tilted slightly on his head.

"I've obviously startled you," the deep voice offered. "My apologies."

Harry straightened himself, trying to regain his composure. The man moved closer and the dim light bulb revealed his face.

"I'm Reese Orchard. I spoke with Bob Moore from the insurance agency and he said I might find you here. I'm the new owner of this mess. You must be Harry Turner?"

Harry relaxed a bit, stepped forward, and extended his hand. "Yes, hello—nice to meet you." He tried to give his best construction-guy handshake but it came out weak. "Bob said you would be stopping by soon to take a look at the place."

"Yes," the tall man replied. "I wasn't sure if you would be here this late, but I was in the area . . ."

Reese took off his hat and rested it on a nearby ledge. He was a large man with broad shoulders—well-dressed, clean-shaven, and very smooth-looking.

Moving toward the center of the room, Reese peered at all the debris and probed around a bit with the toe of his shoe. He bent forward as he moved around, to avoid bumping his head on anything hanging down from the ceiling.

He turned to Harry. "Really a shame, you know. This place was in such superb condition and now look at it—really a shame." Harry nodded as Reese Orchard circled around the room. After a long pause, he began again. "You know, what seems really odd—there is no evidence of how the fire started! Have you got any ideas?"

"I'm sorry," Harry apologized, "I really don't, at least, not yet."

"Well, before the fire I was hoping to sort through some of the things collected here. I still don't quite know what I will do now."

Well, Harry thought, *you've chosen a set of building plans and hired me to rebuild it—that's a start…*

Harry suddenly felt uneasy standing between Reese Orchard and the chest. He tried to think of something to say in order to break the silence. Attempting to conceal the trunk behind him, he took a deep breath. "Well, it's getting late for me. Long day, you know?" he offered, looking especially weary.

"Of course you're right," Reese replied. "It *is* getting late and I did not mean to keep you. I just, you know . . . well now, that's an interesting item!" As he spoke, he walked around Harry, who tried to look nonchalant.

"What have we here?" Reese asked with sudden curiosity.

Harry quietly stepped aside as Reese knelt down next to the chest and ran his fingers across the surface of the lid.

"Fascinating—it's untouched! Is this what you were leaning over when I walked in?"

Before Harry could answer, Reese Orchard casually lifted the entire trunk with both hands and carried it closer to where the light bulb hung from a ceiling joist. He set it down directly beneath the bare bulb and lifted the lid just as Harry had done moments ago.

"Hmm . . . nothing. Just an empty old trunk," Reese exclaimed. "Was there anything in it, Harry, I mean, when you found it?"

Harry attempted to hide his discomfort. "Uh, actually, I was just about to take a look when you walked in. We hauled out quite a bit today. Unfortunately, anything that might have been worth saving was destroyed in the fire."

"Right," Reese said with a noticeable tone of regret. "Well, I should probably be going— sorry again to have kept you. And Harry—do let me know if you find anything of interest, okay?"

"Of course. Would you like me to set this aside for you?"

"I'm not interested," Reese answered. "You may have it if you like. It was nice meeting you, Harry. I'm sure we'll talk soon."

Harry nodded as Reese handed him a card, retrieved his

hat and abruptly exited the basement.

He studied the card. It said something about real estate and had Reese's name on it. Placing the card into his shirt pocket, Harry peered through the large opening they had created. He heard the quiet hum of an automobile and stepped out into the driveway to see Orchard's BMW disappear. Something very odd had just occurred but his brain was having trouble sorting it out.

Walking back into the basement, Harry examined the chest. How could this thing be empty? Earlier that day, they couldn't get it to budge. Then Reese Orchard just strolls in, effortlessly lifts it up, and carries it closer to the light? *Something was wrong here!*

Harry grabbed the box with both hands and lifted. The empty container came up easily and he held it for a moment, level with his waist. *This is too strange!* He moved the chest back to where it had been and set it down. He looked at the floor to see if there had been something holding it in place. Nothing. Finally, he sat down on the lid, lowered his head between his knees, and let out a long sigh. He felt as if he could just fade away and fall asleep right there.

A few moments passed. Again, Harry had the strange sensation of a breeze, except stronger this time. He lifted his head up slowly and stared directly ahead.

The essence of it was unnatural. An intoxicating odor enveloped him, with an instant calming effect which relaxed his entire being. The fear that welled up was accompanied by a wonder that seemed to subdue the sudden horror he felt. He had the faint passing notion he should be terrified, but instead felt as though he were in a dream and could only watch as it unfolded before him. Still, even under this spell, he thought he might become sick with this unusual mixture of fear and wonder. He wanted to cry out.

Instead he simply sat there captivated, watching in silent trepidation as a vaporous vision collected before his eyes. It was a kaleidoscope of color and light, pulsating and growing and filling the air in front of him. As he watched the image moving and forming into a shape, he was compelled to be still and only observe. The figure before him continued to thicken and solidify. Gradually Harry recognized a human form, but strangely different. Unexpected sounds emanated from the mouth, which was just now becoming discernible. Harry started to hear them as words.

"W-e-l-l . . ."

The mouth closed, then opened. Again, out came the gravelly, watery voice.

"Well now . . ."

There were eyes now, peering through the milky light while the voice coming from the form continued.

"Hello . . . Harry Turner," it said with a hollow, bubbly sound.

Harry sat there on the chest, stupefied.

"Yes," the vision spoke again, taking on a fuller shape

while the voice became clearer.

"Salutations—"

Harry heard the words but he himself could not speak.

"My name is Narcissus." This time the voice had a stronger deeper tone. The being paused as Harry watched the misty form oscillate and congeal into a more solid exterior. Again the figure spoke. "This *is* the proper greeting, is it not?" The voice was fluid and calming, like moving water.

"Hel—lo," Harry thought he heard himself say as he watched the figure increasingly take on a more distinct appearance.

The deep masculine voice continued. "Excuse me . . . I have been quite weakened by my long season of inactivity! It is truly an exquisite feeling to be freed from the confines of that . . . chamber!" The ethereal features of the being's face were now becoming even more tangible. A prominent nose, sharp cheekbones, and full lips began to emerge.

This face was beautiful!

Now Harry saw radiant eyes of light looking directly at him. He felt as though the whole scene was set in slow motion and he was caught in it like a trance.

"Do not be afraid."

"O—kay," Harry muttered dumbly.

"You *are* Harry Turner . . .Yes? And you are wondering why you are not terrified. *But you are!* You see, I have temporarily mollified you. You are not dreaming as you may even be wondering, although I understand your current unwillingness to accept my presence as reality."

The creature paused and glanced around at the immediate surroundings. There was a fierceness in its countenance which urged Harry to back away but he could not pry himself from the chest.

Again the creature spoke, but in a more formal tone. "Let me attempt to explain. I am, or was . . . a member of the Seraphim."

"What?" Harry managed to mumble.

"I am a Seraph...a celestial being. Listen to me, Harry Turner, and try to understand! I do not wish to frighten you, but let me give you a sincere warning. Even in my weakened state, I am powerful. I still have the ability to manipulate and even beguile the most influential and elite."

With this, Harry watched the creature's form darken and glow with a heat that he could actually feel.

"But I am not here to deceive you! In fact, I have been elected to be a guide, if you will."

Harry opened his mouth but nothing would come out. The being leaned forward with a curious expression and spoke again. "What is it . . .?"

Harry sat transfixed before the angelic figure. It was fully formed now and moving closer. The creature was extraordinary in every detail, its magnificent face evoking deep emotion within Harry. A fearful symmetry radiated from the contours of black shoulder-length hair and stern forehead. Its distinct cheekbones and majestic nose were evenly positioned above a solemn, virile mouth, a resolute jaw, and a sharp chin. Youthful and mature, the combined features appeared ageless.

Harry made the mental transition from "it" to "he." Although not human, this creature clearly possessed personhood. His body was perfect in each aspect—not overly large, but authoritative and strong, with broad shoulders, a trim torso, and beautifully sculpted hands and feet. This was surely a formidable figure, yet even the smallest movement was filled with grace. He was dressed in a simple robe fastened with a wide sash. The most wondrous thing of all, though, was the strange warm glow that flowed through both his body and robe. It was as though the angel himself was composed of light. His crystalline flesh seemed to pulse with varying intensities when he moved or spoke.

As Harry gazed at this figure of extraordinary beauty, he perceived that Narcissus was right. He did feel a distinct terror underneath the calm that had been imposed upon him by some external source.

The exotic scent grew richer as Harry faced this marvelous being. He tried to formulate his feelings, to think of some way to respond, but he was at a complete loss for words. What he really wanted to do was fall flat on his face, cry, run and hide, and weep uncontrollably. His body shivered and convulsed. He faced the creature with no idea of what to say or do, cleared his throat, and looked into Narcissus' radiant eyes. He wet his lips with his tongue and opened his mouth, but still nothing would come out.

Finally, Harry managed to whisper, "What do you want from me?"

Narcissus' gaze darted around the room cautiously and then focused back onto Harry. Suddenly he grinned. "I have no wants or desires that any human being could fulfill. It is *you* who is in want, Harry Turner, and I am here for you." The creature moved even closer to Harry and leaned down. "I understand you have many questions. In time I hope to answer them all, but it is late now and I'm afraid you are fading away."

All at once, Harry's mind *was* flooded with questions, but none of them seemed to make any sense. The mixture of fear, wonder, and fatigue overwhelmed him as he felt his legs buckle. With no strength left, his body slumped down onto the concrete floor.

Narcissus reached out and took hold of Harry's arm. "Let me help you." He lifted Harry up and carried him out to the truck, seemingly sensitive to the fact that the man was exhausted. After setting Harry into the passenger seat and closing the door, the strange visitor returned to the basement, turned off the light, and returned with the chest, which he placed into the rear of the pick-up before climbing into the driver seat. Harry leaned over to see Narcissus start the engine and put the truck into gear.

"I—didn't imagine you knew how to drive," he said

wearily.

"There are a multitude of things you do not know about me," Narcissus responded as he pulled the truck out of the driveway and drove up onto the road.

Harry was listless during the short drive home. Once there, Narcissus moved his ward inside and placed him on the bed. He then positioned the chest on the floor at the foot of the bed. After seeing everything was in order, the creature effortlessly altered his form, moved through the walls of the apartment, and vanished into the air of the night sky.

3
Getting Through the Weekend

The next morning Harry awoke to the sweetest fragrance. *What was it?* He pulled the covers back to see the sun shining through the window. *What time is it?* Harry was usually up before the sun, but this morning was different. For some reason he felt unusually relaxed. Hopping out of bed, he headed toward the bathroom to begin his usual routine.

After a long shower, Harry proceeded to make a pot of coffee. He loved the smell of fresh ground beans, especially on a Saturday morning when he could unwind from the work week over several cups. Working on a weekend was forbidden. A full week of manual labor was enough after all, so the weekends were committed to himself. He observed the living area while grinding the aromatic French Roast. The bedroom, living room and kitchen were all one large open space with the bedroom on a level higher, two steps up from the main floor and separated by an iron rail.

With a cup of strong coffee in hand, he stretched out on his sofa, picked up the music remote, and clicked on his favorite Celtic collection. Soft Scottish rhythms began to fill the room. The familiar sounds of lutes, recorders, and fiddles soothed Harry's mind while he savored the rich flavor of the fresh java.

As Harry enjoyed the warmth of the sunlight coming through the windows, he surveyed the room. Everything was in order. His modest home was unusually tidy for a bachelor, but something seemed peculiar—something he couldn't quite put his finger on.

Then all at once, the events of the previous night came rushing into his consciousness. The aroma of his coffee paled now in comparison to the exotic fragrance filling the room. There at the foot of his bed was the chest! He nearly choked as he caught sight of it.

"Narcissus!" He managed to whisper. *No! This was too much!* He jerked himself up off of the couch. Something was clearly wrong here. He was instantly dizzy and his legs began to feel weak. Grabbing the nearest chair, he slumped down into it. With his head between his knees, he took a few deep breaths. Guardedly, he looked back up at the chest. How could it be? This sort of thing just didn't happen . . . in the *real* world!

You have stepped over the edge.

But he remembered everything. Each detail became lucid—every word spoken, every gesture and look and thought. All the memories from the previous night were fully intact, and all too real. His mind raced as he strained to control a feeling of panic.

There's no way this really could have happened to me! See? This is the way it begins: First you think you've seen an angel. Then it will be your mom or dad, or maybe even Jennifer who visits you. And then, if you really go off the deep end, the ghost of Christmas past will appear! This is exactly how you end up in Eastern State Hospital or some other loony bin with a strait jacket on and a minimum wage nurse who forgets he left you strapped to the toilet seat—.

But still, as Harry sat there dumbfounded, he remembered everything just as though the previous night's events had truly happened. Last night could not have been a dream . . . could it? The sweet odor in the air was familiar now—it seemed to emanate from the chest. But this was *too* fantastic—it was unbelievable! He fumbled with the cup of coffee and then set it down. He slowly stepped over to the chest and gingerly lifted the lid.

"Narcissus," he repeated aloud, staring at the empty container. Whether the experience was real or just something he conjured up, the Seraph was gone and he was alone now.

He picked up the coffee cup and staggered over to the kitchen sink to rinse it out. The water and the remaining coffee swirled down the drain in a spiral motion, and Harry felt himself spiraling down as well. As he stood hunched over the sink, running the water mindlessly into the cup, he noticed the flashing red light coming from his land line. Relieved to have any distraction, he set the cup down, turned the water off, and pushed the message button on the phone's answering machine.

"Hello, Harry," the deep voice began. "This is Reese Orchard. I'm sorry for calling so late; I figured you'd be home by now and maybe still up. I forgot to mention earlier that I have another project you might be interested in. Give me a call over the weekend if you like. My number is on the card. Thanks, Harry!" The message ended with the usual beep and the machine clicked off.

Without hesitation, Harry retrieved his jacket from the floor next to the chest and found the card in his pocket. He felt an urgency to get out, to take any opportunity that would divert his attention to something else. Lifting the receiver, he dialed the number on the card.

Instantly, there was a voice on the other end.

"Hello, Reese Orchard here—"

"Uh, hello, Reese, this is Harry Turner."

"Harry! Right—I'm glad you called. I know this is short notice but I'm working on a project you might be interested in, that is, if you're available."

"Well," Harry considered, "I'm always available for the right job. Can you tell me a little about it?"

"Glad to! But it might be easier to show you. I've got a set of blueprints. Could you possibly meet me for lunch this afternoon? It would mean a great deal to me. I'll give you all the details and you can let me know what you think. How about it?"

"Sure. That would be fine."

"Listen then, Harry, why don't you meet me at that little cafe downtown on the corner of First and Pearl, say, twelve thirty?"

"Sounds great, Reese—I'll see you there."

"Right."

Harry heard the receiver click and set the phone down. He looked at his watch. He would have just enough time to get dressed and get to the cafe. He put on some clean jeans and found a shirt he hoped would be appropriate. Reese Orchard appeared to be a successful businessman and he didn't want to look too unkempt. He grabbed his cell phone and punched in the password. The screen lit up and beeped. He checked for messages—none.

As Harry got ready and headed out the door, he found himself fighting off a sense of urgency. Who was this Narcissus, and would he appear again? What was he to do in the meantime? Just go on with life as though nothing had happened? Just go on, not knowing whether he was delusional . . . or *the chosen one!*

He made his way down through the rustic streets of Isles End. The small community was still charming, even with the downtown looking slightly neglected. Through Harry's eyes, the town was just underdeveloped. He recalled his first impressions were that of a small fishing village. There was a harbor, a pier, and some fishing boats. A cluster of steeply pitched rooftops gathered in the center, showing their age. Nearby, there was a splintered wharf with various types of small vessels gently rocking along its worn sides. The town appeared quiet and slow, and in some way veiled, like a shadowy watercolor. *Jenny would call this picturesque*, Harry had thought, then mildly scorned himself for allowing the interruption.

Discovering Isles End had really happened by accident.

Climbing into his truck just to drive somewhere had become a ritual before he left his home in the city. That particular day, the sky had been pale, clear, and surreal. He recalled the scenery passing by his window like an old moving picture. The warm breeze flowing through the cab, washing over his face and his pain, inviting him to come further, without thought or concern. The freedom of driving was a wonderful thing!

Plane Goes Down . . .

It was over a year ago now, near the outskirts of town, he had stopped at an intersection and turned up a narrow road with a street sign that read, "Top of the Hill Road." He followed it a couple of miles to the summit where he parked and got out to stretch his legs and inspect the view. Tall grass covered the clearing like a wild green crown. All around the back side of the perimeter, fir and alder trees grew uniformly as if they'd been planned, circling the clearing like a fortress. He walked toward the edge where he could see the town and sat down on the rim of a large boulder to enjoy the view. Isles End looked almost ancient from this vantage point. Except for the cars on the roads and the wires on the poles, he imagined he could have traveled somewhere back in time.

Harry recalled gazing down at the view for a long time, giving in to thoughts of Jennifer, and of his mom and dad. They would not be back, he reminded himself. He thought of his sister Gwen and the few close friends he had back in the city. *They would understand . . . they would have to.* Either way it didn't matter; his mind was made up. Within days Harry had packed, and before a month was over, he had purchased a small home just outside the downtown area.

Part of him hoped Isles End would remain the peaceful, sleepy little town it was. But his builder's instinct saw the potential it had for a bustling tourist town, right there on the edge of the small ocean bay. He imagined various shops and antique dealers, cabarets, beer gardens and art galleries. This place could be a goldmine for a smart investor with the funds to make it happen.

But in the meantime, Isles End lay undisturbed by the rest of the world and had enough activity to keep Harry and other local business owners busy. For now, that was all he required.

Harry turned his truck onto Pearl Street and began his descent into Isles End. There was a beautiful view there where most of the town could be seen below. To his left, a small bridge crossed over Isles Inlet to the more rural side of town. Underneath, a constant stream of fresh water quietly flowed down into the bay. He continued past the ancient-looking dock with the quintessential fishing boats and sailboats bobbing up and down along the sides. As Harry drew closer, he could see a couple of kids at the end of the long ramp with their poles hanging out over the weathered sides of the pier.

At the bottom of Pearl, Harry turned past the cafe and pulled into the rear parking lot. He was starving and realized he hadn't eaten breakfast. Walking around to the front of the building, he peered through the large front windows and could see Reese was already seated. Giving a wave, he continued over to the front door and stepped inside.

"Thanks for meeting me on such short notice," Reese said, as Harry pulled out a chair and sat down. "You're probably wondering what's so important that it can't wait. First I want you to take a look at these." He handed Harry a set of blueprints. "I hope you don't mind— I've already ordered for both of us."

"Not at all," Harry said as he scanned the prints.

"Harry, what we have here is a pretty good-sized commercial building. I purchased it awhile back, in an area that was recently bought out by a small but well-established corporation. Right now we're negotiating a plan where I can maintain some interest—possibly some sort of lease option. I'm not sure of the details yet. It's some sort of biotech enterprise involved in what sounds like very interesting work. I guess they expect to go public soon, but you know how *that* is."

"Oh, yeah," Harry responded, pretending to understand. As he watched and listened to Reese, he wondered if the man was always so matter-of-fact and business conscious. Harry wanted to ask him about his personal life. What else did he do? Did he have a family? What were his interests? Did he live *in* Isles End? But he could not seem to find an opportunity to change the subject. Apparently Reese was not interested in Harry's private affairs, or at least he did not broach the subject. Harry's focus came back to Reese who was still speaking about the project at hand.

"—and so I've found keeping my real estate license current has come in quite handy, and that's how I came across *this* deal. Anyway, Harry, you can see the proposed modifications." Reese directed Harry's attention to the blueprints. "Not a whole lot of changes here, just some renovations and alterations that will meet the needs of these people during their occupancy. For example, here—" He pointed to a section of the plans, but was interrupted by the waitress.

"Here you go, gentlemen," she said as they cleared the table for their food. She carefully set down the two plates. "Is there anything else I can get you?"

"I think this will do just fine, thank you," Reese said politely.

Harry smiled gratefully as the girl bustled off and then turned his attention to his plate. It was a large club sandwich with a small salad. *Excellent*, he thought as he remembered his empty stomach. He looked up at Reese, who was already garnishing his meal with condiments.

Harry ate and listened while Reese shared more of the details. Reese explained there was not an enormous amount of work to be done, just some detailed specifications which needed to be performed according to the customer's instructions. Harry looked over the plans as Reese pointed out some of the objectives; they needed some small cubicles built, and special plumbing with sinks which could supply and drain various chemicals and contaminants. There were electrical diagrams requiring intricate circuitry for highly sensitive instruments, and more wiring for audio and video monitoring systems. Reese also explained to Harry that this was a somewhat classified project. If Harry should become involved, all information concerning the project would need to be confidential.

"No problem," Harry assured Reese. He could tell it would not be a difficult job and was confident he could manage. Besides, he wanted very much to build a relationship with this man. Contacts mean contracts, Harry's dad used to say, and if you had good contacts, half the battle was won.

Of course, he explained to Reese, this might slow him down just a bit on the Ivory Lane project, at least until he could secure some additional help. But that did not seem to be a problem for Reese who insisted his priority was the Biotech project.

They finished lunch and made plans to meet at the commercial building on Monday morning. Reese handed him another card with directions on the back and then hurried off to another appointment, leaving a good portion of his meal untouched. Harry considered eating the half sandwich on Reese's plate but didn't want to appear ill-mannered. He added to the generous tip already left by Reese, thanked the waitress, and left the cafe.

On the way home, Harry stopped at Isles Market to pick up some needed groceries. He was starting to recognize some of the market's employees— friendly people, always busy stocking the shelves and tidying up. He made some small talk as he went through the checkout line and realized he was already becoming well-known.

"You're the new builder in town, aren't you?" one woman questioned.

"You start that job up there on Ivory Lane yet?" asked an old-timer who apparently had become fused to a chair by the front entrance.

"Hey, I've got this door that seems to be outta kilter. Is that somethin' you do?" the checker wanted to know. Harry was beginning to feel like a regular local.

He loaded his provisions into the back of the truck and headed home. Once inside, Harry took pleasure in the mundane task of sorting out the many items. Doing something *ordinary* seemed to give him comfort. Separating the dry goods from the perishables, stacking cans in the cupboard, and putting milk and eggs in the fridge all contributed to an overall feeling of normalcy.

When he was finished he called Ed and explained that he might be taking on another project soon. Would Ed consider a position as foreman in his absence? Of course Harry would be there when he could, but he would need someone dependable to make sure the Ivory Lane job stayed on track. Ed was thrilled, which was no surprise to Harry. The prospect of more money and less physical labor? Who wouldn't go for that? Besides, Harry had complete confidence in Ed who had once been a foreman for a large construction company.

With that business taken care of, Harry had nothing left to do. It was five o'clock on a Saturday night, but he had no interest in going anywhere. He really had nowhere to go and besides, he felt very comfortable just staying at home . . . usually. But this night he didn't really know how he felt. How was he supposed to feel? How does one act, following the visitation of a celestial being—or, the possible departure of one's own mind?

He thought about calling Gwen, but that could only create further problems. His sister already worried about him—she would surely think he'd lost his senses if he shared anything about last night. And if he had indeed *snapped*, he wasn't sure he wanted anyone to know about the encounter, at least not right away. Maybe the whole experience could be his own little secret. The thought he could go on living in some sort of mentally deluded state and keep it a secret from everyone made him laugh aloud. But that's what he decided he must do for now anyway— just go on with life, business as usual.

But the more Harry deliberated over his situation, the more unsettled he became. He spent time absentmindedly straightening up the kitchen. He could not accept the idea that he was having some sort of mental breakdown, yet that possibility had to be considered. He swept the floor twice. Maybe this incident was the result of a latent response to having lost the three most important people in his life, and it was finally surfacing after being dormant for almost a year. Could it be possible?

He sat down at the kitchen table, his face close to the oak surface, and stared at the grain in the wood. He thought about how calm he had been with Narcissus, remembering the fact that the angelic being had sedated him somehow. The thought made him uncomfortable, although he supposed he would have completely lost control otherwise. The memory caused a sense of panic to rise up from his gut and he fought it back.

Could he have overworked himself and somehow imagined the whole thing? He'd heard of that sort of thing happening to people who had become delusional due to fatigue or stress. More information would be helpful. He would go online soon and explore the subject. In the meantime, he needed to find something else to occupy his time.

To occupy my time, he thought; one of the darker phrases he had leaned on for over a year now. Something we must all do, he consoled himself—find ways to occupy our time.

He organized a bookshelf and took care of some bills. But even after a long hot bath, he could not relax. Finally, he got into bed, turned off the lights, and fell into a restless sleep.

The next morning Harry felt like he hadn't slept at all. He spent the entire day inside. He read for a bit, napped, fixed himself a meal, slept again and, as usual, continually had his music playing. Not really a typical Sunday.

Several times he went and lifted the lid of the chest and felt around inside. The compartment held the most intoxicating fragrance, unlike anything Harry had ever experienced. He felt compelled to lean down into the cavity and inhale deeply, then hold his breath and slowly exhale. Finally, after several rounds of this, he put an old lock on the chest where he had cut the other one off, and moved it into his closet where it could not be seen.

Throughout the evening, he could not stop thinking about the angel and the strange recollections from the other night.

Narcissus . . .

He had heard the name before. He remembered something from school; was it Greek mythology? Something about a guy who fell in love with his own reflection? He only remembered thinking it was a bit silly, though he understood the idea of being "narcissistic", but what did that have to do with this creature?

Whatever the case, Harry was frustrated and almost angry about the whole thing. Underneath the surface of his consciousness, he felt a deep foreboding fear.

What happened to me?

The light of the sun was finally waning. Harry lay down on his bed, still thinking about his otherworldly visitor. He recounted each moment from the prior evening. Was it just two nights ago that he had been confronted by the celestial creature? He struggled between accepting it all as reality and complete disbelief. Somewhere in this struggle, a new fear began to collect around him. He realized he was more afraid now about the possibility that the whole experience had actually happened!

Did I hear something?

Harry jumped up from his reclined position and strained

his ears. Then he slipped out of bed and walked over to the door. Placing his ear to the door frame, he held his breath and listened. There was nothing. He carefully eased the door open and peered out. All was quiet, not even the sound of wind interrupted the silence of the yard and street. Harry closed and locked the door again and went to the fridge. He grabbed a cold bottle of beer, popped the cap, and tipped it over his lips. He didn't stop until half the bottle had poured down his throat. The cold ale calmed Harry's anxieties. Two more gulps and the bottle was empty. Feeling exhausted, he quickly took care of his evening duties and got back into bed. Soon he was fast asleep and before long his dreams brought him back to his childhood, which was not an unusual occurrence. The images that Harry's mind conjured up during the night often caused him to visit the special places he had known as a child. This night he dreamed of one such place.

He was ten years old and his mother was seeing him off to school. She handed him his lunch and kissed him good-bye. As he turned to begin the half-mile walk to school, she warned him to be careful and shouted a short prayer that his guardian angel would protect him. He laughed and waved to her; she looked so lovely as she smiled proudly and waved back.

He continued down the steep road. Everything was completely familiar. He had walked this path so many times: the stone wall that ran along the roadside, every cracked square of sidewalk, every twisted tree, the road signs, every bird—they all knew him. They all belonged to him!

But as he neared the bottom of the road, the landscape began to change. Suddenly things were no longer familiar. Ahead of him was a small bridge. He remembered now being told not to go near that bridge, but as he walked, there was no other way to go. If he kept moving, he would be forced to cross. He could see far down below where a stream ran under the structure. At the last minute, just before he reached the ramp, he jumped off the side of the road and slid down the bank of the ravine towards the stream. He watched the water rush up towards him until he splashed into the moving current which immediately gripped him. Gaining his balance, Harry realized the water was only knee deep. He was almost under the bridge now where the small creek flowed.

Fear and uncertainty filled his thoughts. This was a bad place—he was not supposed to be here.
He looked around anxiously to find another way but there was nowhere to go except under the bridge. Against his will he moved forward into the dark arched opening. Directly ahead there appeared to be something . . . someone . . . it was an ominous figure looming, waiting for him. With increased anxiety he tried to stop, to break free, but the current propelled him forward.

There before him appeared a huge beast of a figure with shiny ebony skin, glowing crimson eyes, a fierce expression on its face, and awful wings which sprouted out of its shoulders and draped down around its sides like a cape. The creature smiled maliciously at Harry and held out its hand.

"Come, my young friend," the apparition urged. *"You appear to be a tasty morsel. I would like to feast on you tonight!"*

Harry awoke with a jolt. He was soaked with sweat and felt like he couldn't breathe, but he managed to suck in a deep breath. Taking a moment to calm himself, he told himself it was just a dream.

No, it was a nightmare! A horrible nightmare!

Harry studied the room. It was still dark, but the light of morning would be coming soon. His alarm clock began to ring. Fumbling, he managed to shut it off and checked the time—six-thirty. The weekend was over. It was time to get up.

4
Advanced Bio-Cell

The room grew light as Harry prepared to leave. He put a potato in the microwave and went to take a shower. Eight minutes later his shower and breakfast were done and he was out the door.

It was six miles to Ivory Lane. The sun was still coming up over Isles End awakening a brilliance of color from the landscape as Harry's truck moved down the winding road. The rooftops were wet and glistening with swirls of steam rising up like large pots of stew scattered across the countryside. Everywhere Harry looked, the colors of the trees were changing hue. The locals could often be heard praising the beautiful Indian summers of Isles End and the fiery change of color as the leaves turned, and now summer was over and the autumn leaves were making their entrance.

When Harry turned down Ivory Lane he could see Ed's red pickup already in the driveway. There were Ed and Butch sitting in the rusty truck enjoying their morning coffee. Harry pulled his rig up behind Ed's and tapped his horn. They both replied by raising their cups. He got out and walked over to Ed's window.

"Mornin' partner," Harry said in his best country accent, rubbing his hands together.

Ed cracked his window. "Hey, you're late, pal."

"Where's my coffee?" Harry responded with a false

frown.

"We didn't think you were coming, so we drank it," Ed joked.

Butch leaned forward and held up his cup. "You can have the rest of mine, boss."

Harry could see the donut crumbs floating on the surface. "That's okay, Butch—you go ahead. I guess you guys just spoiled me last Friday and I'm going to have to get over it."

"So, what's up Harry?" Ed asked. "You working with us today or what?"

"Actually, no. I just stopped by to see if you guys needed anything. I've got a new job to look at."

"Well don't worry, Harry, we'll be fine. With my supervision, Butch will have this mess cleared up in no time at all."

Harry scowled. "That's what I'm afraid of! Butch, how do you put up with this guy?"

"Aw, it's easy. When he gets too far outta line, I just smack him upside the head until he behaves himself. I usually look for a kiln-dried two by four—they work pretty good. One with the right weight and not too much snap!"

Harry laughed and Ed frowned, rubbing his head.

"Well," Harry said, "let's see if we can get some bodies added to this crew. If I get this other job, we're going to need more bodies—speaking of which, I'd better get going. I'm supposed to meet Reese Orchard at eight o'clock. Call me on my cell if something comes up."

"All right—see ya, Harry," they both chimed.

Harry climbed back into his truck and carefully backed out of the driveway. He drove up to the top of Ivory Lane and turned towards the highway while he checked the directions on the back of the card. *This can't be too difficult,* he thought, as he reached the on-ramp for Highway 303. He headed north, away from Isles End. The road stretched across miles of rolling green hills and pastures, beautiful scenery with small farms interspersed among sections of forestland sprawling down from the hills. Soon, the land became perfectly level in all directions. The large area had recently been zoned as commercial property and most of it was still undeveloped, but on the north end there were a dozen different new buildings and warehouses, all in close proximity. Highway 303 ran right past this development and continued north to the interstate and eventually, to the city.

It took Harry forty-five minutes to reach the project. He could understand why this was such desirable real-estate. It was a perfect location with easy access to the interstate. He reviewed the directions again. Interestingly, all the streets here had recently been named after well-known artists. As he neared the first set of buildings, he turned right at Van Gogh Boulevard. To his left, there were a series of unusual looking, sky-blue stucco buildings that appeared to be empty. He drove further up the road and took a left onto Parrish Avenue. Here, they had just put in a foundation and had begun framing with steel. Harry noticed a sign in front:

"Future site of ABC Incorporated." *That sounds a little simplistic*, he thought. He continued up to the end of Parrish and turned right onto Escher Lane.

A quarter of a mile up on the left, he saw Reese's BMW parked next to a large multi-level building. The structure was larger than he had imagined and nicer, too—not like the stucco buildings he had seen earlier. This was very contemporary with a smooth exterior and reflective glass windows all around. It had previously been occupied by a pharmaceutical company. Now the old sign lay beside a large commercial van parked by the entrance.

Two men pulled at cables as a new sign was hoisted up over the archway of the complex. It read, "Advanced Bio-Cell, Inc."

He parked next to the BMW and made his way around the sign equipment and up to the front door.

"Careful, bud—the lettering on that glass is fresh," called one of the workers.

"Sure thing," Harry replied, looking mindful as he opened the glass door and stepped inside.

Despite having been occupied, this place looked and smelled new. He walked into a large foyer with a twenty-foot ceiling and natural stone floors. There was some furniture off to the side and in the center someone had begun assembling some sort of stone pillar. Up ahead, two women were unpacking office supplies and loading file cabinets in a large reception area. He made his way in their direction.

The woman closest to him looked up. "Can I help you?" she asked, smiling politely.

"Yes, I'm uh . . . here to see Reese Orchard," Harry stuttered, suddenly caught off guard. She was lovely he thought, quickly realizing that he was staring at her dumbly.

"Oh, you must be—" She picked up a card and glanced at it, "Harry Turner?"

"That would be me." Harry smiled back nervously and tried to project some confidence.

"Well, Harry Turner, I've been instructed to take you to Mr. Orchard as soon as you arrive. If you'd be so kind as to accompany me—" She smiled at him again as she made her way around the work station. He followed her down a corridor to where there were two elevator doors. She pressed one of the buttons and stepped aside to wait.

Harry was still staring. She had a lovely rounded face with beautiful green eyes and straight brown hair that went half way down her back. He caught himself and took a step back in an attempt to focus his thoughts. He managed to put some words together.

"So, I don't think I've had the pleasure of meeting you yet," Harry said boldly, immediately wincing at the sound of his own eagerness.

"Hi, Harry. I'm Beth Fairbanks." She offered her hand.

"Pleased to meet you, Beth. " He took her hand and gave

it a slight squeeze. It was soft and delicate and warm. The way she looked at him so trustingly, he felt he could have continued holding her hand and she wouldn't have minded. He forced himself to let go and was surprised to find his uneasiness fading. Her gaze seemed to have a calming effect. Feeling unexpectedly relaxed, he made a second attempt at conversation. "So, have you been working here long?" *Great— Another half-witted effort,* he thought, realizing this company hadn't even fully moved into the building yet.

"Actually, I've been in Isles End for a while, but I just started working with Advanced Bio-Cell. You know, they've relocated here from another state—expanding, I guess. I'm not even sure yet exactly what all they do, but from what I've gathered, it all sounds very exciting!"

Harry nodded. He was listening to her, at the same time wondering if he would be able to say anything that had some semblance of intelligence. He decided to be daring.

"You know, Beth, I don't know if you can tell but I'm actually a bit nervous right now. This could be a good opportunity for me. But being here with you . . . well, I can't seem to keep my foot out of my mouth! How am I going to behave when I meet your superiors?"

"Oh, I'm sure you'll do just fine . . . but, here, let me—" She reached her arm up around his neck and straightened his collar. "Sorry, just a motherly instinct kicking in I guess." She suddenly blushed and stepped back.

There was a ding, and the elevator door opened. Harry stepped back courteously. Beth entered and Harry followed. She chose their destination and, as the elevator began to ascend, she asked Harry about his occupation. But before he could tell her very much, there was another ding, and the door opened to the third floor.

They stepped out into a massive open room. It was almost an entire floor, completely empty with a high ceiling and windows all around. On the far side were several men, among them Reese Orchard. He noticed Harry and Beth and motioned them over.

"Ah, Harry, I see you've found us okay, and right on time—once again, I'm impressed!" Reese turned abruptly toward Beth. "Thank you, dear—I'll take it from here." He swung Harry around toward the other men while Beth dismissed herself and walked back to the elevator. Harry twisted his head back to see her. He wanted to say good-bye or something, but she was already stepping through the door.

"Gentlemen, this is Harry Turner," Reese began. "Harry, I'd like you to meet William Algren, CEO of Advanced Bio-Cell."

Harry waited to see which of the three men would step forward. The eldest, another tall man with rough features who appeared to be in his mid-sixties, approached Harry with a warm greeting.

"Pleased to meet you, son," he said, shaking Harry's hand

firmly. "Don't let the big title fool you. I'm really the Chief Executive *Old-timer* of ABC. I know, it sounds more like the name of a children's toy block company—simple and easy to remember, though! Anyway, please call me Bill."

"It's a pleasure, Bill," Harry said smiling as he studied Bill Algren's rugged features.

"And this," Reese continued, "is Dr. Shushi Yang."

"Hello, Mr. Turner," the second man said dryly, giving Harry a curt handshake. He looked to be about the same age as Bill but was half his size, with a full head of thick white hair.

"Dr. Yang is the head of the research department and a brilliant scientist as well," said Reese. Harry nodded politely.

"Hi, Harry," the third man interjected extending his hand. "I'm Preston Hart. I guess I'm the CFO and, sort of, well . . ."

"My right hand man," Bill Algren interceded. "Props me up when I look like I'm going to teeter over."

"Well, yeah." Preston's large round glasses slid down his small sharp nose as he chuckled. "I guess I do a little bit of everything around here."

Harry shook Preston's hand. "Glad to meet you . . . all of you." He looked around and made eye contact with all his new acquaintances. He was impressed with this group and somehow felt honored to be in their company.

"So you've had a chance to look over the plans, Harry?" Bill asked.

"Briefly, sir."

"Harry, please… call me Bill. It will make me feel like I've got at least one friend around here."

They all laughed and Reese cut in, holding up a copy of the blueprints. "Harry, this is the floor that will need to be divided into small work stations. What do you think?"

"Yes, the cubicles? Actually, this will be the easiest part of all," Harry explained. "We'll frame up all the walls with metal studs, do the wiring, drywall, and drop the ceiling. Piece of cake."

Following Bill's lead, the five men walked along near the large windows of the outside wall while Harry continued. "Now the wiring and plumbing on the lower floor—that will be a little more complicated. Luckily, I have some great sub-contractors— they won't have any trouble at all!"

"So you've done a lot of this type of work before," Preston said as more of a statement than a question.

"Oh yes," Harry ventured. "My first nine years of experience were all commercial. But for the last year, I've chosen to focus on residential work. It doesn't pay as well, but it allows for much more creativity."

Reese gripped Harry's shoulder with a smile. "Why don't we go take a look at the basement?" he suggested.

"Sounds good," said Harry.

"Gentlemen?" Reese gestured toward the elevator.

William Algren held up his arm apologetically. "Shushi and I have some other business waiting for us. Preston, why don't you accompany Reese and Harry and see that they are clear on all our needs."

"No problem, Bill. Will you still want to see me later this afternoon?"

"Absolutely,"

They all crowded into the elevator and Bill pushed the button for the main floor. Within seconds they arrived and the door opened. Bill and Shushi stepped into the lobby, and Bill turned back to Harry.

"Nice to have met you, Harry. I'll look forward to seeing you soon. By the way, can I ask how old you are?"

"I'm almost thirty—"

"Huh, just about the same age as our Beth." Bill winked and turned toward Shushi who was already half-way down the hall.

"Right," Reese smirked.

Harry had a funny feeling they could read his mind and were subtly teasing him now. Was his instant attraction to Beth Fairbanks that apparent? Preston pushed a button, the door closed, and within a few seconds they were in the basement.

"*This* is where we will be performing our most important work," Preston announced.

"What exactly will you be doing here?" Harry asked.

"Well, it's rather complicated, Harry," Preston responded, adjusting his glasses. "We have many interests, but our primary concerns are focused on the human cell. Currently we're experimenting in the field of genetic engineering."

"Wow! That sounds futuristic."

"Well, yes and no. What *we* are doing is definitely cutting edge, but altering genetic material by way of recombinant DNA is not new at all."

"Recombinant?"

"Yes, it's uh . . . well, we call it gene splicing. There are various techniques for inserting DNA fragments from the genes of *one* organism directly into the chromosomes of another, thus changing or improving the genetic makeup. The process has been used quite a bit in producing vaccines and hormones, but we are hoping to take it to a whole new level of possibilities."

Reese touched Preston's arm with a slightly agitated look on his face. "Excuse me, Preston, but why don't we show Harry the existing utilities and see if they'll meet your needs."
Harry nodded as Reese led him to an area where there were several types of plumbing pipe stubbed up out of the concrete. They also found a large electrical panel nearby with other multi-colored cables, each serving various purposes.

"Much of the equipment we have is self-contained. I'll make sure to get you a copy of the blueprints we've had made up," Preston offered as Harry looked around and took some notes.

"I'd like to get my electrician and plumber out here by the first of next week if I can, and get their approval. I'm sure it will be no problem getting things up and running."

"Great, Harry, that's what I was hoping to hear," said Reese. "Do you need to see anything else while we're here?"

"No, I think this will do for now. I'll arrange to get some estimates so that I can submit a bid to you."

"Oh, we want you to do the work, Harry. I'm sure your fees will be fine. I'd like you to get this started as soon as you can. Don't worry about Ivory Lane—there's no hurry over there."

"Well, Reese, I'll do my best to get them both done in a timely manner."

"Are we through then?" Preston asked.

"Yes, I think that's it," Reese answered.

"Very well—upward and onward," Preston gestured toward the elevator.

They nodded and followed him to the lobby. Back on the main floor Preston said good-bye and disappeared down a nearby hallway. Reese thanked Harry for coming by and promised to meet with him soon.

As they entered the lobby, Harry looked for Beth. He stalled for a minute, pretending to study his notebook while Reese made his way towards the entrance of the building. He watched Mr. Orchard walk out the front door and then turned back to the large reception desk where he had first seen Beth. Now, only the other woman was there. He paused for another moment, apparently having trouble getting the notepad into his briefcase. Scanning the area again, he hoped to find Beth somewhere, but she appeared to be gone. Finally he gave up and headed in the direction of the front door.

"Mr. Turner?"

Harry swung around to see the woman at the desk waving to him. *Me?* He gestured by raising his eyebrows and pointing to his chest. She smiled and nodded her head as she wiggled her forefinger, motioning him to come to her. He glanced around nervously as he approached the workstation where the young woman stood waiting.

"You must have made a good impression on my co-worker."

"Really?"

"Yes, she told me that she enjoyed meeting you. I just thought you might like to know." She smiled and then turned back to her work.

With that bit of information, Harry found a chair nearby and began to scribble a short message:

Beth,

I hope I'm not being too forward, but if you would like to get together sometime, I'd be honored to spend a little time with you. I don't have your number, but here's mine, if you don't mind calling me.

~Harry

He marched back over to Beth's co-worker. She paused from what she was doing and looked up at Harry with a quizzical expression.

"Would you mind giving this to Beth when you see her?" he asked, offering the note.

"I'd be happy to." A tiny giggle escaped her lips as she accepted the folded piece of paper, then she abruptly turned and continued about her business.

Feeling self-conscious, Harry strode quickly out the front door, under the new sign and over to his truck. He unlocked the door and climbed in. Would Beth take the initiative to call him? Now he wondered how he could find her phone number. She might not want to call him first, even though *he* had made the offer. *Why are these kinds of things so complicated?* he thought.

As he drove his truck away from Advanced Bio-Cell and headed home, a touch of anxiety tainted his exhilaration while he considered the possibility of having a date with Beth Fairbanks.

5
Beth Fairbanks

Once home, Harry went over his notes and made a few calls. He left messages with some long-time contacts hoping he could get them started right away on the ABC project. With that out of the way he sat by the phone for a few moments and fidgeted with the cord. He hadn't been able to think of anything except Beth since he'd left the note for her. He wanted to call her but he didn't want to appear too anxious, and besides, he didn't have her number. He began to fantasize. The scene was a picnic on a hillside by a lake or a romantic dinner by candlelight in a small café, somewhere they could enjoy an intimate conversation together, undisturbed. She sat enamored as he shared his hopes and dreams.

Why am I having these ridiculous thoughts? I don't even know this girl! What if we have nothing in common? What if she's not my type?

But she had told her co-worker how much she enjoyed meeting him! And then there were those stunning eyes of hers—how could those eyes fool him?

She IS my type, he proclaimed to himself. *There is something about me that she liked.*

"Alright, here we go," he stated aloud, and grabbed the slim Isles End phone book. He flipped it open and began working down through the names. Fahey, Fayler, Fair, Fairbanks—Beth! That was easy! Right there in the open for anyone to see. What did he have to lose? It had been several hours now, would she be home already? Harry punched out the numbers. He heard the ringing and fought back the urge to hang up. He listened: one ring, two, three . . .

"Hello?"

He recognized her sweet voice.

"Beth?"

"Yes?"

"Hi, it's Harry Turner."

"Harry!"

"Yes—I found your number in the phone book. I didn't want you to feel pressured to call me, so I thought I'd give you a call and see what you're up to—"

"Right now?"

"Sure," he ventured.

"Well, I'm rearranging the furniture in my front room."

"Really?"

"Actually, I was thinking about calling you. But I wasn't sure if that would seem a bit anxious, even though you invited me to. I wanted to leave my number for you at the office but then I ran into the same problem."

"What problem is that?"

"Not wanting to appear forward, I guess. Or worse, to be perceived as some crazy girl who gives her number out to any stranger. So . . . I decided to move some furniture around."

"Do you?" he questioned.

"Do I what?"

"Give your number out to *any* stranger?"

"Well, only a select few," she teased.

"Hmmm, didn't your mother teach you that—you know—whole thing about strangers?"

"Of course, Harry, but my boss told me he had already done a thorough background check on you, and you passed the test."

"*Really*, the Chief Executive *Old-timer* of ABC told you *that*?"

She laughed.

"So what else did he tell you about me?" he probed.

"Not much, really—he said you reminded him of himself when he was younger."

"Well, I guess if your boss approves of me, I can't be all bad!"

"*I'll* have to be the judge of that," she quipped.

Harry chuckled. "So, I was going to ask you if you'd like to have dinner with me."

"I think that would be nice."

"Great," Harry said with instant confidence. "Is there somewhere you especially like?"

"Well, Harry, this is a small town. We don't have a lot of choices unless we go to the city. We could meet at Belmar's—you know, just up from the cafe?"

"Of course."

"Or," she continued slowly, "another option would be to have you over to my place . . ."

"Oh—"

"Harry, normally I would never consider having a guy over to my home for the first date, so to speak. Now I feel funny saying that. But my boss did give his approval."

"You're referring to the background check?"

"Yes."

"He really *did*?"

"Oh yes!"

"I wasn't sure if you were actually serious or just teasing."

"Bill already treats both Valerie and me like we are his daughters. He's very protective. But back to our plans—I'm just thinking it would be nice to have you over. You could see my little house and I could make something simple. I just didn't want to create any added pressure on either of us, so soon, you know?"

Harry hoped to quickly put her at ease. "Beth," he said, "I would be very happy to meet you anywhere and I'm flattered that you would be comfortable enough to have me over to your home. I promise I'll behave myself . . . *if* that's what you decide you'd like to do."

"Behave yourself? Well, don't get carried away—you'll take all of the fun out of it!"

They both laughed as she continued. "So, Harry, it's *my* place for dinner?"

"Great."

"Okay, how about tomorrow evening, say six?"

"Can I bring something?"

"Actually, yes. You could bring a bottle of merlot."

"That's some sort of wine, isn't it?"

"Yes, Harry—"

"Anything else?"

"Hmmm, yes, you can bring some salt water taffy."

"Really?"

"Sure. As long as you're going to the trouble, you may as well bring something I really like."

"Consider it done."

"Well then, I better let you go, Harry."

"Wait a minute, what are you going to make for dinner?"

"It's a surprise—"

"Okay, if you want to see that taffy, you'd better tell me how to find your house."

Beth agreed and gave Harry directions. He recited them back to be sure he had them right and then said good-bye. Flopping down on the sofa, he let out a long sigh. He couldn't believe he had not only called Beth Fairbanks, but was having dinner with her tomorrow night. And he was amazed at how well their conversation went. He was always so clumsy and nervous around women, before and after Jennifer. Somehow this woman had a way of making him feel at ease. For the first time in a long while he had a feeling of excitement and hope.

Even as his enthusiasm grew, regarding his plans with

67

Beth, memories of Jennifer began to surface. Over time, he'd learned to turn his thoughts to somewhere safe where the grief could be held at bay, but now he felt compelled to let it flow.

He couldn't help recalling the crush he'd had on her through high school. At first, her innocent, childlike features had caught his attention. Her smooth skin, her long silky hair, and her profile . . . flawless. By the end of high school she was nothing short of radiant, marked with a purity that had attracted Harry and every other boy who laid eyes on her. Unfortunately for Harry, having a crush on any girl at that age never materialized into anything outside of his own mind. That's what had happened with Jennifer—he worshiped her from afar. It wasn't until years later, that she had unexpectedly come into his life again, and he had never been happier, especially those few months after they were engaged. He recalled how funny it was, whenever they went out, they always seemed to hook-up with his parents. At first, double dating had been Jenny's idea, but after a while the four of them almost naturally seemed to end up doing something together every week. This arrangement seemed to spark up something new in his folks too. The way they would hold hands, laugh, and whisper things to each other, it was as though *they* were the young engaged couple rather than Harry and Jennifer.

Would he always torture himself with the past? He wanted to focus on the future but Gwen had explained to him, this reflecting was just part of the healing process. *Don't try to stuff it down, Harry, and don't isolate yourself!* But that's exactly

68

what he did. Thankfully his sister had taken care of most of the logistical details of his parents' effects leaving Harry free to work through the more emotional components of recovery. There were, of course, bills to pay, funeral arrangements to make, and all the matters of the estate. But Gwen seemed to have the strength, the skills, and the motivation to attend to all the details. Harry couldn't understand how she managed, but he guessed it was the way she found *her* healing, and he was grateful for her unselfish efforts.

Harry allowed himself a few more minutes to reminisce and realized the process didn't create the usual anguish he was used to. He wondered if his Jenny would approve of Beth Fairbanks. Somehow, he thought the answer might be yes. Even though they had just met, he could tell right away there was something special about this girl. But what was he thinking? He'd hardly spent twenty minutes with her! Entertaining these sort of thoughts was plain nonsense.

I've got to keep things in perspective, he warned himself. *Play it safe . . . Mmm-hmm!*

6
Out of Body

It was time to call it a day. Harry tried not to think about his date with Beth while he got ready for bed. He needed to concentrate on starting the framing at Ivory Lane *and* getting the bids in for the new Advanced Bio-Cell project. This would be a busy week. He made a couple of last minute notes and then turned out the light and climbed into bed.

Under the blankets, Harry stretched out in every direction until his body surrendered to the release of all tension. He might even allow himself to think about Beth . . . or dream about her. Soon, he felt himself drifting off and his mind began to wander. He was in another place, with someone, doing something—was he with Beth? He was just conscious enough to realize he was beginning to dream.

The images filled his mind as all other concerns were left behind . . . *and he walked out onto the balcony of the small apartment and surveyed the buildings below. He was having dinner with Beth and he could hear her humming inside while she prepared a meal.*

"Harry," he heard her call. *He turned around to respond, but the woman he saw inside wasn't Beth.*

"Come on, Harry—supper's ready." the woman said with Beth's voice.

I've got to get out of here, *Harry thought. He climbed up*

onto the rail of the balcony and gazed down at the ground, many stories below.

"Harry?" she called again. He turned back and this time the woman appeared to be Jennifer. She looked lovely, as she always did in his dreams. He wanted to go to her.

But instead, this time he thought, No! I can't see you any more, Jenny. You're not real, and I'm alive! He looked down again and took a deep breath. I've done this before, he reassured himself as he held out his arms and jumped.

He sailed out into the air, slowly and lightly, maintaining altitude as he glided over the building across the street. He looked further ahead. Down below, on the flat rooftop of the next building, there was someone waving. He appeared to be motioning for Harry to come over. I can do that, he thought. He simply tipped his left arm up and began to spiral downward toward the figure on the roof. He landed perfectly, straightened himself up from his flying position, and looked ahead. There in front of him was Narcissus.

"Hello, Harry."

"Narcissus, I'm so glad you're here. I was about to have dinner with Beth— you haven't met her yet—but suddenly the woman wasn't Beth, but she had Beth's voice—then she turned into Jennifer! Anyway, I had to get out of there, and so I jumped off the balcony and flew away. Then I saw you—but what are you doing here?"

"You're dreaming, Harry," Narcissus smiled.

"What?"

"You are currently in your bed asleep, having a dream, that is, unless you're in the regular habit of jumping from buildings and flying over rooftops."

"Oh, I see. Are you part of my dream?"

"No. I'm visiting you while you are in your dream state. I didn't want to wake you. I decided I could take this opportunity to see you without disturbing your slumber."

"How do I know this isn't all part of the dream?"

"You will know. There are some things I would like to show you. Will you come with me?"

"Right now? I mean, shouldn't I wake up first?"

"There's no need. Where I'm taking you, it will be better if you're sleeping."

"I'm confused, Narcissus!" He looked around the top of the building and then up at a cloudless sky and a feeling of panic began to grow. He looked back at the angel. "I'm afraid!"

Narcissus stepped forward and took both of Harry's hands in his. The heat from the angel's glowing flesh had an instant calming effect.

"Take your hands and place them over your eyes," Narcissus said. "You will feel that your eyes are closed."

As Harry obeyed, Narcissus added, "And now keep them covered."

Harry could feel that his eyelids were shut, yet he was still looking into the angel's face. He pressed his hands firmly over *both his eyes and looked down to see that Narcissus was still holding his hands. He pulled them away apprehensively.*

"What does this mean?" Harry asked.

"It means you are asleep as I have said. But where we are going, you will have no need of your body. Now, if you are willing, come with me into the supernatural."

Harry was torn between fear and exhilaration. "All right," he answered.

"Then take my hand again," Narcissus said and reached out his own. Harry took hold and instantly the image of his dream melted away.

At once, Harry felt weightless. As far as he could tell, he still had a body but it had been altered somehow. His surroundings had also changed. There was nothing immediately in view.

"Where are we?" he asked.

"We have just crossed over from the natural to the supernatural," explained Narcissus. "From here, we can see things that have been, things that are, *and* sometimes, even things that *could* be."

"But *this*," Harry gestured to himself, "I'm different . . . it's—"

"Of course, let me show you." Narcissus steered him around a short distance. Then, just like opening a window, his room appeared. All his things were just as he'd left them, and there in his bed he saw himself lying fast asleep.

"Strange!" Harry remarked as he continued to stare at himself as though hypnotized.

"Come," Narcissus urged. "I have things to show you."

Harry acquiesced. As he turned toward Narcissus, he saw the window of his room fade.

"Will I be okay?" he gestured back toward his room.

"Of course. You're with me."

Together, they sped off like radio waves through space. He could feel himself moving, but there was nothing to visually confirm it.

Within moments, another window appeared before them. Harry watched as the frame opened up into a radiant and picturesque garden. He and Narcissus were perched in the opening and could see far in every direction. From the first glimpse, the sights and smells were utterly delightful to all the senses. Down below was a row of immense, majestic trees. Giant ferns of bright yellow and gold and royal blue fanned out and draped over the ground like huge carousels of lucid bloom. Exotic flowers of unknown origin sprouted from everywhere with sequined petals and generous blossoms. The aroma was more fragrant than plumeria, filling the air with an intoxicating perfume. All around the well-manicured trails was an unusual variety of wild fruit growing in abundance, ready to gather. A cool and gentle breeze blew through the trees and vines, spreading the rich scents all around, while a stream of crystal clear water flowed down from the higher country. The stream made its way through the garden, creating pools here and there as it followed its gravitational course. Harry became swiftly aware of the refreshing music of the small songbirds—beautiful sonnets, freely cast to the wind, each a unique and simple ballad of thanksgiving.

This garden was the most sumptuous scene Harry could ever have imagined. He sat with Narcissus, in awe of the splendor, when out from among the trees stepped a woman.

She was radiant.

Harry almost blushed realizing the woman was unclothed. He glanced at Narcissus who beckoned him to pay attention. He watched curiously as she stepped out into the open like a doe, carefully walking amidst the plants and flowers. Without fear she began to sing softly. Her beautiful melody drifted through the air, without words, invoking extreme passion. Like a siren she called, and the garden answered her. Water gurgled around her, flowing from one pool to the next, while songbirds flitted about her and joined in the chorus. Like fairy music, they seemed to follow the theme.

Harry tried not to focus on her nakedness, but it was impossible. Her body was that of a goddess—pale, milky white moonlit skin. She had a slender but voluptuous figure, curvaceous and wholesome in every respect. Her hair was brown and thick, all curled in ringlets, falling down to the small of her back.

She turned suddenly and appeared to look directly at

Harry. He flinched as if discovered by her, but Narcissus calmed him, reassuring him of their concealed position. He studied her face—nothing short of stunning. Her simple smooth features were all wrapped into a wise expression of innocence, serenity, and alertness.

Bending down, she picked up a large hand-woven basket and began gathering fruit. She seemed selective as she made her way, choosing only certain pieces. Harry noticed now there was something in her gait. He sensed the slightest bit of apprehension on her part, which increased as she continued towards the center of the garden. Still confident, she moved purposefully to a certain gnarled little tree, which appeared to stand alone in a solitary clearing. The outgrowth on the tree was a scant red fruit, nothing impressive.

She thoughtfully set her basket to the side and hesitated before the knotted limbs of the twisted bush. Then she spoke, personally addressing the tree.

"Oh, beautiful tree—where is your Keeper? I have come to say, after careful consideration, I have not been able to find any reason why I should not accept your gift. I *must* know what you have to offer—I want my eyes to be opened. Yes, I will taste of your fruit."

She studied the fruit and then plucked one of the larger selections from its limbs. She glanced around nervously and then eagerly bit into the flesh of the swollen form. The red juice splashed like blood out onto her neck and chest as she let out a faint sigh of pleasure. But no sooner did she find satisfaction than she immediately became agitated and tense. She placed the remainder of the piece of fruit into her basket. There she stood, still for a moment. The garden had become quiet and still. Then, with her bushel in hand, she trudged back up the trail from where she had come, paused suddenly before a large fern, and examined the plant. Setting down her bundle, she proceeded to tear several of the giant leaves from it and fashioned them into a wrap, with which she immediately covered herself. She stepped over to a pool of water and stood there, leaning over, staring at her own reflection.

To Harry, she looked ravishing. The gold and blue ferns were like an exquisite gown, but her face revealed something lost. The blank expression she wore gave no indication of her thoughts. A single teardrop fell from her face and hit the water, blurring the beautiful image. She looked up.

"Adam!" she whispered, and seizing her basket, she ran off into the trees.

Harry realized he was gripping Narcissus' arm tightly and released him. He wiped his damp face with his hands.

"Was it *real?*" Harry exclaimed. "Did this really happen?"

"Just as you saw it," Narcissus answered.

"What does it mean, Narcissus? Why did you show me this?"

"What this means is that no matter how beautiful or

intelligent or *innocent*, every human being is susceptible to deception."

"She *was* innocent, wasn't she?"

"She had been expressly warned."

"What do you mean?"

"You don't know the story, Harry?"

Harry looked uncertain.

"Harry, this is about deception. And the one *certain* thing about deception is that when one is being deceived, he or she is never fully aware of it."

"Really?"

"Of course. Either that, or one has *allowed* himself to be deceived in an effort to gain some desire. Either way he or she is still oblivious."

"I see," said Harry, soberly.

"In this case," the angel continued, "I believe that any human being placed in *her* position and circumstance would have done the very same thing."

"So she had no choice?" Harry asked.

"Of course she had a choice," Narcissus countered. "I just mean that given the same conditions, anyone else would have chosen as she did. Don't fool yourself into thinking that there's someone out there who would not have been tempted. This is the nature of free will, to *know* what one is choosing. The problem is by knowing something or gaining the understanding—say good and evil—one must have aligned oneself with that position, at some point."

"Really?" Harry looked confused.

"Of course! Light and darkness cannot occupy the same space, can they?"

"All I know," Harry said with his head bowed, "is I feel sorry for her."

"I understand," Narcissus whispered. "At times, I feel sorry for you all."

7
The Bank and a Very Dark Place

Harry wasn't sure how much time had elapsed since the window to the garden had faded. For all he knew, minutes or months could have passed. He knew they were "outside" of time, but what did that mean? He was still so overwhelmed by the vision he could hardly think of anything else.

Eve?

He wanted to go back and help her—to save her somehow. But of course he could do nothing. Then something interrupted his thoughts—it was Narcissus touching him—no, holding him. "Narcissus?"

"Yes, Harry?"

"I'm okay now," Harry assured the angel, pulling away uneasily.

"Are you ready to see more?"

"I suppose so. What is it?"

"It is *this*," Narcissus answered, stretching his hand out with a gesture as another window began to appear before them.

Harry instantly recognized the building in the scene—the Isles End bank. It was the newest building in town, very attractive with beautiful stone columns, a covered wooden deck, and old-fashioned benches to each side of the front door. Flowerpots overflowing with lobelia and petunias hung all along the front of the building.

"Hey, that's my bank!" Harry exclaimed with surprise.

"Yes, now pay attention," the Archangel responded soberly.

Standing near the front door, Harry saw two elderly women speaking to one another. As the scene moved in closer, he noticed something peculiar about each of them. The smaller frail-looking woman was hunched over and seemed to have some kind of strange growth near the top of her back. Behind the other healthier looking woman, a tall stately figure stood radiating light around her like a shield. The vision gradually brought Harry closer to the two women until he was able to make out their conversation.

". . . yes, it's really something," the stronger woman said, smiling.

"I don't know," said the hunched-over woman. "I'm having a difficult time getting around these days—my back, you know."

Harry shuddered suddenly as the growth on the woman's shoulders began to squirm. *What in the name of . . . !* Now, as the vision moved in closer still, he recognized the growth was in the form of a small head growing out from between her shoulder blades. It was whispering in her ear.

"I just don't have the energy I used to," it spoke.

"I just don't have the energy I used to," she repeated.

"Oh, my dear," the fit woman implored, "you don't know what a good outing can do for you!"

Now the lump on the smaller woman's back growled and bared its teeth, while the angelic guardian of the other stepped forward. The head whispered again, and the weaker woman echoed, "I'll give you a call if I change my mind."

"I'll give *you* a call either way," the other woman countered. "I worry about you, dear." Was she oblivious to the ugly thing protruding from behind the smaller woman's neck? "Somebody's got to check up on you once in a while."

Then she reached out her arm and patted the other woman gently. The head cringed horribly and shrunk away until the robust woman and her defender walked down the deck towards the parking lot. The vision followed the smaller woman into the bank where she waved to a man behind a large desk.

"Hello, Mrs. Matson! Please come over and have a seat." The man politely helped her to a chair. "Can I get you anything? How about some coffee?"

"I guess you've forgotten already—I prefer tea," she said as she struggled to make herself comfortable.

The banker left, and then returned shortly with a cup of tea on a saucer which he placed in front of the elderly patron. He sat back down in his chair and leaned forward.

"See, I haven't forgotten. Here you go—Earl Grey with a little honey, right?

Her features softened as she accepted the cup.

"So, how are we doing today, Mrs. Matson?" the banker asked.

"Well, you know why I'm here, Mr. Hauser."

It was Mr. Hauser . . . of course!

Harry recognized the man from his own visits to the bank. He seemed different now that Harry was watching him from an alternate perspective. As he studied the scene, it became apparent that the back of the banker's chair was moving. But then . . . it wasn't the back of the chair at all, but a dark shrouded form, almost like a cape with a large turned up collar wrapped around the man while he spoke.

"Yes, of course. I've got all the papers ready for you to sign," he smiled wryly.

The head hissed something to her and she repeated, "Mr. Hauser, we spoke about some High-tech and bio-tech stocks that were going public soon? You mentioned a couple we could still purchase privately—"

The dark veil around him now hid his features as he leaned back. "Oh, yes, Mrs. Matson, the documents are right here—prepared for you just as you requested. You may take this home if you like and review it at your leisure. One in particular looks to be a very auspicious opportunity, and is still available privately—we just bought three point five million shares." He pointed his finger halfway down one of the forms in front of her. "Here it is: Advanced Bio-Cell, Incorporated. Yes, take special notice of that one."

Again, the deformed creature spoke purposefully into the woman's ear, and she resounded obediently with a swift change of manner.

"I'm looking for a simple answer, Mr. Hauser," she complained, sipping her tea.

"Yes, Mrs. Matson—"

But before he could respond any further, she continued.

"I don't want to take 'special notice.' That's why I've retained you. And I don't want to take anything home, either. Let's put it this way—you have a lot of *my* money. If you want to *keep it* that way, then you need to make it multiply, however you do that. Let me sign these papers, and *next* time I come in to see you, show me some results!"

"My dear Mrs. Matson," the banker spoke calmly, unaffected by her brusque behavior. "Let me assure you that your portfolio is in the best of hands. Some of the recent acquisitions we have made in some of the most innovative new companies in the world are going to make us very, very comfortable."

"Well, that's wonderful, Mr. Hauser. It's comforting to know there is someone like *you* looking after my best interests," she said as she scribbled her name at the bottom of each document. The dark shape enveloped Mr. Hauser as he received the signed forms from Mrs. Matson.

Harry watched as the banker helped the old woman out of her chair and out to the front door. As she exited the building a young gentleman approached and Mr. Hauser paused to hold the door open for him. A tall broad-shouldered being of light accompanied the man. Harry looked around and became aware of other people in the building. Nearly all of them were chaperoned by various apparitions, each appearing to have different degrees of commitment to their prospective hosts. Some came and went like bees pollinating a field, airy and intangible. Others had become permanent appendage-like fixtures of their victims, as in the case of Mrs. Matson.

One man who was struggling to breathe had a very heavy-looking form attached to his waist and dragging behind him. A woman at his side had a thick cloud of smoke enveloping her head. As Harry studied the scene, he could discern that some of the spirits clearly had honorable intentions while others appeared to have darker motives. One thing was sure, he thought—they all moved about as though it were business as usual.

Harry turned to Narcissus with a disturbed expression on his face. "What is all this supposed to mean?"

"What do you make of it, Harry?"

"It appears there is much more going on than meets the eye. I wonder if this too, is all *real*?"

"The scene is exactly as you observe, except you are seeing things through spiritual eyes,"

"I never imagined—"

"You know, Harry, just because you can't see something doesn't mean it isn't there." Narcissus turned away from the vision as it began to fade. "Consider the wind. You can't see it, but the power of it moves ships across the oceans, tears buildings violently from their foundations, and erodes mountains into dust."

"I never thought of it that way before. But what about these people, Narcissus? Don't *they* have a choice? Or must they be subject to any or every entity which chooses to prey upon them—or to assist them?"

"Look at it this way. Counsel and direction are presented to them daily from every venue of life. Even from moment to moment, they are faced with decisions—some complicated, but usually simple: what to eat, what to wear, how to respond to any given situation. Generally, human beings will listen to the advice they *want* to hear. So you see, whatever these souls have acquired, as you've witnessed, they have invited themselves. You have also recognized not *all* of the "entities" are harbingers of ill will."

"You're right, Narcissus—there is *you*!" Harry looked at his angelic guide with wonder. The angel smiled back, possibly for the first time, Harry thought as he gazed into the Seraph's glowing features.

"Narcissus, I'm wondering . . . well, I guess *you* didn't have access to me, before I found you, but have I ever been a *victim* to any of these . . . undetectable advisors?"

"Actually, you are one of those who has lived without gaining the attention of any type of spirit. Due to your inimitability, I don't believe you've ever been approached. In other words, Harry, you are unique."

"Really? What do you mean, exactly?"

"Well, you are different, though there are still many others like you. I believe we shall soon see exactly how and why. But having had no conscious knowledge or real contact with anything, say, *mystical*, still you have done well intuitively. You've made decisions in your life that have kept you shielded. There is the work of a greater power or decree imprinted on your being. Does this make any sense to you?"

"Well, not really."

"Harry, why do you think I'm here with you?"

"That's what I'm trying to figure out." Harry said with increased confidence. "This is all new to me. I'm completely amazed and questioning my sanity at the same time. When you're with me, your presence feels real. But these last couple of days have been anything but normal! I still don't understand what your purpose is. You haven't given me much of an explanation, you know?"

Narcissus was quiet for a moment, then, "I promise to explain more soon."

Harry's agitation erupted. "Narcissus! Are you here to help me? Is something going to happen to me that you already know about? Are you some kind of guardian angel? Did you know I would find you in that—?"

The Seraph raised his hand and Harry paused.

"Am I here to help you? Yes, but maybe not in the way you might think. I am here to offer you guidance. Let me tell you something. There are many spirits searching this world. Now, even here in Isles End, you have seen a variety of spirits who have direct interaction with men. Some are here to help while others merely want to manipulate and control. Harry, you have a calling but this is not uncommon in itself, for all beings have purpose. You might say that I am here to help you discover what your purpose is."

"So, you are like the 'light guardians' I saw at the bank?"

"Very good—but look! *My* veil has been lifted. We are able to see and communicate with each other face to face. I can give instruction, but like all men it is up to you to choose how you will follow the path which has been set before you."

"Okay, so the purpose of this recent revelation about Isles End is . . . ?"

"To see for a moment beyond what is physical and to understand the deception that continually surrounds you."

"Beyond what is physical," Harry repeated. "Is it like this everywhere?"

"You'd be amazed."

Harry considered for a moment. "And what am I supposed to learn from this revelation?"

Narcissus looked at him intently. "Why don't you take some time to think about that question?"

"Okay," Harry answered with a half-formed grin, "I'm thinking about the reference to Advanced Bio-Cell we heard about in the bank. Should I plan to buy some of this stock? I mean, was this the intention of this vision?"

"No, it was not the purpose at all! Are you—" Narcissus paused, wondering if Harry was really being serious with him. Then he continued, "It's obvious that investors all around the world are putting their assets into new technologies. *How* the funds are routed in specific directions could be interesting to speculate upon. But when it comes to the art of accumulating wealth, men don't need a lot of help from unearthly sources— they actually do just fine on their own. Now on the other hand, the ability to manipulate and control the financial institutions and those in power could serve well those whose desire is to direct nations, empower governments or pursue any other degree of domination. But listen, there is only so much I am able to share. Do you understand that you have been given a great opportunity here? Look! You have a natural ability to discern what you see without any help. I would recommend that you cultivate *that* gift."

"Hmm..." Harry lowered his head in thought.

"If you're feeling satisfactory, we have one more objective. Are you alright?"

"Well, I'm a little short on time—will this take long?" Harry raised his head and grinned.

Narcissus pressed urgently, "I understand your jest, Harry, but I'm sorry to say our next destination will be rather grim."

"And what would you call the *last* two visions?"

"Bear with me, my friend."

Harry looked at Narcissus with sobriety and concern as a new window opened before them. At first, the image was indiscernible. Harry gazed through the opening and tried to make sense of the shadowy landscape that appeared before him. He could see miles of countless spherical objects all about, shiftless and unconnected. But he realized there *was* no landscape. He could only see the defining line between a vast sea of idle drifting forms and the dark space above and around them.

"It looks like an ocean," Harry remarked, but Narcissus kept silent.

The immensity of the scene was almost overwhelming. In fact, Harry felt dizzy and was nearly sick for a moment and had to look away. Clearly what he witnessed did not abide in the physical realm at all, like the visions before. This was somewhere far removed from the world he knew. He watched with mixed emotions of curiosity and foreboding as the vision became clearer.

Again, the window seemed to transport them nearer to a specific area, right up to the edge of where the surge of spheres began. Harry could see each orb was clearly independent of those around it. They all appeared to be floating together in stasis, swaying slightly to and fro, but remaining together as though magnetically held by opposing forces. They looked like enormous eggs.

A sea of eggs. An ocean of stagnation. How many were there? Thousands? More!

The area was vast, Harry guessed as he gazed across the expanse of endless space. Another peculiar thing, the entire scene was void of color and sound. Only various shades of gray could be discerned. He wondered how he was able to *see* anything at all. There was no source of light to be found.

Harry turned his attention to the orb closest to him. There was something detestable about it. The object was quivering silently and almost appeared to be breathing as it expanded and contracted. Having to watch the alien looking organism became almost intolerable and he felt he might be sick again. He was about to ask Narcissus what this meant and if they had to stay any longer when he was distracted by a sudden bright light.

The radiance appeared directly before him. At first he felt a sense of deja vu, but then knew exactly where he had experienced this phenomenon before. There was a fragrance, accompanied by a subtle breeze. He turned to Narcissus and then back to the light. The familiar transformation was much quicker this time and the scent was different, but this presence was undeniably another angelic being. As the figure rapidly formed, the delicate zephyr produced was striking in this mute landscape.

Like Narcissus, this creature was extraordinarily beautiful to behold. Noble and strong, its body glowed in the same way as his angelic friend, but rather than a simple robe, the being wore a magnificent full length gown with many folds in rich shades of blue and lavender that lit up the entire area. The colors were even more brilliant in this gray and colorless void.

The being stood tall and fearless as it somberly viewed the expanse. Then it opened its robe. To Harry's surprise, a man emerged and stood before the godlike creature. The man was naked and appeared small and insignificant before his host. The Seraph looked solemnly down at the man and spoke with a voice of command.

"This is the final destination of the path which you have chosen!"

The small man gazed around at the endless gray sea of orbs and began to moan. He turned back to the angelic being.

"Where are we?" he managed to gasp.

"This is Gehenna," the Seraph replied.

The man fell on his knees, choking. "Is there no other choice?"

"You have had your audience—"

The man coughed for a moment and then spoke bitterly.

"Yes, my audience . . . I thought I was going to die right there! I heard my own tongue confessing my failures. I saw clearly the *many* opportunities I'd been given to choose life, and I *knew!"* His body began to shake and he lowered his head as he whimpered. "So many times—I see now . . . I allowed myself to be mislead."

At this point he began to weep desperately while he continued. "Who am I?" he pleaded with a gurgling cry, "What have I become?" The words grated out painfully. "I intentionally concealed and perverted the truth with the intention of misleading myself and others as well. And I refused to allow the truth to ever come too near. *Why?*"

He bowed his head in shame and began to shake. The Seraph stood above him waiting quietly.

"Still, I do not wish to be here . . . " The man's voice was hardly audible, as the words bled out like an untended wound while his face emitted immense torment.

"It is time," the magnificent Archangel spoke.

"But wait," interrupted the man, his teeth grinding. "Is there any way my family can be warned? Otherwise, how will they know? Please, sir, I can't stand it—the thought of them—ending up here, like *this! PLEASE!"* he wailed.

"The work has already been done," the Angel boomed.

Then he leaned forward and lowered his voice, "The truth has been written all across creation. The wonders of His works have been placed on display everywhere you look. They cannot be hidden, only ignored. Your family, your friends—they have been given every sign they need. But now," the formidable Seraph thundered again, raising his arms, "IT IS TIME!"

The man shrieked horribly as the Archangel opened his mouth. From his jaws came a sword of seething light which struck down and enveloped the man. His convulsing body could be seen momentarily inside the molten casting, which was now forming into a spherical shape all around him. Inside, it was fiery, but the surface quickly cooled into a dull gray, while his image disappeared inside. A few moments passed, silent and still, then without hesitation, the newly formed orb floated idly over to join the rest of the shiftless drifting spheres. There, it quivered briefly and settled into place.

The air was still again, and the brilliant Archangel stood with authority over the Sea of Gehenna. In a strange way, it was awe-inspiring to see him standing there, shining so radiantly over a place of such desolation. But then the Archangel closed his robe and vanished as quickly as he had appeared. The light vanished with him and once again the scene no longer held any attraction. Colorless and quiet, dull and dark, the ocean of spheres took on a different guise, sickeningly empty and lonely. Now Harry felt the anguish and despair. He looked out over the vast landscape and guessed at the continual torment of isolation and regret. He understood there was no immediate threat to him in this place, yet he was still overwhelmed with fear and gloom.

Narcissus stepped back and the vision began to fade. He considered the expression on Harry's face.

"I'm sorry, Harry, if all this seems overwhelming to you."

"Overwhelming? Yes! But I think 'horribly dark and hopeless' would describe it better. Can we leave now?"

"Are you so troubled?"

"Narcissus, will that man be forever encased in that . . . tomb?"

"Every creature with a soul must abide somewhere."

Harry could not hide his horror. He looked up at Narcissus with dread. "I don't think he ever could have chosen

94

that!"

"But you see that he did. Ultimately, all things must be fulfilled, *one* of them being justice. For those who expect little, much will be given, but to those who demand their portion, even a small portion shall be denied. This man finally knew the wrongness of his choices and the penalty that was due, just as all creatures will someday fully understand their road has led them to their final destination."

"Still, Narcissus, will he be forever alone?"

"Ultimately, this truth holds true for every creature—for a design to be separated from the designer means the design will be desperately and utterly alone."

"I don't understand."

"Think about my statement, Harry."

"I don't understand eternal separation! It seems incredibly harsh," Harry responded sadly.

Narcissus thought for a moment and then said, "Tell me, which would seem more harsh? Me . . . forcing you to accompany me, or instead, letting you decide to follow or not to follow?"

Harry answered quickly, "The first one of course . . . to be forced."

"There you have it—see? You've answered your own question."

"But if I *knew* that by *not* following you, it would lead to ultimate isolation—"

"Yes," Narcissus was ready, "Exactly why I would have warned you ahead of time, but would you listen to me? Would you believe me?"

"I don't know, Narcissus. I suppose you're right. I just feel sick," he muttered and closed his eyes.

"And you're not the only one," the angel continued. "I would joyfully remove this place from existence if I could, but truth and logic necessitate it. You see, Harry, the truth is, every action and choice that is made has a result—a reaction, if you will. If you have committed a crime and have no one to stand in for you or take your place, you are responsible for your actions and must suffer the consequences. And who will do that? Justice dictates the penalty for wrongdoing must be paid. What would happen in a universe where evil deeds had no consequences, where no one was accountable for what he did or for how it affected him or others? Life on earth would surely be chaotic; but as you can see, the earth and the cosmos is not filled with chaos. The opposite in fact is true, this universe is well thought out, planned and orderly. The need for justice is no stranger to men. Even your courts do not allow unlawful deeds to go unpunished."

Harry nodded thoughtfully in agreement.

"Harry," the Archangel continued, but now with a different purpose in his manner, "I must take a moment to make my intentions clear to you. I have been given instructions regarding you. It has been my purpose to enlighten you with the specific images you have witnessed, in order that by doing so, you will be more fully aware of true reality. First, that anyone can be deceived, regardless of how good or pure or smart he or she might seem—in fact, someone of *this* nature might be even *more* susceptible to deception. Secondly, the condition of being deceived is commonplace, actually accepted and even invited on a continual basis. There are many who court deception regularly, to the point they are betrothed to it. Thirdly, there is a permanent result for the one who allows himself to be deceived—it is not something for which he is unaccountable. In other words, if one is deceived, he is *still* responsible and must accept the consequences for his actions."

"Have I been deceived, Narcissus?"

"Do you mean right now, or ever?"

"I don't know—how about right now? Am I being deceived right now?"

"Do you mean, by me?"

"Well yes, sure. I'm just asking—"

"What do *you* think, Harry?"

"Well, I guess—and you can probably understand—I have had my concerns. I mean, I have wondered if I am even in my right mind! But, if you are real . . . and I'm sure you are. . . and since I believe in you, then I wonder if I can be deceived by you. But I feel a trust with you and everything seems to make sense. Otherwise, why would you be sharing these things with me? So, I believe I am not being deceived by you. But now I'm confusing myself. Sorry if I—"

"Don't be sorry, Harry. It is your duty to measure and discern each experience you encounter and to trust the gift you have. Once again, cultivate this gift—let it mature and grow."

"Narcissus, it just occurred to me, I think one of my difficulties has always been that I feel very weak. So often I am not sure about many things that I ought to be sure of. If I were stronger, I'd be more confident in myself and less likely to be fooled or misled."

"Yes?"

"So, what's wrong with me?"

"There is nothing wrong with you, outside of being human. Trust me! The acceptance of your weakness is a good thing. Accepting weakness is the first step to becoming strong."

"Okay, I'm going to have to think about that one for a little while, but somehow I think I do understand."

Narcissus reached out and put his hand on Harry's shoulder. Instantly, Harry felt a strengthening.

"Now I *know* I was tired," Harry said, looking refreshed. "But how is it possible for me to be tired in this out-of-body thing? I felt almost completely exhausted a moment ago and now—"

"You *were* tired, Harry, maybe not in a physical way, but mentally and emotionally, yes! We are finished for now, but we will continue this conversation later. Come."

Narcissus motioned Harry towards another window just ahead of them. The place in the image was strangely familiar. As they stood together, gazing forward, the window frame began to expand before them until they were swallowed into it. Harry realized they were back on the rooftop of the building in his dream.

"Wow, how did you do that?" he marveled.

Narcissus grinned. "A simple parlor trick. But I forget—you are still easily impressed."

"I am impressed, Narcissus. That is, when I can accept you as real and not some twisted part of my imagination that's snapped under the pressures of my weak life. By the way, when are you planning to impress me again—with your presence, that is? I mean, it would be nice to know when I could expect to see you again, whether it's in a dream, or maybe—"

"I can't say right now, Harry, exactly when I will return to you, but I promise it will be soon. In fact, you can expect to see me within seven days."

"Thank you, really! That's all I needed." Harry sighed.

Narcissus looked at his earthly friend and smiled fondly. "If you go into that doorway," he pointed to the only entrance on the roof, " you'll be lead to a room where you can immediately rest. Otherwise, you may dream on; it's up to you. Until I join you again, I wish you peace, Harry. I hope the visions of this night will give you deeper insight into the struggles you must all face here in this world and also into your own personal plight."

Narcissus reached out and touched Harry's shoulder, and again Harry felt a surge of energy flow out from the Archangel.

"Now watch this, Harry."

The Seraph laughed and threw back his robe. Two enormous wings flared out from his shoulders and in one great flutter, Narcissus shot straight up into the sky and disappeared.

Harry laughed aloud, but just as suddenly as his exhilaration flourished, he returned to a somber state of mind with more unanswered questions. For one, he wanted to know what his "plight" was. There didn't seem to be a whole lot going on in his life that he would classify as a serious dilemma or predicament. He accepted the fact that he would have to wait, and though he was refreshed and currently sleeping, he welcomed an exit from this place. He walked over to the doorway and stepped through it. There was a short hallway and another door, which he opened. Inside was a room identical to his apartment, and there at the foot of his bed was the chest he had moved into the closet. He smiled and closed the door behind him. Climbing onto the bed, Harry instantly faded away.

8
Taffy and Merlot

Harry opened his eyes and sat up in his bed. For a moment, he stayed right there and gazed around his room. It seemed like days or even weeks since he'd been here. It was hard to believe that just yesterday he'd made plans to meet with Beth—and tonight was the night!

Climbing out of bed, he went to put a potato into the microwave, and nearly fell over the chest at the foot of his bed. Had he taken it back out of the closet? No, but in the dream— Narcissus must have moved the box! He checked the lock—it was still intact. He turned the combination just for good measure and lifted the lid. Again, there was the unique scent of the angel, but something else was in the box. He reached down inside and lifted the object from the bottom. He held a large branch, a fern of the most unusual and magnificent shades of blue and gold. Harry knew exactly where it had come from. He sat there for a moment recalling the scene of the splendid garden and the beautiful woman.

Eve!

He nearly swooned at the thought of her.

He studied the golden cerulean wand as he held it ever so carefully in his hand. The branch was fresh and real, and somehow very old, he realized. Was this the Seraph's way of telling Harry he wasn't losing his mind? Maybe a small memento of something tangible which he could not *possibly* explain any other way. He soaked in the rich colors for a moment and then carefully placed the branch back into the chest.

In a way, this made matters worse. How could he even try to explain these experiences to anyone?

Yeah, I visited Eve! You know, EVE . . . the original woman. . . the mother of the human race? And I've got this fern leaf to prove it!

He could see the straight jacket being made ready.

Once again, Harry wondered how he was able to treat the entire affair with such calmness. Every time Narcissus came to him, he felt clear headed and unafraid, but after each visit he couldn't help but wonder if the whole experience had been his own strange fantasy. All he could do for now was put the whole experience out of his head and try to concentrate on the day at hand.

In an effort to regain his focus, Harry spent most of the morning trying to put together a schedule for the projects he was running, but he continually found himself inundated with memories of the time he'd spent with his angelic host. The garden. . . the bank. . . the sea of spheres . . . *and what they contained!* Narcissus said it was all about recognizing deception.

Finally, he got on the phone with Ed, who had now officially assumed the position of foreman. They made arrangements to hire a couple of temporary laborers and discussed the upcoming schedule. They agreed to have the entire mess cleaned up that week and then begin framing. Harry's focus became sharper as he went over the details of the project with his anxious friend. He thrived on the process of setting everything in motion and then watching as the wheels turned and his ideas became reality. And so, by discussing business, he felt himself coming back down to earth.

Harry followed up with some other calls to trusted sub-contractors in the city and arranged to meet with them at Advanced Bio-Cell the following day. He was amazed at how well things were working out and found himself wondering if Narcissus had a hand in any of the trite circumstances of his life. By late afternoon, Harry had the rest of the week planned.

He decided to head into town for the bottle of merlot and saltwater taffy Beth had requested. He knew very little about wine and so opted for the slightly more expensive, twenty-five dollar bottle of merlot. He was not a wine drinker and didn't really appreciate the dark red stuff, but he figured he could suffer through a glass or two. The taffy was easy—a small handful of every flavor placed in a bag and he was ready to go. His stomach began to knot up as he made his way toward Beth's place. Maybe a glass of wine would come in handy after all.

As he crossed the Isles Inlet Bridge, he wondered how much Narcissus knew about Beth. Or for that matter, what did the Archangel know about Reese Orchard, or Advanced Bio-Cell, or its other employees? Did Narcissus have any idea about the type of spiritual influences any of *these* people might have? Who was whispering in *their* ears? Had the celestial being already looked ahead through a window to see the outcome of Harry's relationship with Beth, assuming there would even be one?

He didn't want to worry about the future. In any case, there was no sense in worrying. There was nothing *he* could do anyway. Besides, Narcissus seemed trustworthy and he believed the angel would warn him if something dangerous were about to happen. He made a mental note—ask his angelic companion about all these things at their very next visit. For now, he decided to relax and enjoy the company of the very lovely Beth Fairbanks.

Her home was a charming little cottage on a small lot across the river from town. Plum trees grew in the back yard, planted evenly along an old wooden fence that enclosed the property. There was a large corkscrew willow in front, partially draped over the roof on one side and the fence on the other. Smoke curled up out of the chimney and the shuttered windows in front were all steamed up. He saw her smiling face appear in one of the windows as she wiped the steam off the glass with her hand and waved to him. He parked next to a pearl white Karmann Ghia. *That's got to be Beth's car,* he thought. He shut off the engine and hopped out of his truck. Before he reached the front door, she was standing there waiting for him.

"Did you find me okay?" she asked as he wiped his shoes on the doormat.

"No problem," he answered. Fumbling with the wine and

taffy he stepped inside and she followed him, closing the door behind her.

Inside was warm and cozy. There was a fire burning in the fireplace, and the smell of something good coming from the kitchen. Then, the sweet sound of Beth's voice.

"So, what have you got there, Harry?" she asked playfully.

"Oh . . . *this* is for you," he replied, attempting to set the wine and the taffy onto the kitchen counter.

"Here, let me help you," she intervened by taking the bottle of wine out of his hands and glanced at the label. "Oh, this is an excellent wine, Harry. You know . . ." she hesitated, and then continued. "It was really nice of you to bring the wine and taffy, although I didn't give you much choice, did I?"

"Oh, it was my pleasure! In fact, my mom taught me to always bring something when invited into someone's home."

"Hmm, sounds like your mom taught you well—can I get you anything?"

Harry was thinking a soda would be good. "Sure, whatever you're having."

"Well," she said, "why don't we have a glass of this wine now, and we can save the rest for dinner."

"Dinner, yeah! It smells great. What is it?"

"My mom's recipe for pot roast. She used to make it for us almost every Sunday. It's a simple meal to prepare, but don't tell anyone!"

Harry nodded with a grin as Beth poured two glasses and carried them into the living room. There was a small coffee table in front of the fireplace and a stuffed chair to either side. Harry followed her as she placed coasters on the table and set the glasses down.

"Come on, Harry, have a seat."

He sat across from Beth as she lifted her glass and held it up over the table. "How about a toast?"

"Sure," he replied. Feeling a little pressure, he promptly held up his glass and announced the first thing that came to mind.

"Here's to Advanced Bio-Cell."

"Yes," she responded swiftly. "May they have incredible success, and bring us many beautiful and extremely smart children."

Harry clearly had a stunned expression on his face as he weighed Beth's statement with his glass still held high.

"Harry, I'm being facetious!" she quickly added, laughing due to the expression on Harry's face. "You *know* they work with cell structure and genetics, right?"

Hearing this, he immediately redirected his demeanor to humor.

"No, I'm with you. I just didn't realize you wanted so many children. I was thinking maybe only eight or ten."

This made her laugh again and Harry laughed with her. He watched her tip the glass to her lips, and while doing likewise, he realized how much he enjoyed the sound of her laughter. He found himself feeling very relaxed, his guard down and his nervousness fading.

Good wine, he thought, as he let it coat the inside of his mouth.

Harry had a sudden resurgence of self-confidence. As he swallowed the first drink of merlot it occurred to him that Beth actually reminded him of Jennifer. Physically she was built similarly and seemed to share the same kind of boldness and self-assurance Jenny had always displayed. But he didn't want to be reminded of Jennifer now, nor did he want to replace her. He liked Beth and hoped to discover her without the memory of his beloved Jenny . . . interfering. It had been well over a year now, he reminded himself. Wasn't that considered a long enough wait—avoiding the proverbial "rebound" relationship? Not that he'd had a whole lot of opportunities as of late. Either way, he couldn't wait forever.

For the time being, he did not have a difficult time putting away these thoughts. Here was Beth, sitting in front of him, sipping her wine and smiling, looking extremely lovely in her ironed blue jeans and white blouse. Now this girl, he thought, could make him forget about anything—if he needed to. But the fact was, there was currently nothing he needed to forget. He felt he was facing an attraction he could not possibly ignore and was enjoying the experience immensely.

He watched as she set her glass of wine down on the coffee table and started towards the fireplace.

"Do you need some help with that?" he offered.

"Oh no, I'm fine. When it comes to fires, I'm sort of a pyro," she stated with a grin.

"Oh, really?"

"Oh yeah," she continued. "Growing up, I was the oldest. Whenever we went camping, I got to be in charge of the fire."

"Ah, the eldest child?"

Beth nodded as she easily placed another log onto the fire. "Yes, I've got two younger sisters who live in my folks' old place. I was with them until last year when I moved here to be on my own. I have an aunt who lives here in Isles End. She helped me find this place."

"So where are your folks?" Harry ventured.

"Well, we lost my dad to cancer about a year and a half ago," Beth looked somber. "It happened very quickly—everything seemed fine until he became ill and was diagnosed. The whole episode lasted about four months and then he was gone.

"Not long after that, my mom fell and broke her hip—things went downhill quickly after that. She . . ."

Harry watched her face begin to twist.

"I'm sorry. You don't need to—"

"No, Harry, I'm okay," she said as she rapidly blinked her eyes and pinched the top of her nose. "Yes—my mom, she quickly began to lose interest in all the activities she used to enjoy. I think she just missed my dad so much that she wanted to go and be with him, somehow. One morning we got up and she had gone in her sleep during the night."

"Wow," Harry whispered. "I'm really sorry."

"It's okay—I'm . . . *almost* fine now. I mean, I still miss them terribly sometimes but I have peace about it. I imagine they are together somewhere, you know?"

Harry nodded.

Beth returned to her chair and leaned forward. "I feel a bit odd telling you about my parents," she added. "I haven't talked about them or shared my loss with anyone for quite a while, but I think it's healthy."

"Yes, I agree," Harry smiled softly. Thank you for sharing with me. Actually, I didn't imagine I'd be telling you this tonight, but I lost both of my parents too, just over a year ago."

"Oh, Harry!" She exclaimed sadly.

"Yes, kind of a depressing coincidence, isn't it?"

He then proceeded to share the very basics of his parents' accident, skipping a few details, such as the fact that his fiancée had been on the plane with them. He almost felt like he was being dishonest by not including that part of the story, but he just couldn't bring himself to talk to Beth about Jennifer . . . not yet, anyway. So, at the same time as he felt awkward about it, he was also feeling deeply moved by the fact that they had something so tragic in common. He could tell Beth was touched, too. As they finished their first glass of wine and he helped her set the table, he sensed a somberness in their movements. It was as though the meal they were about to share had taken on a deeper meaning.

They sat across from each other in the small dining room. Beth lit candles and replenished the wine glasses. Harry wanted to carve the roast but Beth explained to him that the beef would just fall apart. While she fixed him up a healthy plate of meat, carrots, onions, and potatoes with lots of gravy, he asked her about her home. Did she rent or had she purchased it? She explained how her dad had invested wisely. After her mother died, the three girls inherited the old home and a sizable portfolio, including a considerable sum of insurance money. So when she decided on a place of her own, she was able to pay cash for it. She didn't seem to be afraid of discussing her personal finances with Harry and so likewise, he shared with her the similar circumstances of his financial condition.

As the evening progressed, Harry was continually amazed by the commonality of their experiences. It was uncanny how they were both currently working for the same company, so to speak, and they had recently moved to the same town, and then, the loss of their parents.

He was also pleased to find they shared similar tastes in literature and music. Beth had a book of art from the Symbolist period and Harry had the same copy on his bookshelf. They spent half an hour looking through Beth's copy and noted their favorite artists and paintings.

They shared their immediate and long-term goals, their careers, and their plans to move on with their lives with new experiences and changes of scenery. They both admitted escaping to Isles End to be removed from the pain and loss they experienced, and had also chosen the town because of its quaintness and remote setting. Of course they mutually agreed that Isles End was quite beautiful, still unaffected by what Beth referred to as the fast-food world.

Wherever their conversation went, the words flowed with ease. A friendship was rapidly forming. At one point, Harry almost wanted to ask her what she thought about celestial beings or angels but decided against it. He still wasn't completely sure how *he* felt about his recent experiences with Narcissus and didn't want to scare her away on their first date.

Before they realized it, the meal had been consumed, the bottle emptied, and the evening was getting late. Harry was not ready to leave but he knew he couldn't stay much later. After dinner, they moved to a small couch across from the coffee table and the fireplace. Beth called it the love seat. They sat there now and watched as the last remains of the fire crumbled into coals. The art book lay open on his lap and taffy wrappers were scattered all around. Beth chewed on a piece of peppermint taffy.

After a few moments of silence, she looked at Harry and asked innocently.

"What are you thinking about?"

He grinned back, "I was wondering if you were going to eat the whole bag of taffy tonight!"

Beth made a fist and struck him lightly on the shoulder.

"The bag wasn't that big!"

He faked intense pain and responded, "Okay, I'll have to make sure to bring a bigger bag next time."

"Oh yes!" she laughed. "I can't wait."

"Actually," he continued, "I was thinking that it's getting late."

"Really?"

"Well," He closed the book and set it on the coffee table. "I can see that you are wide awake and perky but don't you have to work in the morning?"

"Oh yeah, that!" Beth frowned as she began picking up the taffy wrappers.

"Yeah that," he repeated as he stood. "And I've got a meeting there tomorrow. I don't know what time you need to be up, but it's just past midnight now."

"You're right, Harry."

They both got up and Beth followed Harry to the door. He stood at the doorway and paused. Turning toward her, he looked into her eyes.

"Thanks for having me over," he took her hand in his and held it for a moment. "I had a really nice time."

"So did I."

"Can I give you a call soon?"

"I hope you will," she answered, and as he stepped away she added, "Good night, Harry."

"Good night, Beth. See you tomorrow at work," he said

smiling and turned toward his truck.

9
William Algren

William Algren sat behind a beautiful mahogany desk in his new leather arm chair and watched as the sun came up, bringing its warmth and light through the windows into his office. Everything in the room was shiny and new. The furniture, artwork, bookshelves, and computer equipment had all been delivered and set up the night before. Leaning forward he noticed his reflection in the glossy surface of the desktop. His rough features stared back at him with just a hint of a smile. He leaned back and considered the feel of his new space. The perspective he had from his desk felt powerful as he considered the placement of each article. His smile broadened as he acknowledged the plaque over the mantle of a small slate covered gas-log fireplace. It read, *Honoring Nature by Imitation.*

He swiveled the chair around to the window view.

This time of year the countryside was especially beautiful in the morning with the light and color reflecting off the distant hills. But more importantly, this land was conforming to the scheme that had been planned—a design for which Bill was directly responsible. Modeling the complex exclusively after the contours and lay of the terrain, he had been instrumental in designing the blueprints and every aspect of development. In regards to environmental concerns, he was keenly aware of the delicate balance between progress and growth, as well as the very ecosystem of nature.

This will be my modern-day Eden, he had declared to himself the day they signed the closing papers.

He remembered the look of intrigue on Reese Orchard's face when he described his vision for this large portion of real estate, to purchase the whole area and devote it entirely to new technologies. It would be a virtual Mecca of cutting edge science, physics, and chemistry—all research and development, and entirely related to genetics in one form or another.

Not only that, but all the buildings, streets, and landscaping would be completely harmonious with nature in every respect, utilizing the most current and innovative approaches to water and energy use, run-off and sewage treatment, as well as environmentally smart buildings. Above all, the entire area would be aesthetically pleasing to the eye in every way. All the landscaping would be colorful and lush. Fruit trees, flower gardens, waterfalls, and walkways would frame the buildings and line the streets. Rooftops would be gardens to trap the rain and siphon it through purifying systems. The windows would collect and store heat. There would not be a power line in sight. This would be his crowning achievement. A work of art with even the streets named after his favorite artists.

But this served only as a foundation to usher in something far greater than the world had ever seen. He knew it sounded incredibly bold, but he considered it to be true. He could hardly contain his excitement as he watched the groundwork of his vision coming to life from the office window on the top floor of his lavish headquarters.

When Reese Orchard heard of William Algren's plan, he was clearly pleased that he had a financial interest in the commercial buildings, even though he only leased the property on which they sat. And Bill was happy to keep Mr. Orchard involved. Reese had many valuable connections in Isles End, and the town would soon be expanding due to this very project. He estimated there would be several hundred employees by the time Advanced Bio-Cell was fully up and running, and surely more following the completion of their current project. Developing good friendships with the business people of Isles End would be a great advantage.

He swung the chair back towards his office and surveyed the room again.

Yes, this was going to do just fine!

At that moment, there was a tapping on his door and Preston Hart stuck his head in just a little.

"Good morning, Bill," he said, adjusting his glasses.

"Preston, come on in and have a seat," Bill replied waving him over. Preston entered the office with a wide-eyed look and sat down in one of the two smaller chairs in front of Bill's desk.

"Ah, these are comfy!" he remarked, leaning back and sliding his hands across the leather arms of the chair. He gave a quick glance around the new office. "This turned out nicely, Bill!"

"Yes, it'll do very well—for now, anyway," he responded with a mock smug tone. "So, what can I do for you this morning, Preston?"

"You called *me* in, Bill," Preston said, looking puzzled.

"Oh, of course, you're right! I wanted to know if you could fill me in on our current status in regards to the opposition."

"Ah yes . . . well, the gap has narrowed slightly, Bill. It could end up being close—I won't try to kid you about that." Preston spoke directly as he leaned forward and folded his hands on the edge of Bill's desktop. "Gen-1 Corporation has received a healthy dose of public funding recently which has helped their cause considerably. But our sources tell me they still have some hurdles to jump through before they catch up with us. It's still a race I believe we will win."

"Of course we will, Preston. Any news about our computers and equipment?"

"The shipment is due to arrive the first of next week, maybe sooner—then our entire staff of scientists will be arriving and getting their stations organized."

"Can we get it all set up that soon?" Bill asked excitedly.

"Well, that partly depends on whether our new general contractor can get the job done in time, but I'm optimistic. You know, I still don't see why you decided to use him when we've got so many other experienced contractors already available for the project."

"Actually, Preston, he's stopping by later today with several other subs of his own. I'm not sure what you're worried about. I have a good feeling about him, and I have reason to place some confidence in him. Reese has assured me that Harry Turner is hardworking and reliable and will be an asset to our company. It will also be beneficial for us to have connections with local people. Harry is a part of Isles End and he'll be useful in other ways."

Preston leaned back in the chair and stretched out his arms. "You're right, just so long as we keep up with our schedule. I keep assuring Shushi that it will all work out, but he's become increasingly agitated. You know how he felt about this move, just when we were getting so close to completion."

"You know . . . we've been over this before," Bill said with a subtle weariness in his tone. "Shushi will just have to be patient. He knows we were hard-pressed for space *and* needed more equipment in order to move forward. I don't know what he expects."

"Bill, he's got more than a dozen scientists and technicians twiddling their thumbs. I think he's afraid they are all going to lose their edge. They had their work suddenly pulled from underneath them, just when they were so close . . . Is it any surprise they are restless?"

Bill looked at Preston and frowned. "We hit a brick wall. Shushi knows that! We didn't have the facilities to move forward. We would have died in our tracks if we had continued to work in such cramped conditions. He ought to be pleased we found this location and thrilled about the private financing we have. As soon as we are up and running, he'll be back on track with nothing left to interfere. He should be thankful he's not working for our competition, controlled by some government bureaucrats, without nearly the level of creative freedom he enjoys here."

"I wouldn't say that too loud, Bill. I think the success of this project is more important to Shushi than even a Nobel prize, not to mention money and fame. You know how focused he can be. It wouldn't surprise me at all if he's been tempted to go *anywhere* there would be zero restrictions or limits on his work. There are opportunities out there like that as well!"

"But there are no restrictions now! He's not focused, he's obsessed! And you know, that's partly why I appreciate him so much." Bill chuckled wryly. "I'm sure you can keep his enthusiasm up."

"Of course . . . I *am* the lead cheerleader here, right? I've made sure that Shushi has his hands full right now, and that's the important thing. In a couple of weeks he'll be back in his environment and working at his peak."

"Very good, Preston, very good," Bill responded as he opened a drawer and pulled out a note pad. "I have something else here for you—two things in fact: an outline for you to review, and a list of concerns I would like you to add to our critical path. If all goes according to schedule, we have a press conference coming up in about four weeks. If we have to postpone, so be it. Otherwise, I'll be looking forward to making our announcement—to the press, and to the world."

Algren passed both sheets over to his colleague. Hart held one up and adjusted his glasses again.

"Ah, yes, your speech. Let's see . . . " He studied it for a moment and then began to read aloud:

Ladies and gentleman, honored guests, fellow associates, nations of the world. We are honored and humbled to be the first to announce the completion of an incredible work—a milestone, if you will, for human achievement. As many of you know, we played a large part in successfully mapping and sequencing the human genome.

In 1916, it was discovered, through the study of the fruit fly, Drosophila, that the genes are located in the chromosomes. But it was only just recently that the fly's entire genome was fully sequenced. Through the help of computer technology, and in a reasonably short period of time, we have unraveled and coded the entire human DNA strand. What this means to the world is yet beyond imagination and superlative in the possibilities it has to offer.

Soon, we hope to be the first to introduce to you

and the world, the first cloned man . . . the "Adam", if you will, of the cloning age.

I understand the many concerns expressed in regards to cloning and genetic experimentation, but we cannot ignore what science has revealed and now has made available to us all. What this means to the world is phenomenal. We are looking at great leaps in farming and agriculture, in nutritional value and the volume of production—food for the world! Also, imagine the potential cures for existing diseases—growing limbs, and growing organs to replace defective hearts, livers, kidneys, and lungs. We could see an end to cancer, heart disease, and diabetes. Why, we may even be looking at a new age where disease will eventually become non-existent.

In addition, the wealth of great minds from the past, could be the great minds of the future. Until now, this information has only been known and understood by . . . Mother Nature. Now, this knowledge is at our doorstep. What we have here, and are about to receive, is—in essence—the human book of life!

There are those who will immediately oppose—

Preston paused and silently scanned over the rest

of the manuscript and then looked up at Bill. "It's good," he said, removing his glasses and massaging his eyebrows. "Let me take this to my office and look it over further. I'll get back to you."

"It's just a rough draft," Bill stated. "We've got plenty of time to polish it up. Let's just hope we have the goods in time to present it."

Preston returned the large round frames to his face and glanced again at the items on the other page. "Well, I can see I've got my work cut out for me—I'd better get moving. Onward and upward—right?" he questioned, rising up from the chair.

"Yes, onward and upward," Bill mimicked as Preston left the office and closed the door behind him.

He swung his chair around toward the window to see a group of gray clouds moving in to block the sunlight.

"Must be something we can do about *that* . . . maybe someday," he mumbled. As he looked out his window across the broad landscape, he imagined how it would soon be transformed. Just as he began to close his eyes, a beep sounded from his desk. He reached over and pressed a button on a small intercom and heard the voice of Beth Fairbanks.

"Good morning, Mr. Algren. Harry Turner is here with several other gentlemen—"

"Yes, good morning, Beth. There's a set of plans there on the counter marked for Harry. Maybe you could show them around, just as a courtesy. I think Harry knows what they need to see."

"Sure thing, Mr. Algren. I can take care of that. Anything else?"

"That should do it, Beth. Thanks."

"Yes, sir," he heard her say, and the speaker clicked off.

10
Abaddon

Abaddon's crimson eyes glared down from above and watched as a seemingly unimportant group of men left the new offices of Advanced Bio-Cell. His scarlet gown billowed around him as though huge gusts of wind supported his position there in the sky. But it was his own mastery over the very air that kept him hovering high above.

He was, after all, a prince of the air.

In league with the many that had long ago inherited the space above and below and all around the small repressed planet, he accepted his position as a poor substitute for the grandeur he once enjoyed.

His vermilion face and body pulsed with a dull glow, giving his rich dark form an enchanting and irresistible appeal. Of all the many facades he had created for himself, this was currently his favorite. He was provided with a measure of glee when reflecting on the human expectation of how a creature such as himself might appear. But the expression of his sharp cold features confirmed he was no average spirit. He exuded power and calmness. Fierce, elegant and admirable, he studied his surroundings with keen awareness.

Even though undetectable, he employed a level of caution above the small group of men. He had been studying these creatures since the very beginning. Humans were all the same for the most part—small and self-absorbed. Currently his attention was focused on one man in particular.

Abaddon had become curious to the point of agitation, though he was not ready to question the authority of his superiors just yet. Why had this little man become part of *his* assignment? Didn't his own track record show many successes of far greater value than this insignificant *adamite*? After all, he had charmed and seduced some of the most elect and elite of many generations past. Was he not currently doing quite well with his minion in this fascinating little biotech company? The answer, of course, to all of these questions was a resounding, *YES!* He had exhibited time and again throughout history, a level of mastery in the art of deception and manipulation that was rivaled by few. He was able to guide, direct, and even control the actions of men, even to possess them—and *all* with their full consent.

Now he was in a quandary. Was there something about this individual which he was missing? What was it about this Harry Turner that had the attention of his superiors? From all outward appearances, this carpenter was a small fish, but in submission, Abaddon had gone ahead and helped facilitate some potential connections between this man and the executives at Advanced Bio-Cell.

He could not conceal a grin as he watched Harry Turner move away from the small group and enter a pick-up truck. He held back his pride and decided to lean on what little patience he had learned to employ. *Yes*, he thought, *patience… a dreadful thing but sometimes necessary—a little patience can go a long way. I will continue to find out more about this mortal, and he may yet turn out to be a tasty morsel to feed upon after all.*

Abaddon glided above the pick-up as it moved out of the parking lot and headed down Escher Ave. He surveyed the rest of the territory as he followed Harry. He considered the different comrades he would need to add to his employment as dozens of workers began filling the new ABC building and others surrounding it.

As they neared Isles End, Abaddon had a sudden awareness, the presence of a familiar spirit. He turned back and noticed a small dark form approaching from the north. Almost immediately he recognized its shape.

"*Scratch*," he muttered irritably.

As the figure neared, Abaddon stopped still in the air for a moment while Harry's truck disappeared down the road. Then he shot straight up into the clouds and swelled himself up in an effort to appear larger and more forbidding.

The dark form followed.

"I see you!" the small corpulent creature spoke. "I know my presence is unwelcome, as usual."

The larger dark angel said nothing.

"Abaddon, you look well-kept, as always," the small creature spoke again as it boldly moved forward and stopped directly before the formidable scarlet lord.

Abaddon glared down, his expression apprehensive.

"Scratch, your company is, let's say, *necessary,* I presume?"

"I might have suggested we skip the formalities," the diminutive demon responded, "but as it is, I see you already have!"

Abaddon continued to stare at his uninvited guest. He sought to maintain a neutral expression on his face, but found it difficult to hide his contempt for the deformed imp. He had never been very tolerant of this fiendish little messenger, and ever since it had been scarred, he was repulsed by the demon's very presence.

"Well," he said flatly, "I *am,* as usual, very busy—as you may have noticed? But I suppose I can sacrifice a minute of my time for you."

"Your politeness increases along with your lordly appearance," the small demon said with a tone of disdain.

"Why are you here?" Abaddon cut to the chase.

"Yes, let's get right to the point. I am only here to inform you that your overseer has summoned you. Gorguol requests your presence—immediately."

"Gorguol? What does he require from me now?"

"That's his business, but he has insisted that I escort you."

"*What?*"

"He wants us to return together!"

Scratch drifted up so his eyes were level with Abaddon's, invading the larger demon's space. "Are you ready?"

"You haven't changed, have you?" charged Abaddon.

"Oh, but we all change! We all improve with time—don't you agree?" Scratch queried with sarcasm.

"With experience," Abaddon grated, "some of us become more adept at our skill. Others only stagnate in their rank. The latter would be you, Scratch. You remain banal and petty. The service you perform is inconsequential and could be filled by a thousand other waif-urchins. The only reason Gorguol keeps you around is because you are so predictable. And the only reason you stay is because you hold no authority on your own! Besides, few would be willing to put up with the permanently twisted expression Gorguol so appropriately bestowed upon your visage. So you thrive on the scraps from the table, and this makes you feel very important, doesn't it?"

"Abaddon . . . " Scratch countered with an attack of measured slowness. He needed to choose each word methodically, as though he would be graded by his superiors in his ability to show viciousness and distain in his ridicule and mockery. He spat out each acerbic word with precision and intent.

"For a once-radiant Archangel, your vision seems to have become quite flawed. You overlook the sweetness of my arrangement—or more accurately, maybe you are just jealous. I have ears in the private quarters and am privy to a great deal of information. I honestly believe you are envious, my Lord! We know information is power, my dear Abaddon, and power is an appetite for which I know you desperately hunger. Besides, you assess too highly your own position and abilities. You think your successes from the past have earned you permanent status which should be recognized by all. You're working too hard and not realizing enough reward. You long to rest, but are afraid of losing your rank!"

Abaddon wanted to squash the swollen creature, but in light of his overseer's wish to have him escorted by the vile little wretch, he controlled his rage. The mere effort caused him to quake.

"Am I hitting a nerve?" Scratch asked with a hint of glee. "Am I a little too close to home? Is my keen insight making you squirm just a bit?"

Abaddon held his tongue.

"And as to my appearance, don't be so sure that the same wages could not be paid to you. It is *Gorguol* who seeks your audience! Remember?"

"Yes," Abaddon said, still holding back his fury, "but I don't need *you* to lead me to Gorguol. I know where to find him."

"You do not listen well," Scratch charged. "Or perhaps you are deaf because of too many distractions? It is Gorguol's request that *I* deliver you. Besides, he has taken up residence at a new location."

A new location?

"That's . . . unusual," Abaddon responded. He tried to appear calm but a look of nervousness tainted his countenance.

"I don't have time for you to sit and consider the issue indefinitely. Unless *you* are in need of some facial reconstruction yourself, I would suggest you accompany me immediately," Scratch warned as he turned his podgy body around and darted away.

With mixed emotions of wrath and dread, Abaddon followed Scratch at a distance. He didn't want to lose him, but he still felt soiled by having been in such close proximity to the nauseating creature.

Scratch led him north, over the hills and away from Advanced Bio-Cell. He made a beeline towards the city where Gorguol's new domain resided. The drive was usually forty-five minutes from Isles End, in human terms, but at their speed they were there in seconds.

Abaddon narrowed the span between Scratch and himself as the lesser devil began to weave down around the tops of the skyscrapers. The city proper had been built with careful planning, right on the edge of the circular ocean bay. At night it looked like a crescent of rising light reflecting beautifully on the water. It was dusk now, and though the sky maintained a slight blue hue, the moon and stars made their entrance high above the silhouette of the metropolis below.

Scratch slowed, and then graceful as a butterfly, he landed on the top of one of the older and more unusual structures in the original section of the city. An old stone monolith projected from the building's top, forming the shape of an irregular pentagon. The apex was like a jeweled crown, with a collection of steeply pitched and multi-colored turrets, each shooting upward like a crowd of angels toward the stars. Below, they were surrounded by a contemporary garden of fountains, benches, and small manicured trees. A short stone ledge enclosed the entire bastion. Various sizes and types of gargoyles crowded the circumference of the small wall, perched over the edge, as though guarding the top of the building from any intruders.

Abaddon came down alongside Scratch and hovered just above the surface.

"Come along," Scratch said, his bent smile gleaming. "Don't be afraid!" He lightly sauntered over to a small doorway on the side of one of the parapets.

"This way," he prompted again, his head twisted back toward Abaddon, this time with a more devious expression on his face. Then he turned to the opening and disappeared.

The crimson demon hovered in the air just above the surface of the rooftop. He considered his position. The advantage he held with ABC was possibly one of the most interesting opportunities he'd had yet, being with men who were destined for high places—men who would someday be associated with the upper echelon of the world. Gorguol's domain in the city was a stagnant effort to maintain old positions using law firms and a slew of greedy corporate officials. Abaddon much preferred the arrangement he had cultivated on his own with Advanced Bio-Cell.

He had not yet had a chance to fully examine the employees at ABC. However, he had managed to find a permanent advantage in one of them, and through this minion had worked with the others long enough to see these supercilious fellows would soon be the desired guests, the cream of society and even the leaders of nations. Abaddon knew too well that the knowledge they were so close to understanding was inevitable. The long awaited marriage of science and biology to technology would soon be in full bloom, and he was highly elated to be assisting them, even if his contributions were measured out in controlled portions. Now it was only a matter of time before *someone* figured out the secret to completely duplicating a human being. How he hoped his protégé would be in the forefront of this discovery, thus ensuring inclusion in the ushering in of a new age!

Unfortunately, the dark creature and all his companions were at a disadvantage. Unlike their adversaries, he did not have access to the same knowledge they did, nor did he have the freedom to pass on certain information over to their lower servants, man. How grand to bestow upon mankind any sort of advanced knowledge before the proper time—anything to speed things along towards a favorable future.

Abaddon also knew his work was more effective when he kept his active participation hidden. Currently, it had become a popular belief among the men of this age to see creatures such as himself as make-believe fictional characters, created for the amusement of men or to put fear into children. More importantly though, to debunk the antiquated ideas of a crumbling religious empire. The delusion was perhaps, the smartest strategy *they* had come up with yet.

Abaddon was convinced of ultimate victory. His group had gained too much ground to believe anything different. How else could they have made such progress, except that their opponents had demonstrated weakness on so many occasions? With careful planning, someday Abaddon's kind would rule the created pets of the enemy. In time he and his own would control all things, even if by no other force than sheer cunning and determination.

The dark lord set his thoughts of grandeur aside for the moment and touched down onto the textured surface of the roof. Striding over to the opening where Scratch had disappeared, he held up his hand and pressed his palm onto the surface of the door. He recoiled instantly from the heat and the murky presence within, but quickly managed to regain his composure. Forcing himself to be focused and alert, he stepped through the opening and was immediately immersed in the dark and sinister domain of Gorguol.

11
The Overseer

The Overseer—an Archangel of the highest order of angels, the Seraphim—was a magnificent being of light. Far above the earth, her domain shone like a star, brilliant and impenetrable, yet entirely undetectable to the natural eye. She governed her position over the planets with awesome power and authority, directing planetary movements with perfect cadence and seeing that time itself flowed uninterrupted. The perpetual rhythm of finite change was under her continual scrutiny.

But this was not the only appointment of the Overseer. A host of celestial beings were at her disposal, moving to and fro across the earth as each ministering spirit fulfilled its every instruction. Though they were in her charge and steadfastly obedient, she was not deified or exalted by them in *any* way, for she, like them, was also a servant.

In her court, the Cherubim, who were of the second order of celestial beings, entered and departed respectfully. Each in turn contributed and shared in the collective purpose of their being, greeting the Overseer regularly and continually moving forward with their directives.

The court was a spectacular array of color, light, and sound, each complementing the other as the myriad of creatures blended together like a beautifully arranged symphony. The combined expressions of these celestial beings emerged as an integral and distinct entity—harmonizing, controlled and balanced, rising and falling—now soft and sweet, and then swelling in an awesome display of perfect symmetry. The resplendent Cherubim erupted into spiraling choruses interwoven in the ongoing, triumphant and continually escalating celebration.

In the center of the court there appeared a small, dimly lit figure.

"Please come," invited the Overseer.

The small figure moved forward into the presence of the brilliant Archangel.

"Narcissus . . . it's so good to see you," she said. "Will you share with me?"

"I am honored to be here," Narcissus spoke humbly. "I have made acquaintance with the man whose name is Harry Turner. I've explained to him briefly who I am and why I have come to him. He understands very little and will have many questions, should I be directed to return to him."

The Overseer drew Narcissus closer. The heat and the light of the Archangel emanated out to Narcissus and filled him with courage and strength.

"Elohim shows you great favor," she spoke gracefully.

The smaller angel began to weep.

"Receive this bequest of joy and light," she continued. "It is a gift."

Narcissus felt the offering come to him. As it entered into his being, he was instantly refreshed and had a fuller sense of completeness. Revitalized, he straightened up and spoke.

"Shall I be returning then . . . to Harry Turner?"

"Of course you shall return to him," the Overseer confirmed. "Now take notice," she said, and as Narcissus gazed forward, a vision appeared before him.

He could see the beginning of Harry Turner, his body being formed in his mother's womb. Narcissus watched and understood as each fiber was woven together to make Harry the unique being he was. The scene was of perfect love being given and received. He watched Harry's birth and saw how the parents' hearts were filled with joy. He observed as Harry grew from crawling to walking and speaking. As the years scrolled by, Narcissus absorbed every nonchalant *and* intimate moment of Harry's life until he knew Harry almost completely. Even some glimpses of the future were implied. Harry's ultimate destiny could not be seen, but Narcissus understood what his own liberties and boundaries were. Still, it would be Harry's own choices which would guide him to his eventual destination.

When the vision faded, the Overseer spoke again.

"Into your hands, Narcissus, has been given a precious assignment. You've been chosen to provide guidance and instruction to a man in the hope that, with your aid, he may come to know the truth. You will also have the opportunity to triumph over a formidable adversary. I will caution you though, you *must* refrain from interfering in the slightest way with this man's decisions. *He must choose!*"

"Of course," Narcissus answered soberly.

"It is difficult for *us*, who are outside of time, to accept the finite thinking of mankind. The decisions they make, based on such temporal input, often seem like folly to us. Our desire to intervene must be tempered with wisdom. From the beginning of time, the free will of each and every created being has determined *who* they are and *what* they will become. You may soon be giving Harry Turner a measure of eternity, but still . . . *he* must choose."

"Yes," Narcissus agreed.

The Overseer reached out and caressed the angel's face with the palm of her right hand.

"Go with serenity," she said, filling him with an increased portion of wholeness.

With a distinct and lucid understanding of his purpose, Narcissus withdrew from the presence of the Overseer and flew like a shooting star back down towards the quiet blue planet.

12
The Omelet and the Great Fall

It was late afternoon when Harry pulled into the driveway of the remodel on Ivory Lane. Having spent most of the morning with several sub-contractors at Advanced Bio-Cell, he wanted to be sure that things were moving along with Ed and Butch.

He stepped out of his pick-up truck and studied the building site. Now that all the debris had been removed and the framing had begun, the project was beginning to look more like new construction rather than a remodel. Ed and Butch were busy finishing up for the day. Harry could see despite all Ed's joking, he still made great progress.

Harry walked past a load of lumber and over to the future entryway.

"Hey, guys," he shouted over the sound of the air compressor as he stepped up onto the edge of the new floor. They both looked up and greeted him.

"Hey, boss," Butch said smiling as he extended his large hairy hand. Harry noticed a heart tattooed on Butch's forearm as they shook hands. He stared at it for a moment and then glanced back at the rough looking man.

"That's from the old days," Butch explained.

"Any special meaning?"

"Nope. Just a large needle and too much time on my hands, no pun intended," Butch grinned.

"Hey, Harry," Ed called as he finished sawing off the end of a two-by-six. "We've got a couple of young guys lined up to give us a hand—they'll be out first thing tomorrow morning.

"So, are you saying that you guys don't need me anymore?" Harry teased.

"Oh, we can put you to work right now if you want," Ed responded in his usual jesting manner. "Just depends on how fast you want to get this thing framed."

"Well, I was actually looking forward to being out here with you guys, but now it looks like I'm going to be a full-time coordinator. That means you're my foreman now, Ed. I know we've already talked about it, but I guess today it's a reality."

"Very cool," Ed said, looking quite pleased.

"I was going to ask if you needed anything, but it looks like you have everything under control," Harry commented as he surveyed the site. "And by the way, the place looks great!"

"Thanks!" Ed responded with pride. "The only problem so far is the inaccuracy of the plans, but what's new?"

Butch took the opportunity to chime in. "These architects spend too much time at a desk and not enough on a job site."

"Yeah," Ed agreed. "What's their favorite saying, Butch?"

"Can't see it from my house!" the burly man announced with a smirk.

Ed laughed forcefully and then looked at his watch. "Hey, we were just gonna take a five-minute break and then finish up.

You ready, Butch?"

"You bet," the stocky man answered and slumped down into a shady spot, tipping a jug of water to his mouth.

"Hey, Harry," Ed began as he fashioned himself a seat with some plywood scraps. "When we were cleaning out the rest of the basement, we noticed that old chest is missing."

Harry was caught entirely off guard.

The chest! What could he say about the chest?

"Oh yeah, I, uh—I took it home," he explained.

"What the heck was in that thing?" Butch demanded. "If I couldn't budge it, it must have been filled with something like concrete!"

Harry didn't know what to say. He thought quickly and pulled an answer right out of thin air. "Gold! It was . . . filled with gold."

Ed laughed loudly, and then stopped. "Seriously, Harry, what *was* in that thing?"

"It was very strange," Harry explained. "The other night after you guys left, Reese Orchard stopped by. When he noticed the chest, he walked over and lifted the thing up like it was light as a feather—and when he opened the lid, it was *empty*!" At this point Harry had to wonder how this explanation could possibly fly. "The chest must have been wedged into the floor somehow," he continued, "because after that, I lifted it without any trouble and carried it out to my truck."

"That's weird!" said Ed. "Nothing?"

"Yeah, completely empty," Harry said scolding himself for not sounding more credible—but it was as close to the truth as he could come.

"Harry, you *sure* you're not—? " Butch began, but then stopped, noting the seriousness of Harry's expression.

There was an awkward moment, and Harry just shook his head with a puzzled look on his face.

"Well, break time's over," Ed broke the silence. "Let's get this place cleaned up so we can get out of here," he added as he pulled himself to his feet.

They all stood up and Harry turned toward the entryway. "I'll stay in touch with you guys—keep up the good work. Call me if anything comes up."

"You got it," Ed replied while Butch grunted and offered a wave.

Harry climbed into his truck and drove home.

That was close!

He regretted having been slightly less than honest about what really happened. A sense of anxiety crept over him. His desire to tell someone about the whole affair was growing, but who would believe his story? No, it was the same argument he had already gone over in his head many times. At some point, he would have to confide in someone.

As Harry drew closer to home, his thoughts turned to Beth. *Ah! Was it only just last night he'd been with her?* And today on the job, forcing a professional manner, and having so little time! He walked up to his door when his phone gave a chirp. It was a text from Beth!

Fumbling with the keys, Harry got the door unlocked and hurried inside. He flopped down onto the couch and anxiously read:

> *I had a wonderful time with you last night. Thanks again for the wine and taffy. Weird at work today, wasn't it? Not being able to really talk? I wanted more time with you. Call me!*

He wanted to see her. Was he in too much of a hurry? He reminded himself that he still didn't know Beth very well. Yet, at the same time, he wanted to cast all concerns aside and go for it. Why was there so much apprehension? Maybe the loss of Jenny contributed to the fear of being vulnerable. But there was no anxiety when he was with Beth, so there it was! Narcissus had told him to use his ability of discernment, and that's exactly what he would do.

After a shower and some left over pizza, Harry stretched out on the bed. Taking a moment to relax, he punched in her number and waited. No answer. After a few minutes he tried again. Still nothing! He reflected on their conversation from the night before, recalling and savoring each moment. He was gazing into her lovely eyes as he closed his own and fell into a very pleasant sleep.

Harry dreamed of many things, including Beth. They were all scattered and fragmented, but peaceful and pleasurable, the kind where you awake with fond memories, even when you don't recall the details.

He woke with a start, still on top of the covers, still dressed, and feeling slightly confused. Feeling disoriented, he pulled his cell phone out from under his head and rolled over.

Unexpectedly, the smell of onions was in the air, along with the distinct scent of Narcissus. Harry looked down into the kitchen from his bedroom, and there was the angel cooking something!

"Good morning," the celestial being greeted him.

"Narcissus—!"

"Yes, it's me. I hope I didn't frighten you. I thought this might be a good time to visit since you are not occupied with anything."

"No, you didn't, I mean, it's okay. I'm glad to see you, of course! You didn't mollify me, did you?"

"Oh no. I don't think I'll be doing that again. But I am preparing something which I hope you will enjoy. A change of diet from your microwaved potatoes."

"What is it—angel food cake?"

"I like your humor! But no, it's an omelet."

"Alright!" Harry replied with a growing tone of frustrated

sarcasm. "He can drive a van—he travels through time—he even cooks breakfast! It's a very strange relationship we have, Narcissus. What's next? Will you entertain me with some music— maybe you're good with a hammer?" Harry stopped suddenly, embarrassed by his outburst.

"Actually," Narcissus responded calmly, "I *am* well versed in music, although I'm sure it's not the type you are used to. But what's wrong, Harry? You're upset."

Harry came down from the bedroom, slumped onto the couch and tipped his head back. "I'm sorry! I still don't know exactly what to make of all this."

Narcissus remained silent, encouraging Harry to continue.

"You are the big secret I can't talk about, and who would believe me anyway?"

Harry got up off the couch, walked over to the kitchen table, and pulled up a chair. His demeanor took on a milder tone. "I guess it's not every day a man meets an angel. I can't stop thinking about you. Where do you go? Are there others you've also been *assigned to?* I have so many questions. I just don't—"

"Harry," Narcissus said softly. "Be at peace."

Narcissus walked over to where Harry sat and placed his strong hands on the shoulders of his friend.

"I know this has been difficult for you. It is I who must apologize. I have had no experience in dealing with men, but you must trust me. I am real, and I have nothing but your best interests in mind. Please believe me."

Narcissus stepped back and continued to speak softly. "There is no one else I have charge of. My time away from you is spent in meditation and council and doing the will of my Overseer. You are of utmost importance to me, not only because I have been assigned to you, but I care about you and have come to understand you better than you know. In a fashion, I have known you since your conception. Harry, you are my friend—do not doubt *that* for a moment. You must bear with me. You must have faith!"

"Okay," Harry said, staring back into the angel's glowing face. His expression was compelling, his words convincing. Harry suddenly felt foolish about doubting this very real and personal being.

He made an effort to stand and Narcissus stepped back to give him room. "So, what's in the omelet?" Harry asked leaning toward the stove with a grin.

Narcissus smiled. "Well, let's see—onions, mushrooms, sausage, and cheese. I believe it's a combination your mother used to make."

"Yes," Harry said, his eyes watering.

"May I serve it to you?"

"Please," Harry responded taking a seat back at the table.

Narcissus turned toward the kitchen counter and returned promptly with a plate which he placed in front of his friend.

"Thank you," Harry said as he carved a large bite with his fork and carefully placed the food in his mouth. "Wow . . . it's just like my mom's! What did you do—go back in time and take cooking lessons from her?"

"In a way, I did," the angel said, "but it is no more than an omelet, Harry."

"I see—so it's not going to make me super powerful or anything?" he joked.

"No, just satisfied, I hope," the Archangel said as Harry savored each bite.

Narcissus let Harry finish his breakfast in silence before he spoke again.

"Harry, although I am a celestial being, I am still, momentarily, a flawed being—capable of some error. This may not make sense to you—my visiting and my manner of sharing certain information. Though you may not understand now, I hope that in time, the things I share with you will make more sense."

Harry looked up at Narcissus with concern in his eyes. "This sounds like the beginning of a farewell speech."

"Well, in a sense, it is—my time is limited. I'm here with you now, but soon I will be unavailable . . . for a period."

"Hmm, that's not what I want to hear. I almost brought your name up the other night when I was with a new friend of mine, Beth, but I held back."

"Harry, you will know when you're ready to share your experiences regarding me with someone else. Don't worry about it too much. My advice is, don't be anxious about anything. Be true to what you know in your heart. Live with the peace of knowing you are on a path to wholeness. Remember, one of your gifts is discernment. You just haven't cultivated it yet."

With an increased trust, Harry leaned forward. "Can you tell me why you were held prisoner in that chest?" He pointed over to the trunk that sat at the foot of the bed.

"Yes." The angel moved closer and stood before his human friend. "I have shared with you already, I am a celestial being. I was once a Seraph, a member of the highest order of servants to the One called Elohim, that is, the Author and Designer who is the Divine One.

"Long ago, before there was time as you understand it, there was a grand and marvelous creation, unequaled to anything you have ever seen or could imagine. There was beauty, harmony, and symmetry, and all who abided within, reveled in the brilliance of majestic perfection. Unfortunately, there was one who was finally not pleased with such a wondrous existence. This one—truly the most splendid of all the Seraphim—fell into an abyss, which here in your world is called *pride*. Not pride in something worth celebrating, but rather that of a false nature. This was the first great fall!

"While enveloped in this state of deception, the prideful one planned and orchestrated a fantastic and quite convincing but malevolent scheme to all who would lend their attention. As a result, many were deceived."

As the angelic being spoke, his body began to radiate an increased aura of heat and light.

"In his desire to be recognized—to even equate himself with Elohim—this noblest of all the Seraphim allowed his pride to overwhelm and blind him. In a radical attempt to gain support, he seduced multitudes of both Seraphim and Cherubim by unveiling before them their own extraordinary and unique gifts of wisdom and beauty."

At this point, Narcissus paused and lowered his head. "Harry, I did *not* follow them, but when I was shown my own reflection . . . I was caught in a moment of hesitation."

For a moment, the glow of the angel's flesh weakened. He looked up at Harry, his expression remorseful. "I was not cast out as were the iniquitous ones, but rather, Elohim confined me to a place, as He deemed appropriate."

There was clearly regret and sadness in his voice as he solemnly went on. "Subsequently, I've been isolated—worse, I've been separated from the pure, magnificent, and unequaled presence of the Divine One."

Harry was bewildered. "So, you were held in that chest—for how long?"

"This all occurred long ago, but still, out of time—I understand it's confusing to you. Don't be troubled. The chest has only been like a doorway to come to you."

"But, that's unimaginable!"

"Yes, I *have* been treated with extraordinary mercy!"

"No, I mean, it's horrible! How is that mercy?"

"Well, listen, do you understand that a good father

instructs his child and chastises him out of love, so the child might live with honor?"

"But to be imprisoned for . . . how many years? Thousands—*millions?*"

"Harry, you do not comprehend! To me, a thousand years is like a day, and a day is relative to a thousand years. Beyond this physical world, there is no *time,* as you understand it. But to be removed from the presence of the Creative One, is to be incomplete, no matter the duration. My hope is that I shall be fully redeemed—that I may be in His presence once again."

"I'm sorry," Harry stammered, looking around the room with sudden panic. "I'm not feeling well. Why are you here again?"

"Harry, everything is all right! Be at peace and listen." With this, the angel put his hand on Harry's shoulder and comfort spread over him.

"You have been born into an age of wondrous events, yet there is still nothing new under your sun. Men continue to imagine that their lives will never end while death is all around them. The heavens and the earth display incredible works, but some guess the universe is somehow here by chance, while they themselves bask in their minuscule achievements. You might say they are like clouds without rain, wandering stars without direction, for whom some, there is reserved . . . only that dark place. Remember the sea of orbs?

"Celestial beings were once tried in a conflict far

removed from here. Now this world has also been challenged. Thankfully, there are still some who are strong and have not forfeited their innocence for just a sample of forbidden fruit.

"Your calling in all this remains to be seen."

Harry struggled to understand. "So it's not a mistake I'm here, doing this particular job?"

"Nothing is an accident," the Seraph replied.

"And the house burning down?"

"One could say, in a fashion, it was preordained."

Harry was astonished. He considered this strange revelation, but found himself at a loss for words. "So, where do we go from here?"

"For now," Narcissus replied, "I have time to spend with you."

"Narcissus," Harry prodded bravely, "let me ask you about something else—this 'noblest of Seraphim'. What happened to him?"

Narcissus leaned in close to Harry and looked gravely into his eyes. "His domain is *here!* He has worked cleverly to conceal himself and convince the world he is only a myth."

Harry nodded, "And his followers, they are like the ones I saw at the Isles End bank?"

"In a fashion, yes, they were cast down with the fallen one."

"I don't understand—forgive me, but why are these dark powers allowed to exist, especially here, in a world where there is already so much trouble? Or, are they the cause of it all?"

"No, Harry, they are not the cause, but through their influence, they do make a contribution. Still, did I not tell you? The race of man has been broken and fallen from the beginning. The sons of this world have the ability to create a great deal of struggle all on their own."

13
Elohim and the Supernatural

Harry was silent for a moment. He fought off a feeling of hopelessness as he considered the fallen nature of so many things.

"Forgive me again, Narcissus, but I'm uncertain about this Elohim. If He is the author and designer of everything, can't He just destroy these dark creatures and make all things right?"

"Harry, again you do not understand, but first let me explain something to you. There are literally not enough books to contain all the wonders of the Marvelous One. I will share with you *some* things." Narcissus stepped back from the table as though he needed a little more room, and his form took on a new brilliance.

"Elohim is spirit," he began. "You see, there is spirit, and matter, and there is flesh. You comprehend matter to be something concrete and tangible, but the fact is that matter and flesh are only temporary while the spiritual realm is everlasting, permanent and solid. All you see and know here, is real to you. You can touch and feel it—all your senses support it, yet it is only temporal and will not last. It is all just reconstituted dust, if you will, blowing around with the wind. You know this to be true because you have witnessed it many times in your own life, and the minimal knowledge available here supports this.

"But the mystical things you cannot see—these are

genuine and authentic. The physical world *you* know is only a silhouette of things to come. Consider the profound difference between you and your shadow! That's just a picture of how far removed the spiritual reality is from this shadow world, which is all you know. Yes, there is wonderful beauty here, but it is fleeting!"

The idea of fleeting beauty caused Harry to wince with the thought of Jennifer. He forced his attention back to the angel.

"So, Harry, Elohim is spirit. And though He can manifest Himself in ways understandable to the flesh, this only occurs so the eyes and minds of men will have something to identify with.

"Allow me to share three concepts with you. First, Elohim is *omniscient*—there is no end to His knowledge because He is the author of knowledge, knowing and understanding all things, intimately—everything! See? There is nothing unknown to Him.

"Secondly, He is *omnipresent*, meaning He is everywhere and anywhere at all times. There is nothing hidden from Him, and there is nowhere you can go where He can't find you. If you traveled to the most remote place in the universe, He is there.

"Finally, He is *omnipotent*, that is, all-powerful. His power is infinite and unlimited, if that concept is even comprehensible to you. Nothing exists without His authority. Can you even imagine, Harry? All creation lies at His feet. He is the ultimate architect! There is no one thing more powerful . . . nothing even close. He is incomparable and His creation is incomprehensible.

"Beyond that, there is another thing I want you to ponder—He is bound by His own laws of truth, which He Himself has ordained because He is the embodiment of truth. Harry, this means He is good. He is loving, kind, compassionate, forgiving, merciful, just, and full of grace."

As Harry listened, the light flowing through the angel's body began to grow with an intensity he had not seen before.

"It sounds too incredible," Harry said without thinking, "to know all, see all, and have complete power. It's hard for me to believe, let alone comprehend."

The angel allowed Harry a moment to consider the words, and then went on. "The point is, if space *is* infinite, or at least too large to comprehend, then even more so is the Author who designed it."

"Okay, yes. I can make sense of that."

Harry closed his eyes for a moment in thought while Narcissus gazed at him with a paternal fondness.

"But if He is all powerful," Harry started up again, "then why does he allow so much suffering in the world?"

The angel grinned, having already considered this question many times.

"It's a simple thing. Remember I shared with you how all beings are given a free will?"

Harry nodded.

"So, they are given the freedom to choose—good or evil—"

"But wait," Harry interrupted. "I'm talking about the suffering of innocent people who have no control over their circumstances—like a child born with a deformity, or anyone who is treated cruelly by another."

"The truth is, Harry, this is a cursed world. But it wasn't always. It started out perfect. You saw it for yourself. In every way it was resplendent and balanced, without a hint of imperfection. Elohim—the Creative Designer—designed man into existence out of His desire for intimate relationship and to share His marvelous creation. But what would a relationship be unless it included the free will of both parties? Elohim gave mankind free will so man could freely love.

"Unfortunately, man used his free will to overstep his boundaries and make some regrettable choices. The Divine One understood this logical possibility, and though He hoped that *all* would receive Him, He would not force His hand on anyone. He gives all created beings every opportunity to come to know Him. He knew from the beginning, while some would reject Him, there would be many others with the desire for real relationship.

"It was man—not Elohim—who decided he must know the difference between good and evil. And how can you know evil other than by being exposed to it? Thus, a curse! A curse that not only compels you personally to make bad choices, but which ultimately is an affliction altering everything in Creation. This curse has brought into existence an unsympathetic force that penetrates anywhere it can gain a footing, and there it clings. As a result, man has suffered and experienced much loss and pain. Even with all the incredible beauty this world contains, it *is* lost, you see, and will not last forever. But while it does exist, the sun will continue its generous outpouring of light and heat on both the benevolent and the malevolent.

"The thing to remember, Harry, is that while this short life you have is temporary, eternity is . . . well, let's just say it will last a little longer. Men place far too much importance upon the finite rather than the infinite, because they do not understand that their physical demise is only a doorway to the everlasting. The good news is that justice does prevail—it cannot do otherwise! Every single wrong that has ever been committed, large or small, will be righted someday. There will be true justice, when time is no longer in control."

"Okay, Narcissus, I'm trying to keep up with you, but you still haven't answered my question!"

"What's that?"

"Why is there suffering?"

The Archangel frowned. Then without warning he held up his arm and swung it down on Harry's head, hard enough to hurt.

"Hey! What are you doing?"

"Did that hurt?"

"What do you think?" Harry frowned. "Of course it did!"

His painful expression lingered while he rubbed his head.

"I'm sorry, Harry, but I'm trying to prove a point."

"And you can't do it without clobbering me?"

"Forgive me, but there are those who have tried to debate this issue and have made it far too confusing. Just tell me, who just caused you to suffer?"

"You did!" Harry answered looking perplexed.

"Exactly," Narcissus said, "and so you see that our Intelligent Designer had nothing to do with it. He only allows us the free will to act. Those who hurt each other are always looking for someone else to blame. As for the suffering that occurs as a result, in this world of free will, you must believe it will all be accounted for someday. All beings have a burden in life to manage. One cannot always know the gravity or weight of another's experience, but you will learn that all trials give each bearer the opportunity to grow and become less broken, until finally all things will be made complete. In other words, just as I stated a few moments ago, all wrongs, all suffering, will ultimately be accounted for."

"Do you really believe this?" Harry asked, still rubbing his head.

"It is the absolute truth."

"So every deed ever done by hundreds of millions—or rather, billions of people over all time and history, is recorded and ultimately addressed?"

"Exactly as you say. Incredible, isn't it?"

"It sounds . . . unbelievable!"

"To you it does because you are, for the moment, a finite creature, but nothing is impossible for Elohim. How much more do you understand about life than say, an ant, a dog, or even a dolphin? Let's take a moment and consider the ant. He goes about his business, even as you stand directly above him and study his movements and behaviors, while he is completely oblivious of your presence. You understand much more than any of these creatures, yet how many unanswered questions are there for man which, if answered, would only create a thousand more?

"Harry, do you have any idea how much of your brain you actually use?"

"Not enough!" Harry blurted out, "but yes, I read it somewhere. I understand your point."

"Good, let me challenge your brain by telling you more about the Father of Design," Narcissus continued passionately.

"There is not one single living person who has any idea of the kinds of things Elohim has prepared for those who choose to seek Him. The unbelievable plans He has for all who will come to Him are far beyond anyone's most far-reaching imagination. Think of the most beautiful thing you have ever seen or experienced—then multiply it by millions. Can you even attempt it? Think of the most pleasurable encounter you have ever had, or could imagine having. It is minuscule and immeasurable compared to the rapture you will see and touch and feel and know in the spirit. Have you ever known peace, fullness, or wholeness? They are barely a flicker of what those who belong to Elohim will receive.

"And another thing . . . if all of this sounds too fantastic, I will tell you now, it's still *nothing* in comparison to being in His presence. Just to be near—*even to gaze from afar!* Anything else that one could possibly imagine . . . pales! A thousand suns would be wan in His shadow. He has no needs in order to make Himself complete. *He is completeness!* Still, amazingly, He desires to have the deepest intimacy with all those in His creation, and He will, with those who come to Him. The intricacies of His vast splendor are too deep to comprehend, and yet He is fully approachable. His personal care for each of His creatures is profound and absolute!"

The Archangel's deep fluid voice was almost booming now. He towered now above Harry as he regaled him with his description of divinity—but it wasn't just a message of spirituality or theology. *This was personal knowledge!*

With his arms raised, Narcissus became a beacon with a surge of light, liquid electricity flowing through his facial muscles as he spoke, his flesh glowing so intensely that the angel's features could no longer be seen. Harry closed his eyes for real fear of being blinded, but the light even penetrated his eyelids. He turned his face away and crouched down in his chair as Narcissus continued, but he dared not interrupt the celestial being.

Seeing that Harry was now lying on the floor, the angel forced his brightness to soften.

"You have . . . *seen Him*, haven't you, Narcissus?" Harry asked cautiously, inviting his celestial friend to continue.

"Yes, but not in His entirety," the angel answered. "Very few have, that is, in His fullness. It might be more than any living creature could endure, except maybe a few chosen elect who minister to Him continuously, but even then, I do not know. For one to say he has *seen* Elohim, might be equated to saying, 'I have seen the entire universe'. But it's infinitely far more than that!"

"I think I know what you mean," Harry spoke with confidence—his hands covering his face. "You could look at a book, but not know what it contained inside. And if it was an epic writing, even if you read it many times over, you might still not gain all the understanding."

"Yes," Narcissus confirmed. "I think you *do* have an idea."

"*Really*—I'm intrigued! I've never really thought about eternity—or about this 'Elohim'. I actually feel as though something has awakened in me. A new awareness, or maybe a deeper understanding."

"Yes, Harry. I believe there *is* an increase in your vision!"

Narcissus realized his poor friend was now entirely under the table.

"Ah, I'm sorry, Harry."

The fiery brilliance that still radiated from the Archangel's flesh began to recede. He stood before Harry looking as magnificent as ever—in fact, to Harry he looked like a deity. For a time, Harry found himself mesmerized by the mere sight of the fearful and beautiful being who towered before him. He was ashamed of the way he had spoken earlier. Though he felt very familiar with Narcissus, he realized he was in no position to be at odds with such a potentially formidable adversary. There was no question that this being could be very compelling and persuasive—if not forceful—in order to have his way. But then as Harry continued to gaze at his guest, he saw gentleness and compassion in the Archangel's expression. His eyes seemed to shine in a way that invited trust.

"Narcissus, you said you have limited time with me. Did you have something else planned besides making me breakfast?"

"Oh yes, if you are willing," his glow receding smoothly under his flesh.

"What specifically did you have in mind?" Harry ventured.

"Well," the angel began, "you have seen a bit about how deception can work. How about something different?"

"Why the mystery?"

"No mystery—maybe just a bit of a surprise," Narcissus said with a mischievous expression.

"Mystery, surprise—either way—I'm in," Harry said climbing out from under the table. "Just as long as it's more pleasant than our last outing!"

"Oh, I think you'll enjoy this trip," Narcissus reassured him.

"So, what do I do?" Harry asked, now standing near the

kitchen table.

"Why don't you lie down?"

Harry walked over to the bed, straightened the covers and lay down flat. "How's this?"

"Perfect, said the angel, "now close your eyes."

Harry obeyed, and instantly he was out of his body. Once again he felt weightless, with nothing immediately in view except his angelic friend.

"Are we in the supernatural again?" Harry asked, realizing he was holding the angel's hand.

"Yes."

"This is so *unreal*, and yet it feels natural."

Narcissus nodded in agreement. "That's because it *is* ultimately more natural than anything physical. If you think about it, you might remember feeling a bit heavy after our last experience."

"You're right! I'd forgotten that. So, where's my house?"

"It's still here," the angel pointed.

Harry didn't have to search. His home sat just below.

"Can we go down?"

"Sure. Why don't you lead the way?" Narcissus let go of his hand.

Harry started forward with a jerk and then stopped. "How do I do this?"

"You were doing fine. Just move where you want to go. Use your instincts."

Harry directed his attention to the outside wall of his bedroom. As he focused, he moved himself forward but realized he was going to collide with the building. He looked anxiously at Narcissus, but it was too late. He reached out to stop himself, but instead found himself submerged in the wall, his head and shoulders in the bedroom and his lower half still outside—and there was Narcissus, in the room with him.

"Are you having fun?" the angel asked facetiously.

Harry was still confused as he looked around—at Narcissus, at the bed, at himself lying in the bed. He reached out and willfully grabbed the corner of his dresser and pulled himself down. He watched his legs appear as they came through the wall. "Okay, help me out here!" he pleaded.

Narcissus took Harry's hand, and once again they were hovering above.

"Okay, that . . . was really weird!" Harry cried. "How is it that I can pass right through things—objects—and then at the same time, I can also grasp other things?"

"It is being in the natural and the supernatural at the same time," Narcissus explained. "You can pass through matter, and then manipulate it or pick it up, if you will, because it is subject to your will."

"I'm going to need some practice at that,"

"It's just like riding a bike," Narcissus joked. "Are you ready to go?"

"I think so—let's start pedaling!"

With Harry in tow, Narcissus sped off into the supernatural.

14
Scratch and Gorguol

Abaddon waited. Though he had been summoned, waiting to be invited further in, was customary. He had been through this tiresome routine on many occasions in the past and knew the protocol, but this visit felt different. Gorguol's presence weighed heavily in the air. There was a strong odor to it that Abaddon found abhorrent, yet he inhaled, deeply savoring the fowl aroma. The stench was repugnant, and still somehow pleasing.

He heard Scratch now, whispering, but he could see nothing. Protocol forced him to remain until he was given vision and entry.

His mind wandered as he recalled the many times he had found himself in this position, waiting for Gorguol, usually put off for no other reason than to be shown who was in charge. But Gorguol had been smart enough to hold this venerated position for quite some time. A seat of such power was neither given, nor maintained, without consistent results, and that's what Gorguol achieved regularly.

But I can take a great deal of credit for that, he mused.

But the means of such control is what Abaddon questioned, such as the condition of Scratch's face and overall appearance. Fear was a useful and necessary tool, but there were so many other creative ways to use one's power to achieve the same results. Of course, he couldn't expect everyone to be as clever and cunning as he. Most creatures were not gifted with the high level of inventiveness which Abaddon had at his disposal. Consequently, they were forced to rely on whatever lesser resources they could employ, even if it meant using the most basic tools of unsophisticated and callous cruelty.

Even so, being subject to Gorguol had its advantages, if you were a valuable servant. There was a certain level of freedom available, sometimes to pick one's own assignment or hold a coveted position of authority over lesser spirits who had either failed to achieve success or had simply been groomed for less important purposes. Abaddon decided he could give credit where credit was due, even if his overseer was archaic and simple-minded in his effort to bring about human submission. Whatever it took to get the job done, he supposed . . . but still, he hated Gorguol.

A dull violet light appeared and the smooth walls of a short hallway became visible. Abaddon stepped forward, and ducking under a low arch he entered a large room. Aside from the familiar stench of Gorguol, the air was thick with another smell. Abaddon recognized it immediately—the reek of a human corpse. He glanced around the large tabernacle. The spacious room had minimal adornment, for the most part. On the opposite end sat Gorguol on a plush leather sofa. His dark mauve glow was bathed in a sticky film of sweat. Scratch sat to his right, and two other veiled demons sat crouched to his left. Before Gorguol was a large oak table and two chairs. On the chairs sat two men,

Gorguol's well-dressed attorneys who were clearly held in a state of oblivion. Stretched out on the table was the body of a similarly dressed man. Most likely a client, or even a colleague who had displayed a level of poor judgment. It wasn't the first time Abaddon had seen this kind of development regarding his superior. Gorguol grinned hugely and motioned for Abaddon to come closer. He had not changed, as Abaddon could see him for what he really was. Gluttony, sloth, and obesity were still his close companions.

Abaddon ignored Scratch, who pretended to be indifferent, gazing down at the dead man lying on the table. The scarlet devil strode across the room and halted before his master.

"Abaddon . . . you look well!" Gorguol said in a deep persuasive voice. "As you can see, I do not rely on a facade, nor do I have any concern for putting on airs regarding my personal appearance." He gazed down at his own enormous form and then back up to his noble servant.

"Greetings, Gorguol," Abaddon bowed, ignoring the subject of his master's appearance. "Have I disturbed you?" He gestured to the table.

"Don't be ridiculous—remember, it was I who summoned you! But no, your presence is never disturbing."

"I am glad to hear that, my lord, and happy to respond to your invitation. Still, I am rather anxious as you caught me at a critical juncture. May I politely indulge your good nature and then return to my duties?"

"Abaddon, I do not wish to take up *too* much of your time. However, there are some matters that I feel we need to address, face to face."

"Of course," Abaddon responded with an air of calm while preparing himself mentally.

"Do not be overly anxious. I will be brief. You know I am not one to go on at length unnecessarily, so I would recommend you be careful not to give me the impression that you do not appreciate the generosity of my invitation."

Abaddon stood mute, forcing a pretense of respect.

"Tell me, what do you think of my new quarters? I have put much thought and care into choosing just the right location and design. What is your impression—do you approve?"

"Your Eminence, if I have been neglectful in any way, please accept my regrets. The structure *is* impressive. You have chosen well! With that said, I am mainly concerned with delivering to you my highest standard of performance. I know you will demand nothing less."

"Then let us proceed with the business at hand. The immediate issues have to do with your level of commitment to the man, Harry Turner. My resources indicate that you have spent little time in that effort. Tell me, is there a problem there?"

"Not at all," Abaddon responded, and then added in a more controlled tone, "In fact, I was pursuing him when I was *interrupted*. If I had not—"

"Hold," Gorguol said flatly raising a flabby arm up in

protest. "My first request is that you now begin to give this man your full attention. I will credit your skillfulness later. But that, is the request from above."

"Understood," Abaddon acquiesced.

"Secondly, it has been confirmed that there is angelic interference there. You remember Narcissus?"

"But of course. How could I forget? His name has been a topic of fiction and myth for some time—a satirical hoax at his expense—rather humorous, don't you think?"

"Yes, Abaddon, and I believe you had something to do with that little prank, didn't you?"

"This is true," the fallen angel smiled dryly. "What? Has he finally been liberated?"

"It seems so. Liberated, and even now in a process of redemption! It sickens me!" Gorguol's sonorous voice took on a rumbling tone as he spewed out the words.

"Very curious," Abaddon mused, his eyes taking on a darker hue. "I have sensed nothing of his presence."

"Apparently some sort of covering has been placed over him—until now," Gorguol growled. "It seems he has been exposed—we don't know why. In any case, there are signs, queer things happening in high places all around our little globe. The eyes I maintain are sensing something nearby. Regardless of whether or not our old friend Narcissus has been redeemed, he is involved somehow, and whatever folly he is up to will be at our expense. There are rumors that he has grown powerful, and we

169

shall not take this warning lightly. It is bad enough that this fool has been released, but that he should take up a position against us now? We, with whom he should have conspired—it's ludicrous. So take note, for this defector there will be no mercy!

"Now my next question," Gorguol leaned forward and his eyes narrowed, "Do you require aid, or can you handle this without my intervention?"

Abaddon needed to use caution here. The wrong answer could be detrimental.

What was Gorguol looking for?

If he declined the offer of support, would his abilities be in question—would Gorguol take offense?

Why hadn't he known of Narcissus?

It was because Harry Turner had *not* been a real priority!

On the other hand, would it be an admittance of weakness to accept the offer of aid? Abaddon believed Gorguol was already convinced he could not handle the situation on his own, otherwise he would not be here. Even though he already had the assistance of his own associates, he might eventually require additional aid. He needed an answer that would give him an advantage.

"My dearest Gorguol, it is true I have been immersed in the facilitating of the Bio-Cell project, and I have ample support at my disposal. Your offer to assist me in my efforts is generous. If you are willing to sacrifice some portion of your constituency on my behalf, I would be indebted to you and grateful to say the least!"

"Splendid—splendid," Gorguol's wet face gleamed. "There is apparently something we have missed. I trust you will discover where the problem lies and nip it in the bud, so to speak."

Was that it? Abaddon readied himself to agree with his master and then promptly make an exit.

"Now, on a more positive note," Gorguol leaned forward even further and stretched his neck out, taking in a large breath of the foul odor that hung in the air. "Where was I? Ah, yes, this is an unusual and rare treat! It has been handed down to me that *you* have been given the authority to reveal yourself to the man, Harry Turner, and whomever you deem necessary, in regard to this specific project. Accomplish this task however you wish. The method is up to you. Be as creative as you like!"

"How delightful!" Abaddon beamed as he stifled his urgency to depart. "It appears this is a more important undertaking than was anticipated, but we shall respond to this threat accordingly. Approaching a man—in the flesh, so to speak—has always been a satisfying experience."

"Excellent then," Gorguol said leaning back. "I'm sure you won't let me down. Now, I won't need to sacrifice very much of my citizenry. In fact, I'm convinced only *one* should be necessary, and I have the ideal candidate."

Scratch winced as Gorguol turned his direction.

"Yes, my beloved Scratch. I will try to find a way,

somehow, to get by without my personal aid for a period. I know you will find him to be most helpful. Besides, the fact that you two already have a special relationship will only insure to me the greatest combination for success. My very own protégé and my most elite colleague—working together. How very pleasing this is to me!"

Abaddon kept all his emotion at bay, while Gorguol exuded his delight like a rotten melon being squashed.

Scratch wasn't as good at keeping his feelings hidden. He squirmed as he sat fixed in obedience. His expression betrayed a look of shock and dismay, but he bit his tongue in silence.

"Is there anything else, your Excellency?" Abaddon asked, in an effort to conclude.

"As a matter of fact, there is *one* more thing. To your credit—I really must commend you on your superb choice of this pawn—I believe her name is . . . What is her name?"

One of the veiled demons leaned over and whispered into Gorguol's ear.

"Beth Fairbanks? Yes! A superb bit of strategy! Every time I begin to doubt you, Abaddon, you turn around and surprise me with a stroke of genius. Scratch tells me she couldn't be a more perfect selection. There, you see? We *do* notice the good things as well!"

Abaddon was at a complete loss. How would that little scamp know anything?

Beth Fairbanks?

What was this trickery? The new secretary at Algren's company. What was her significance? What was Gorguol talking about?

"Abaddon? You look puzzled. Is something wrong?"

"On the contrary," Abaddon lied. "It's just, I had no idea you were so well-informed. Yes, thank you. I believe she will work out quite nicely."

"Very well," Gorguol said with a bark, "Why don't you and my little friend here go and see what kind of progress you can make together." He shot a stern glance at Scratch and then tilted his head in Abaddon's direction. "And remember, I am always near—keep me informed. And Abaddon . . . don't be a stranger!"

Gorguol motioned to his aids and closed his eyes. The other occupants of the hall began to stir as though they had been released from some hidden clutch. Now that they were free to move about, the two humans discussed the disposal of the body, unaware of their company, while the two veiled demons ministered to Gorguol.

The room began to dim as Scratch moved towards Abaddon.

"Come—our session is over," he said with his teeth grinding. He brushed past Abaddon and marched toward the doorway where they had entered.

Abaddon turned on his heel and strode after him. As he stepped out onto the rooftop garden, there was Scratch waiting for him with a menacing scowl on his distorted face.

"This is your fault!" the podgy devil seethed.

"What?" Abaddon grated back with instant fury.

"If you had exhibited a thread of real courage," Scratch spat out, "you would have declined the offer of aid. You are truly a bigger coward than I imagined! You have a myriad of qualified and devout devils available to you, but you are more concerned with appeasement. The only help you need is in arrogance management! *Abaddon the artist! Abaddon, the spirit of renaissance!* Do you think for an instant that Gorguol cares in the least how artistically you get the job done?

"*FOOL!* You could have rejected any interference and pledged to handle the whole matter without intervention. Yet, you chose to make it clear that you are incapable of handling even the simplest challenge by yourself. Gorguol is probably planning your replacement as we speak, which will be the only positive outcome of this fiasco."

"You little rodent!" Abaddon lunged forward and Scratch met him head on. "I would reshape you again right here, except that you are *mine,* only temporarily." He bore down hard on the smaller devil. "Right now, I cannot afford to spoil Gorguol's property any further—but I promise you now . . . you will regret those words!"

The two devils were locked together in a livid display of scorching intimidation. They were not engaged in combat, but each held his ground, pressed against the other in ferocity. As they glared at one another with piercing defiance, they both became aware of a movement near the entry to Gorguol's sanctuary. Abaddon could see Scratch was distracted and risked a glance over to the doorway as well.

There, just inside the opening, stood one of the well-dressed men who had been seated inside during the meeting. He walked out into the open and sniffed the air. Both of the dark angels stepped back from each other and turned towards the man with unease. It wasn't until now that Abaddon really got a good look at him. He was very slender, almost gaunt. His cheeks were dark and hollow, his expression indifferent. He looked tired, as though he had not slept in days. The way he was dressed, he could only have been a high-ranking executive, except for the fresh blood smeared on his shirt and tie.

Abaddon and Scratch both became rigid as the man casually strode up to them. He stood and stared at them for a moment and began to laugh, slowly at first, then uncontrollably. In a jerky motion, his laugh turned into a howl as the two devils stood there staring back mutely. Then, just as quickly as he had begun laughing, the man was silent. The bewildered demons watched as the gaunt figure sauntered forward, bearing down on them with his dark hollow eyes. Halting before them, he stared at the two puzzled figures, opened his mouth again, and out crept the deep resonant voice of Gorguol.

"Yes, I do take pleasure in manipulating humans to commit vile and murderous deeds," he said as he looked down and studied the bloody condition of his expensive suit and tie. Stepping even closer until he was inches from the other two, he opened his mouth again.

"You must learn to co-exist in harmony if you expect to accomplish anything." He spoke calmly, but with force. "I will be dreadfully disappointed if I do not see some significant results— *very soon!*" He pushed his face against them so that his flesh made contact. Raising his hand up to his face, he scraped his thumb nail so hard into the skin of his forehead that a gash opened and began to bleed profusely. With that, he added in a barely audible whisper, "*Go now!*"

Abaddon didn't waste any time. Without a word, he pulled away and shot up into the air and across the city sky.

Let Scratch make his own way!

He was sure the foul fiend would have no problem finding him, and then he would deal with the imp in a more personal manner. Right now his main concern must be Harry Turner, and then, this Beth Fairbanks.

Curse that little fool for spying and interfering with his business! If he hadn't meddled where he shouldn't have, Abaddon would not have this mess on his hands. Now, he needed to know all about this woman before Scratch figured out the truth.

He was not in control of Beth Fairbanks—!

If there were any level of outside interference, wouldn't he have known it? What made Scratch believe she was *his* servant? That abominable little spy must have seen *something* that was very convincing.

Curse him!

Abaddon could only surmise at this point that the woman was under the influence of someone else, but who? Clearly, Scratch believed Beth Fairbanks was already doing Abaddon's bidding, and now he must keep it that way. He needed to resolve this matter before Scratch realized the truth—*that Abaddon knew nothing about her!*

Moments later, Abaddon had returned to Advanced Bio-Cell. The angry devil dropped down far below the main building to a place deep in the rock where he had hollowed out a sizable residence for himself. After all, every creature had to abide somewhere. This was his residence for the time being, but just because it was temporary didn't mean it couldn't be luxurious. The underground fortress had all the things an elite spirit might desire to make himself comfortable. And with a view of the entire landscape, he had a perfect vantage point. From here he could monitor every activity, up through the rock, the soil and roots, the contour of the surface, and all that was on it, just the same as if he were high above the ground looking down. Since most of his time was spent manipulating and directing human beings, or seeing that his underlings were guiding them properly, he did not spend a lot of time here, but it was home for now.

Abaddon had made arrangements to accommodate his full entourage. Considering each location carefully, he placed his underlings according to their specific purpose and talent. They were not an unusual collection of devils in regards to their abilities. Their successes were largely due to Abaddon's skill in finding their potential and then directing them towards the desired outcome. Almost all of his servants were well-trained in various arts of wickedness. There were, of course, areas in which they must all be adept, creating envy, strife, deceit, and even murder when need be. Then there were those who specialized in only very specific areas. There were whisperers of lies, spreaders of insolence, spreaders of jealousy and arrogance, and inventors of other evil things. A select few were masters of idolatry, sorcery, and all forms of deception. Currently, these fallen creatures were all set up like chess pieces waiting to be placed in the proper position at the appropriate time—and Abaddon was the chess master.

With the exception of a few recent complications, the stage was neatly set for Abaddon's entire scheme to be put into motion. Soon there would be nothing that could interfere, and he would orchestrate the ushering in of a new age in which he would flourish. He would finally receive the honor and recognition he so truly deserved. Forget the vile indulgences of Gorguol and all his sullied cronies. Their antiquated customs would soon be found tired and lacking. The world would not bend to the old ways much longer. In Abaddon's far-reaching plan, even things like drug addiction and prostitution would be brought to new spiritual and technological heights. The visions of this contemporary society required something more progressive—something more suitable for a race of people on the verge of deity. He would show them all a new and innovative approach— a bridge to a new millennium, a new Babylon, with Abaddon helping to lead the way. And why not! Wasn't it always the artists and the builders, the noble thinkers and philosophers, who guided the rest of the masses toward a truer and nobler vision? Besides, this was for the benefit of *all* mankind. They had never been *consciously* interested in forfeiting free will for servanthood, but just like the proverbial frog in the slowly heated kettle of water . . .

Beth Fairbanks! The name issued from his lips.

He swiftly turned his face towards Isles End.

"Rull," came out of his mouth. The sound moved forward and vibrated and was immediately heard. Within moments a specter appeared before Abaddon. It was black and shadowy and powerful in stature. At first glance, its face appeared to be masked, but in fact it was nearly featureless. The subtle curves suggested that of a gray mannequin, smooth and shiny. There were no penetrations in the demons face save a slit where its mouth was.

"Lord?" the spirit responded submissively.

"There is a woman in Isles End. Her name is Beth Fairbanks. You will probe her without delay and then return to me. Find out—does she have a guardian? Whom does she serve? To what level can she be influenced? Look for anything that

179

might be relevant. Go—and report back swiftly!"

"Yes, Lord," the shrouded demon answered and was instantly gone.

No sooner had the spirit disappeared than another form emerged from the north. It was small and fleshy.

Scratch!

Abaddon did not attempt to conceal himself—if he was ever to achieve success, he must build some sort of alliance with the disfigured courier, even if it was not genuine. Before Scratch got any closer, Abaddon prepared himself mentally for the positive working relationship he would soon be forced to maintain with his new 'assistant'. Once again he would be required to depend on much patience, and *this* time he would be under close scrutiny!

Abaddon watched as Scratch slowed down to a crawl. The little devil showed apprehension as it peered about cautiously. Rather than wait for his guest to come to him, Abaddon opted to show Scratch a willingness to meet him part way. In a gesture of good faith, he made himself very visible as he moved up into the open air and approached the little devil.

"Greetings," he bowed with an eloquence that almost seemed genuine.

Scratch looked around suspiciously. "What game is *this,* now?" he smirked.

"No game," the crimson demon declared with poise. "It has just become very clear to me that we must immediately reconsider the condition of our relationship."

"Well, how generous of you," Scratch responded with thick sarcasm.

"Listen, I know you are bound by Gorguol," Abaddon began diplomatically, "and I am not looking for your undivided allegiance. But if you can see your way to being loyal to this cause, I believe we can both submit to the request of our master and find some common ground—or as he put it so well, 'learn to co-exist in harmony'."

Scratch studied Abaddon's face. In an attempt to gauge the unbalance between sincerity and deceit, he asked, "You already believe I will use every advantage I find to discredit you. Tell me, what do you have for me, should I find your intentions to be remotely sincere?"

"Why not simply tell me what will make you content," Abaddon quickly countered.

"Beth Fairbanks," Scratch said without hesitation. "I want the woman, Beth Fairbanks! You clearly have her—I desire her."

Abaddon veiled his anxiety and quickly formed a refusal.

"This cannot be done. She is an integral part of our strategy. She is already under the guidance of one of my most trusted subordinates," he lied with great finesse. "This kind of compatibility takes time and great effort. Besides, to what purpose could she serve you?"

"As you may already know," the smaller devil ventured, "I have never been given the opportunity to possess a creature, or rather, a human." Scratch spoke bitterly, suggesting a weakness. "I have not been allowed the training which I have desired for so long." His head was bowed and his eyes hidden as he continued, "I have watched her recently. I have seen how cleverly she fishes for this Harry Turner. I have studied her at work. She is sly and cunning—almost *too* perfect! I am impressed at how completely you have beguiled her. She is utterly convincing! And so, here is my chance. I must know the feeling to guide and control!"

"And that is my point," Abaddon forced an apologetic tone, "She is controlled because there is someone who controls her, one with knowledge and experience who has bonded with her. You do not have that ability, yet! Would I jeopardize this entire operation just to satisfy your lustful cravings? What would Gorguol think? Surely you can see the folly of it. There must be something else that will satisfy—"

Abaddon struggled to maintain a look of confidence.

Cursed little fiend! He will concede—HE MUST!

But he mastered his expression with calm and conviction as Scratch seemed to mull over the impracticality of his own request. Abaddon knew if he betrayed himself in the slightest way, he could be in grave danger. But how long could he keep this charade a secret before he was discovered? Or, how long would it take to gain an advantage over Beth Fairbanks? He must come up with a solution soon. Either get control over this Beth Fairbanks, or destroy her.

"You are right," Scratch grated harshly. "So then I must

be trained. I will gain the experience, and you will provide the instruction I require. *That* is my request! Now that I have been forced into this situation, this is what you must do if you want my cooperation!"

"Alright, Scratch, I will do this for you." Abaddon purposefully revealed a portion of his elation, knowing it would be misinterpreted, as he secretly breathed a sigh of relief. "And in return, you will find a way to be supportive of my work and refrain from sharing any information that would be unfavorable to our cause."

This is very good! Find the weak spot!

Abaddon considered the dangerous creature before him. Here was his leverage point. *Something that Scratch deeply desired!* And at the same time, he would keep Scratch away from Beth Fairbanks until he figured out what was really going on.

"And what about our old friend, Narcissus?" Scratch asked abruptly. "What have you discovered about his participation?"

Abaddon concealed his annoyance. "Not to worry, my friend. I plan to deal with him personally, very soon."

"Like you have done with Harry Turner?"

"I appreciate your sarcasm, but now that I have gained your additional expertise, I will be all the more liberated to pursue both adversaries with added fervor. In any case, you need not concern yourself. Now that you are on the inside, you can be sure I will keep you informed every step of the way."

"Well then," Scratch smiled artfully, "let us begin to co-exist in harmony . . ."

15
Preston Hart

Preston Hart's glasses slid forward on his face as he signed the shipping documents for the friendly courier. Simultaneously, several other neatly uniformed men maneuvered the last of the new equipment into the lobby of the lower floor of Advanced Bio-Cell. The redness of Preston's usually ruddy cheeks became blotchy in the coolness of the basement. *It was time to start warming this place up*, he thought to himself as he watched the moving crew at work.

He looked across the large room and imagined it in full operation, running like a finely tuned engine. And he would be right there in the midst of the thrill. He felt as though his hand was on the throttle, he was revving the engine and it was beginning to purr. This achievement belonged to him as much as anyone else. He was the problem solver, the chief advisor, and the mediator. Whenever anyone had a problem, who did they go to? If there was ever a dispute, Preston was called upon to solve it.

He liked to think of himself as the keeper of a zoo. It was his responsibility to feed the animals, each having a different diet, a unique craving or special need. When animals are satisfied, they are happy and perform at their optimum ability. Other times, Advanced Bio-Cell was more like a circus than a zoo, and then he became the lion tamer. Preston chuckled as he visualized himself cracking a lengthy whip.

His excitement grew as he watched the equipment being carefully placed on the far side of the room. The idea of having all these high tech instruments up and running with the best scientists available was overwhelming. It was fantastic! Having been involved in the sequencing of the complete human genome had brought them serious recognition, but it was only the beginning. This was, "The Biology Century!"

There was no question that genetic engineering was the future. Why be afraid of that? They had already moved genes around among plants, animals, and bacteria. Of course they still got the usual complaints. Okay, so the experts had little or no understanding of what the possible consequences might be, but that is how you discover how things work! How else had they come so far already? Why slow down the process and waste necessary funding with over regulated safety testing? They weren't dealing with humans . . . yet!

Or were they?

Preston knew they were. Their own engineers were already modifying the genes of humans. Dolly had been cloned from the DNA of a sheep that had been dead for six years. Human cloning was next.

Lost a loved one? Want to have them back?

Gene therapy and germ-line manipulation were next in line. Imagine treating diseases with genes rather than medicine. Or, how about the next generation inheriting new traits through changes in the prior generation's germ cells? It was no longer science fiction. The possibilities of cloning organs as a cure for so many diseases was almost a reality, technically appealing and financially lucrative. It was so completely astounding to Preston that he couldn't keep from smiling.

It was the new book of life!

The thought was captivating and the possibilities were endless, as long as the naysayers and the so-called Moral Majority did not raise too big a fuss. There was always someone to stand in the way of progress. Where would they be if every time someone came up with a better way to do something, the fearful and suspicious rose up and shut it down? Preston shook his head and laughed silently as he thought about it.

Abject morons!

But there was always an element out there who were incapable of developing beyond the boundaries laid by their ancestors. Ironically, they would only further the cause *this* time with their futile attempts to interfere. The thought was actually entertaining. He could see it now in the headlines:

"Religious Right Rejects Cure for Cancer"

"Moral Majority Marches against Market for Organ Repair"

His thoughts were interrupted as one of the movers nearby motioned to him. Preston walked over.

"That's the last of it, sir," the man said as he slid out the hand truck from under a large crate.

187

"Yes, that's quite a load! There *is* another shipment coming soon, right?" Preston asked, returning the signed forms.

"Let's see." The man studied the paperwork. "Looks like twelve more crates will be arriving tomorrow."

"That sounds about right," Preston said as he did a quick calculation in his head. "Thank you."

"No problem. Thanks for using Care-Freight," the man said politely and turned towards the elevator.

Just then the elevator bell sounded and the doors slid open.

"Perfect timing!" Preston declared as the mover smiled and pushed the hand truck over to the elevator. He stopped abruptly as a short man with a head of thick white hair and a stark white coat to match stepped out of the elevator and hurried past, his head down.

"Excuse me," the mover apologized, but the white-haired man just dashed by, oblivious.

"Shushi, over here," Preston called out, as though his colleague were blind. Shushi looked up and redirected himself towards Preston.

"Where are you going in such a hurry?" Preston asked with a chuckle. "Can't wait to get your hands on this stuff, eh?"

"Our equipment has arrived early!" Shushi said with obvious exhilaration.

"Yes," Preston noted, sharing the enthusiasm, "but we can't do anything until our general contractor is finished. Still, it may speed things up a bit. Good thing there's so much room in here!"

Shushi walked over to where a dozen large wooden crates had been placed against the wall like dominos. He immediately pulled out a note pad and began scribbling as he studied the labels on the different containers.

"When will Mr. Turner be here?"

"Harry Turner?" Preston responded, "I believe he is scheduled first thing Monday morning."

Shushi nodded with partial awareness, his thoughts divided. His lips moved mutely as he studied the room, as though he were having a conversation with someone else. Walking over to the work station area, he made some more notes and looked back at Preston. "I think it would be wise to keep this equipment sealed until Mr. Turner is finished. There's plenty of room in here and I want to keep it free of any dust or debris."

"Naturally," Preston agreed. "I know you're anxious to get started, as we all are. If your team of technicians are ready, we can begin as soon as Harry is done."

"Of course," Shushi agreed, still taking notes. He glanced over to Preston with an agitated look, as though he were about to say something, and then absorbed himself in his notes again. He reminded Preston of a student cramming for a big test, but there was really nothing more he could do for the moment.

"It won't be long now," Preston consoled him. He could tell by the doctor's disposition that he'd gone beyond being self-absorbed in his work. He was on the verge of becoming neurotic. This was nothing new though. Shushi's fixation had actually become a positive condition as far as Preston was concerned.

Shushi began to fidget with the buttons on his white coat as he stood looking like a lost child. *He needs to be fed*, Preston thought.

"Shushi, why don't you take the weekend off—get away for a couple of days. You need some rest and a fresh perspective before you tackle the final stages of this project."

The doctor appeared sharply cognitive. "Don't be ridiculous! What are you talking about? I am even now working on the final preparations—they *must* be complete before we can proceed. Where are the brochures on this new equipment? *That* is what I will be spending my time with over the weekend!"

"Oh, of course. It is all here." Preston stepped over to one of the crates and lifted a stack of folders from the top. "I almost forgot about these," he said innocently, looking through the top of his glasses as he handed the folders over to Shushi.

The scientist glared at Preston with a questioning look of disdain as he took the bundle of material and stepped over to the elevator. "Preston, you cause me concern. Maybe it is *you* who are in need of a rest!" Then, "You know where you can find me. Oh, and turn up the heat in here. It's freezing!"

Preston suppressed a chuckle and waved as Shushi entered the elevator and disappeared behind the doors.

Feeding time and another meal delivered, Preston mused.

The thermostat was in a utility room behind the elevator. Preston brought it up to 72 degrees. Then he made his way up to the main floor and slipped into his new office.

With the exception of a couple light fixtures, his office was nearly complete. The solar tubes brought in ample light for his needs. Though not nearly as elaborate as Mr. Algren's suite, this would serve his purposes, and he did have a partial view of the countryside. This space will do very nicely he thought, as he sat down behind the desk and saw Bill's notes lying there.

Oh yes, the speech.

He had forgotten about it already, though there was no hurry. Bill had done a good job so far. Now it was his responsibility to make the document acceptable for the news media and ultimately the public.

He clicked on his computer and waited for the hard-drive to boot up. Now that it was networked into the system, he could tap into almost every bit of information that ABC had compiled.

Preston hummed quietly as the logo for Advanced Bio-Cell came up on his screen. ABC! A little simplistic, he had thought at first, and surprisingly unintentional, but he liked the way the letters were woven into an eternity symbol, like a sideways figure-eight. The "B" was partially concealed by the intersection at the center, with the "A" and "C" inside the circles, in full view. They had toyed with the idea of working some DNA designs into the image but finally decided to go for the unpretentious and straightforward look.

191

He typed in his password and waited for the response. Almost instantly a page appeared. He scrolled down: Genetic Engineering, Human Genome, DNA, Gene Splicing, Adult Stem Cells, Embryonic Stem Cells, Cell Therapy, Blood Cells, Heart Cells, Brain Cells. The list went on. He clicked on Embryonic, then Fertility Clinic, then Frozen Embryos. The screen read, "left over from in-vitro fertilization procedures." He clicked on Surplus, "currently about 200,000 available." Then Research, "Authorized in Britain, but halted in the United States."

"Fools," he muttered aloud. But it didn't matter. A private company like ABC could do what it wanted without the government looking over its shoulder. He clicked again and a word processing screen appeared. He reached over and picked up Bill's speech.

"Might as well get started on this," he said to no one in particular and began typing.

16
Are You Okay, Miss?

Beth Fairbanks stood at the counter in the large foyer of Advanced Bio-Cell. She watched as several laborers picked up the last of their materials and headed for the exit doors. They had just finished installing an immense water feature in the lobby, and she couldn't take her eyes off it.

A beautiful collection of furniture in rich earthy tones was arranged attractively around a waterfall that cascaded out of the ceiling into a cradle of stone just below. The pillar rose like a monolith, fourteen feet high, in the center of the room. The perimeter of the pool spread out like roots of stone, carrying water to the giant ferns placed all around the furniture. The entire arrangement rested on a carpet resembling grass. The display was like an oasis, so unusual and real looking. It didn't blend in with the rest of the room yet, but given time, Beth guessed it would. She gazed at it, mesmerized.

"Isn't it *lovely!*" gushed the woman next to her.

"Oh yes, Val," Beth answered, her eyes transfixed on the display. "It's amazing!"

"I wonder if they plan on doing anything like that here at *our* work station," the other woman said with a hint of envy. "You know, maybe a large terrarium all around the counter."

They both laughed, but Beth still stared, captivated by the immensity of the exhibit. Like a kaleidoscope, the water swirled and flashed the colors of the multi-faceted stone as it flowed down the sides of the pinnacle. The sound of the water gurgling along the maze of waterways almost put her into a trance.

She turned back to find her co-worker watching her. Valerie was a small blonde woman, well-groomed and professional in her appearance. Her hands were especially noticeable, perfectly manicured and covered with jewelry.

"I'm wondering," said Valerie, "whether the waterfall has enchanted you, or maybe Mr. Turner is *really* responsible!"

"Oh," Beth blushed, "you know, I guess I *was* thinking about him! On the way home yesterday, I sent him a text. I haven't done anything like that for awhile!"

Valerie gave Beth a stern but friendly glare. "You'd better pace yourself," she warned. "Take your time and reel them in slowly, that's what my mother always said!"

"I think it's a little too late for that, Val," Beth answered, inadvertently pressing her hands on her cheeks. Self-conscious, she turned back towards the fountain.

"It's funny, but somehow I knew right away that I was going to like this man."

"Well, you know better than I do—" Val said, turning back to her computer screen. "Hey let's see if we can ignore the tropical garden for a little while and get the rest of these files organized."

Beth turned away from the lobby and sat down. She had only just started working with Val, yet she felt very comfortable alongside the smart looking woman. Val was quick with her hands. While she had already sorted through one stack of forms and was busy with another, Beth was only halfway through with her first. Beth decided to make a serious attempt at concentrating on her work.

But she couldn't stop thinking about Harry. Her fondness for him had developed quickly. It had been so easy! What was it about him? His honesty, his looks and warm nature? That she and Harry could have so much in common was amazing, almost like it was planned. How nice that might be, if it were true!

Again, Beth realized she was getting behind.

Valerie looked over at Beth and could see her co-worker was distracted. "Dear, tell you what—why don't you call it a day? You've already put in more hours than required! We're just about through anyway. I'll finish up and see you back here tomorrow."

Beth looked at her watch. It was almost an hour before quitting time. "Well, I—"

"Oh, go on, Beth. I'll cover for you," Valerie insisted.

"There *are* some things I could do," Beth said, hesitating. "Okay, thanks! I'll see you in the morning," she agreed, grabbing her purse and jacket.

As she headed for the front door, she was tempted to stop and sit in one of the cushy chairs at the base of the fountain. She reached down and felt the carpet. It was amazing—like real grass! She looked back to see Valerie watching her and smiling. Waving back, Beth turned and moved toward the front door.

Minutes later, Beth's Karmann Ghia was purring down the highway towards Isles End. She had quickly grown accustomed to the pleasant drive. The beautiful scenery flew by as she sped home. On her way, she decided to pick up a few things at the grocery store. She thought about stopping by Harry's place but decided against it. He must have gotten busy with something, otherwise she would have heard from him by now.

As she neared the market, a dull ache began to grow in her stomach. Gradually, the throbbing increased, spreading to her limbs. Was she ill? No . . . just worried suddenly, but why? What was there to be troubled about? Her hands gripped the steering wheel as though she were going to tear it off. Loosening her grasp she reached for a tissue and wiped the sweat from her forehead.

You must get hold of yourself!

Snatching several more tissues from the console, Beth attempted to dry her damp face and hands. Where was Harry? She would call him later to make sure he was okay.

Pearl Street came into view and there was some relief knowing she was almost there. The pressure in her head began to subside as she turned into the parking lot of Isles Market. Annoyed by the strange condition that had come over her Beth wondered if she really needed to go shopping. She parked near the front door and scanned the area. Everything seemed quiet. She looked over her shopping list and began to feel a bit more normal. A couple of old folks sitting in front of the store greeted her as she made her way inside. She grabbed a shopping cart and collected a few items as she worked her way to the produce section. The store was nearly empty inside; the few shoppers who wandered through the aisles seemed to move slowly as they methodically filled their carts.

Beth strolled past the rows of neatly organized fruit and selected the necessary ingredients for a fruit salad. When she turned to the vegetables a sense of oppression filled her again. She paused for a moment as the nausea grew, but she was unable to identify any specific symptom. An elderly woman pushing a cart with a small dog in the basket moved towards her, apparently sensing something was wrong. Beth tried to move out of the way in order to avoid any confrontation, but it was too late.

"Are you okay, miss?"

"I'm fine, thank you." Beth feigned nonchalance as she pushed past the woman. The dog began to growl and she twisted her head back to study the small animal. It seemed to be staring.

That dog! Is it frowning at me?

She had a creepy feeling and tried to hurry away, but the overwhelming sense of panic pushed itself towards the surface. She pulled the cart over to the side of the lane and leaned over it to keep herself from falling.

"What is—" she muttered under her breath, but couldn't seem to speak. "I need to get—" she tried to say again, but what little bit of control she still maintained seemed to abandon her as the walls of the building closed in around her. It was no use. Her knees buckled as she gripped the sides of the grocery cart with her hands. An elderly gentleman appeared with a concerned expression on his face, but she was incoherent.

What? His mouth is moving, but . . .

She was already unconscious when her hands let go and she fell back and slid down onto the floor.

17
The Pool

With his body fed and safely napping, Harry glided out of time and space alongside his angelic companion. The feeling was fantastic, being in the company of Narcissus, this time with complete trust, not knowing or caring where they were headed. Funny though, he had no idea where they were going. In fact, he wasn't sure they were even moving at all.

Did it really matter. . . ?

Narcissus had said this experience would be a welcome surprise. For the time being, it was like a carnival ride. They might not be going anywhere, but for the moment, the journey was more important than the destination.

"I like this," Harry commented to Narcissus as they moved along.

"Yes, Harry, being in the supernatural always feels good because there is no time for which we must be accountable."

"How long could we do this?" Harry asked.

"How long do you want to do this?" Narcissus countered.

"How long have we been here?" Harry continued.

"There is no 'how long' . . . we are in the here and now!" the angel stated.

"But how can we be outside of time—is everything on *hold*? I mean, is everyone else frozen?"

"Harry, try to think of it like this, your life is like a

motion picture. We can fast forward or rewind to view or visit most any given point of your life from here in the supernatural. On the other hand, while you are in the natural, you don't know what's next because you haven't experienced it yet. You are in time, so you are bound to stay on track—you can only move forward at the pace which time allows. But when we return, you will be placed right back where you left off."

"Then I am right," Harry said with confidence. "If being in the supernatural is like a DVD, then we are in the pause mode."

"It's not quite like that," the angel laughed. "We might view a point *in* time, but time has not stopped for anyone. It's all continuous."

"Then we are actually cheating time?"

"There is no cheating going on!" the angel stated firmly.

"It sounds like everything I do, or am bound to do, has already been done—so in fact, I have no choice, no free will?"

"Didn't you understand anything I told you about free will? What you *will* choose to do might already be *known*—that's all. You still have free will at all times. Whatever you choose to do in any given situation is your choice. It is still voluntary on your part, and although the rest of the 'story' might be known in the supernatural, it must still be played out by you."

"Then do you know *my* future, Narcissus?"

"I have seen glimpses."

"I don't suppose you want to share them with me?"

"I don't think you would really want to know, would you?"

Harry paused for a moment and considered the question. Would he really want to know his own future? He doubted Narcissus would tell him anyway, but just the possibility that he could know was intriguing. He was instantly thinking of several things that would be to his advantage to know ahead of time. Of course, he thought of the stock market or the racetrack. The possibility of being able to avoid accidents seemed worthwhile, especially ones that could potentially lead to death. How about his own death? No! That would not be a good idea, would it. . .? Somehow, gaining that information ahead of time would almost seem wrong. But think of all the good things one could do!

But it didn't really matter. Narcissus would never tell him anything.

"I can hear the cogs turning, Harry," the angel said, guessing his friend's thoughts.

"Yeah, you probably have a pretty good idea," Harry grinned.

"So, your answer?"

"I guess not knowing is best." Harry feigned indifference with the most convincing tone he could conjure.

Narcissus laughed hard and it took Harry by surprise. He had not heard the angel laugh many times. And the fact that he laughed at Harry's answer troubled him.

"What was that for?" Harry pretended to be hurt.

"You *are* good!" Narcissus said as he continued to chuckle quietly.

"What—you don't believe me?" Harry continued his masquerade.

"Really, Harry, I *do* know you, almost better than you know yourself!"

"Yes, I remember now." Harry gave in and began laughing himself. "I really do understand though. I'm sure I'd be tempted to know too many things, most of which would probably turn out badly."

"I am proud of you," the angel stated. "And you are completely right! At least you have recognized quickly that it would be folly and even ruinous to gain such information."

Harry relaxed and let his thoughts wander. Gliding peacefully through the supernatural with an Archangel as his guide, he allowed himself to be completely absorbed in the moment. Just to be in the company of such an extraordinary being was overwhelming. There was finery and grandeur in the angel's every movement and expression. The more Harry studied his companion, the more his fascination increased. He imagined he could sit and stare at this celestial creature for hours.

Once again, he had a clearer sense they were moving. There was a gentle rise and fall, a shifting in direction, and the coolness of a slight breeze. His heart was light and carefree. But was this moving, or just being? Whatever was happening to Harry felt addictively pleasant.

As the feeling of movement increased, a landscape appeared.

"Where are we now?" Harry asked.

"Below the gates of a city!"

"So we have been actually moving?"

"Yes, Harry. And we have traveled to an actual place."

The first thing Harry experienced was sunlight and a warm breeze caressing his face. Down below there was water everywhere, like an ocean, but very calm with tiny white caps cresting across the surface. Harry held tightly to the angel's robe as they floated downward.

From this position, he could see and hear the ocean water spilling over an immense wall and into a beautiful blue river far below. They started to move quickly now in a downward glide, over the edge, past the river, and onto a grassy hillside. They hovered a few feet above a blanket of deep luxurious grass that covered the landscape. It was teal green—thick and exotic—and gave off a strong, rich scent.

"Look there," the angel pointed and Harry could see ahead of them, high above the pasture, a great wall. The more he raised his eyes, the greater the wall seemed to expand. The height became incalculable and it stretched endlessly in both directions. The color was like bright coals in a furnace, shimmering and fluid.

Gradually, there appeared a gateway. Were they still moving forward? The wall paled as the entrance came closer into view. Harry had never seen such a splendid gate. The intricacies of the craftsmanship were astounding. Interwoven in the shining entryway were swords and shields with strange carvings and inscriptions. There were beautiful mantles and elaborate armor, and—wings—magnificent giant wings, wonderfully mounted on the shoulders of . . .

Angels!

Harry was astounded! But were they . . . living?

Yes!

The entire gate was comprised of living creatures! Winged sentinels, watchful and bound together in a beautiful mosaic, securing the entrance to—a city! Guards to a kingdom that held—*what?*

"Narcissus, this is un—believable!" Harry whispered with a touch of apprehension in his voice.

"You're safe with me," Narcissus assured him. "Have no fear. I have brought you here to take part in a celebration! There is good news! I have been restored, but still not fully. There is more work for me to accomplish before I will be in the presence of Elohim, but in due time I shall be reinstated. Even now, I am being strengthened, and once again," he paused and became larger and more animated, "I am in the service of The Divine One!"

Harry gazed uncertainly into the eyes of the angel. They looked like swirling planets lit up by the sun . . . they were unworldly! He wasn't sure what to say. "I'm very happy for you," he offered.

"Yes, I believe you are! Thank you. It *is* a time to be glad," the Archangel beamed. "But this is not only about me. We will celebrate *you* as well."

"What do you mean?"

Narcissus grinned. "Once I am reunited with my old companions, we will share something special with you."

"Why?"

"Because I have been given permission, and you're my friend!"

Harry felt ecstatic as he hovered with the Archangel over the teal green hillside. Once again, he was distracted by the steady sound of water. He turned around and there below, circling the majestic grassland, he saw the river which he had just passed over, traveling for miles around the base of the blue-green pastures.

On the opposite bank, a stone wall shot straight up three hundred feet high, bordering the entire length of the river in both directions and cradling the ocean above. Harry marveled at the sight and sound of the sea gushing over from so high, like a never-ending waterfall. From north to south, the ocean spilled over into the waterway that stretched along the base of the fertile fields, surrounding the entire realm. From where they hovered, the fields moved upward toward the gate and the immense wall encircling the city inside.

The experience was too much for Harry as he attempted

to familiarize himself with the unusual surroundings, the ocean and river, the golden wall, the gate of living beings, and the big blue sky above. He became faint and nearly swooned. He sensed Narcissus beside him and pulled himself back to the moment. He felt the strong arm of the angel supporting him and looked up to see the being's face gazing down with care and concern.

"I'm sorry—I feel weak," Harry explained, his voice shaking.

"No need to apologize. I will hold you up. Now look, there is more!"

As the angel held him, Harry regained his strength, becoming vibrant and aware. He looked down and realized his bare feet were now buried in the tall grass. He wiggled his toes in the soft reeds and was amazed to feel the same revitalizing effect he had experienced when Narcissus touched him. Energy seemed to flow up through the soles of his feet and into his entire body. He took a deep breath and exhaled loudly. The air tasted sweet in his mouth. But his body wasn't here, he considered. It was back at home in his bed, on earth, wherever that was! But he didn't care. The important part of him was here, now.

He had never felt so complete as he did standing with his angelic friend, in this land.

This dream . . .

Except he wasn't dreaming. It was more like waking up from a dream.

This was real!

As he waited, he watched the great living gate begin to open. Three bright figures stepped out onto the meadow. The gate immediately fastened behind them as they began to walk down to where Harry and Narcissus stood.

"I have brought you here to rejoice with me and also to bestow upon you a special gift," Narcissus explained as the beings approached. "And also to meet my dearest companions. These three, I have known from the beginning. They are Cherubim. We are now reunited, and they shall accompany me and give aid in the work I have yet to accomplish."

Harry admired them as they drew near. They were each very similar, fair and blond, yet distinctly unique. All wore bright golden robes with wide belts and sheathed swords at their sides. They had the same fiery glow as Narcissus but were slightly less formidable in their appearance. Still, they displayed a certain fierceness in their countenance and would certainly be frightening in a conflict. He was intrigued by their childlike appearance. Even though their features were sharp and mature, they were also youthful and ruddy. One looked especially like a young boy. They moved forward with poise and conviction in their gait. Their features translated wisdom and keen awareness, but when they finally stood before Harry and the Archangel, the somberness left their faces and they took on expressions of great joy.

With Harry still at his side, Narcissus knelt before them.

"My dear friends," he began his greeting, "I am so pleased

to introduce you to my friend, Harry Turner."

The three angels faced them, side by side, until the tallest one stepped forward and stood directly before the kneeling Seraph. He smiled wisely and bowed. Then, rising back up, he spoke.

"Narcissus, we are immortal, forever bound and in your service! Thanks be to Elohim!" He shouted triumphantly as he reached out and gripped Narcissus by the shoulder. He was clearly elated to see his old friend but also noticeably reserved.

He then turned his fierce countenance to Harry. "Harry Turner, I am Ranan." He spoke courteously, then stepped back.

The second angel moved up and knelt down before Narcissus.

"My dearest friend, we are perpetual, abiding, and shall endure always! Praise to the Divine One!" he exclaimed, his voice ringing out like a song.

Then he addressed Harry. "Greetings, young man—I am Psallo!" he sang again, his voice resounding in the air.

Finally, the third, youngest looking Cherub jumped up and came close to Narcissus. The Seraph could not keep from smiling now as *this* youthful spirit greeted him. His round boyish face had the broadest grin Harry had ever seen, and his eyes twinkled with fire as he spoke.

"Salutations, Narcissus! From everlasting to everlasting— we are exceedingly glad! All honor to Elohim!" he shouted gleefully, and wrapping his arms around Narcissus, he kissed him on the cheek.

Then he turned his sparkling gaze to Harry. "And greetings to you as well, young Harry. I am Agalliao!" he beamed and fell back in line with the others.

Narcissus stood and announced, "We will soon be meeting with my Overseer. There we will celebrate again and receive added strength as well as instruction. Are you equipped, my friends?"

Ranan gripped the hilt of his sword. "We have already received the summons and have readied ourselves. We know there is work to be done. There is darkness spreading and forces building in number and strength, but when *we* are called, we know there is a greater need. And now that you have been restored—we are not troubled."

Psallo stepped forward. "We have been walking up and down in the midst of the stones of fire. Our blades are sharp and two-edged," he sang out with a voice like a trumpet.

"We are ready!" Agalliao confirmed, a wide grin flashing across his face.

"Well then, enough of this talk!" stated the Archangel. "We are here to celebrate with Harry. We have something for him, don't we my friends? Let us all go down to the water."

Harry followed as Narcissus turned away from the city walls and led them down towards the river. They all reached the water's edge together and stepped onto the sandy bank. Harry looked on with awe at the massive cascade of water that poured down like a mirror of sparkling light on the opposite side of the stream. Droplets of blue sapphire bounced off of the surface and dashed across Harry's face and chest. Immediately, he was perplexed. There was something different about this water. It seemed to have a life of its own. He watched it bead up on his skin and then almost purposefully spring away and sail back into the moving current.

"This is very—" Harry began.

"Come, Harry!" Narcissus urged.

Harry put aside his distraction momentarily and continued to follow the four angels as they made their way along the river bank. The sand was soft and powdery, like flour with a pearl white glow. It could be a path of fresh snow, separating the teal countryside from the deep cerulean stream. A short distance away, he noticed the river opened up into a large pool. At its center, he could see a smooth rock protruding from the water, large enough for several people to stand upon.

The four angelic beings stopped, tall and noble at the edge of the pool. Narcissus motioned for Harry to join them.

"Here, we unite again," the Archangel began, "just as before. We have gone down below the surface to be cleansed and strengthened, and we have risen as purified new creatures."

Ranan continued, "We have stood on the solid rock—that which is raised up and remains always in the center!"

"We are living, breathing, and chosen," sang Psallo as he lifted up his strong arms.

"We are one!" shouted Agalliao, his mouth grinning wide. Then his eyes darted towards Harry, as though *he* was the next one expected to speak out.

Narcissus stepped in. "Harry, this is an anointed pool. Here, many have come to find cleansing and fullness. We come together to celebrate with you and to receive power. It is a sanctuary of healing and unity. We wish to bestow upon you a mantle of strength, if you are willing . . ."

"Well, yes, I am willing," Harry answered, not yet understanding what he was about to receive.

Narcissus saw the apprehension. "You will have no regrets," the Seraph assured him with a comforting smile.

Harry watched his friend step down off the bank and into the water. The angel stood, chest-deep in the sparkling indigo while the others followed suit. One at a time they waded into the translucent pool and stood alongside the Archangel while the water splashed and danced around them.

"This is living water, Harry!" Narcissus said reverently. "Come in—I invite you to drink."

"What will happen to me?" Harry asked with a sudden tremor of hesitation.

"Nothing bad, Harry. You will be refreshed." The angel added, "Trust that I will not let any harm come to you."

The trepidation left him as suddenly as it had come, and Harry calmly stepped forward into the pool. He acquiesced as the water first surrounded his legs and then his waist and torso. It seemed to envelop him in a way he'd never experienced before.

This water was alive!

It began to penetrate all of his pores, into his very being. He stood with the water gleaming and dancing on his skin, while the four angels circled around him and laid their hands on his shoulders and head.

Narcissus spoke, "May this living water nourish you and bring new strength!"

Harry looked confidently at his angelic friend whose eyes were now closed. He looked at the other angels circling him, their faces showing great delight.

As he stood in awe, they began to gently pull him down and he went under. Normally, his first inclination would have been to panic, but he was so relaxed and trusting, he could not be distressed. His eyes were open and he could see all four of his companions were under the surface with him. Their mouths were open and they appeared to be breathing! Harry remembered Narcissus' invitation, "I invite you to drink." He immediately let go of every reservation and fear and opened his mouth. Carefully, he let the water in.

He swallowed—

It was amazing! So sweet and gratifying. He gradually let in more until it began to fill him.

He was breathing water!

I'm a fish, he thought. *I'm like a fish that has finally come back to the ocean!* He let out a laugh. Bubbles escaped his mouth, but most of the air was gone now and pure water was flowing through his lungs.

He could see the faces of the others clearly now. Narcissus' eyes still closed, except that he did open them for a moment and peeked at Harry with a grin. Ranan and Psallo were blissfully floating, their eyes also closed and their faces serene. Agalliao's eyes were wide open however, and sparkling like diamonds. The youthful angel's mouth was also open wide and grinning freely. Did this delightful creature have a permanent smile? He could hear Agalliao now; the angel let out a sound like a laugh and Harry realized that he himself was laughing back. They both sounded like young children as they stared into each other's faces with amazement and wonder. Harry felt completely saturated now. The water had filled his entire being!

The angels parted before him and he could see the pillar of stone below the surface of the water. It was enormous, like an iceberg. Only the level crown protruded above the surface of the water, while the massive foundation was hidden below. Compelled to approach the monolith, he let himself rise up to the surface, continuing to move upward until he found himself standing on the surface of the water. He bravely stepped forward and placed his right foot onto the gleaming surface before him and put his weight on it. Amazingly, he was supported! Harry continued several feet forward until he stepped onto the surface of the stone. The top of the pinnacle was flat and glistened like polished granite. He stood on it and exhaled the remaining water from his lungs. Below, the angels' heads were above the water now, gazing up at him from around the edge of the stone. Turning towards the wall behind him, he was startled by his reflection in the clear sheet of water that cascaded down the sheer wall from above. Gazing at the mirrored image, he realized the transformation. He appeared the same, but something had changed. What exactly had happened in the pool, he couldn't explain, but he was different.

He was new!

"You are shielded now with a covering, Harry. A mantle of strength!" Narcissus called out.

Harry *did* feel a new sense of vitality. There was a completeness within that he'd never known before. It was indescribable! He was not the same man he'd been when he arrived.

"I must allow you to return home," Narcissus said. "And we must be off, as well, to have council with my Overseer."

"Yes," Harry answered, still standing on the rock and looking down on the four angels. He felt as if he was finally home after being away forever. He didn't want to leave. He felt as if he had just returned to his birthplace to begin a new life and was now being asked to leave and return to something that did not exist anymore. Yet, as he considered all things, he knew he *must* go back. He had a life to resume. A new sense of duty to live fully and with determination filled Harry's being! Yes . . . of course he would return.

The drops of water collected and rolled off of his skin and he was dry. The three Cherubim swam back to the edge of the pool and floated up onto the shore. Narcissus elevated himself up out of the water, his feet resting just on the surface and stood before Harry.

"Good-bye for now, my good friend. I will see you again when the time is right. Until then, remember these things I have told you." Narcissus spoke somberly. "You have a natural ability of discernment—cultivate it."

Harry listened attentively.

"Beware of deception. Don't be anxious. And, be true to what you know to be right in your heart. Will you remember these instructions?"

"Yes, Narcissus. I will try—or rather, YES! I *will* remember! You've done so much for me. I still don't fully understand why, but thank you!" he added warmly.

"Harry, I have only attempted to nurture what was already there." Then he turned and walked right across the surface of the water over to where the others waited for him.

"Narcissus . . . wait!"

The noble Seraph looked back. "Yes?"

"How do I get back to my room?"

"Simple! Click your heels together three times," the angel answered with a stern look.

"What?" Harry questioned, looking bewildered.

"Sorry, Harry—just my expanding sense of humor,"

Narcissus broke a smile. "When you are ready, simply lie down and close your eyes."

Harry watched as Narcissus joined the others. They were gathered together on the sand, and he could see the angel whispering something to the others. They all chuckled for a moment. Agalliao's grin was stretched wide, and then the youthful angel winked at him playfully. The sparkle that flashed out of his eye was the last thing Harry saw before they shot upward into the blue sky and disappeared beyond the golden walls of the city beyond.

Harry stood for a moment in awe and then began to laugh aloud. He couldn't help himself. He laughed at the sky and at the water, and laughed even harder as he realized that Narcissus had been cleverly funny. Click your heels together? They must have all been laughing about the joke when they were whispering together!

Then he began to wonder what would happen if he didn't lie down and close his eyes. What if he stayed? Could he walk closer to the wall or up to the gates of the city? Would the beings of the gate notice him? Maybe they would invite him in? Probably better not to find out! He sat down on the rock and let his feet down into the water. He began to kick them up and down, watching the water splash all around him. The droplets pulled together knowingly and found their way back to the pool. Tired, Harry leaned back and closed his eyes.

18
Jinn and Rull

Abaddon took care in creating the perfect lodging for his new guest. He would offer the imp a space unlike anything the poor creature had ever personally enjoyed. The splendor and stateliness of his new accommodations would surely surprise the little devil and hopefully give him the sense of being elevated. It was all about strategy, so forfeiting a portion of his estate was a small sacrifice. Besides that, the arrangement would allow him to keep an eye on the little fiend.

He realized that in order for this to work, the smaller devil would have to receive real training and ultimately be of some real use. Otherwise, Scratch would know he was being patronized. Even worse, Gorguol would know. There was no question—he must use Scratch in a significant way so there would be no suspicions about Beth Fairbanks or any concerns about his own handling of the Bio-Cell project.

There was no room for error!

Abaddon did not have to think very long about a tutor for Scratch. As soon as he had the malformed imp comfortably settled in, he summoned one of his most trusted subordinates. Again he spoke a word, and another spirit came forth and stood before him.

"Lord!"

"Greetings, Jinn," the dark lord said. I have a special task for you— something challenging as well as satisfying. You remember Scratch? Of course you do."

The spirit nodded distastefully.

"He has joined us for a period," Abaddon continued. "He must be entertained, but in a fashion where he is truly being trained in the practice of control and possession. In addition, he must be convinced that he is an actual player in the game. Of course, you and I both know the process of capturing the human heart is a delicate, complex, and time-consuming process, especially when our adversaries are involved. But in this case, we will let Scratch's own arrogance deceive him into thinking he has more of a gift than he actually does. You will take him on as your protégé. Convince him he is gaining special knowledge by giving him exactly that, only in measured doses. You see, Jinn? In the same way you would train any apprentice, you will take Scratch under your wing and instruct him in the arts with a level of accuracy that will attract no suspicion, while at the same time finding a foothold—a weakness!"

"Sire, what if he *is* gifted?"

"We already know he contains some mysterious talents and we shall use this to our advantage. Then we'll give him just enough rope—"

"Master, is there a specific victim you have in mind, as practice?" Jinn interrupted.

"I will leave the specifics up to you. Ultimately, I do have a specific plan in mind but, for now, practice on whom you wish.

218

Weak and simple minds will be perfect—find someone who is already sponsored by one of your underlings. Begin with the basics: minor temptations, whisperings, subtle suggestions, you know—the usual. We will find out what this distasteful demon is capable of."

He paused and studied the spirit's face. Jinn was a ghoul whose nature was complex and whose devious methods of control and possession were revered by many and even feared by some. His evil features were monstrous and could not be disguised very well, but Abaddon could read him clearly. In many ways he reminded Abaddon of Gorguol, except Jinn was progressive in his ideas about dealing with men—*and* he nearly worshiped Abaddon.

The crimson angel moved closer to Jinn in an effort to avoid any misunderstanding. "Jinn, this is a critical assignment! It must be managed with extreme care. If it is mishandled, we will *all* face Gorguol, and I guarantee . . . it will be under the most uncomfortable circumstances."

"Understood," Jinn winced at the mention of their master, but remained focused and alert.

"Can you take *pleasure* in this assignment?" Abaddon asked.

"Absolutely!" The dark ghoul nodded with conviction.

"Then I am assured without a doubt, that you will handle this affair without any risk of failure."

"I will do it, and I will savor every moment," Jinn's

gruesome features beamed confidently. "To ultimately bring down that pompous little scamp will be my sincere pleasure."

"First we must succeed in raising him up—take great care!" Abaddon warned. "He may be far more devious than he appears. As Scratch's new comrade, it will be to our advantage if you temporarily move your quarters closer to his new lodging. It will be more convenient for both of us if you are readily available."

"Excellent."

"I knew you would find this mission pleasurable. Now, take some time to formulate your strategy, and then inform your new assistant of his upcoming schedule."

"Yes, my Lord," Jinn saluted his captain and was gone.

This would work out nicely, Abaddon mused. Having Jinn and Scratch in close proximity was a wise decision. He was confident that Jinn was perfect for the task. With Scratch under this devil's supervision, Abaddon could focus on the more important matters of Beth Fairbanks and Harry Turner.

No sooner had Jinn departed than another familiar shadow approached the crimson devil.

"Rull! Welcome. Do you have good news?"

"It is puzzling," the shrouded apparition spoke. "I found the woman, Beth Fairbanks, but I detected nothing. There was no sign of the enemy, nor did I find any indication of influence. It is as though she has been concealed or sheltered her entire existence. Perhaps there is the possibility of a protective shield—

something hidden. As you know, it is quite rare to find a—"

"Enough!" Abaddon barked.

He took a moment to refocus and then continued with a small measure of self-control and sarcasm. "Alright—tell me more about what you did *not* find!"

"I searched her thoroughly," Rull snarled, "and found nothing. Her entire being was—" he paused and then choked it out, "—pure and innocent! She was overwhelmed by my presence almost immediately and, to my surprise, she fell unconscious. With that, there was nothing more I could do. I did not make myself known to her, ever. I am certain she suspects nothing of my brief examination."

"Rull, do not be dismayed," Abaddon responded. "This is not your fault. There is something diabolical here. Our enemy is most certainly involved but somehow has escaped detection. This is just the beginning of our work here. It's only a matter of time, and then we shall see. I want you to keep a close eye on this woman. Watch her carefully, but be very discreet. Do not interfere by any means and remain fully veiled—*that means to everyone!* Do not leave your post unless I send for you. Do you understand?"

"Yes, Sire," Rull's thin slit of a mouth answered obediently.

"Go then, but be aware! Under the circumstances, there may be eyes everywhere!"

"It shall be done as you say," Rull answered and made a

tactful departure.

This demon was one of his best, but even now Abaddon was considering a back-up. Another veiled shadow to duplicate Rull's assignment might not be a bad idea at this point, both committed to extreme caution and stealth while studying the same human—each completely unaware of the other. As difficult as it was sometimes, he must learn to depend more on the many talented devils he had at his disposal. He wished he had the time to monitor Beth Fairbanks himself, but he already had the Archangel Narcissus and Harry Turner to deal with. Besides that, he had already neglected his personal ward at Advanced Bio-Cell for far too long.

Abaddon went back to work with something he never grew weary of. Moving upward until he entered into the Bio-Cell building, Abaddon surveyed its current condition. Everything seemed to be in order. Much of the equipment had arrived and several of Dr. Yang's scientists had stopped by and begun preparing themselves for the following week. By then, hopefully, the basement would be close to completion.

The new waterfall in the foyer looked spectacular. He quietly acknowledged a few of his underlings busy with their usual chores. Giving them nods of recognition, he let his presence be known throughout the complex. Once confident the machine was running smoothly, he moved into the office of his most finely tuned instrument.

"*Miss me?*" he whispered deviously to his protégé as he

slipped into position. "Ah, the seat is still warm—almost as though I never left!"

It's like autopilot, he thought as he looked through the eyes of his most favored pawn. He fed the man some pleasurable thoughts. The poor creature sighed with satisfaction over his own brilliance while Abaddon made himself comfortable. Masquerading as a human could provide some great results, but there was no better place to abide than within the warm body of a real flesh and blood human being.

19
Galileo and Isles Market

Beth Fairbanks opened her eyes to see the grocery clerk staring down at her. He was speaking to someone else as he studied her.

"She's waking up!"

"Do we need to call an ambulance?" another voice questioned with concern. It was the elderly woman she remembered, with the smiling dog.

"No, please . . . don't . . . don't call an ambulance," she moaned groggily as she tried to lift herself up. Her head was throbbing as she pressed her hands against the hard floor and pushed herself up into a sitting position.

"Are you sure, ma'am?" the young clerk asked.

"Give her a hand there, young man!" an older fellow pleaded.

She looked around. There was a small group now, gathered around her, staring. She must have attracted everyone in the store.

"Really, thank you, I'm fine. I don't know what happened, but—I'm sure I'll be fine." Beth pulled herself up and grabbed the handle of the cart she'd been pushing.

"Young man, could you please get her some water? And hurry," the elderly gentleman urged again, stepping closer. While the clerk hurried away obediently, she remembered the face of this man as well. Had he been outside the store earlier? Yes, but his was the last face she remembered before she fell. The rest of the shoppers began to move away as he offered her his arm.

"My dear, please come outside and sit down for a few minutes. I don't know what happened to you, but you look a bit pale. It might do you good to rest a bit and get some fresh air before you do any driving. Here you go—" He smiled widely and extended his arm again.

Beth was too weak to argue. Besides, he seemed friendly enough and genuinely concerned for her. She complied as he helped her to her feet. Together they walked out the front door and he led her to one of the benches that lined the front of the store. She took a seat as the clerk returned with a bottle of water.

"Thanks, son—I'll take it," her benefactor said kindly, taking the bottle as he handed the clerk a couple bills. "That should cover the cost." He turned to Beth. "Here, young lady— try to drink some of this."

Beth smiled weakly as she took the bottle and tipped it up to her mouth. The cold water was soothing and seemed to strengthen her as she swallowed it down.

"This looks like the fancy imported water," he smiled broadly and winked. "Probably better than our local well water— and it should be, for the price! But I'm afraid I've forgotten my manners. My name's Leo— it's short for Galileo—I know, an unusual name," he said with a sparkle in his eye. "I'm sure you've heard of the famous astronomer and philosopher? Well, no relation, but I *am* known to be a bit of a philosopher on my

225

own . . . are you feeling any better?"

Beth took another drink. "Yes, much better. Thank you . . . Leo. My name is Beth. I really don't know what came over me. I was okay earlier. I haven't been sick or anything!"

"Hmm," Leo pondered. "I've heard rumors of some sort of virus going around here lately—something in the air."

"Oh, really," she responded with more energy now. "That doesn't sound good."

"I wouldn't be too concerned, Beth. It may have been nothing, but I still suggest you go home and rest for a while, just to be sure. Would you like some help?"

"Oh no. I'm alright now. Thanks Leo, you've been very kind."

"Well, let me give you my card, just in case you do need something—anything. That's what I do—I help people." He reached into his shirt and produced a gold colored card, which he extended towards her.

"Okay, Leo, thanks!" Beth was still a bit light-headed. She took the card from his hand and couldn't help noticing how smooth his hands were, strong and youthful in appearance. She held the card up. It simply said: Galileo—Isles End.

Strange, she thought. No phone number?

"It's on the other side," Leo said as though he'd read her thoughts.

She flipped the card over in her fingers and there on the other side was the phone number. She looked back at him and

226

somehow he looked younger than before. She studied his face. Behind his well-aged features was a serene expression blended with a covering of gold and silver hair, but his age was a contradiction to the strength he seemed to have concealed under his casual attire.

"Have we met before?" she asked.

"No, I don't think we've formally met, but I'm sure I have seen you around. You moved into town about a year ago, didn't you?"

"Yes, though it doesn't seem like it's been that long."

"Well," Leo said, patting her shoulder gently, "I hope you're feeling better. I've got to get going. I have an appointment to meet up with some friends, but I'm glad I was able to help you. Please don't be afraid to call—I'm always available." His eyes twinkled again as he stood. Then he flashed a broad smile and strode away.

"Okay," she called back. She had completely forgotten her incident in the store, and in fact, she wasn't dizzy at all now. As she watched Leo disappear, the clerk stepped out with her groceries.

"Ma'am, I rang these things up just in case you still wanted them."

"Oh, thank you, yes! My car's over here." She motioned towards the Karmann Ghia and he followed. After placing the bags in the front passenger seat, she wrote him a check and he hurried away.

"Just a minute, please," she called.

The clerk stumbled to a halt and turned. "Yes?"

"Do you happen to know that gentleman who helped me out of the store?"

"No, I've never seen him before."

"Hmm . . . okay. Well, thanks!" she said, and he turned again and hurried away.

Beth sat in the parking lot for a few minutes and finished the water. She looked around to see if there was still any sign of Leo, but he was nowhere in sight. The late afternoon sun painted broad brushstrokes of red and orange across the horizon.

She let out a long sigh, pulled out of the parking lot and turned down toward the bridge. Built out of stout timbers and tied together with heavy steel, the old structure had originally been used as a railway. Now it only carried the few automobiles of locals who lived on the dead-end road. As she passed over, the sparkling water below gave her a sense of calm. She watched how easily it flowed down into the bay. That was how she wanted her life to be, slowly but steadily moving at a peaceful and easy pace.

Beth wondered if her instant fondness for Harry might interfere with the simple life she had come here to find. It wasn't that her future didn't include a man. She had every intention of finding someone to share her life with, but she refused to be in a hurry. The real challenge had been getting past the loss of her parents, then making the transition from being guardian of her younger siblings to being a single and potentially available woman.

Some of her friends had suggested her expectations had been set too high, or maybe just higher than the character of single men they knew. One of the things so attractive about Harry was that his confidence wasn't tainted with arrogance. She was tired of men who needed to announce they were available . . . for the time being. The implication was that you had better respond quickly, because they were valuable commodities and might not last for long. Worst of all, they seemed to think that their expensive toys would be more of a lure than their character.

Not so with Harry. He seemed to have a genuinely healthy, positive opinion of himself—not an over-inflated one. He believed in himself for what he knew he was capable of and nothing more. Also, he was fun to be with because the time spent together wasn't all about him.

Her thoughts turned back to what had taken place at the store. That had certainly been an unusual experience! As she replayed the whole scenario over again in her head, it seemed strange now. She was more curious about Leo than she was about passing out in the market. How odd! Well, she was fine now. Maybe she would give Leo a call soon.

Within minutes, she could see her home. There was comfort as she pulled into her driveway and her concerns began to fade. Even though it was still early, she put the groceries away, got undressed, and climbed into bed.

20
Abraham Dante

Harry opened his eyes to find himself back in his bed and reunited with his body. It was late afternoon. He must have slept long after his return from . . . where had he been? Outside the gates of a city—a wonderful, magical place that he never even entered! He still felt incredibly strong as he recalled the pool. Taking in a deep breath and letting it out, he observed his lungs were clear and healthy. *The result of breathing living water?* He wrapped his arms around his shoulders and flexed.

A mantle of strength, he thought as he stretched out his arms and clenched his hands. What exactly did it mean?

He closed his eyes for a moment and found himself back at the pool on the surface of the rock. The memory was so fresh! He almost believed he could open his eyes and find himself back there.

Climbing out of bed, Harry was aware of his physical body. It was heavy again and very different from being in the supernatural. He also realized he was still in yesterday's clothes. Stripping them off he entered the shower. As the water splashed over his back, he was back at the pool again. The experience began to wash through his memory. Time slipped away as he leaned against the tile wall, sedated under the flow. When his stomach rumbled, he was pulled back to reality. The last thing he'd eaten was the omelet.

Showered and dressed, he wondered what he could squeeze into the rest of the day besides food. He considered stopping by the Ivory Lane project to check on Ed and Butch, but they were probably already finished and gone by now.

Then he thought of Beth. They hadn't spoken since . . . when? Was it yesterday at Advanced Bio-Cell? Yes, but they hadn't really had a chance to talk. She had sent him a text. He decided to give her a quick call.

"Hello?"

He was pleased to hear her voice. "Hi, Beth, it's Harry!"

"Hi! Where are you?"

"I'm home."

"Harry, I was just thinking about you! I wondered if I might see you at Advanced Bio again. Did you get my text?"

"Yes, I tried to call you but your phone must have been off—I fell asleep trying to reach you."

"Oh, I was on another call and didn't realize you were calling. You should have texted me! That was sweet though—sorry I missed you!"

"Me, too. How are you? How was work?"

"Fine. Things were a little slow so Valerie kicked me out early. After I left, I started feeling funny, and then I got sick on the way home. I actually passed out in the Isles End market."

"You what?"

"It's not as bad as it sounds. I'm okay now. I've been lying down."

"Beth! Are you sure?"

"Yes—I think so, anyway."

"Is there anything that I can do for you? Do you want me to come by or bring you something?"

"No, Harry, really. I'm pretty tired, though. I just got into bed a little bit ago."

"Oh, I hope I didn't wake you."

"I don't mind."

"Well then, assuming you're okay, what would you think about doing something tomorrow night? Friday—no work the next day!" He tried to sound tempting.

"You don't have to twist my arm!"

"Great! Shall I give you a call around five?"

"That sounds fine. What do you have in mind?"

Harry thought quickly. "How about a night on the town? You know, Isles End has a pretty exciting night life!" The sound of Beth's giggle encouraged him to continue. "We could start out at Belmar's—it may be the only nice restaurant in town, but it's unusually sophisticated, really. After that, we could take a walk out on the pier. I understand they're doing some squid jigging out there after eleven or so, and I hear it's going to be a full moon. I might even spice things up with a six-pack of micro brew. Could be pretty wild!"

"How could any girl say no to that?" Beth laughed.

"No girl in her right mind would!" Harry replied convincingly.

She laughed again.

"You better get some rest now, if we're going out tomorrow. I'll see you then, and I want to hear all about your episode at the market—you *sure* you're okay now?"

"I'm sure, Harry. Thank you, and have a good night."

He wished her well and hung up. For a few moments, he sat and recalled all the details of his out-of-body adventure. It was amazing he could function at all, but he *did* have the mantle of strength . . .

Harry's stomach growled again. He decided to go out for dinner. Since they would be having dinner at Belmar's tomorrow night, he decided to dine at the café.

Harry passed the bridge that led to Beth's home and turned the corner to the café. He parked in the rear as usual and walked around to the front, pausing to admire the beautiful sunset. The bay was peaceful and relatively calm. A couple of boats moved around on the water and he could hear the wake splashing against the bulkhead across the street. The town was quiet except for the cries of a few seagulls.

Once again, Harry wondered how long it would be before some investor showed interest in the empty buildings down along the water. He could see a profit there for someone who had the vision to renovate and make the property attractive enough to occupy. In his experience, waterfront had always been considered prime real estate. This could be a gold mine. Of course, it would take some time before the investment might pay off, but Isles End couldn't remain this way for long. Progress could spread quickly, especially with William Algren's project in mind, and it was only a matter of time before this town exploded. Funny to think of anything exploding as he surveyed the town from the café. It probably hadn't changed in over fifty years. He would have to talk to Reese Orchard about it. Maybe together they could come up with some ideas.

Stepping into the café Harry found a table by the front window where he could enjoy the view. He placed his order with the waitress. The Thursday evening special was pot roast. The memory of dinner with Beth made him warm inside.

While he sat at the window, Harry recognized Reese's BMW up the street on the waterside of the road. Funny, he hadn't noticed it before. It was parked in front of one of the buildings that he'd just been thinking would make a great investment.

The pot roast arrived shortly and he wasted no time carving into it. He ate slowly, reminding himself he was in public. The food was good, but not quite as perfect as Beth's.

This is just what I needed, he thought to himself as he sat there in the café window—*a relaxing evening, a meal, and a view*. The last of the sun dipped down below the horizon and splashed a final layer of red and orange across the muddled blue sky. As he carefully dissected the meal, he noticed Reese stepping out of a door on the side of the building and hurrying over to his car. Behind him, another gentleman followed. Harry had never seen this man before. He was tall like Reese except trimmer, with a robust build.

That figures! Harry thought to himself. He couldn't believe it! That is, if he was correct. Could Reese and this man already be negotiating a deal with those buildings? He watched them exchange a few words, then Reese got into his car and pulled away. Harry almost waved as Reese passed the café.

He turned his attention back to the other gentleman who had begun walking toward the restaurant. The man appeared to have a set of blueprints under one arm and a slender brief case in the other. As he neared the front of the café, the man looked up and seemed to stare right through the glass at Harry. Feeling a little awkward, Harry diverted his attention out toward the bay, but he could see that this fellow was walking up to the front door of the restaurant. The man stepped inside while Harry concentrated on the darkening horizon. From the corner of his eye, Harry watched as the man chose a table right next to him. He decided to look over and make eye contact as the stranger pulled out a chair and sat down.

"Hello," the tall man said tersely.

"How are you doing?" Harry responded casually.

The stranger immediately picked up the menu and began to consider his options. Harry tried to ignore him and concentrated on his meal and the last of the sunset. A dark violet haze hung above the skyline and a couple of stars were visible. He looked back over toward the man at the table. The fellow had just given the waitress his order and was already examining the set of blueprints. Harry didn't know much about clothes, but he could tell this guy's suit was far from average: silk tie, one of those fancy handkerchiefs sticking up slightly out of the breast pocket, and a very tailored look to the jacket. Must be something European, Harry thought. The man looked up and caught his gaze. Harry coughed purposefully and decided to make an attempt at conversation.

"I noticed you walking out of the old building up the street. Are you a developer?"

"I am, at times," he spoke curtly and quickly resumed his study of the prints.

"I was just thinking today," Harry continued, "about the possibilities of that real estate along the water there."

"Oh, really," the stranger replied, looking up briefly then returning to his plans.

"Yeah," Harry persisted. "I've seen property like that become very valuable when it's been properly renovated."

The man ignored him and remained focused on the prints. Harry found himself slightly irritated now. Was this guy too good to have a casual conversation? Harry decided to press further and see whether the man would warm up a little or continue with his boorish manners.

"Of course, you've got to know what you're doing," Harry said, forcing a smile. "There can be lots of unforeseen costs in projects like that."

The smartly dressed gentleman looked up now and glared

at Harry.

"So . . . do *you* know quite a bit about developing real estate?" he questioned with mild disdain.

"Well," Harry began modestly, "I've had some experience. In fact, I've worked on several projects for some very successful investors."

"So, you're a builder?"

"I've been a general contractor for awhile, though I'm still a bit new here in Isles End," Harry explained with an air of confidence.

"Oh, *really!*" the stranger leaned forward with a hint of interest.

"In fact, I happen to be currently working on a couple of projects with Reese Orchard," Harry went on boldly. "I believe I saw you with him just a few moments ago."

"That would be correct!" the man said with obvious surprise.

Harry wasn't about to let up. "So, are you an associate of Reese's?"

"I hardly know him," the man stated quickly with a slight frown. "One of my aides contacted him for me in regards to these properties. I guess Mr. Orchard knows the owners, but they haven't wanted to put the properties on the market. I guess they are among his many pocket listings."

"Hmm," Harry let out the sound of acknowledgement. His knowing Reese Orchard had caused this upper class snob to change his tune a little. He continued to pause with reserve for a moment of satisfaction. This seemed to make the man feel the need to continue.

"I'm sure that a suitable offer will speak the right language to the owners. I just need to decide whether I'm really interested in investing in this area in the first place." The man paused while the waitress delivered his meal and then continued. "So, you've been working with Mr. Orchard?"

"Only on a couple of projects," Harry admitted.

"You know, Reese said he had a builder with whom he was highly pleased. I believe he mentioned a Mr. Turner—"

"That would be me," Harry gave a hint of a smile. "My name's Harry."

Now the man fumbled a little as he attempted to shift his conduct to a more gracious tone.

"Mr. Turner . . . Harry, I'm very sorry. I had no idea! Forgive me. I feel I'm at a slight loss. Please allow me to introduce myself. My name is Abraham Dante."

Suddenly the man stood, slightly taller than Harry, and extended his long arm outward in Harry's direction. Harry felt slightly foolish, as though he'd judged the man too quickly and stood to meet him halfway between the tables. The man shook Harry's hand firmly and then sat back down.

"You know," Mr. Dante said, "Reese spoke so highly of you that I have your name on my list of immediate contacts. It's very coincidental that I should happen to run into you tonight. He suggested that you might be in a position to start expanding."

"Well, I don't know about that—but I'm in a position to consider it," Harry responded with some uncertainty, realizing his business was growing rapidly.

"It was only just over a week ago," he confided, "that I was working by myself—now I'm wondering how many employees I'm going to need just to keep up with all the new work!"

"Yes," Mr. Dante concurred, "I know from experience that sometimes change comes all at once. But this is the true test of a good businessman—to have the ability to recognize the right time to expand or to cut back, before everyone else does."

"So, is this the right time for *you* to expand—here in Isles End, Mr. Dante?" Harry asked bluntly.

"That is the question I'm considering right now. What do you think? Is *this* the right time for Isles End?"

Harry's expression became flat. He almost felt he should say it wasn't a good time at all. Just a flat *no!* Why should he encourage this stranger to move in on an idea that *he* had thought of on his own and might be able to coordinate by himself—well, if he had the funds. Or maybe Reese Orchard would be interested in collaborating with him somehow. On the other hand, Harry thought, this guy might be willing to share some sort of partnership, or at least share a fair part of the profit with someone who had the experience and know-how to supervise the project. Did it really matter whether he teamed up with Reese or this man? But then, why wasn't Reese already on board with Mr. Dante? *Good question*, Harry thought.

"I think it's a great time and a perfect location. But tell me, Mr. Dante, why aren't you and Reese already working together on this?"

"Please call me Abraham. Yes, that's a good question— the same one I had. It seems that Reese has his hands full with a large portion of real estate just outside of Isles End, as well as several small residential projects—you probably know more about it than I do. Besides, I'm not looking for investors, nor do I require any help with the funding. I have all the financial backing I need and I think Mr. Orchard would prefer to turn a quick profit in this case—with as little association as possible."

"That makes sense, I suppose," Harry agreed. "So did you have any sort of arrangement already in mind? I mean, there are probably many ways to approach this."

"You are exactly right," Abraham agreed. "And what I'm looking for is someone I can trust who is capable of overseeing the entire venture. Ultimately, maybe a partnership would be ideal. That way I could have minimal involvement myself in the responsibility of contracting and offer someone else a high return of profit for supervising the complete project."

"And so, you were thinking I might be a potential candidate?" Harry ventured, attempting to mask his enthusiasm.

"Currently, you are at the top of my list," Abraham replied without hesitation.

Harry leaned forward, looking pensive. "I would think someone like you would already have access to at least a few reliable contractors."

"Someone like me—?" Abraham answered with a hint of a smirk.

"Well," Harry added nervously, "I only mean—"

Abraham Dante cut in. "No worries, Harry. I understand what you mean. Yes, I do have good contacts from other projects I've done, but I prefer using people from the immediate community. I've found that using hand-picked professionals from the local area nearly always guaranteed success. And in most cases they are interested in more than just the money—they take a personal interest in the quality and completion of the project."

"You're probably right about that," Harry agreed.

"I am," Abraham assured him, as he turned his attention to his meal.

Harry glanced over at Abraham's plate and recognized the pot roast. He thought it best to allow Abraham Dante the opportunity to finish his supper, and as he was finished with his, he left an ample sum of cash on the table and moved to get up. He glanced out at the sky. The sun was gone now and all the color had faded to gray. He wondered how he might finalize his discussion with Dante when the tall man stood and spoke.

"Mr. Turner . . . Harry," he said pausing from his meal, "It seems fate has brought us together tonight. Do you have a card?"

"Uh," Harry mumbled, feeling around his pockets, even though he knew he had no cards. "Just a minute," he said reaching for a napkin. He scribbled his name and number down and handed it to Abraham.

"Excellent," Abraham said. "A napkin and a handshake in a small town has always worked for me." He extended his hand once again. Harry complied, feeling that somehow he had just signed some kind of contract.

"You'll be hearing from me soon," Abraham added as he seated himself back down.

"I'll be looking forward to it," Harry said politely and turned toward the front door.

"Good night," called the waitress.

Harry drove straight home and quickly got into bed. He tried to go right to sleep but couldn't seem to relax. Forty-five minutes went by and he lay awake while his mind raced through the events of the last week. He couldn't believe how his business had grown so suddenly. He'd gone from being a small-time contractor doing remodel and residential work, to working on medical buildings and commercial projects, almost overnight. He'd seen it happen before to other builders, but knowing firsthand how it felt to reach the next level was exciting. And now, with Abraham Dante and his interest in the downtown area, who knew where it might take him? He mused over the possibilities.

But was this what he wanted when he moved to Isles

End? He remembered his original intentions: *To run away—find a place to hide.*

He had managed to succeed with his plans so far. For a whole year he'd remained under the radar without any trouble at all. Even his few close friends had eased their efforts to maintain regular contact. Somehow he had imagined an uncomplicated, secluded life in an obscure quiet town. Stay small. Keep it simple. One day at a time. That is what he had thought he wanted, but now he wasn't sure. Things had changed quite a bit lately. . . or was it he who had changed?

A therapist had told Harry a year ago, recovering from the loss of his loved ones might take some time. How long? It was different for everyone. *Be productive*, the doctor had advised. *Stay in touch with your remaining family and friends.* Well, he hadn't fully complied with that order, but was he feeling better? He shuddered to imagine what that doctor would think about Narcissus!

Hmm, an imaginary friend? A super human friend? An angel? I see . . .

Yes, he could see the doctor's notes, "Harry has created a 'friend' to fill the loss—" At first he had almost convinced himself he had done just that, but no longer. He was sure Narcissus was as real as anyone else. His last venture with the angel had proved to be more authentic than anything he'd ever experienced. At this point, if his experiences with Narcissus were just a delusion, he didn't care. He felt better now than he had in a long time.

He was ready to move on with life!

If not, could he have opened up to Beth like he had? He was trading in the painful memories, the loss of Jennifer and finally turning his thoughts toward living, instead of living in the past.

As he drifted off, his thoughts settled on the image of Beth, the sound of her voice, and her last words on the phone, "I'm sure, Harry—thank you and have a good night."

21
Beyond Devious

Abaddon never tired during the time he spent directly with one of his minions. The difficult art of appearing in various forms on his own was thrilling and useful, but there was nothing quite as tantalizing as the feeling of a servant's total submission. It was a familiarity he could not compare to anything else, to be so in touch, to possess so fully, to the point of complete surrender—an intimate melding into one. Such was the relationship he currently enjoyed. Whether during the cherished moments of contact, or even when he was removed from his host, he always felt a special closeness, a kind of mystical connection. The merger was exhilarating. He was the drug of choice for this man, he mused, and an addiction this disciple could not refuse.

Abbadon's schedule was currently full though, and he realized he would have to get used to sacrificing some of his special time. Even now, after only a brief reunion, he was interrupted. He yielded to the intrusion.

"Lord?" It was Jinn, and the anxious expression he wore revealed a deep concern.

"Come," Abaddon spoke as he slipped away from his human host, looking back briefly to see the man wince at his departure. He motioned Jinn to follow him to his quarters where they could ensure privacy.

"Sire, it is about Scratch," the lesser demon was hesitant.

"Well, it is this—he is beyond devious! Even with much training, I don't know how he could have gained such abilities as he employs—except that he is a prodigy! Not only does he already display an unusual ability to beguile almost any human with minimal effort, but he also boasts a natural talent in the art of transformation and appearing in human form."

Abaddon did not speak. Jinn waited patiently as his master considered the information. Abaddon's expression was void of emotion and did not reveal the slightest hint of a reaction. Finally the scarlet lord spoke.

"I am not surprised," he said blankly. "There is something—hmmm—curious here."

I have let my personal distaste for this imp blind me to his deeper purpose, maybe . . .

"Remember, I warned you of this creature's cunning. It seems clear that Scratch is unusually gifted but I suspect now he has had more instruction than we believed. But continue to encourage him, still. Show natural surprise—even admiration at his craft. Remember to look for his weak spot—every creature has one. Continue your tutoring. Feed him, just not too much, too soon. Allow this smart little creature to sharpen his skills even further and assure him he'll soon have the chance to show them off."

"Do you wish to witness his abilities prior to his first outing?"

"No. I trust your judgment. Only inform him immediately

that he is to be used in a very important matter. Tell him we shall require his services very soon."

"And what guise shall he prepare to take, Sire?"

"I am not sure yet."

"Lord?"

"I assure you that whatever position I choose, it will be a challenge. Tell him exactly that."

"Consider it done—but my Liege, I can assure you he shall prove to have no problem performing any task. This urchin is a *wunderkind!* I'm afraid to say that his brilliance is almost baffling! I never saw it coming . . . I feel at a loss."

"Jinn!" Abaddon growled, "*Remember who you are!* Be strong and do not debase yourself so easily!"

"Of course, Master, you are right," the hideous looking demon snarled in response.

"I will contact you as soon as I have made a decision. Right now, just make sure Scratch is aware that his talents will be put to the test, and he will need to perform with the greatest expertise."

"I promise you, Master," Jinn's face twisted into a sardonic frown, "he will be ecstatic!"

Abaddon's blank expression turned into a defiant smile as he motioned for Jinn to go. If things went according to plan, he had nothing to fear. Should Scratch prove to be successful, it would only help further his cause. If the assignment was muddled, who could be to blame except Scratch himself?

Naturally he would protect his new comrade from any backlash from above. He would not allow his new charge to be found lacking, at least not too soon. Whatever Scratch's biggest weakness, Abaddon was confident Jinn would discover it. Of course, there were the obvious things: Scratch's lust for power, his desire for recognition, and his fear of Gorguol. But was there something more? No matter. In the meantime, they would have to stick together like true devils in arms. It was flawless!

As all seemed to be in place for the moment, Abaddon decided to take some time to meditate rather than rejoin his host. In the privacy of his domain, *he* was all that he needed. He stretched out and gazed at himself. He studied the perfection and balance of his form and superior intellect. How exquisite was the handiwork that had gone into his creation. The depth of color and illumination pulsing through his veins was spectacular. He expanded his consciousness out into the vast space of his underground asylum, basking in the immensity of heat that radiated from his being. He was far too beautiful to be hidden like this. The day would soon come when he would be on display, and admired by all . . . but then, he must guard himself from becoming too *narcissistic*, he laughed to himself, and gloated quietly.

22
Dinner at Belmar's

Friday morning Harry was up early. He stepped into the shower and adjusted the temperature. As the water splashed over him, he was mentally transported for a moment back to the pool.

Could he ever think of water in the same way again?

He took and held a deep breath as the water poured over his face, remembering how he had inhaled the water from the pool as though it were the air he needed to breathe. Would he ever visit that heavenly shrine again? The events of the past week flooded his thoughts. Looking at anything in the same way again would be difficult. He was surprised how quickly things could change. Hopelessness could turn to hope. Sorrow into joy. What else?

Loneliness into love?

He looked outside and was pleased to see the sun shining down over Isles End. He quickly dried himself and stepped into the bedroom. There was a hint of anticipation as he looked through his dresser drawers: jeans, tee shirts, socks, and shorts. In the closet, there were work shirts and a couple old dress shirts. His wardrobe had become rather sparse. He would need something suitable for his date with Beth, and there was a nice clothing store downtown. If he could take care of business in time, he would attempt to upgrade his attire. Then there was the entire weekend, free! Maybe a whole weekend with Beth?

Harry's first stop was Ivory Lane. He spent more time than necessary with Ed and Butch, but enjoyed every minute of it. They were nearly done framing the first floor, and it looked great. He really wished he could be there, pounding nails and raising walls, but he knew his efforts elsewhere would be putting money into their pockets for tomorrow.

At Advanced Bio-Cell, Harry couldn't help admiring the new waterfall feature in the foyer. Though it was extraordinary, he was really more interested in seeing Beth, but she was out running errands. He would have to call her later.

He was also scheduled to meet with Preston Hart and Bill Algren, but no one seemed to know where they were. While waiting, he was nearly knocked over by the bustling, short-statured doctor. Shushi was in such a hurry he only said, "Mr. Turner, you will have the lab ready according to schedule, correct?" and disappeared down a hallway before Harry had a chance to respond. Preston finally showed up, only to be interrupted a few minutes later by a new employee begging Preston's attention.

"You don't need me for anything else, do you, Harry?" he said hurrying off without an answer.

Well, it wasn't anything that couldn't wait until later. On the lower floor, the framing crew had shown up early and were making great progress. He was confident they would have this place operating before the end of the following week. The third floor office cubicles would follow. He made a few last minute notes and took the elevator back to the main floor.

"Beth is still out," the woman at the front desk said as Harry approached her.

He checked his watch. There would be just enough time to find something to wear besides his jeans and work shirts.

On the drive back to Isles End, Harry thought about his celestial friend. What were the chances that Narcissus was watching him now? Was it possible the angel could observe him from afar? He rolled down his window and hung his arm out. He looked up at the blue sky, grinning at the thought of Narcissus looking down at him from somewhere up above. He raised his arm up and let it push against the force of the wind, as though he were waving.

Hello, Narcissus, if you're there . . .

At the local department store, Harry found plenty of help upgrading his wardrobe. The two sales girls were intent on doing a complete makeover on him, and he found himself thankful for their help. He left with two very nice shirts, two pairs of pants, two ties, and a dark brown blazer. He hurried home to clean up. With an ice cream sandwich to hold him over until dinner, he went to call Beth.

He was surprised to see a missed call icon on the screen. He started to retrieve the voice mail when the phone began to vibrate. No wonder he'd missed the call. After silencing his phone at Advance Bio-Cell earlier, he had forgotten to restore the volume.

"Hello?"

"Hi, Harry!"

"Hey, I was just going to call. How are you?"

"I had a pretty hectic day. They had me running all over. I don't know how I'm going to keep up if the pace continues like this. But whatever happened to me yesterday seems to be gone— I mean, I feel much better."

"Well that's good to hear. I was concerned."

"I know—thanks. I'm okay now. So, are we still on for tonight?"

"I hope so! I'm almost ready to pick you up."

"Well, I'm home and ready," Beth said with equal enthusiasm.

"Give me just a few minutes and I'll be on my way," he pressed the end button.

He forgot about the waiting voice mail, finished the ice cream sandwich, and considered his new wardrobe. He decided to go with the combination the young women at the store had recommended. He checked himself in the mirror. He hadn't seen himself cleaned up like this for quite a while.

Harry felt confident in his new attire as he climbed into his truck and headed towards the Isles Inlet Bridge. Another beautiful fall afternoon was gracing the landscape. The sun was still up and a cool breeze drifted in through his open window.

When he got to Beth's house, she was waiting outside by her car, looking stunning. She motioned for him to park alongside the Karmann Ghia.

He stuck his head out of the window. "You want me to park there?" he said, motioning with his arm.

"Sure, but would you rather take my car?"

He pulled into the driveway and got out.

"Harry! Look at you!" She exclaimed walking toward him.

"What—?"

"Nice blazer! You look so . . . different. Come here."

"Is that a good thing?" he asked with mock suspicion as he complied with her request. He stopped in front of her and she circled him.

"It's a very good thing," she giggled. "Shall we go?"

"You're the driver."

"No, you're driving, Mr. Turner," she tossed her keys into the air.

Harry eased his lanky frame into the small car and quickly familiarized himself with the instruments. Beth smiled at him as she fastened her seatbelt. Harry pulled carefully out of the driveway and took the only route back into town. The setting sun still sparkled brightly on the water. They could see a couple of small fishing boats coming in with their catches. The parking lot for Belmar's was full, so Harry had to park a half-block away, next to the pier.

"Look at the size of those fish," Beth said as she climbed out of the car and pointed toward the boats. The fishermen were laying out their catch and weighing them on a large scale just outside of a small shed at the head of the dock.

"Yeah, those are nice," Harry responded.

"Salmon, right, Harry?"

"Yes, gotta be Chinook."

"What's that?"

"The larger breed of salmon, also called Kings," Harry explained. "Do you like salmon?"

"Very much," Beth confirmed.

"Should we go get a fresh one right now and bring it home?" Harry suggested facetiously.

"Oh . . . maybe another time! Right now I'm ready to be wined and dined."

Inside Belmar's, Harry and Beth waited for a nice table to open up. There was the usual crowd of weekend patrons in the main dining area, but in a separate dining hall on the other side of the restaurant there was a large party in progress.

"Someone's birthday?" Harry questioned the hostess as they were being seated.

"Oh *that?*" she glanced over to the dining hall and then back to Harry. "Yes, it's hardly ever this busy. There's a good-sized gathering here tonight, some bigwig celebrating the purchase of those warehouse buildings down the street."

Harry hid his surprise as she guided them to a nice table by the window and handed them menus. Beth surveyed the room.

"This is nice, Harry! I had no idea it was so elegant

inside."

"You've never been here?" Harry asked with honest surprise.

"No . . . well, I haven't really had the occasion to come—" she stopped, nearly blushing, "I haven't been out a lot since I moved to Isles End."

"That's fine," Harry responded, hoping he hadn't made her feel uncomfortable. "I've only been in here once by myself. Actually, I was just a little curious one night and also . . . a little lonely."

Beth studied Harry's eyes. She could tell he was being very sweet.

"Hmm," she paused, "You were hungry too, I imagine . . . so, what did you have to eat?"

Harry smiled. "I remember very well because it was so good, halibut stuffed with smoked salmon—makes my mouth water just thinking about it. On the side were three separate portions of marinated vegetables; string carrots, sauerkraut, and green beans. It might sound odd, but that dish was very distinctive and tasty—I'll never forget it."

"Wow," Beth commented, "I guess there's no need for me to waste any time looking at the menu. I already know what I want, if it's still available."

"You won't be disappointed."

Just then the waitress came.

"Would you like to start with something to drink?"

Harry turned to Beth to allow her to make a choice.

"I won't make you drink merlot again, Harry," she quipped with a grin.

"What do you mean? I liked it," Harry countered with a teasing smile.

"Actually, I'd like a glass of water."

"That sounds good to me, too," he agreed, addressing the waitress.

In no time at all, their water arrived and they ordered their meals. They watched with interest as people mingled back and forth from the other side of the restaurant, which was obviously used for more exclusive gatherings. Harry was anxious to confirm his suspicions. He hadn't seen anyone he recognized yet, but he had more than a strong hunch about the whole thing.

"Harry, are you looking for someone?" Beth interrupted his thoughts.

"Well, I—sort of," Harry stuttered. "I think I know the man who was going to be involved in a real estate deal with those buildings, and I'm sure this party must have something to do with it."

Just as the words came out of Harry's mouth, Reese Orchard and Abraham Dante stepped in from the larger room. They were laughing and talking vigorously when Abraham noticed Harry. He immediately said something to Reese, and they both hurried toward Harry's table.

"I'm surprised and happy to see you," Abraham

approached their table.

Reese was right behind him. "Hello, Harry," he said smiling, "Hello, Beth."

Abraham placed his hand on Harry's shoulder. "I tried to reach you on your cell phone earlier!"

Reese nodded with a look of confirmation.

Abraham continued excitedly, "We are celebrating the acquisition of five properties here on the water. I wanted you to know, since I'm hoping you'll be the one to manage the project. I dearly hoped you would be able to join us. But, I'm sorry, I have forgotten my manners." He stepped toward Beth and extended his arm. "Hello, I'm Abraham Dante."

"Very nice to meet you," she smiled back, taking his hand.

"Forgive me," Harry interrupted. "Abraham, this is Beth Fairbanks."

"It's a great pleasure, Beth."

"Well," Abraham continued, looking back at Harry, "as I was saying, I left a message on your cell phone inviting you to join us here tonight—and what a coincidence, here you are! The party came together so quickly that my head is still reeling just a bit. I had hoped to introduce you to some of my friends and colleagues tonight—I'm sorry," he glanced at Beth, "I really didn't mean to intrude."

Harry sensed that Beth wasn't sure how to respond.

"It's really no intrusion at all," Harry answered. "We

were just going to have some dinner, but I'm sure Beth will enjoy hearing this exciting news. It's quite all right, isn't it Beth?"

Beth looked at Harry, knowing his personal interest in this venture.

"Yes, of course! We'd be more than happy to join you."

"I have an idea," Abraham responded. "Why don't we have your meals delivered to the other room? Come and join us now—we'll find you a table."

Together, they all headed toward the large ballroom. As soon as they entered, Abraham grabbed Harry by the arm.

"I must introduce you to my secretary before she has to leave—where is she?" He surveyed the crowded room.

Harry glanced over to Beth. He already felt awkward about their date being interrupted. Beth looked as though she wanted to say something but Reese stepped in.

"Here, Beth, shall we find a nice table for the four of us?" he asked politely.

"Yes, Reese," Abraham agreed. "Maybe you can entertain Beth for a few moments. I just want to make a couple of quick introductions here while we still have the opportunity. You won't mind terribly, will you, Beth?"

"Not at all," she answered, and graciously submitted as Reese drew her attention over to an empty table nearby.

"I realize this is a little awkward—almost uncouth—I'm sorry, Harry, but I do hope you understand. This will be a very profitable endeavor and we must start out on the right foot."

Harry wanted to keep Beth at his side, but before he could formulate a polite refusal, he was pulled away and suddenly found himself being introduced to a most unusually beautiful woman who seemed very intent as she set her gaze upon him.

"Ah, here she is. Harry, I'd like to introduce you to my close friend and project manager, Rachael Sapphire—and yes, she is a jewel!"

Harry hardly heard a word. His attention was so instantly fixed on this dazzling creature. She stood before him with a hint of a smile on her ample lips, waiting patiently for him to respond. He fumbled for some words.

"It's very nice to meet you, Rachael."

"Hello. Is it Harry, or Harrison?" she purred.

"It's Harry Turner, dear," Abraham interrupted. "I mentioned him to you this morning. I hope he'll accept the position of General Contractor on this project."

"Well," she said, "Abraham doesn't waste any time choosing his associates. But then, he does seem to have a knack for it." She took a step closer to Harry and spoke softly. "So, what do you think, Harry—are you ready to get started?"

Harry was mesmerized. She was lovely to behold. Her skin was tanned and glowing, her eyes were deep dark pools, her plunging neckline revealed a field of small goose bumps across her shoulders and neck and . . .

Ready to get started?

"Well," Harry said, pulling his thoughts together, "Yes! I

am . . . though I haven't officially accepted the position yet. I just—"

"And why not?" she asked bluntly, with a look of genuine curiosity.

"Well, I only just met Abraham last night," Harry explained, "and I'm in the middle of a rather full schedule—but I *am* interested."

"Let's not pressure Harry too quickly," Abraham offered. "He should naturally require some time to consider any proposition, even a grand opportunity such as this."

"That's part of it, Abraham," Harry explained, "I want the job—no question. It's just that before I make a commitment, I want to be able to assure you, as well as myself, that I can give it my best."

"Well, Harry," Rachael contributed effortlessly, "that just makes me want you all the more, and I'm sure Abraham appreciates your sincerity. But I really must say, after all the nice things Reese has said about you, I don't think we will want to proceed without your help!"

"I really appreciate that, and I'm going to do everything I can to make this work, Miss Sapphire," Harry promised. His eyes began to wander again.

"Please, Harry," she implored, "With our potential partnership at hand, you must call me Rachael. And if you haven't figured it out already, this project is going to be the biggest thing this town has seen in years. Have you noticed how many of the local shop owners are here tonight? They all want a piece—and who can blame them? I can't wait to get started on it myself," she added. "This town is going to grow, and if you want my opinion, the downtown waterfront is just the beginning."

This woman is in control and entirely confident, Harry thought. He wondered what kind of relationship she had with Abraham. He wanted to divert his eyes. There was something very exotic in the angle of her cheekbones, the curve of her eyes, and the way she looked into his with some unspoken language.

"Harry?" He heard her saying his name.

"I'm sorry—yes?" He answered.

"I think it might help if we could meet soon and look over some of the plans together. I already have some ideas I'd like to share with you. Could we do lunch sometime this coming week?"

"Yes," he agreed. "That's a good idea."

"Great! Then I'll be in touch with you soon, okay?" she looked past him briefly, "Oh, looks like your dinner is ready," she added, pointing over to the table where Reese and Beth were seated.

He turned his gaze away from Rachael and located Beth across the room. She gave him a little wave and he could see their plates had arrived.

"You'd better get going while the food is hot!" Rachael urged him.

"Yes, thank you—uh, it was very nice meeting you, Rachael, and I'll look forward to seeing you again . . . if you'll excuse me?"

"Yes, let's get you back to your date," Abraham said. "Rachael, I'll see you in the morning—"

"Right, Boss," she answered and turned back to Harry. "It was very nice meeting you too, Harry. I'll see you soon then, hopefully."

She turned and strolled away. Harry felt compelled to watch her as she gracefully navigated her way past the other guests. Had he heard a word in that entire conversation? He felt uncomfortable, yet he wasn't sure why. He hadn't done anything wrong that he could identify. Had something just occurred that was inappropriate? Not at all; it was purely business. Why then the concern, as though he had just done something shameful? She just happened to be a very attractive and polished businesswoman, that was all. He dismissed his apprehension and followed Abraham back to the table where his meal waited. Beth smiled as he took a seat beside her and picked up a napkin. There was a sudden impulse to avoid her glance, but when she looked at him with such softness, he felt instantly redeemed.

"You were right, Harry. This dish is fantastic! If you had taken much longer, I might have had to help myself to your serving, too."

"Well, why do you think I returned when I did?" he countered, picking up his fork and turning it down to the plate.

"Right," Reese spoke as he stood up, "now that you have safely returned, I'm going to make a more serious study of the hors d'oeuvres. Please excuse me."

"Well then, just a minute and I'll join you," Abraham Dante chimed in. "Harry, we won't leave you two alone for very long. Just enough time to give you both a moment alone with your supper—then we'll return, I promise. Otherwise, we may as well have left you back in the other room!"

The two men shuffled away towards several large tables across the room. That seemed to be the popular meeting place, and there appeared to be more there than just a light array of appetizers offered. Aside from the usual spicy meats, fish, cheeses and spreads, all carefully arranged on various shaped crackers, there was a second table of main course items, and a third table of desserts.

These people spare no expense, Harry thought. Glancing around the room, he recognized many of the guests. Somehow, Reese and Abraham had managed to round up quite a few locals on short notice. The mayor and police chief were busy with crackers and caviar. The owner of the gas station sat and discussed the smoked salmon spread with the guy who chartered fishing boats. There was the café manager from across the street, the proprietor of Isles End market, and also both of the young women who had helped Harry with his wardrobe earlier that same day. He secretly hoped he wouldn't have to chat with those two, even though they had been so helpful.

He glanced over at Beth. She was also entertained by the busy scene. She must have sensed his gaze because she turned toward him.

"So, Harry. How are you doing?"

"I'm good."

"How's your dinner?"

"Well, to be honest, I've been so distracted I haven't had a chance to savor it like the first time."

Beth frowned in sympathy. "Well, mine is exquisite, if that helps at all. No worries though. Even though we might have preferred a more intimate dining experience, I'm convinced this is a big deal. It's important that you are here to be a part of it."

"Beth, you are so sweet . . . thank you, really. Even so, I would have preferred the intimate dining experience!"

Beth smiled back at Harry. Somehow, her lovely smile made it all worthwhile. They ate in silence for a few moments, making only 'Mmmm' sounds back and forth to each other as though it were their own private language. As they were finishing up, a clanging sound got their attention, and they looked up to see Abraham standing by the main entrance to the room. He had closed the double doors and was enthusiastically tapping a spoon against a wine glass. The chatter of the room quickly hushed and as soon as he had everyone's attention, he spoke.

"First, let me take this opportunity to thank you all for coming down on such short notice, especially since I am virtually a stranger to you all.

"I want you all to know how grateful we are to have this time with you. It's not often an opportunity comes along with such charm attached to it, but that is what we see here in Isles End: a chance to take something with intrinsic value, restore it to its original beauty, blending classic style with innovative design.

"As we move forward with this project, we want to be sensitive to all your concerns. We hope to invite your opinions and ideas since you are, in essence, the heart of Isles End. In addition, I want you all to rest assured, we do not intend to deprive any of you of revenue or the customer base you have worked hard to build over your many years here. We have explained to most of you what our basic plans are for the waterfront and the five warehouse buildings south of here. This is why we will be offering you first options for leasing or renting any of the shop spaces available. We'll make sure you are provided with any financial help you may need to expand or relocate. Some of you may choose to stay where you are. We can help facilitate a face lift for your building as well. In addition, we put covenants in place to insure there will be no threat to existing businesses from other bigger retailers or shops selling the same products.

"There you have it. We have fallen in love with Isles End. We do not wish to change it or harm the town in any way. We only wish to improve on a good thing and be a part of its continued and unavoidable success, alongside you. We will make ourselves available for any suggestions or concerns any of you might have.

"Finally, we will be opening up an office very soon, just

up the street in what I understand was once the original drug store. I know it's been empty for quite some time and the building will need some work, but we intend to fully restore the landmark to its original condition. I assure you, the finished product will be lovely! We will remain available to all the local businesses who are interested in this project, in whatever capacity they choose.

"In closing, let me thank you all once again for taking the time to join us tonight. I look forward to meeting you all again and helping you in any way I can as we work together towards the restoration and preservation of Isles End. If you wish to contact me, my cards are on the table by the door. Please enjoy the rest of your evening, and don't be shy—there's plenty of good food here to be enjoyed by everyone.

"Thank you all again, so much!"

Abraham's speech was followed by a round of applause, somewhere between lively and polite, which Harry and Beth joined vigorously.

"Hey, Harry," Beth whispered as the appreciation died down, "that sounds pretty cool, huh? Especially the part about fixing up the old drug store. Have you seen that place? Other than the fact that it needs a serious face lift, you can tell it was once a beautiful building!"

"I know," Harry answered with enthusiasm. "I've actually thought more than a few times how much fun it would be to give it a complete makeover."

"Yes! And imagine the kind of attention the contractor will receive who handles that renovation!"

"You know what, Beth, you're right. Any carpenter who has any love for architecture would die for the chance to restore that building. It might sound funny, but I literally fantasize about the possibility every time I drive past."

Beth leaned forward, "Is there any reason you can think of *not* to jump on this?"

"Not really," he answered pensively.

"Harry, who was the woman Abraham introduced you to earlier?" Beth asked with no intention to change the subject.

"Oh, his secretary—uh, Rachael something."

"What did she have to say," Beth continued curiously, "if you don't mind me asking?"

"Well, she wants to sign me up immediately to oversee the entire project on the waterfront—so does Dante."

"Hmm, interesting. She's a very stunning woman, Harry—don't you think?"

"Um, well, yeah, if you—"

Just then, Abraham and Reese returned to the table. Reese had a healthy plate full of exotic and mostly unrecognizable cuisine—Abraham had only a glass filled with a rich red liquid. They both sat down and it was quiet for a moment, except for Reese's crunching. Harry found himself staring at Abraham's drink.

"Campari and soda," Abraham exclaimed, answering

Harry's unspoken question by raising his glass.

"Oh, it's so red!" Harry responded not sure what else to say.

"And quite delicious," Abraham added, gazing over the table. "Well, how are we all doing? Did you two enjoy your meals? I do hope you will forgive me again for interrupting your time together this evening. I honestly didn't know what else to do!"

Beth looked like she was about to say something, but Harry beat her to it.

"Abraham," Harry began, "I just want to say I've been thinking—I've decided I don't need to delay my decision about this. I've had ample time, and actually I can see no reason not to participate with you in this project immediately. To be honest, this is exactly the type of work I excel in.

"And Reese," Harry continued, "I want you to know that this will not hinder me in the least from putting a hundred percent into your projects as well."

"Oh, no worries there," Reese chuckled through a mouth full of raw fish. "As far as I know, we're ahead of schedule on everything—and by the way, the Ivory Lane house looks superb. You've got my blessing!"

Harry looked at Beth, who had been quietly listening. She was holding back a grin.

"What do you think, Beth?"

"I'm thinking—congratulations—? But you might want to

check first with Abraham."

"Of course," Harry turned back to Abraham Dante. "Abraham, I'd like very much to accept your offer to work on this project with you! What do you say?"

"Frankly, Harry, I'm thrilled!"

Reese stood again, this time with a glass of champagne in his hand, "I believe this deserves a toast."

At some point during all the activity, champagne had been delivered to every table. They all stood and raised their glasses as Abraham Dante offered a nod and a, "Here, here."

"My friends," Reese said with his glass held high, "here's to Harry Turner, Isles End, and success in all our ventures!"

They all clinked their glasses and tipped them to their mouths. As Harry felt the champagne tickle its way down his throat, he couldn't help but feel elated by the whole affair.

The rest of the evening was spent making small talk as the crowd thinned out. Both Abraham and Reese left together after they finished drinking their champagne. Harry and Beth stayed for a while longer to have a little time alone. Ironically, they ended up chatting with the two women from the department store who had helped Harry with the beginning of his new wardrobe, which was embarrassing for Harry and humorous for Beth.

When they finally left Belmar's, it was dark outside, but the street lamps lit up the downtown area like a runway. Beth offered to drive this time. They circled past the old drug store first, just to take a look, and then past the five large warehouses.

All the way back to her place, they talked about their vision for Isles End and how exciting it was to be included. When they pulled into Beth's driveway, it was midnight. Harry walked Beth up to the front door.

"I wish it were earlier," Beth said tiredly. "We were sort of robbed of our evening together, but I understand it was a great opportunity for you. I still had a wonderful time and I'm glad I got to share the experience with you."

"Well, thank you, Beth. That's very generous of you, and I feel the same way! Maybe I can find a way to make it up to you sometime soon," Harry offered smoothly.

"Hmmm, what did you have in mind?" Beth pretended to be coy.

"I'm not sure yet, but I'll think of something."

"Well, can I give *you* something to think about on your drive home?" she asked as they lingered in her doorway.

"What did *you* have in mind?"

"This," she answered and reached up and gave him a quick peck on the cheek and then stepped away. "Thanks again for a very nice time."

"Thank you!" Harry smiled stepping away and turning towards his truck.

"I'll let you know when I have a plan," Harry said tilting his head back in her direction.

"Bye-bye, Harry."

"Good night, Beth."

Harry had plenty to think about on his drive home, but when his head hit the pillow, he was out like a light.

23
Rachael Sapphire

The weekend came and went without incident. Beth had already made plans with her aunt who needed help with cleaning and running errands. Harry spent that time doing payroll and writing checks for job materials at the Ivory Lane project. By Sunday night he still wasn't finished.

The following week held no relief. Harry's schedule was packed. And though he had no doubts that he would be able to handle the load, he was still anxious.

There were now four framers on his crew, in addition to Ed and Butch. They were starting on the second floor now and he needed to schedule the truss package for the roof system.

The crew he hired for Advanced Bio-Cell had also worked through the weekend and were nearly finished with the steel framing. In a few days, the plumbing and electrical would be done, then drywall. He was afraid the process might take a little longer than Shushi Yang had the patience for, but it couldn't be hurried. He'd decided to focus on the basement so they could begin operations sooner and then move to the upper floor.

He spoke with Abraham Dante, who insisted Harry meet with Rachael Sapphire as soon as possible. The only available time he had left on his schedule was evenings. He wondered how he would squeeze in time for Beth, which had recently become a priority. Besides, with all the pressure to get things finished at

ABC, William Algren had Beth working overtime. He would have to be patient—on his own behalf and hers.

Following up on Abraham's request, Harry agreed to meet with Rachael Sapphire on Wednesday evening at the old corner drugstore. She would already be there with the city inspector who had agreed to go over some changes with her, even though applicants were usually required to come into the planning department for such things.

When Harry pulled up to the old building, the inspector was just leaving. He gave a wave as the man drove away and then walked up the path to the front door. Just as he approached, the door opened, and there was Rachael looking just as splendid as she had the first time he met her.

"Well, you're right on time, Harry," she greeted him, turning aside to let him in.

"Thank you," he said stepping into the foyer.

"I just met with the inspector," Rachael announced. "It was really nice of him to come down, don't you think?"

"Yes, a little unusual, though. You must have some good connections around here."

"Well, I didn't have to beg," she explained, "I think they're very pleased about this project."

"So am I," Harry said already studying the framework inside .

"Here, take a look at these plans . . . it's alright that I call you Harry, isn't it?"

"Of course," he nodded as he accepted the set of prints.

"As you can see," she continued, "we aren't going to do much structurally, only these walls, here, and here, will be moved," she pointed at the changes on the prints. "So, we'll need the structural beams installed to support these areas once the walls are gone, but other than that, it's mostly the interior trim and exterior siding we're concerned about. We want it be as close to the original as possible. See, here are some pictures of the drug store in its prime."

This wasn't so bad, he thought. He hadn't stumbled or stuttered once yet! Why had he felt so intimidated by Rachael the other night? Was it just her appearance?

Or was it because Beth had been waiting for him at the table . . .

Rachael *had* been dressed rather provocatively, but even now wearing clothes that left a little more to the imagination, she was still enchanting.

"Let me show you around," she suggested. Harry followed her as she began a tour of the main floor. He took notes while she explained what each room would be used for.

"It's important," she explained, "that we restore every detail of this building to period perfection. Even though we'll only use a small portion of this building for actual business, it's really a notable landmark to the town and community and must be treated with careful consideration. We will build trust with the residents as they notice our careful approach to the restoration of this prized landmark."

"I see you've really thought this through," said Harry.

Rachael paused and looked up intently at Harry with her large dark eyes. "I just know people, and generally they don't care how much you know until they know how much you care."

"That's very insightful—"

"Thank you. You know, Harry, I earned a degree in psychology, but rather than pursue a career there, I realized that one can help people in whatever field they choose. I've always been gifted, if you will, with a natural ability to read people. I have an inborn sense of what their individual needs and desires are—what their struggles are, and their goals and dreams. In addition to designing and planning, I'm also involved in marketing and PR work. Using my gift gives me the opportunity to be a benefit to all my clients."

"That's quite a gift!"

"I hope so."

"So, are you ever wrong?"

"Not very often. The thing that I've found is that most people want to be understood, so it's not hard to gather information. Beyond that, it does take a special skill. Take you for instance; I think I already have you pretty well-figured out."

"Really?" Harry said as he followed her lead up the staircase to the second floor.

"It's not rocket science. Most of the basics, anyone can see. I can gather that you are fairly new here in Isles End. You like people, but you're somewhat reclusive. You have the ability to be very business-minded, but you have refrained until recently from reaching toward higher goals and bigger challenges."

At the top of the stairs Harry walked behind Rachael to a small dormer with a window seat. She sat down and motioned Harry to sit beside her. Like most of the buildings downtown, this window had a fantastic view of the harbor.

"But this is where I believe I can go deeper," Rachael continued. "You don't mind, do you, Harry?"

"Uh, no, please go ahead—"

She had a mystical look to her as she continued, her head leaning forward with her back to the window. Her exotic features were shaded by the setting sun, making her even more enchanting.

"I sense that you have been hurt terribly, not too long ago, and you still struggle with some kind of loss. That's why you moved to Isles End, is my guess. I also sense something has happened to you more recently that has had a tremendous effect on you, so much so that you even question your own capabilities. The woman you were with the other night—you are quite fond of her, though you are only recently acquainted with her. *I know,* that one is a no-brainer, but am I close? I certainly don't want to be too presumptuous!"

He sat there silently looking down at the floor, considering what Rachael had just said. He didn't want to reveal his astonishment, but he was taken aback. There were elements in her choice of words that could not have been guesses. How could she have known? He tried to think of anyone he might have shared personal information with, and how it could have traveled to Rachael.

"Harry?"

"Yes—"

"I'm sorry if I've stepped out of line," she placed her hand on his lap.

"Oh no, I'm fine. It's just that you caught me a little off guard," he answered, looking up at her. "So, you haven't been talking to anyone about me?"

"Oh no, Harry. I wouldn't do that."

"Well, you really do have a gift! You're not some kind of a fortune teller on the side?" he asked with half a smile.

"Of course not, but, so does that mean there is some truth in what I shared?"

"More than you know."

"Well, maybe, if you're comfortable with it, we can explore these things again next week. This little project here will be fun and relatively simple, but we're going to have to spend some serious time together planning our strategy on those buildings across the street, and I'll be counting on you for lots of input and professional advice."

"Of course," Harry agreed, though he wasn't sure how he felt about the 'serious time together.' There was something about her that was very alluring. If he hadn't just met Beth, he thought suddenly—but quickly put it out of his mind.

They stood and she walked him through the rest of the rooms upstairs, which were lined up on either side of the hallway so each had windows with partial views of the bay. They were all in good shape. The floors would need refinishing and the trim would need to be replaced. New plumbing fixtures in the bathrooms, but the electrical fixtures were in surprisingly good condition. They discussed details, but there was something funny in the air. The level of comfort wasn't entirely normal.

How is she able to read me so well?

But she claimed to have that talent with others, too, he reminded himself. Still, he wasn't used to having beautiful women taking such an interest in him.

They finished up, but Harry didn't want to leave. Nor did he want to discuss any further details of his personal life. He just had this desire to spend a little more time. It was Rachael, however, who suggested that Harry should be getting home.

"Thanks again, for meeting me here this afternoon, Harry. I appreciate it very much."

"No problem. Hey, we had to get it done, and it worked out fine."

"You're really very kind. I'm headed back up to the city. I still have to meet with Abraham tonight. He'll be glad to know we have these details worked out. He wants to get this place finished right away so we can set up housekeeping here—you know, temporarily."

"Really," Harry said. "I didn't realize that you were going to be living here—the two of you?"

"Not exactly. First, I should explain—Abraham's not my companion. We will have our own separate rooms. He and I have a great working relationship, but I could never imagine being involved with a man like him. For one, there's no attraction between us, though he's brilliant and very exciting to work for. He's the kind of man who is so driven by all his pursuits that I don't think he would know how to make a woman happy, even if he wanted to."

She began picking up her things while she continued.

"We will stay here when it's convenient or necessary, once things start to get busy across the street."

"I see," Harry said.

"I'm looking forward to spending some time camping here. It'll make my job that much more fun, especially after you're finished. The city can be very tedious at times!"

Harry opened the front door for Rachael and she stepped out into the last light of the fading sun.

"Oh, I almost forgot," she added, as she began searching around in her purse. "I've got a couple things for you."

Harry waited as she rummaged through her bag. He still couldn't take his eyes off her. Everything she did was interesting and bordered on captivating. Thick ringlets of long dark hair fell forward and hid her features as she searched through her purse, making her look even more mysterious. *What was it about some women*, he considered, *that they had such an effect?*

"Here we go," she said with delight. "There's a key to the front door of this building, and also a check to help you get started. Abraham will see you soon and you two can work out your financial arrangement. But trust me, Harry, the only thing you will be concerned with is that he's paying you too much. " She handed Harry the keys and the check.

"Well, goodnight," she offered, holding out her hand. But before Harry had a chance to take it, she pulled it away.

"Oh, Harry!" she blushed and then stepped up close and hugged him. All he could do was reciprocate.

He watched as she walked away down the sidewalk and into a nice looking Cadillac he hadn't noticed before. Then he climbed into his pick-up and started the engine. He flipped on the light and nearly choked when he saw the check. It was made out to H.T. Construction for exactly twenty thousand dollars.

After a moment of recovery, he drove the short distance home and got ready for bed. He checked his messages. Nothing from Beth. He rang her number but she didn't pick up so he left her a voice mail.

Disappointed, he stepped around the empty trunk that was still at the foot of his bed and was reminded of Narcissus. It seemed like forever now since he'd seen his celestial friend, though only a few days had passed. He knew from what Narcissus had told him that the angel wouldn't be around for awhile. He should have been more persistent in trying to find out when Narcissus would return. But were things falling into place for him now because his angelic guardian was looking out for him? The thought was comforting and perfectly logical too. His life was coming together because he had a powerful spirit protecting and guiding him. Now he must make the best of all the opportunities that continued to come his way.

Under the covers, Harry adjusted his pillow and assumed his usual position. He thought about Beth again, but it was too late now to call her. As he started to drift off, he had the images of many faces appear in his mind: Narcissus, Beth, Abraham and Rachael, Reese Orchard and William-Bill Algren, Preston Hart and Shushi Yang, his dad and mom...and his forever lost Jennifer. As he began to dream, they all faded away and he traveled back to a familiar place from his youth.

It was the same dream he'd had a week or so ago. He was about eight years old again and his mom was seeing him off to school. She handed him his lunch and kissed him good-bye. As he turned to begin the half-mile walk to school, she warned him to be careful, just as she always did. Once again, she teased that his guardian angel would protect him. He laughed and waved back; she looked beautiful as she smiled and waved in return.

He continued down the steep road. All the familiar signs were there. He had walked this path so many times over the years, in real life and in dreams. But then, like before, as he neared the bottom of the road, it became twisted and unfamiliar.

Ahead of him was the small bridge. He remembered again

that he was to stay away but as he walked, he was once again forced to go forward. Soon, he would have no choice but to cross. Far below, he could see the stream running underneath.

At the last minute, just like before, he jumped off the side of the road to avoid the bridge and slid down the bank of the ravine towards the water. He watched it rush up towards him until he splashed into the moving current and it gripped him. Gaining his balance he realized the water was only knee-deep. He was almost under the bridge now and the stream became a trickle. Even though he'd been caught in this scenario before, he was still trapped and the same fear came over him. He started to panic as he realized there was nowhere to go except under the bridge.

He was forced into the dark opening. Directly ahead, he recognized the same ominous figure as before, except there was something different this time. The creature was still large and beastly. He had the same ebony skin and crimson eyes, with the same fierce expression on his face, but instead of the cape-like wings sprouting out of his shoulders, he wore a dark tailored suit. He smiled again and extended his hand.

"Come, my little man," he urged. "You still appear to be a tasty morsel, and my appetite will not wait much longer!"

Harry lurched forward and nearly fell out of bed. He looked at the clock. He had hardly been asleep for an hour. Getting up he wiped his face and neck with a damp towel and got back into bed. He should have asked Narcissus about the dream, but he had nearly forgotten about it himself. Did it have any meaning? Why was this menacing figure invading his sleep? Harry found himself unexpectedly irritated. Why wasn't Narcissus able to stay?

Maybe he didn't really deserve the continued aid of an Archangel. He considered the stark reality. He, Harry Turner, was no important leader or statesman. He hadn't even made class president! What was it about him that caused the release of a spiritual being who had been bound for centuries? Why, after all that time, should the angel be set free for the benefit of one man, only to visit him three or four times and then be gone? It seemed odd, and he was surprised he hadn't thought of his experiences with Narcissus in this way before. Could this creature, who seemed so intent on the subject of deception, be somehow deceiving him in the process?

No!

He'd been through these doubts before. Still, why had Narcissus forsaken him? Without warning, the promises he had made to the angel came to the forefront of his thoughts—several promises, actually. He had promised to be patient. He would cultivate his ability to perceive what was true and what was false. He would be wary of deception. He would cultivate his "mantle of strength."

Finally, after an hour of tossing and turning, he dozed off again and this time slept undisturbed through the rest of the night.

The following day Harry found himself supervising all

three jobs he was now contracting. It was amazing to him how busy he was and he hadn't even picked up a hammer! He was sure he'd find a few minutes somewhere to talk to Beth on the phone, but every time he remembered her, something urgent came up. A whole week had gone by since he'd visited with her!

Finally, he found himself sitting in his truck at Ivory Lane after the guys were gone, with four phone messages sent and nothing to do until responses came back from at least two of them. It was late and Beth ought to be home by now. This might be a good time to call if he could get hold of her *and* if he didn't have one of the return calls interrupt. He sat there in his truck and waited while her phone rang.

"Hello?"

"Beth, it's me."

"Oh, Harry!"

"It's nice to hear your voice. Seems like forever since I've seen you!"

"I know. I can't believe it's been a whole week! I guess we've both been busy."

"Yes, I know. I've been swamped," he stammered. He suddenly felt awkward, like he'd lost his place in a book.

"Me, too! They've got me running around everywhere down at ABC. I'll be racking up some nice overtime this month. Are you doing okay?"

"Oh yeah," Harry said, "but I miss you."

"I miss you, too. I've meant to call you several times, but

whenever I try, something interferes."

"I know what you mean. Hey, maybe we can get together this weekend? Find somewhere to go where we won't get interrupted?"

"I'd really love to, Harry, honestly, but you know this last weekend I spent with my aunt? Well, she's not doing very well. I'm afraid she needs me again."

"Is she okay? I mean, is it something serious?"

"I'm not sure," Beth said with obvious concern. "It's only been just recently that she's had any trouble at all. Now, one moment she's okay and then it's as though she's very ill. We've never experienced anything like this with her before. I know she must miss my folks very much, and with them gone now, I get the feeling she thinks her time must be coming soon as well. She never discussed it at all before, but now she talks about death often."

"Hmmm. It must be tough. I'm sorry."

"Well, the thing is, she has pleaded with me to spend this next weekend with her. She's very dear to me, and I know she must be lonely. I feel responsible for her. We've always enjoyed each other's company, but with her recent troubles, she seems to have become much more dependent."

"Was she ever married?" Harry asked.

"She was," Beth answered. "She was widowed at an early age and never married again."

"She's very lucky to have someone like you."

"Thanks, Harry. I feel as though I'm very fortunate to have her. In some ways she has filled a void in me, you know, since I lost my parents."

"Really—yes, that makes sense," Harry said. "I'm glad you have her, too, Beth."

"Thanks for understanding. I hope we'll get to see each other sometime soon!"

"Me, too. I'll give you a call again when I can, okay?"

"Alright, Harry. Well then, I'll see you—"

"Bye."

Harry pushed the end button on his phone and sat there. Why had he hung up so soon? He wished he had talked with her longer. Had *he* ended the call? He had wanted to tell her about the plans for the corner drug store and the hefty check he had received. But more importantly, about how much he enjoyed their night out last week, and saying goodbye to her that night. Why not just call her back? He held the phone up, but before he could redial, it began ringing.

It was the lumberyard. While he worked through that order, another call came in. The plumber from the city was filling him in on their progress at Advanced Bio-Cell. Then Ed called. Even though Harry's thoughts were elsewhere, it was nice listening to Ed, who did most of the talking. Other people had lives too, he reminded himself. As timing would have it, just as he said goodbye to Ed, there was another call. He didn't recognize this number but answered anyway.

"Well hello, Harry, it's Rachael."

"Oh, Rachael!" Harry responded. He hadn't given her his cell number yet, though he had no reason not to. It was nice to hear her voice.

"You know," she began softly, "we talked about the importance of meeting soon to begin working on the plans for the waterfront buildings?"

"Of course," Harry replied, hoping to conceal his troubled thoughts.

"Well, my weekend has just opened up," she said with a lilt in her voice, "and I'm thinking it would be perfect if we could conspire together on this project as soon as possible. I know Abraham would be very impressed. Do you have any plans yet for this weekend?"

Harry thought about the twenty thousand dollar check he still had in the glove box of his truck. Maybe that should give him a little incentive.

"You know what? I just happen to have the entire weekend available—let's show Mr. Dante some real progress!"

He heard a little giggle.

"Really? That's great, Harry. Okay, here's what I'm thinking. There happens to be the most extraordinary group of buildings up here, on the waterfront, that I think would be perfect in design for what we want to accomplish in Isles End."

"Excellent!" Harry hoped he didn't sound too excited.

"Yes! So why don't you come up Saturday morning, and

287

you can spend the day, or even better, we can put you up for the night. We can take what we learn back to Isles End on Sunday and consider plans for *our* waterfront buildings. What do you think?"

"Sounds good," Harry answered without thinking. It made sense, he thought. Besides, if anyone knew Abraham Dante's vision for those waterfront warehouses, it would be Rachael. Harry had some ideas of his own, of course, but seeing exactly what Rachael had in mind would be a great benefit. "Let me know when and where to meet you and you've got a deal."

"Wonderful," Rachael squealed and gave Harry the directions.

"Well, I can promise you, Harry, this project is going to involve some work," she added, "but with you on the team, I feel certain we'll have some fun, too."

"Building is always work for me, Rachael, but I do love it. If we can have some fun at the same time, that's just an added bonus."

"You just leave everything to me . . ."

Harry clipped his phone to his belt and decided he'd better get to the bank and deposit that twenty thousand dollar check. Most of it would be eaten up right away in materials, but he still felt good about the trust they had placed in him. A few minutes later, he was sitting in front of the Isles End bank. The last time he'd seen the bank was when he viewed it with Narcissus. It didn't look so creepy now—there were no spirits

288

clinging to humans, or guardians of light keeping their eyes on things. He walked up to the front door with the check in hand. Opening the door, he nearly collided with a man who was leaving. It was the banker he had observed speaking with the elderly woman who had the talking lump on her back! Up close and in the light, Harry realized it was the same clerk who had opened his account.

"Excuse me . . . I'm sorry," the man said lurching away to avoid running into Harry.

Harry stepped quickly to the side. "My fault!"

The man studied him. "Harry Turner, right?"

Harry stepped back further and smiled. "That's right—"

"Yes! I'm very good with names! I'm Alex Hauser—I opened up an account for you last year some time . . . but I haven't seen you around much."

He didn't look at all sinister like Harry remembered from the vision, in fact, he was rather friendly. Harry extended his hand nervously. "Yes, I remember—good to see you again."

"Thank you," the banker said shaking Harry's hand. "Feel free to come by and see me anytime. We've got some great CD's available now and also some other attractive investment opportunities you might find interesting."

"I will," Harry promised, and the man brusquely hurried away. After depositing the check, Harry drove through town looking at all the buildings scattered along the waterfront. He began to envision the entire downtown area completely renovated—new siding and stone and paint on all the shops and stores. Knowing he would be so instrumental in the process of restoring Isles End was exciting.

Saturday morning arrived and Harry found himself driving north. He had the directions on his GPS and reviewed them several times. He had rarely visited that part of the city even when he had lived there, but some of the street names sounded familiar. He had already passed Advanced Bio-Cell, and would soon be sitting in a small cafe with Rachael Sapphire.

Part of his nervousness was because he hadn't been near his old home since he'd left over a year ago. Gwen had come down to visit him on two occasions, but he hadn't been back at all. He felt guilty now, having made no plans to stop by and say hi to his sister while he was in the area. She had always been so caring. He wondered if she had anyone who fussed over her as much as she had done with him.

Just south of the city, he drove past the crash site where his dad's plane had gone down. A familiar feeling came over Harry as he remembered that day, and the pain came creeping in uncontrollably.

I lost my parents and the woman I loved!

But then, just as quickly as the sorrow had come, it was gone. Not long ago, grief and sadness had been a daily occurrence, but time really did have a way of healing some things. As Harry drove on, he could see the beginning of the sparkling city below lining the bay. Calmly and quietly he let a couple tears escape, wiped them away, and put those thoughts behind him.

24
The City and The Kiss

The transition from the scenic countryside to the glistening city was abrupt. Harry carefully made his way through the traffic and down to the water. There were skyscrapers everywhere and the streets were busy with people hurrying about their business. As he moved into the older district, there was a sudden transition from contemporary buildings to gothic stone architecture. The buildings here were not as tall as the newer ones, but they had a solid and artistic appeal. The doors and windows were all wrapped with carved stone, and heavy bronze street lamps lined the cobbled streets.

A large iron sign proclaiming, "Welcome to Old Towne," stretched across an entire intersection, boldly announcing the entrance to a historically significant part of the city. Beautiful arrangements of flowers hung in large baskets from every street lamp and created a colorful contrast to the dark bronze and ornately carved stone that dominated the rest of the scenery.

Harry left his truck in a parking lot and tripped over the uneven cobblestones of the old street and came to a stop in front of a large corner building. The sign over the door read, "The Froggy Dog." The windows displayed an array of sculptured porcelain animals. He stood there for a moment, intrigued with the artistry.

"Hello there," said a young man in the entryway holding a

guitar in his hands.

"Hi," Harry answered.

"Need some help?"

"I'm looking for a place called 'Geese and Friends.'"

"Ah, it's just a few shops down," the young man said, pointing. "Awesome soup there!"

"Thanks," Harry nodded as he turned in that direction.

This part of the city was obviously a popular area to visit. There were shoppers and tourists everywhere, shuffling in and out of the various boutiques and restaurants. Half a block down, Harry found a sign over the entrance to a small café which read, "Geese and Friends." He didn't see Rachael anywhere outside so he went in.

A young woman with a big white goose embroidered on her blouse stepped up to Harry. "Can I help you?" she asked.

Harry studied the goose. There was a small crowd of tiny people huddled around the bird's feet.

"I'm meeting someone here for lunch."

'Would you like to take a look around inside?" she suggested.

"Sure," Harry replied, and made his way to the dining area. The café was small so it didn't take him long to see that Rachael hadn't arrived. He found the waitress again.

"Could you seat me at a table for two, please?"

"Sure. Right this way." She led him over to a window table.

Harry checked his phone but there were no messages. He realized he had Rachael's number on the received calls list of his cell phone, but decided to give her some more time before he bothered her.

"Would you like something while you wait?" the waitress interjected as she passed by.

"Yes, thank you—how about a coffee?"

"I'll be right back," she answered and disappeared around the corner.

Harry looked out at the bay. The view was amazing. The harbor was almost a perfect half circle, and the city had been built right up to the edge of the water with a continuous bulkhead from one end to the other. It was funny, he thought, that he'd never really spent much time in this part of the city before. Of course, for years he'd seen pictures and post cards of Old Towne, mostly of the bright lights at night—but the view of the bay from here was spectacular in real life, sparkling in the daytime and glittering at night.

Harry was enjoying the atmosphere when his phone rang.

"Harry, it's Rachael."

"Hi, are you—"

"I'm sorry, Harry. I had a meeting this morning that went longer than expected. I'm just up the street. Did you find the cafe? Will you wait there for me?"

"Yes, of course," Harry said.

"Good— I'll just be a few minutes. I've found something

I think you will find extremely valuable— go ahead and order for the both of us. I trust you."

Harry said goodbye and looked over the menu. What would Rachael like? He saw the waitress and waved her over.

"Ready?" she asked.

"Yes, my friend, or associate rather," he corrected himself, "will be here shortly. I've heard your soup is awesome."

Harry made his selections and sipped his coffee while he waited. He was anxious to see Rachael. More than that, he found himself eager, and he had to tell himself that it was only the anticipation of this project that had him going. But when he saw her enter the front of the café, his excitement grew. He stood and admired her as she approached.

"Harry, you look well. Can you take these things?" She offered him a bundle of drawings and folders and sat down across from Harry. "So what do you think of this place? Can you see Isles End with a waterfront like this someday?"

"That would be quite something," Harry admitted.

"I don't know how I got so lucky, but there in that bundle are the photographs, drawings, and blueprints for this entire block. Can you believe it?"

"Wow! That *is* amazing," Harry responded. "How were you able to find these in such a short time?"

"I know, I amaze myself sometimes. But it does help to know important people in high places. Still, I had no idea I'd have these in my hands today. I think this is nearly everything we need, Harry! But we can still take some time to look around. We've got the whole afternoon free, if we want."

After they finished their soup and sandwiches, Harry and Rachael walked up and down both sides of the street and took notes on the shops and types of products being sold. About halfway down the main street, they found a walkway leading to a park with a very large pier.

"Let's take a walk out there," Rachael urged, grabbing Harry's hand and tugging him down the walkway. The touch of her hand was both pleasant and troubling. He was wondering how it would look if Beth suddenly appeared. She wouldn't understand and he would feel terrible. Yet he was drawn to Rachael in a way he could not describe.

She might be attractive, but this was strictly business. Since there was nothing improper going on, there was nothing to worry about.

This particular street was originally designed for traffic, but now it was a wide lane for pedestrians only, lined with old wooden benches and full-sized bronze sculptures of people and animals. The pier was also clearly meant for foot traffic. There were more benches and light posts with hanging flowerpots. Manicured lawns and flower beds were planted along the front of the pier, transitioning into wood decking that stretched out over the water. Couples walked hand-in-hand down the wooden planks, while others sat close to each other on the benches, gazing out at the view.

Harry walked with Rachael out to the end of the pier where they found an empty bench.

"We ought to look over some of these plans and photos, but it's so lovely here it's hard to think of work, isn't it, Harry? Can you see all this, transplanted right onto the waterfront of Isles End? We are going to transform that old wharf into the most charming and profitable part of town— then just watch the rest of the area take off!"

"Yes, I can see it too, Beth—or—Rachael! Wow," Harry stuttered , "I'm sorry, I . . ."

"It's okay, Harry," she responded softly. "It's quite all right. You know, it's no secret that you have feelings for her. Why so nervous?"

"I'm not sure," he answered. "I guess I feel a little awkward being here with you. I know there's no reason to be concerned, but I'm not sure how Beth would feel."

Rachael looked troubled. "Harry, I sort of wondered if this subject might come up. I've heard that she's really—a very nice girl, and I don't mean to intrude, but I can't help but be concerned for you."

"What do you mean?"

"Well . . . gosh, Harry, I suddenly feel very uncomfortable myself . . ."

"Please, just tell me—what is it, Rachael?"

"I hope you'll forgive me—I'm really sorry to bring this up. It's just that, it seems to me that Beth ought to end one relationship before beginning another. "

"What?"

"I wasn't going to say anything, honestly, and it occurred to me that you might already know. I usually don't get involved in other people's affairs, but it would be very difficult for me to keep a secret like this for long and still continue working with you. I'm rather fond of you, and I'd hate to see you get hurt."

"Please, what are we talking about, here?"

"Reese mentioned something to Abraham, and he shared it with me. It may not be that big of a deal. It's just, I guess she's been seeing someone else. I think it might have started before she met you, I'm not sure. I don't know if the relationship is serious, and she may have already broken it off, but it seems to me you should know about her involvement, especially if it's still going on."

Harry couldn't think of what to say. He just sat looking out at the bay. He forced his attention onto the city and how it circled the water like a crescent moon. A warm breeze came up and drifted over the two of them as they sat in silence, but Harry was far from comfortable. His stomach was tightening up in a hard knot. He looked at Rachael and attempted a weak grin and then looked away again.

"Oh, Harry, I can see now that you knew nothing about this, and I'm really sorry. I shouldn't have said a word, and honestly, I don't know the particulars. Please forgive me."

"Knowing how perceptive you are," he said, "I doubt that

I could hide my feelings very well from you, but however disappointed I might seem to be," he paused and took a deep breath, "let's not let this ruin a perfectly good day." He paused and studied the sparkling water in an attempt to gain control of his emotions. "I'll be fine, really. You know, I haven't known Beth very long. It's not like we're exclusive yet or anything."

What am I saying?

"I've only been out with her twice," Harry   continued, "but listen, you're right. It seems we don't know the facts here . . . let's just keep it—" He stopped himself, with the feeling he was beginning to ramble and wondered how much of what he was saying was really true. He looked down at the folders in Rachael's lap. "Here, let's take a look at some of these pictures."

"Are you sure?" Rachael asked.

"Of course. Let's see what we've got here."

Harry pulled out the photos and Rachael slid a little closer.

"Yes, these are nice," Harry said, shifting his focus. "Very nice. We won't have any trouble passing these designs through the city commerce or building departments."

"I thought you'd agree."

"Has Abraham seen them yet?"

"Not these photos—but he's seen these buildings many times and likes them very much. Even so, he wants *us* to be the ones to make these decisions."

Harry sat beside Rachael, collaborating over their ideas

for the rest of the afternoon. They looked through all the photographs, drawings, and prints. If Harry hadn't had Rachael's company, he didn't know how he would have dealt with the news about Beth.

Could this really be true?

He did his best to steer his thoughts away from Beth—being with Rachael helped with that—but during the lulls in conversation, he couldn't help wondering if Beth was really with her aunt these last two weekends.

Was it possible she would have lied to him?

"What's the plan from here?" Harry asked in an effort to move things forward.

"Well, finding all these plans and photos saved us a lot of time and work. We could have spent half the day just taking pictures, and who knows how long it would have taken to get this stuff from the building department. So, here's my idea. I took the liberty of getting you a room in the same building where I live, just in case you decide that you're not up to driving back to Isles End tonight. If you like, we can go check in, and then maybe think about dinner."

"Alright," Harry said, still stunned. In light of the disturbing news, he wanted to escape the pain that was seeping into his heart. He pulled himself up from the bench and began organizing the bundle of plans that had accumulated in his lap. "That sounds fine. Let's do it."

They walked back to the lot where they had both parked.

Harry followed Rachael as she made her way into traffic. They had only driven a few blocks when she turned abruptly into the parking garage of an old stone building. Harry gazed up to see that the building was quite tall. All around the top, a crowd of ancient stone gargoyles leaned out over the edge, staring back down at him. Above the creatures, Harry marveled at the half a dozen colorful turrets crowded in the center, shooting up into the clouds. The architecture was a fascinating combination of gothic and renaissance design.

He heard the blaring sound of a horn and quickly turned his attention back to the road. Braking suddenly to avoid a near collision, he jerked his truck into the opening, following Rachael into the dark passageway. His eyes adjusted and he sped up a little until he saw her Cadillac parked near an elevator door.

"C'mon, Harry, and don't forget your luggage," she called.

"You don't waste any time, do you?"

"Oh, I got used to city driving a long time ago."

While they rode up the elevator to the lobby, Harry realized it wasn't so long ago that he was in the elevator at ABC when he met Beth for the first time. The thought made him ache as he pushed it out of his mind. There was Rachael standing quietly next to him. She had been so kind, he thought as he studied her. Why not enjoy her company while he was here? What harm would there be in finding a friend in her as well as a business associate? She had been honest with him, and as he thought about it, Harry began to appreciate her in a deeper way.

Moments later, the elevator door opened to reveal a large foyer dominated by marble columns and floors. The room was empty except for a small pale man who stood like a statue behind a massive granite counter. Harry followed Rachael as she stepped out and walked toward the man.

"Good afternoon, Miss Sapphire," he said as they approached him.

"Hello, Roman—you're looking gaunt," Rachael said politely.

"Thank you," Roman said.

Harry wondered at the odd exchange but decided to keep silent.

"Did you find a nice room for my guest?"

"Of course, madam. It's all ready for you. Here's the key."

Roman held out a thick gold card with a plume of red tassels dangling from one corner and dropped it into Rachael's hand.

"Enjoy your stay, sir," the man spoke blankly in Harry's direction.

"Do I need to sign anything?" Harry asked.

"It's all been taken care of, Harry," Rachael interjected, handing the card over to him. "Follow me."

Obediently, Harry followed Rachael back to the elevator and up they sped. This time when the doors opened, Harry was looking at a long dark red hallway with embroidered cloth covering the walls and large heavy wooden doors on both sides.

"Here we are," Rachael said. "Your room should be down here on the right. Let's check it out." She stepped into the corridor.

Harry grabbed his bag and tripped out of the elevator. "Where's your room?" he asked as he recovered himself.

"I have an apartment, Harry, up on the next floor. This is the last floor of rooms in the building. There are only a few condos above, and of course, the penthouse." She moved briskly forward and paused a short way ahead. "Here it is, Harry—room 104."

Harry pushed the heavy door open and let Rachael enter first. The room was pleasant and richly furnished. Large windows faced the bay and the last of the sun's rays were streaming in through the half-open blinds.

"Wow, this is really something!" Harry exclaimed as he strode across the thick carpeting and set his suitcase down by a stone fireplace. He had expected a nice room but this was more like a luxury suite. There was a large living area with a kitchenette on the far end and a separate bedroom and bath on the other side.

"It *is* rich, isn't it," Rachael responded with a carefree laugh. "And take a look at that view!"

Harry walked over to the window and gazed out at a fantastic panorama of the entire bay. He could see the buildings nestled all along the water's edge in both directions. Directly below was Old Towne, and as he studied the buildings, he couldn't help visualizing them all sitting on the waterfront of Isles End.

"Look, Harry, there's the dock where we sat this afternoon," Rachael nudged his shoulder.

"Oh yeah! I see it. And there's the place where we had lunch," he said, pointing.

They both stood there for a moment, silently studying the scene below. Isles End seemed far away now, and Harry felt oddly out of place as he looked down at the city and then over to Rachael who was standing so close.

Her eyes locked in, and without a word Rachael turned to Harry and edged in closer. Then, very slowly, she wrapped her arms around him and pressed her body up against his. Almost without thinking, his arms responded as though they were compelled to give comfort, and he embraced her. As she pulled herself to him, he managed to turn his face away slightly, back towards the window to see the sun falling down on the horizon.

"Oh, Harry," she whispered, and with her arms wrapped around his neck, she leaned in closer and kissed him gently, just to the side of his mouth. "Don't worry," she crooned.

Her lips lingered there, brushing the edge of his, until he turned his face ever so slightly to meet her. The taste of her mouth was intoxicating as her lips pressed up hard against his. He lingered there while the seconds dripped by like thick honey. Her body felt warm and inviting as she pressed in harder, making herself more available. Somewhere in the back of his mind, he could hear a voice saying, 'Harry, what are you doing?'" His head felt like a lead weight as he pulled his mouth away and focused his gaze again, out into the dark bay.

When Harry finally dared to turn his gaze back to Rachael, her head was down, her face pressed against his chest. He stood there silently holding her, not sure how to respond now. She finally relaxed her hold and eased back.

Harry turned away from the window and gingerly wandered across to the other side of the apartment.

"This is quite a room you've chosen for me," he said trying to sound casual.

"You can thank Abraham for that," Rachael said, gathering herself. "He always takes good care of his business associates—and even better care of his friends."

"I can tell!" Harry said glancing nervously around. "Will we be seeing him tonight?"

"I'm afraid not, but he *will* be back in Isles End in a couple of days, and I know he'll be looking forward to hearing about our plans.

"Hey, Harry—"

"Yes?"

"Why don't you make yourself comfortable while I go to my apartment and freshen up. I'll be back shortly and we can decide what our plans are for this evening."

Before Harry had a chance to answer, she hurried away. For a moment, he wasn't sure what to do. He placed his hand on the side of his mouth where Rachael had kissed him first and realized he was very warm. In an effort to shake off the anxiety that had crept over him, he browsed around the room for a few minutes admiring the furnishings. Wandering into the bathroom, he decided a shower might do him some good. He popped open his suitcase on the large bed and found his razor and lotion. As long as Rachael was freshening up, he might as well shave, too.

The shower was luxurious. He'd never seen anything like it, with a ceiling head, a fixed head on the wall, and body sprays all around. There was also a steam unit, which he switched on immediately. Inside, the enclosure quickly filled with steam, while hot water massaged Harry's body from every direction. Once again he was reminded of the living water he had been immersed in and had breathed into his lungs. He wondered again about his Mantle of Strength. Up here in the city, on this night, swimming in the pool with angels . . . seemed like ages ago.

I must never forget that day.

Once out of the bathroom, Harry tried to keep himself occupied until Rachael returned. He wondered about the intimate encounter he had just shared with her. Did he do something to bring that on? He felt very uneasy. He hadn't come there for any other reason but business, but after what had just taken place, he began to question his own motives.

Again he heard the words echo in his mind, *"Harry, what*

are you doing?"

I don't know what I'm doing, he answered himself. He felt like he was still under a spell. What was it about her that was so alluring? Her beauty? The way she responded to him? Again he considered their very recent and warm embrace. The texture of her skin . . . the way her mouth moved when she spoke . . . the way her body quivered as he held her . . . the touch of her lips . . .

Finally Harry tore himself away from what felt like a trance. He was afraid of where this evening might lead. Where was this relationship going?

Again, Harry's thoughts turned back to the Mantle of Strength he'd received and he wondered if he could somehow rely on it now. Immediately he felt a measure of resolve growing from inside. He took a deep breath and felt instantly stronger. He wondered if he really needed to stay the night here at all. What would happen if he left the city and drove home tonight?

Back in Isles End, would he find Beth home, or maybe with her aunt? Whatever the truth was, he didn't want to do anything now that would jeopardize the relationship he had begun with her. So, what was he doing kissing a woman he hardly knew?

His thoughts turned back to Rachael. What was taking her so long? Women might have a reputation for taking longer to get ready than men, but what could be keeping her this long? Another half an hour passed and he started to wonder if something might have happened to her. She had said her room was on the next floor up. He decided to see if he could find her.

After packing his things, he stepped out of his room and into the dark hallway. He pushed the elevator button and immediately the door opened as though it was waiting for him. Feeling a little nervous, he stepped in and pushed the button that should take him up one floor. In seconds, the elevator eased to a stop and the door slid silently open.

The hallway in front of him was so dim that the burgundy carpet seemed to disappear just a few feet ahead. He stepped out and tried to adjust his eyes to the faint light. How was he going to find her door? He didn't even know the number. It seemed terribly dark and he wondered how anyone could see in here at all when a door just ahead of him opened slightly and light streamed out into the hallway. He walked forward and peered into the opening as he treaded softly past. There was someone moving inside. Unsure of what to do, Harry kept walking and quickly hid himself in the recess of the next door down. With a sudden jolt, the first door popped wide open and a man stumbled into the hallway. Harry ducked deeper into the recess as the man lunged forward and jerked his way toward the elevator.

Then, nothing but silence.

The man could not have gone far, Harry thought. He never heard the elevator door open. Maybe the man had used the stairs?

It was too quiet!

He wanted to walk back down the hallway to investigate.

Maybe he would find the man and at least ask him if he knew Rachael—find out where her apartment was. Where could she have gone? Somehow he had to find out. He leaned forward and peered into the dark passage. The door was still wide open and the light from inside lit up the hallway just enough to see the form of the stranger leaning against the elevator door.

Harry kept still and waited to see what he was doing. The man looked asleep as he leaned there, motionless. Then in the same fashion as he had first appeared, he started to lurch back towards the open door. Harry pulled himself tightly into the alcove once again, but the man walked past the open door and came to a halt directly in front of where Harry was hiding. He was lanky and thin with tired, hollow eyes.

"May I ask what you are doing here?" the man said staring into Harry's face. "I don't recall seeing you here before." His expensive looking suit was quite wrinkled and he bore an ugly cut across his forehead. There were blood stains on his shirt and tie.

"I was looking for a friend," Harry answered matter-of-factly.

"A friend?"

"Yes—her name is Rachael Sapphire. I believe she lives on this floor."

"No, there's no one here by that name."

"Okay," Harry stammered. "Well, she's got to be around here somewhere. This is her apartment building."

The man just stood mutely.

"Are you feeling alright?" Harry asked.

"I don't know," the man said with a puzzled expression. "I admit, I'm feeling somewhat confused at the moment. I've been putting in long hours. I've probably had too much to drink, too."

"Did you have some sort of accident?" Harry asked.

"No," he countered with a scowl. "Why?"

"It looks like you've got some blood on your shirt."

The man tugged on his collar and peered down at himself. "I must have cut myself shaving—I'm a mess, aren't I?"

"I've seen worse."

"What's that supposed to mean?"

"Nothing. Look, do you need some help?" Harry tried to hide his growing frustration.

"Yeah, you can help by getting out of here and leaving me alone," the man answered as he staggered backwards and hit his head on the opposite wall.

"Very well. I'm going to see if I can find my friend on the next floor up," Harry said curtly. He stepped into the hallway and faced the stranger who had repositioned himself in the middle of the hall.

"There is no other floor, friend," the man said, glaring.

"There's a penthouse up from here," Harry argued.

"Wrong—but go ahead. Be my guest," the man countered and stepped aside as he waved his arm like a traffic cop, motioning Harry to move forward.

Harry brushed past him and marched toward the elevator.

"Good bye, then," the man called out, but Harry ignored him. As soon as the elevator door opened, he stepped in and quickly studied the controls.

Shouldn't there be a button that says "penthouse" or "top floor?"

Harry waited for the door to close and then let out a sigh of frustration. The man appeared to be right. There were no other buttons going up.

25
Auntie

Beth carefully placed a bowl of clam chowder and a cup of hot tea onto the silver tray and carried it into the living room where her aunt was waiting.

"Here you go, Auntie," she said, placing the tray on her aunt's lap. She unfolded the napkin and spread it out. Was she forgetting something?

She glanced around, wondering what she had overlooked. It was such a cozy room, she thought as she tried to remember what had been on her mind. This house was exactly what she would want when she was older. It had always been a place where she could go and feel like nothing had changed. Somehow, there was security in that. She recalled the many visits she had made there throughout her childhood. She and her sisters would always run in and immediately look for the certain things they loved, and they were always there: the calico cat on the mantel, the little butler doorstop, the old lady cookie jar, all the knick-knacks that filled each space so appropriately. Now it had such a rich sentimental feel. Every item had its place, and for the most part, had been there as far back as Beth could remember. Each and every object had been well-cared for and was always right where it belonged. The place was like a museum where no one really lived, with the exception of one aged widow who was very meticulous about her things. And since Beth's parents had passed away, she had become even more adamant that everything be regularly cleaned and put in its proper place.

"Ah, thank you my dear," the small elderly woman's voice creaked as she smiled and repositioned the napkin.

"How are you feeling, Auntie?" Beth inquired as she pulled her thoughts back together.

"Oh my," the older woman answered as she tried to straighten up. "Not too good, I'm afraid. My back's giving me some serious problems again."

"I'm so sorry. Is there anything I can do? How about your chair? Can we adjust it a little?"

"No, but a hot meal always seems to help in some way, along with my medication, of course."

"Oh, that's what I forgot! Coming right up," Beth responded, smiling, as she hurried back to the kitchen.

"And Beth, don't forget a glass of water," her aunt called out. "You know I don't want to try to swallow those horrible things with my tea. It's just a waste!"

"I seem to be having trouble finding your pain pills, Auntie," Beth called as she fumbled around in the medicine cupboard.

"Didn't you have them last?"

"I suppose I did. I thought I put them right here."

"Well, you know what I always say . . ."

"I know, 'There's a place for everything and everything in its place,'" Beth answered back before her aunt could get it out.

"Yes, that's right."

"Oh, here they are, right by the sink where I left them." Beth grabbed her own bowl of soup, a glass of water, and the meds, and hurried back into the dining room where her aunt sat waiting.

"You don't need to wait for me, Auntie," Beth said as she removed three tablets from the bottle and placed them on her aunt's tray along with the water.

Her aunt held the pills to her mouth and paused. "You know how I feel about mealtime. One must never begin before one's company is ready."

"Well, I'm ready now, so let's eat."

Beth's aunt swallowed her meds, and then they both sat quietly for a few minutes while they broke crackers into the chowder. Her aunt quickly consumed half her bowl, wiped her mouth, and let out a long sigh. "That was delicious, Beth! You are going to make someone quite a good wife someday, but in the meantime, you can always be my personal chef!"

"Well, thank you, Auntie. It did turn out pretty well, didn't it?"

"Yes, dear, and speaking of you making someone a good wife, let's hear about this young man you seem to be so interested in."

"Well, his name is Harry—"

"Hmm, it's a nice name."

"Yes. We have only been out twice, but it's amazing how

314

much we have in common."

Her aunt paused from sipping her tea. "Really?"

"Yes! He actually lost both of his parents in a plane crash around the same time that we lost mom and dad. *And*, he moved here to Isles End about the same time I did. Isn't that kind of amazing?"

Beth waited for a response while her aunt worked on the rest of her chowder. Finally she said, "Yes, I suppose you could say that."

"I met him at work," Beth continued. "He's in charge of the remodeling. And Auntie, he's really nice! I think you'd be very impressed with him."

Beth's aunt pushed the tray away, dabbed her mouth daintily and studied Beth for a moment. "Beth dear, it sounds to me like you are quite infatuated with this gentleman already, and yet you really hardly know him, isn't that right?"

"Sure, I guess I don't know him very well yet, but I feel I can trust him. I'm happy when we're together—he's so sweet. And sometimes, you just know, don't you?" Beth paused, waiting for another thought to surface. "And my boss thinks very highly of him."

"Even so, Beth, don't be hasty! You can't know the character of a man after just a couple dates. You're still very young—and, in fact, quite inexperienced."

Beth stood and reached over to pick up her aunt's tray. "Auntie, I *am* an adult and also a pretty good judge of character.

You mustn't worry about me."

"Just be careful, dear. You know . . . you experienced a great loss not so long ago, and you're still vulnerable, whether you understand this or not. I want you to know there are men out there who will seek out just the right kind of woman whom they think will make easy prey. A woman must be very careful these days. One just never knows the true intentions of strange men!"

Beth's stomach muscles tightened as she carried the trays back into the kitchen and began cleaning up. While she did the dishes, she thought about her time with Harry. Had she been *too hasty?* Could she be wrong about him? She didn't even want to consider it. There was nothing to worry about, she told herself. Her aunt was just being protective and that was all.

She thought about the first time she'd seen Harry in the elevator and how he was so adorably awkward. And then, how special their time had been when he'd come over to her home for dinner. They had discovered they shared so many things in common. The more she thought about him, the more she realized how disarming and warm he was and how relaxed and special he made her feel. Their dinner at Belmar's was another example of how very attentive and kind he was. Everyone there liked him and trusted him, too. She added it all up as she put the last dish into the washer. There was no reason to be concerned about Harry. It was almost as though they were meant to find each other here in Isles End.

"Beth, dear," her aunt called, "Are you through yet?"

"I'm just finishing up."

"Well, you know I ate quickly so we could run some errands."

"I know," Beth answered. "I'm ready."

"I don't mean to hurry you, but I need to pick up some things at the dry cleaners, and also, it's very important that I stop by the bank before they close. I have some funds that need to be deposited today."

"We'll be fine, Auntie—not to worry."

"It's just that—oh my!"

Beth looked to see her aunt tumbling out of her chair.

"Auntie!"

She raced into the other room and began to lift her aunt back up.

"Are you okay?"

"Well, I don't know," the elderly woman responded, wincing in pain. "It's my back! Oh my—I'm afraid it just isn't getting any better."

Beth frowned. "I don't like the look of it, Auntie. I think we ought to be taking you to the hospital instead of the bank!"

"Oh no—I'll be fine," her aunt said with a twisted look. "It's just the way it is, dear. Nothing can be done about it— nothing."

26
Dr. Shushi Yang

Doctor Shushi Yang fidgeted with the buttons on his white coat as he studied the labels on every container that had been delivered. Then he studied them again. He scribbled notes on his clipboard, confirming that every piece of equipment was accounted for. Shushi was always very thorough that way. Measure twice, cut once. He'd heard that said on a construction site years ago and the saying stuck. He scanned the room. So far, he was very pleased with the progress, but that didn't mean he had to let anyone else know it.

Keep the pressure on!

That was the only way to guarantee results. Shushi knew this from experience. As long as he maintained a constant level of energetic obsession, he knew it would be contagious. If he appeared a little neurotic, they would have a higher level of respectful fear for him, and that was a good thing. Of course they all had the same goal, but there was no doubt in his mind that he alone truly understood the nature and scope of their work.

Of course he knew that money played a strong role in the motivations of men, and this effort was sure to create plenty of that. But while the men he competed against and worked with on this project could certainly find more toys to buy, they did not need any more money. Recognition and fame played a larger role for those in the forefront. *And let's not forget about power*, he reminded himself. Shushi had seen it many times, the leaders motivated by appreciation and acknowledgment, those who strategized and struggled to keep their heads above the crowd would gladly soak up the spotlight . . . while he remained in the shadows. It was okay. Shushi actually preferred it that way. For Shushi Yang, none of those things mattered. It was the mystery itself—or rather, the unraveling of a mystery and the ways it could change the destiny of mankind—which truly intrigued Shushi. Somehow the idea sounded funny, but it was terribly true.

But for now, there were more serious things to consider. Simply put, Shushi struggled with the very fine line between the good and the bad. The beautiful and wondrous possibilities on the one hand, and the potential for dangerous and disastrous calamity on the other. When it came to genetic engineering, there was, of course, the obvious good: finding cures for disease and illnesses, replacing defective body parts, and giving people a quality of life who otherwise would never know what it meant. There was also the world hunger issue: raising crops that were larger and more abundant, growing virus resistant crops, and genetically altering food products to make them grow faster and with higher nutritional value.

But what about the potential dangers of unknown variables? The long-term effects? Shushi was well aware that tampering with genes might interfere with the most natural patterns of the earth, at the most fundamental and dangerous levels. The basic chemical codes of genes determine the physical nature of all living things. Shushi wondered how many people were aware of the plant-animal hybrids that already existed and could be on the shelves soon. Tomatoes containing fish and tobacco. Potatoes containing chicken, moths, and other insects. Corn containing fireflies. In time, other vegetables would very likely include human genes. Of course, having regulations in place to inform the consumer of these minor details was already looking like an uphill battle. Vegetarians might take issue with eating vegetables that contained meat, but what would they think about eating vegetables that were part human being? Again, Shushi wanted to laugh, except that it was all seriously real.

And what new viruses and bacteria could be created by geneticists and released without any regulation at all? Shushi had recently said to Bill Algren that the level of molecular breeding currently surging forward around the world was enough to make a timid, aging Buddhist reconsider and propose mass murder. Bill didn't laugh. The issues surrounding germ and biowarfare—and now bioterrorism—were all too chilling to think about.

What the problem boiled down to was that the miracle of biotechnology could also be spawning a terrible monster, and Shushi knew he was on board with the cutting edge of the effort.

But to clone a human being!

What a monumental achievement, to actually recreate life, a specific and exact duplicate of a completely unique and one-of-a-kind being.

Mary Shelley had to be turning over in her grave—but with excitement. Shushi laughed aloud at his joke. She had written about bringing a dead body to life, but had she ever thought about the possibility of cloning?

Would they succeed in being the first? Was it possible that, like Dolly the sheep, they might clone a human being who had been dead for six years? Or how about sixty years . . . or maybe six hundred? There was no doubt in Shushi's mind—he was sure of it.

But who would be the candidate?

Of course they had talked about it. Even joked about who could be cloned. The joking, however, had a serious edge to it, considering the possibilities were so close to becoming reality. The names of many great thinkers had been bandied about, as well as many celebrated artists, writers, and poets. They had, in fact, a long list of great men and women with great ideas and renowned talents. With the right DNA available, anyone—dead or alive—was a potential nominee. Of course, they had thrilled themselves through many conversations with the idea of cloning some of their favorites, such great minds as Plato or Aristotle. Or how about more contemporary thinkers such as Einstein and Edison? World leaders like Ghandi, Washington, Lincoln, Jefferson, or even Ronald Reagan and Martin Luther King? Artists and musicians like Da Vinci, Mozart, and Van Gogh, poets such as Keats, Yeats, Wilde, Dickinson and Blake—really, the list was endless.

Bill said he liked the idea of having ten other Preston Harts available to do his bidding with the same mild-mannered efficiency. But who of the living would want a duplicate of themselves walking around? And would the clones be identical in genes only, or would the cloned human naturally have the same talents, interests, and even personalities as the original? They would certainly have the same brain, with the same available aptitudes and capacity for greatness. Still, nobody knew for sure, yet. Cloning replacement organs for specific individuals was one thing, but when recreating an entire person, they would have to be considered as an individual with rights, wouldn't they?

Then there was the idea of adding a DNA mix of one or more other individuals to your next offspring. In the same way DNA could already be added to specific plants, human DNA could also potentially be added to other humans. Would parents soon be considering not only the choices of potential eye and hair color or height, but additionally, a small measure of borrowed greatness to be added to their natural gene pool? Hoping to raise a math wizard with an artistic side? How about a DNA cocktail to include a little Einstein or Steven Hawking along with some Picasso and Rembrandt? And for added beauty … the list was endless. What parent wouldn't want a brighter, taller, healthier, and more attractive child?

I'd like you to meet my son, Billy Einstein Da Vinci Cruise Smith!

Yes, things could get out of hand. But that was where

men like Shushi would continue to play a large part in the process. Someone would have to take responsibility for some level of rational control, some fundamental rules and guidelines for the industry to follow—that is, if it wasn't already too late.

But they *had* rushed ahead, avoiding many safety precautions just to reach their goals on time.

They were rushing now!

Shushi wasn't in a hurry to make mistakes, but it was a race that he desperately wanted to win, at almost any cost, and to a large degree had already won.

Shushi headed back towards his office to make himself a cup of tea and get back to work. He knew that if they were going to be ready, he needed to review every bit of information they had gathered to date. His team would be relying on his preparedness to move them forward, and this would be happening at a rapid pace, very soon. When they found out what Shushi already knew, they would fully realize their position.

In another week they would be having their first meeting in the new building, which would include all of the scientists, as well as Bill Algren and Preston Hart. They would discuss their critical path, make projections for completion of studies, and, also, discuss the grand finale—the preparations for the beginning of a new life. This meeting would also give Shushi the opportunity to share the most recent results of his studies. How would they respond when they found out that Shushi had already discovered the correct equation for their first "Dolly"? The results were conclusive, and so now it was just a matter of putting them into practice. The team would be elated, of course, but that didn't really matter to Shushi. What mattered was that he had the answer and knew it would work.

Shushi knew the best place for him to be right now was in his office where he would not be disturbed or distracted. He arrived without any interruptions along the way. There were only a couple of polite hellos from staff people who knew better than to interrupt Dr. Yang with any unnecessary questions.

Once inside, Shushi went to his personal sink and filled a cup with instant boiling water, one of the small perks that the head scientist was allowed. The small degree of clutter surrounding him was annoying, but understandable under the circumstances. Moving was always a chore, and although Shushi was meticulous when it came to his lab, he wasn't quite as concerned about his office space. Moving past the mess, he dropped a bag of black chai tea into his cup and added two tablespoons of blackberry honey. Now he was ready to focus. He sat down, lifted his teacup to his lips and sipped. A mild rapping on his door disturbed his swallow. Before he had a chance to say a word, the door opened.

"Well, Shushi," came the calm friendly voice of William Algren. "Sorry I didn't buzz you first. I was passing by and realized that I wanted to talk to you before I left for the day."

"No problem," Shushi responded with a mild huff. He did not like to be interrupted, even by the head of the company.

"What is it you wish to discuss?"

"Oh, it's nothing specific. I haven't seen you for a couple of days and I wanted to know how you're holding up—make sure you have everything you need."

"I am fine," Shushi responded, pushing the thick mop of white hair away from his forehead, "I've been staying busy and trying to remain focused until we can resume our work. That's all."

"I know, Shushi—you've been great," Bill said, pulling up a chair, "and I want you to know how much I have appreciated your patience during this relocation period. I know it hasn't been easy."

Bill paused to give Shushi a chance to sip his tea. "I also wanted to ask you, how do you feel about our steps forward?"

The doctor had already planned the answer for this question. He'd already heard it, posed ten different ways. Bill would hear the good news soon enough, but not just yet . . .

"So far, I'm impressed," Shushi said, leaning back in his chair. "You know I was really concerned at one point about losing our momentum. But now the progress we are making looks very good, though I'd prefer you didn't share this tidbit with anyone else just yet."

"I know, Shushi, I know." Bill's leathery features seemed to send a message of understanding and his eyes showed sympathy for his colleague. "You want to keep everyone on their toes. But you have to remember; it's part of my job to encourage our staff and make them feel positive about our developments."

Shushi smiled pensively. "Yes, Bill, you do your job well. Maybe a little too well with some."

Bill looked puzzled and then gave a hint of a grin. "Okay, Shushi, what's going on?"

"Well, you might want to pull in the reins on your sidekick, just a little bit."

"Is Preston getting under your skin again?"

"Nothing that I can't handle. If anything, he is *too* positive."

"Shushi, you're annoyed!"

"Is that a big surprise?"

"No."

Shushi straightened his coat as he leaned forward in his chair. "Preston seems to have more energy at times than he knows what to do with, and it does tend to spill over—"

"—and become irritating," Bill finished for him.

"Well, if you say so."

"Shushi," Bill began, "you and Preston have worked together for quite a while now. I'm sure you can maintain a cohesive and professional relationship as long as—"

"Of course we can," Shushi interrupted. "I make the effort on a regular basis. What I'm saying is maybe you can give him a little warning—a subtle suggestion—which will hopefully allow me to do my job and move freely without his friendly interference. If you can manage that, then I won't have to do it myself—and I promise I won't ask for anything else."

"I understand, Shushi. Not to worry. I'll have a talk with him in such a way that he won't even realize we had the talk."

"Perfect. Now how about our upcoming meeting?"

"Yes?"

"You know I'm doing everything I can to be ready—"

"Yes, and you're doing a phenomenal job!"

"What I'm getting at, Bill, is the name, or list of names for our potential candidate."

"Shushi . . ?"

Dr. Yang's soft features tightened. "When are you going to tell me the name?"

"The name . . ."

"Yes!"

"I never said I was going to share that information at the meeting."

"You inferred—"

"Listen, Shushi," Bill leaned forward, his eyes narrowing in on the smaller white haired man—friendly, but focused. "The truth is, I don't know yet. We have narrowed the list down to just a few nominees but nothing conclusive so far. The decision may very well have more to do with genetic qualities. Our choice may be someone who has never been heard of. We're still waiting on more information from several sources before we can make a final confirmation. This will be, as you know, a very important decision. It has taken a lot of thought. But even if I *did* have that knowledge, I couldn't share it with you just yet. You know that."

"I do not know that!" Shushi countered with controlled frustration. "I don't understand it, nor do I agree with it. I am the lead scientist. If anyone should know, it ought to be *me!"*

"Please, my dear doctor, you have to understand the concerns we have. We've been over this before. This information is basically . . . no, it's *completely* clandestine, at least until we have actually succeeded with our mission. Until then, no one, not even those with whom we are consulting, can know the name of our candidate. Soon we will make several DNA purchases. Once they are in our possession, we will decide which to use, thereby keeping our final decision completely hidden. We've taken all of your ideas into consideration, and everyone else's, too. That's it, Shushi. Let's be reasonable and not make an issue out if this. You must be patient, my friend. There are many things at stake here. I think you understand what I mean.

The still-angry look on Shushi's face communicated everything his silence did not.

"Look, Shushi, here's what's going to happen," Bill continued persuasively. " You will do your usual excellent job regardless of the origin of the DNA sample we choose. We will move forward without a glitch. When the time is right, you will be the first to know. Don't let this become a stumbling block for you. The answer to your question isn't really the important issue. I know this is difficult for you, but I implore you—you must trust me through this!"

"And you must trust me, Bill!"

"Shushi, you know that I do."

The doctor fiddled with the top button on his collar as he stared back at Bill. His face would have been nearly unreadable to the average person, but Bill could see the tumultuous battle between irritation and acceptance brewing just beneath the surface. Bill recognized this as a signal to turn the conversation onto a positive track but in a fashion that would achieve far superior results than Preston's cheerleading style of encouragement.

"Shushi, we are on the brink of greatness. You know that! And you are instrumental in the process. Yes, there are many spokes in this wheel, but you are the primary core. Without you, we could not turn. I want you to excel like you never have before. I want you to focus like you are on the final leg of your life's quest. Put this insignificant issue behind you, really, for your own good, and prepare yourself for something that few men will ever know. I'm counting on you, Shushi, and I have full faith that you are the one person who can and will achieve this greatness that you so unequivocally deserve."

Shushi studied Bill's face warily. "You're not trying to pull a 'Preston' on me, are you, Bill?"

"Heavens, no," Bill erupted with a short burst of laughter. "You know me better than that—don't you?"

"Alright. You have me genuinely motivated now—not that I needed it, but I *am* anxious to get some work done."

"By all means. Carry on, my friend," Bill said, standing to exit. "I'll leave you to your work and catch up with you later."

"Thank you," Shushi answered, turning to a stack of papers.

Bill closed the door quietly and Shushi leaned back in his chair. He considered Algren's words.

They all underestimate me!

Was he truly the primary hub of the wheel? Did he really deserve greatness? Well, if he *was* the chess master as Bill had once suggested, then Bill was in for a few surprise moves. The simple fact was that Shushi was ready now, but he was not about to move any piece into its final position without knowing its origin. The very idea was ludicrous. Before he ever made the final move to breathe life into anything, he would know who and what it was. Fortunately, he had his own means of gathering information. Soon, he would know everything Bill knew.

He put his teacup to his mouth and tipped it up.

"Cold," he mumbled and got up to make a fresh cup.

27
Don't Panic!

The elevator suddenly seemed very small as Harry considered his position. He felt trapped and nauseous in the confined space. If he couldn't find a button to go up, his only alternative was back down to where he had already been—not a great option. As he leaned forward, studying the panel, he had the uncomfortable feeling that the small room was closing in on him.

Don't panic!

Harry reminded himself that he wasn't claustrophobic as he began to break out in a sweat. He'd worked in many cramped places in construction without any problems, but the need to get out of this elevator was growing rapidly.

Where was Rachael?

He leaned forward and studied the controls on the elevator panel again and pressed the button for the next floor down. Was anything happening? Yes. He could feel the elevator moving. Before he knew it, the doors opened and he wasted no time getting out. He stood there in the dimly lit hallway and waited for the door to close. He didn't want to go back to his room. The taste of her still lingered, but it was accompanied with regret. What if Rachael had returned for him while he'd been looking for her?

He hurried down the hallway to his door and reluctantly went inside. The room was empty. He walked back to the elevator door. Only a few steps away, he saw what he was looking for—the door to the stairs. Why hadn't he noticed it before? He opened the door and peered inside. The stairwell was noticeably brighter than what the hallway offered. He knew he could go down, but did he really want to go *up?* He let the door pull itself closed behind him as he started up the stairs. Another door . . . okay. He didn't really want to open it, guessing it was the entrance to the floor he had just left. Why hadn't he noticed a door when he was up there?

But here, the stairs continued up!

He turned away from the door and cautiously climbed up the next flight of stairs.

Another door!

Or was it? In shape and size it resembled a door but there was no knob, and the surface was gray and rough. He ran his hands over the finish. It was cool and surprisingly damp. He pushed lightly to see if it might open. Nothing. He felt around the edges looking for some kind of latch or grip. Still nothing.

What now?

This unusual entryway must open somehow. Harry pressed both hands against the coarse face of the door as he considered his options. Thinking he was ready to give up and return to his room, he pulled back, but his hands had somehow fused themselves to the irregular surface. He was abruptly inundated with such a disturbing sense of dread that he fought to stifle a yell. A dull ache radiating from the stony material traveled up through both his arms with increasing agony. It was more than just physical. This pain was accompanied by a deeper burden of mental depression. It closed in around him, enveloping his thoughts and oppressing his will. As the invisible assault increased, Harry began to yield to the crushing force.

But then something in him rose up and began to fight back. A courageous sense of defiance he had never fully realized before caused him to resist with conviction. A fresh surge of strength increased his resolve and he regained focus. He recognized with a new clarity, the source of the pain. Of course, it was the door! With a renewed sense of power, he ripped himself free and stumbled back furiously rubbing his hands on his legs.

Then . . . he panicked!

Harry staggered away from the dark slab, nearly falling over. He tumbled down the stairway like an animal fleeing a trap. Barely maintaining control he reached the floor where his room was located, but he kept spiraling down. Around and around he circled downward, flying, jumping several steps at a time. Desperate, he continued in a frenzied flight, his hands and arms aching. He had only one goal, escaping whatever it was that had just nearly overpowered him. What sort of sinister things were at work here? Harry could not guess, but he knew he must get as far away as possible.

How many floors had he descended? He had no idea. As fatigue set in, he began to slow down just a little to keep from falling over himself. Turning corner after corner, Harry finally lost his balance and plunged into a doorway on one of the turns landing hard on the concrete platform. He gathered his senses and reaching for the doorknob he pulled himself up. There, on the door, were the words, "Street Level." Feeling the panic rise again, he tore the door open and flung himself out onto the pavement. He raced forward blindly and found himself on a collision course with a tall, raggedy man holding a cardboard sign. It was too late to stop. Harry tried to soften the blow by ducking down, but doing so only made the impact worse. He plowed into the man like a bowling ball.

Immediately following the collision, Harry's momentum was halted abruptly by an all-too-rigid parking meter. His victim was sprawled out in the gutter, partially under the front end of a parked car. The pain from the fall almost matched the throbbing that still burned in his hands and arms. Harry had never been struck by lightning but he wondered if it felt anything like the way he felt now. He attempted to pull himself up and realized he couldn't see clearly. He slumped back down and let out a deep groan. It was the culminating gasp of the day. He felt sick again. He was sick about Beth and the idea of her seeing anyone else. He was confused and agitated by Rachael's disappearing act. He was angry with the fool who lied to him up on the floor where Rachael's apartment was supposed to have been. And now he was in extreme pain, his arms aching from some horror he had no understanding of. He felt like he'd been hit by a Mac truck, and as he lay there half stunned, he wasn't sure he even wanted to live to tell about it.

And now, who was this oaf who had to be in the wrong place at the wrong time, at this hour of the night? As if to answer the question, he heard the man speaking.

"Are you hurt?" he heard a voice asking politely.

"Am I hurt? What do you think?"

"Here, let me help you up." The man's tone was gentle, almost soothing.

Harry could feel the stranger's hands reaching under his arms in an attempt to lift him up, and it was instantly painful.

"Hold it," Harry blurted out.

The man relaxed his grip.

"I don't need your help," Harry muttered. All his anger felt like it was ready to explode. "Just give me some space!"

"I'm sorry," the stranger answered.

"Well, didn't you see me coming? I don't know what you're doing just standing around on the sidewalk at this hour."

"It's not that late, friend."

"Well it's dark. And I'm not your friend! Why are you out begging after dark, anyway?" Harry continued his assault. "Do you think that anyone can even read your cardboard message or that anyone really cares to read it?"

Harry had seen this type before, unshaven and dirty looking guys with poorly scrawled messages on scraps of cardboard. "Homeless and hungry, please help—bless you."

Translated, what they really meant was, "Will accept your hard earned money for alcohol, drugs, and tobacco. Thanks, chump." He generally looked on these beggars with some disdain, never giving them a dime for fear of encouraging their profession, convinced that most of them had come to depend on the good will of the naive who somehow believed they were actually helping by giving them a hand-out. Harry wondered how many bleeding hearts allowed themselves to think they were performing some kind of good deed when, really, their giving was an effort to feel good about themselves.

"I apologize," he heard the man responding. "I've had a rather difficult evening myself. I wasn't begging."

"Look," Harry said, gripping the meter pole and pulling himself up, "Just keep your hands off me."

Harry could still feel the burning sensation in his arms but it was beginning to subside. He rubbed his eyes hard for a moment while he stood there hunched over the parking meter like a cripple. When he was able to see clearly again, he lifted his head and glanced around to get a better look at the homeless man he had run over, but he had disappeared! Strange, he hadn't heard him leave.

Bitter regret swept over Harry. After all, it was he who had caused the accident. He had acted in a foul and vulgar manner. It was just one more thing to be agitated about, except this time he was angry with himself. The man had been plowed over from out of nowhere, and when the poor guy tried to help, he was rebuked. Harry winced at his own insensitivity. He realized he couldn't feel badly about everyone who got hurt simply by being in the way, but, still . . . he felt he owed the fellow an apology.

Night had fallen and Harry wondered what to do now. There was no way he wanted to return to his room. After what had happened up there, he didn't want to have anything to do with that building. He was even unsure about going back to the parking level for his truck, but what else could he do at this point?

Again, Harry looked around for the missing homeless man. He still couldn't get over the stranger's sudden disappearance, and he was feeling even worse now about his own behavior. He shook his arms and rubbed his hands together in an effort to relieve some of the lingering pain. As he gathered his thoughts together he realized there was something strangely familiar about the ragged beggar. He'd hardly had a chance to really look at the man but now it was the voice that had Harry puzzled. He thought for a moment. A visual image of the stranger's face began to appear in Harry's mind. Did he actually know him?

Narcissus?

No! Was it possible? Why would the angel visit him dressed like a vagrant? The more he thought about it though, the clearer it became.

It *was* Narcissus with whom he had collided—but why?

Harry looked up and down the street again to see if he could find his angelic friend but the streets were deserted. He walked down the sidewalk to the corner and peered in both directions. There was no one in sight. Of course Harry knew that Narcissus would not have to walk anywhere to get away. He felt more confused than ever.

Limping back to where he had fallen, Harry noticed something. There, in the gutter, half hidden under the front of a car, he could see the corner of a section of cardboard. He lifted it and held it up in front of him. It read, "Will work for friends." What? He flipped it over and on the other side, in smaller letters, there was more— "Be careful, Harry."

Be careful? It WAS Narcissus!

But where had he gone? Harry was filled with a barrage of questions that wouldn't quit. Why would Narcissus visit him in disguise and then leave so abruptly? He wished he had responded differently and wondered if he would have recognized the Seraph if he had let the angel help him up. But why had Narcissus departed so suddenly, especially when Harry really could have used some help? Now he felt even more discouraged. When he really needed help, Narcissus had disappeared.

And again the question, where was Rachael?

Nothing made sense.

A feeling of shame and disappointment came over Harry as he stood there silently aching. He looked up at the dark building next to him that had denied him entry to the top floor and looked terribly menacing now. He would just have to go find his truck and drive home.

Then he remembered his suitcase was still back up in his room. The last thing he wanted to do was go back inside, but he had to have his things.

Be careful, Harry! The cardboard sign shouted a warning to him.

Harry took the sign and hurried to the parking area. He found his truck and placed the cardboard inside the cab. Then he took the elevator back up to his room. All was quiet as he walked down the dark hallway. He wondered if he might find Rachael finally, but the suite was still empty. Though his head ached horribly, he felt better as he gathered his things.

It occurred to him that he had Rachael's phone number logged into his cell phone. Why hadn't he thought of it before? He scrolled down to her name and pressed the button. He waited for her response but instead heard her recorded message. Well, at least he could leave her a voice mail. The message was brief; he was leaving and hoped she was all right. Then he wondered if he should have called the police? What if she had run into some trouble? But he realized immediately that the police would do nothing about someone who was late for a dinner appointment. He decided he could check with the pale man in the lobby, so he left the suite with a sense of relief.

Once Harry was back in the elevator, he pressed the button that said "Lobby" and waited a few moments until the door opened. He stepped out into the large marble room but there was no one around. It seemed strange that the place was so deserted. Sure, it was a bit late but, still, was it unusual that there were no people stirring anywhere? The entire building could not be vacant! Yet Harry realized the parking garage was mostly empty too, as he steered his pickup truck out onto the street.

It would have been nice to find Narcissus waiting for him at the exit, or on the corner, or a block down the street. After a mile or so, he gave up on getting any help from the angel. He needed to make a plan of his own. The idea of driving back to Isles End tonight was not very attractive. Pulling off the road, Harry made sure his doors were locked and closed his eyes.

28
A Visit with Gwen

It suddenly occurred to Harry that maybe he could stay with his sister, Gwen.

Of course!

He got his cell phone out again and waited while it rang.

"Hello?"

"Hey, Gwen, it's Harry."

"Harry! What a surprise! How are you?"

"I'm fine, and I happen to be close by."

"Are you really? What are you doing?"

"It's a long story. I was calling to see if you would be interested in putting me up for the night."

"Of course, Harry, I'd love to have you over," Gwen responded excitedly, adding with a touch of concern, "Are you okay?"

"Yeah, I'm fine. How are you doing?"

"Me? Oh, I'm doing okay. Just being a home-body tonight—no plans or anything. I've really missed you!"

"Well," Harry said, "I'm not too far away. I could be there in twenty minutes."

"Really? So get over here. I've got the guest room all tidied up. I'm so glad you called!"

"Okay, I'll see you in a bit," Harry replied, and pressed END.

This was *perfect*. Her home was nearby in the area where they had grown up and she worked at a local pharmacy. He had been missing her already and felt bad coming up and not making plans to see her. There was some guilt too, about not keeping in touch, but he *had* been busy . . .

As he drove across town, old memories surfaced as certain landmarks and roads became familiar. The anticipation of seeing Gwen helped him to relax while the pain in his head and arms receded.

The idea of talking to her about his latest activities had crossed his mind before and he was thinking about it again as he neared her house. There had been several times already when Harry had nearly called and told her everything. Each time, however, he had decided against it. Why cause her more heartache and concern than she was already carrying for him? So once again he decided to keep silent. Besides, there were other things he could share. Gwen would be thrilled to hear about Beth.

With a stab, Harry remembered what Rachael had told him. Could Beth really be seeing someone else? What would he tell his sister now?

I've been seeing this woman I really like, but she might still be dating someone else?

The idea of trying to explain all that was not very appealing, either. But then again, maybe it *would* be good to talk to Gwen about Beth. She had always given good advice in the past.

I kissed another woman tonight . . .

Harry tried to focus on the present. Gwen's house looked exactly as it always did. Not very visible from the street, the yard was surrounded by a tall green hedge. Once up the driveway and into the yard, it was like a garden somewhere out in the country. The Victorian home was painted a dark green and practically blended into the rest of the yard.

Harry parked and went up to the front door. He smiled as he pushed the nose on the elf and heard the door bell ring inside. Just as the door opened, a gust of wind picked up and the chimes that hung from the gutters began to ring out their happy announcement that he had arrived.

"He arrives with a song," Gwen grinned as she stood in the doorway sizing up her brother.

"Hi, sis," Harry greeted her, opening his arms wide.

They shared a long hug and then went inside.

"Glad I caught you at home," Harry told his sister. Though tired, he felt extraordinarily happy to see her.

"It's nice to see your smiling face, Harry. You look a bit frazzled, but good—you know, healthy, like you've been eating," she said. "It's a little past meal time but I've got some hot food ready anyway. Have you had dinner?"

"Actually, no, and I'm starving!"

Harry had completely forgotten about the dinner plans that had fallen through. The pain in his body had made him weak and a hot meal sounded pretty good.

"So," he asked her, trying to sound casual, "what are you doing home alone on a weekend?"

"Oh, I originally had plans to go out with a girlfriend from work, but she came down with something. I've been working on this photo album for some time and I decided to stay home tonight and see if I could make some progress. I mentioned it to you a while back, Harry—do you remember? I think there are several pictures here you've never seen."

"I remember," Harry said. "I wasn't sure that I wanted to see them, if I recall correctly."

"I know," his sister responded. "I just thought at the time that it might do you some good. You know, maybe seeing some photos of Jen, and Mom and Dad, might help."

"Hmm, help me sink into the past," Harry added. "But then, you might be right. Maybe it'll be good for me."

Gwen pulled a chair closer to the coffee table and motioned for Harry to sit.

"Sorting these photos," she said, "has helped me accept what happened and face the reality that they are gone. Finally, putting together this photo album gives me peace, Harry." She looked at him with a half sorrowful smile. "But that doesn't mean I don't miss them. I do—but let's get some food on a plate first. Then we can talk."

Harry joined Gwen in the kitchen. Soon, they had the table set with spaghetti, garlic bread, and chardonnay.

"So, what do you mean . . . the pictures give you peace?"

Harry asked, as he sprinkled parmesan cheese over his plate. "I thought you recovered, so to speak, a long time ago."

"No, Harry, are you kidding me? I still struggle," she admitted, pausing to sip her wine. "I guess I have a different way of dealing with things. I tend to keep busy during difficult times. I want to know the troubles of others. I guess it helps me take the focus off of myself. You know me—I don't like to burden anyone, especially my little brother, with my own loss. I mean, we both lost people very dear to us and I think we were able to lean on each other for a while. But your loss was greater—you know that, don't you? And it's okay, we both understand that's the way it is."

"Sure, I understand."

"Okay, so I'm not going to keep giving you the same pep talk, except to say that I'm sure they would all want us both to move forward, live our lives, and find happiness."

"I know, Gwen, and that's exactly what I've been doing. I know it's probably hard for you to believe, but even recently I really have been moving forward."

At least, trying to—

"I'm really glad to hear that, and . . . Harry! What has happened to your arms?" Gwen seemed to forget what she was saying as she noticed the marks on his forearms.

"Huh? Oh, that." Harry tried to play dumb. He hadn't noticed it, but both his arms were quite bruised, all the way up the insides from his wrists to his biceps. He quickly found an excuse. "I was moving a very heavy piano and some other things recently on a job I'm doing. I guess I overexerted myself—"

"It doesn't look very good, Harry. I've never seen anything quite like that before. Are you sure you're okay?"

"I'm fine—really! It looks worse than it is."

"Alright then, if you say so. But what brings you up here tonight?"

"Oh." Harry's mind continued to scramble. He didn't really want to talk about it. In fact, he preferred to forget the whole evening. "I was here on business, looking at some buildings in Old Towne. I'm working for someone who wants the same type of building designs down in Isles End. It's a new project I've taken on. We're just in the beginning stages."

"That sounds great!"

"Yeah, I've actually got several projects right now.

"Also, I guess I can tell you—I met someone recently. We've been out a couple of times. I think you'd like her."

Gwen perked up. "Really? That's wonderful."

"It's still pretty new. Who knows where it will go—"

"Even so, Harry, I'm thrilled to know you are getting out and meeting people. *And dating!* Tell me about her."

Harry described Beth, giving Gwen the basics: where they met, and a few other details.

"She sounds very nice, Harry. I've been seeing someone too. His name is Michael, and he works in the music store across from the pharmacy. We've been going out for a few months now, and he's been really great."

Harry already liked him. He could tell, listening to Gwen, that she was happy. There was a gleam in her eye when she said Michael's name. Harry had a strong feeling, even though Gwen would never admit it, that she had avoided relationships for quite a while after the accident so that she could be there for him. This news was good. Harry might not feel like such a burden to her.

"So, what do you say, little brother, are you ready to look at some pictures? You don't have to, you know."

"Sure, I'll give it a try, sis," he replied, finishing up his meal. He wasn't really sure how he would feel. Was he stronger now with his mantle of strength? There was one way to find out.

They moved over to Gwen's small living room where Harry could see she had been going through pictures. They were spread all over the coffee table in front of the couch. He sat beside her as she organized some folders and switched on a nearby lamp.

"Here, Harry, sit closer to me so we can look at these together. These are the most recent. I took them with a disposable camera the day they went up. I only had them developed a couple weeks ago. Can you believe it?"

She set a stack of prints on the cover of a photo album that their laps shared. The first one showed his dad and mom standing with Jennifer next to the wing of the small aircraft. Instead of the anticipated pain that Harry was sure he would experience, he felt a surprising feeling of joy. There they were, three big smiles. Jennifer's hair was blowing in the wind—mom's arm around her. His father was holding his mother's hand, and in the other hand—a fat cigar. Harry looked over at Gwen to see tears streaming from her eyes. She looked back at Harry.

"I'm sorry. I wasn't going to do this," she said, wiping her cheeks with her sleeve.

"It's okay, sis—"

"It's just that I realized this is the first time that I have seen the two of you together since before the accident."

What she said sounded strange, but Harry understood what she meant. He flipped the picture over and they looked at several more that had been taken that same day at the airport. Some were from inside the airport café. There were still other shots of Jennifer trying on different wedding gowns.

"Oh, Harry, we can skip over these, I forgot—"

"I'm fine," he assured her. "I want to see them."

The more pictures Harry saw of Jennifer and his parents, the more he realized that his sister was right. The photos were having a positive effect on him. He had no tears and felt increasingly stronger. Gwen, on the other hand, had enough tears for the both of them.

"I'm sorry, Harry," she kept apologizing.

"It's okay," he reassured her. "Just let it all out."

They sat there until late into the evening, looking at photos dating back to their youth. Harry felt like they were time traveling, as though they'd left the room and were moving through the supernatural, like he'd done with Narcissus.

When Harry saw his sister's eyes close and stay shut, he helped her up and walked her to her room. She was already in her nightgown, so he tucked her in like she used to do with him.

"Harry," she said when he kissed her goodnight. "Yes?"

"I had a dream about you."

"Really?"

"Yes. You were flying, somewhere—"

"You mean in a plane?"

"No. You were using your arms."

"Hmm—?"

"Good night, Harry."

"Good night, Gwen."

He cleaned up the dinner dishes, left the pictures on the coffee table, and retired to the guest room. So, his sister dreamt that he was flying? What could that possibly mean? Well, he was too tired to worry about it. The bed was comfortable and it felt good to finally lie down.

The peace he felt was surprising. Gwen always had that effect on him, putting things into perspective. After all that had happened that day, he was surprised to find himself so ready to put it all to rest.

Just before losing consciousness, his angelic friend came to mind, and a sense of concern began to surface. "Narcissus," he heard himself speak in a whisper, "Why didn't you stay and help me tonight? I don't know why you were there, but you could have at least explained things to me."

Could you visit me tonight?

The next morning, he awoke to the smell of bacon. He could hear Gwen singing softly in the kitchen like she always did when she cooked. Now there was coffee in the mix. Were there fried potatoes and onions too? He couldn't decide if he wanted to get up right away and see for himself what was on the stove, or just lie there and enjoy the smells that were drifting into his room from the kitchen. Finally he decided to get up. Hopping out of bed he threw on a robe his sister had laid out, and headed to the kitchen.

"Good morning, Harry!" Gwen said cheerfully.

"Hi, sis."

"How did you sleep?"

"Like a baby."

"Hungry?"

"Oh yeah!"

"Well, you've come to the right place!"

"Need any help?" he offered.

"No. Everything's under control. You just get yourself a cup of coffee—the cream's over there—and find yourself a comfortable place to sit."

"Yes, Captain."

"You haven't called me Captain in years, Harry!"

"Well, then it's long overdue!"

Harry found a chair and sat down, tipping it back so he could put his feet on the kitchen table. "So, what was it you were dreaming about...me flying?"

"What?"

"Last night when I tucked you in, you mentioned a dream where I was flying, with my arms."

"Oh, I remember now. I was staying somewhere, looking out the window, and suddenly I saw you up in the air with your arms outstretched, gliding down from a taller building. I had this sense that you were trying to escape from somewhere, but you didn't seem too troubled—you were smiling. Then I saw someone on a roof nearby waving to you. You flew down and landed right next to him."

"Wow...is that all?"

"No. I watched while you spoke with the man for a while. Then you both just disappeared.

This is really strange!

Harry looked at his sister with an anxious expression. "Well? What then?"

"That's all I remember, except I had this funny feeling that you were okay—like, you were leaving on some adventure and I wasn't worried about you."

If you only knew!

"Harry? You have a funny look on your face! Does it mean anything to you? You know, sometimes I wonder if my dreams have a deeper implication or if they are just a bunch of nonsense."

"I don't know much about dreams, but I've had some flying dreams lately!" Harry had never heard of anything like this before. How could she have such information? Now he wanted to tell her everything. Did Narcissus have something to do with this? What else could explain his sister's ability to connect with him in a dream? Unless there was some strange ability that siblings might potentially share? He had no idea where to begin and decided to wait until he felt stronger. "Gwen, you know I've always had flying dreams. You just finally incorporated the idea into your own dreams."

"Is that so?" Gwen responded with a quizzical look. "I guess that makes pretty good sense. But I mean, dreams can mean other things right? Like they can be metaphors, you know?"

Harry thought about it. If he was careful, he could do this. "Yeah, I think your dreams can tell you things about yourself. Like in this dream, my first idea would be that you saw me flying, which could be compared to me moving away after the accident, and you said that I seemed to be escaping—that makes sense. As far as me meeting someone on a roof and then disappearing, maybe you were imagining me meeting new people and moving on—just an idea. Either way, you were probably worried about me and this was a way to put your mind at ease."

"Harry, you should have been a psychologist!"

"Well, that one was easy," Harry said, still perplexed by

his sister's revelation. He wanted to continue the conversation without giving anything away.

"My dreams have never seemed to do much more than keep me from waking up. Like, if I'm hungry, I dream of food. If a dog is barking outside, there's a dog in my dream. Or if music is playing, I might find myself at a concert."

"Really, Harry! Now I know why it's always been so hard to wake you up! But, still, I'm wondering. Is there something more to dreaming, like some kind of spiritual aspect of it?"

"I really don't know," Harry interrupted. "Hey, looks like that food is about ready—"

"Why don't you grab a couple of plates from over there," Gwen pointed.

She served up a healthy serving of bacon, eggs, and fried potatoes, while Harry filled his cup with more coffee.

"So, when are you going to invite me down to visit you, Harry? You know it's been a while."

"I knew you were going to ask me that. Anytime, really. You know you are always welcome."

"Really?" Gwen sounded surprised. She had tried to arrange a visit several times before but it had never been the right time. "You *have* moved forward, haven't you!"

"I think so."

"Maybe I will have a chance to meet this new friend of yours—Beth?"

"Oh," Harry paused from chewing. "Sure, we could

probably figure something out." He hoped things would work out with Beth and still wondered if there was good reason to be worried. It seemed like a long time since he'd seen her. The relationship was so new, and felt so sweet, but considering the things that Rachael had shared recently, he was unsure.

They finished breakfast and Harry helped his sister clean up again. There were a few things to sort out, but doing the dishes with Gwen made life seem normal for the moment. He could have stayed all day, but Gwen had to work and Harry had his own business in Isles End. Gathering up his things Harry promised his sister he would call her soon and make plans to have her down for a visit.

Pulling out of her driveway Harry realized he wasn't sure what he would find back in Isles End. He followed her several blocks and waved goodbye as they turned to go their separate ways.

29
In the Master's Chamber

"Alright," Abaddon whispered darkly, "tell me everything."

The reservation in the demon's voice made him all the more daunting to the host of devils that gathered around him in quiet submission. Deep under the foundations of Advanced Bio-Cell, they met in the dark room, a place designed for privacy. Being the deepest of all the quarters in the red prince's domain, his lair was well-guarded and safe from uninvited guests or any prying ears that might become too curious.

Rull stood to Abaddon's right and Jinn to his left. Eight other shadowy spirits circled them mutely, intent to hear every spoken word. In the center was Scratch who looked as though he had been horribly beaten.

"You want to hear everything?" Scratch moaned. "Where shall I begin?"

"First," Abaddon's eyes narrowed, "before we go any further let me say we've been very surprised with your abilities. You've surpassed our expectations. In fact, it's almost as though you had some rather extensive training prior to joining us. We know we did not send a novice to do the work of a professional, and so we are sorry to find you under these difficult circumstances. However, I assure you, we will get to the bottom of this, and someone will be held accountable. But before you give us your report, do you know the whereabouts of Gorguol?"

Scratch looked squarely into Abaddon's eyes. "I do not."

"I see," Abaddon continued. "Can you tell me where he was last seen?"

"Of course—in his penthouse. You remember his new accommodations?"

"Yes, and his latest business?"

"The usual—he was working with the head attorneys of a law firm. But other than that, I know nothing. He was there when I arrived with Mr. Turner, and then suddenly he was gone."

This was not bad news to Abaddon. He carefully concealed a measure of delight as he considered his verbal strategy.

"Scratch, you have a story for us. Why don't you begin at the point where you left Isles End."

"Yes, I went directly to meet with Gorguol, where I was momentarily detained. This nearly made me late for my appointment with Harry Turner. Once free to pursue Mr. Turner things went quite smoothly."

"Wait," Abaddon raised his arm. "Did Gorguol express any concerns to you about *our* mission?"

"He did have one interesting question," Scratch answered. "He wanted to know why I had been assigned to lure this adamite, Mr. Turner, *away* from Beth Fairbanks when you have groomed her so well already."

"You see what happens," Abaddon responded, "when you are outside the loop and try to second guess a very detailed strategy?"

"And what has been your strategy regarding Miss Fairbanks?" Scratch asked flatly.

"Since it is clearly not apparent to you, my friend, and I'm not saying that I expect that it should be," Abaddon paused with a mixture of vivacity and sarcasm, "I will explain it to you.

"Our first effort has been to confuse Mr. Turner," Abaddon lied. "You see, the more positions we gain around Mr. Turner, the better the chance we have of manipulating him. The more confused he becomes, the more he will rely on someone to whom we have access. That means we will gain his trust through *you*, or we will gain his trust through Rull, who already maintains a strong foothold in Beth Fairbanks."

Abaddon had already decided to name Rull as the operator of Beth Fairbanks. That was of course, a lie, but it worked out nicely as it was Scratch and Gorguol who had wrongly assumed it in the first place.

"Ah, I guessed immediately that it was you, Rull," Scratch interrupted smugly as he turned his crooked smile towards the demon whose smooth mannequin features barely suggested an acknowledgement. "But I'm still confused. Why have you not made an effort to control Harry Turner directly?"

"Of course that has been tried," Abaddon replied, "but he was found to be protected and somehow, 'untouchable.' We have some suspicions as to why . . ."

"Yes, I've heard of cases like this before," Scratch

357

responded, his face still wincing with the pain of his recent beating. "No sign of angelic interference or involvement?"

"Not yet, but that doesn't mean anything."

"Very interesting! But forgive me for interrupting, Lord Abaddon. I need to understand something here. I have been compliant—and will continue as such—but was I groomed as a backup—or a replacement—to supervise Miss Fairbanks?"

"Did you not hear me moments ago? I told you, this is about confusing our opponent!"

Scratch looked down for a moment. "Of course…you speak correctly."

"So then, the answer is precisely both!" Abaddon answered with glee. It appeared that Scratch had bought the lie, and now, whether Gorguol ever returned or not, he seemed to have succeeded in convincing his overseer's assistant that he *was* in control of this situation—so far.

"Very good," Scratch said. "So you have appointed Rull as manipulator of Miss Fairbanks, and I will continue as Miss Sapphire!"

Abaddon smiled sardonically.

"But," Scratch continued, "it seems that you failed at the one thing that should have been the most important item on your list—"

"And what might that be?" Abaddon recoiled.

"NARCISSUS!"

Abaddon struggled to hold back his contempt. "What is it

that I am missing here?" he spat out.

"Pardon me, Sire, allow me to refresh your memory." Scratch let the words out with false humility. "When I signed on, I asked you specifically just how you would be dealing with Narcissus—this was upon Gorguol's request."

"And?"

"You said you were going to deal with him personally! You said that with my assistance you would be liberated to pursue him with greater dedication."

"As I have—"

"AS YOU HAVE NOT!" Scratch snarled back.

"Scratch!" Abaddon's swelling veins glowed under his crimson flesh. "It seems that we have some broken pieces here that need to be put together! You had better tell the rest of your story now, so that we are no longer in the dark—"

"Gladly! I met with Mr. Turner and spent the afternoon with him. All went well. I had his full attention, if you understand my meaning, and quickly had him confused and second guessing the authenticity of Miss Fairbanks' interest in him. You might say that I had him eating out of my hands. You know from your own experience that I am powerfully convincing as a seductive and alluring femme fatale."

Abaddon cringed. "Yes, Scratch—as a woman, you are convincing as well as drop-dead gorgeous! Please continue."

Ironic that such a repellent creature could become so visually stunning in human form!

"We spent the afternoon at the Old Towne wharf and then went up to the room that was provided for Mr. Turner. We nearly had what one might refer to as a romantic interlude. The exchange was most enjoyable . . . I left momentarily to check in with our master who waited in his penthouse above, and I would have returned promptly to continue my work," Scratch's face suddenly twisted in pain, "but I was horribly waylaid!

"Upon entering into my master's chamber, I found Gorguol's personal human host, the head of the firm, unusually confused. Gorguol's presence was not with him, and the bloody fool had no idea what he was doing. I found one of Gorguol's aides and inquired as to our master's whereabouts. He had no answers and neither did any of the other lazy ghouls who were hanging around without supervision. Gorguol had disappeared and none of them knew a thing.

"But what happened next took us all by surprise! Without warning, four formidable beings appeared out of nowhere. You, my Lord, know them all by name. Old friends of ours, you might say—"

"*Narcissus?*" Abaddon asked with reluctant expectation.

"And three more!" Scratch grated. "You remember Ranan? Yes, a most powerful warrior—one of the fiercest. I know personally that he was instrumental in casting you out, once upon a time."

Abaddon contained himself in silence but could not hide his dour expression.

"Ranan was accompanied by Psallo, the musically gifted one, also keenly aggressive and swift with a sword."

"I remember him," Rull interrupted. "An arrogant hack!"

Scratch frowned. "Arrogant, maybe, but he is no hack! You might remember that he's had some time to improve his skills since the last time you encountered him. And finally," Scratch continued, "you will remember the angel, Agalliao. He was the fourth member of their force."

"Yes!" Jinn cut in with a sneer. "The one with the wide, impish grin."

"Yes, but the strange thing, Sire," Scratch continued, turning back to Abaddon, "Narcissus was clearly the leader . . . *and the strongest of them all!* I know he was once a Seraph, but his abilities are more than fully restored, in fact, he is more powerful than ever!"

"What then?" Abaddon urged. His features appeared calm, but underneath there was a maelstrom of rage. His murky scarlet veneer radiated around the room. His emotions were an even balance of hate and pleasure: hate for those who had infiltrated his overseer's keep, and pleasure for the weakness of Gorguol's position. He heard Scratch's voice continue and focused in quickly.

"Everyone scattered," Scratch spat out the words like acid. "The three Cherubim chased after Gorguol's key aides and the rest of the small troop. It was embarrassing the way they fled. Only a few stayed to fight for their master's quarters. It was fortunate for me they did, as Narcissus had actually come for me alone. We tried to band together, and for a moment believed we had the advantage—but there was trickery I did not understand. We were all pulled upward suddenly, away from the fortress, high above into the heavens where we have no authority. We were held there powerless and I could only watch while the others were crushed. I do not know where they were finally sent, but I am sure we will never find them again. Then I was pummeled with such light as I've never seen. The results are obvious! The only reason I was spared . . . to some degree, was to deliver a message to you, directly from Narcissus."

Abaddon studied the smaller demon. Scratch had already been malformed, due to the discipline of Gorguol, but now his features showed further mutilation. Abaddon recognized these specific wounds being the result of more than just exposure to light. They were the consequence of being flouted and jeered at. Even a devil such as Scratch was still a proud spirit and could not endure ridicule or failure.

"And his message to me . . . *WHAT IS IT?"* Abaddon growled impatiently.

"You are in peril, my Lord," Scratch recited from memory. "You are commanded to cease and desist in all of your campaigns, remove yourself from these premises, and hide where you think you cannot be found, or you will be removed and chastised justly and forthrightly."

"Is that it?"

"Yes, master, that is the entire message."

"Tell me, whom do you serve now that our master seems to have found some other diversion more important than his work here?"

"*WHAT?* I can't believe what I'm hearing!" Scratch cursed. "Is that your first concern? That I now turn my allegiance to you? Begging your pardon, Lord, but you have had my loyalty. Oh, you are *arrogant*—and after *you* have failed *me!*"

Abaddon restrained himself as Scratch raged on.

"Here is our current position, as I see it. *We are under attack!* This is because you have not followed up in regards to *your* responsibilities. Narcissus and his band of Cherubim move freely, and they are highly dangerous! It is obvious now—there is clearly a connection between Narcissus and Harry Turner. If you wonder why Mr. Turner seems so impervious to any darker influence, you might put the two together. Now, where these bold assailants will turn up next is any demon's guess. Possibly here!"

Finally the dark lord spoke. "You would do best to hold your tongue, little one!" he warned. "While you have been busy doing your master's work, we have not been idle. Finding an unfallen angel who has been vacant for centuries is not such an easy task as you might think. And, apparently your precious Gorguol did not find it convenient to stick around. I would suspect that he had some idea of the imminent threat and conveniently chose to be somewhere else. So be careful how you choose to shoot off your mouth, my loyal friend. At this point, I may be the only supporter you have, and if we are going to recover from these devious threats and surprise attacks, we *do* need to band together. This would suggest that *my* allegiance to *you* might be a more valuable commodity than you are giving credit."

Under the circumstances, it was hard to read Scratch's face. The damage sustained by Narcissus would take some recovery time. Still, he would probably not be affected in regards to his ability to take on human form. As Abaddon considered his smaller associate, he knew Scratch would still be a useful tool in their mission. Creating false trust was always an intricate art, especially when dealing with someone close, but he had become a master over time and had the patience to appreciate the future benefits. He would not let a weaker creature such as *this* interfere with his greater plan. He must continue with poise, maintaining the delicate position he had gained with this Machiavellian little specter.

"Scratch, let me say first that I do not place blame on you for the unfortunate circumstances in which we find ourselves. On the contrary, you have exhibited exemplary abilities and I want to commend you here in the presence of this company." Abaddon paused to bow, slightly. "You have shown bravery in the face of danger, and your talents have been of great value."

Scratch could not conceal the slight glow that pulsed brighter with those words of praise.

Abaddon continued, "Now, as to our current condition,

we are not as weak as some might think. We may not know exactly where our enemies wait, but we do, however, have certain knowledge of their movements. Do not assume that our opponents move about freely. They are bound by certain laws and rules of engagement, which we ourselves are not.

"There has clearly been a breach in our lines, and for *that,* I'm guessing we can hold accountable our most excellent overseer, Gorguol. Until he returns to give us further instruction, or we hear otherwise from a higher source, we will continue as planned, strengthening our defenses and keeping a wary eye out for any who would work towards our demise.

"I understand that it may be hard for you to see this in your current condition, my most excellent Scratch, but we still maintain a strong position. With our Excellency's fortress in decadent disarray, Narcissus and his cronies clearly found a weak link. But they will certainly find a different sort of welcome here, should they dare to even come close."

Abaddon paused for effect. The strength that exuded from his dark form permeated each of the demons surrounding him and gave them increased confidence in their abilities to do their work. Abaddon knew this and allowed time for the effect to sink in.

"Sire," Scratch spoke up finally with improved conviction, "what shall I tell Mr. Turner when he asks Miss Sapphire what happened to her? Surely he will want to know immediately what kept her from returning?"

"Scratch, impress me—I have no doubt you will come up

with something that is not only imaginative, but also credible.

"As for the rest of you," Abaddon said with an air of self-assurance, "stay at your posts and keep a constant vigil. Very soon, we will visit Gorguol's lair, clean up the mess, and recover our position there. Rull, you will tighten your grip on Beth Fairbanks." He peered sharply at the devil with an understanding of their shared lie.

"And Jinn," he said, shifting his attention, "you will be available to aid Scratch and help create an advantage for us." Jinn understood this to mean, 'Keep close tabs on our crafty companion.'

"I myself," he paused again for effect, "will make every necessary effort to locate and disarm the Seraph, Narcissus. Together, we will see that this angel and his ill-guided minions will have no further success in disrupting our plans. And regarding Mr. Turner, I will be dealing with him as well. In fact, I have already had more than a few encounters with that small fish!"

Abaddon flashed a menacing smile across the room, focusing for a brief moment on each of his shadowy associates.

"Be strong, my devils. We *will* have the upper hand. I am not afraid of Narcissus or his band of Cherubs. His warning to me only reveals his over-expanded view of himself. He may be powerful, but in his pride, he has underestimated *my* abilities!"

This was a win-win situation for Abaddon. His overseer had fled the scene and abandoned his post. He could only guess that Gorguol had not been prepared for such an onslaught and was too distracted by his own gluttonous ambitions. Until he had further notice from a higher source, he could assume greater authority. As for Narcissus and his comrades, they would not find *him* such an easy target.

After Abaddon dismissed Scratch and the other demons, he asked Rull and Jinn to remain. The inner sanctuary was the only safe place to continue a deeper discussion of more specific strategy. They stood quietly in Abaddon's private chamber where he invited them to . . . relax.

"My devils," he began. "We are at an important crossroads here. We have come this far because we have shared trust and loyalty together. I have depended on the both of you to follow my orders, and you have executed them flawlessly. Do not be deceived by my flattering words to Scratch. I do not consider him to be even remotely in the same league as you. He is crafty and astute, to be sure, but he is still your pupil. We will not make the mistake of underestimating him, as we allow him to utilize his talents to *our* benefit. He will be quite fortunate to gain any position here, which, by the way, will be far more comfortable than anything Gorguol would have ever offered him. But still, you two are my most trusted and faithful ministers. When we reach critical acclaim, it will be the two of you who will stand with me and receive the most coveted positions imaginable.

"With that said—Rull, you indicated you have some crucial information for me?"

"Yes, your Eminence," Rull spoke enigmatically, his countenance hidden behind his slick, black, featureless face. "I am still waiting for more evidence, but regarding Beth Fairbanks, we have clear evidence of angelic influence. My generals, Siren and Tumor, have an idea of who the perpetrator is, assuming there is only one."

Abaddon kept his instant rage silent as the demon continued.

"I am convinced now that even when I first investigated her, an angel's presence was there, only so carefully disguised that it was undetectable. We are watchful now with constant surveillance."

"Interesting," Abaddon said dubiously. "Do you have any conjecture as to who the culprit might be?"

"We believe it to be one of Narcissus' group of Cherubim. We hope that soon they will stumble in some way and be detected."

"Very good, Rull." Abaddon leaned back.

"But even more interesting," Rull added, "are the striking similarities both Beth Fairbanks and Harry Turner, seem to share."

"Please continue," The dark lord responded. "This is becoming quite fascinating."

"Master, we know there are beings of light all around us on a regular basis. We are forced to cross paths with them regularly, and we can even move among them without incident.

Rarely do we see the offspring of Adam moving without some sort of accompanying spirit, whether it be of darkness or light. But these two are clearly among a small few who have no apparent fealty to any master thus far—yet they still seem to live and survive unblemished by any outside influence. It's as though they have been set apart . . . but why? I still have not yet gained an understanding of this!"

"Yes," Abaddon hissed. "*Why they have been set apart . . . is the question!* If they are not committed to our enemy, then why are they not available to our influence? It is because they instinctively do things that are pleasing to our adversaries! As a result, we cannot penetrate them easily."

"I have heard this before," Jinn interrupted, "but whatever the reason, to me it is irrelevant! We must crush them—bring them to their knees and control them all, however we are able."

Abaddon grinned and then continued. "Yes, Jinn, and that's exactly what we shall do. What puzzles me, though, is that these types are usually of no concern to us. This interest in Harry Turner has been confusing. He still does not seem to have any real relevance against our cause, and so what is his threat? "

It is the fact, Abaddon silently answered himself, *that Narcissus is here protecting this Harry Turner, but why?*

"There is yet more, my lord," Rull interrupted. "We know of another small influence that may be indirectly involved here which may work to our benefit."

"Go on," Abaddon urged.

"It is a small controlling demon—a lesser devil who was appointed to Isles End by Gorguol long ago—the usual routine, planted here to abide and grow."

"What devil is this?" Abaddon asked.

"The creature's name," Rull answered, "is Choke. He is stronger than any poltergeist, but can only involve himself with one victim at a time."

Abaddon considered this news and spoke. "I do not recall having ever been personally acquainted with one named Choke, but do not underestimate it, especially if the creature is a subject of Gorguol's. These seemingly unimportant spirits can play a major role in weakening the human condition. Their behind-the-scenes efforts may often go unnoticed by us and our overseers, but their work is part of the foundation of a much larger picture. If a pyramid is only laid waste one grain at a time, it is still ultimately destroyed!"

"It does appear," Rull said, "that Choke has maintained a permanent home in Isles End."

"Then keep me informed," Abaddon responded, "but here, let us bring our focus back to Mr. Turner. Why is Narcissus available to provide assistance to someone like him? Who is this man, that they should feel a need to protect him more than any other adamite?"

Rull suggested an answer. "Mr. Turner *does* happen to be linked to the ABC project, though his role is minimal. But we know our opposition has great concern over the project itself, do we not?"

"They have *always* feared what we might do with science," growled Jinn.

"They *do* fear this project," Abaddon agreed, "but what can they do? The advancements in cellular biology are global."

"And," Rull interjected, "all efforts in this field are being fought over by both sides."

"Do they believe they can stop it?" Jinn seethed.

"They do not want to *stop* the effort," Abaddon said, raising his voice. "They want to *control* it. They think they will use the newest technology for all their noble causes, but of course they are mistaken!"

Jinn leaned forward and spoke with subtle urgency. "Lord, place me in a position to battle against Narcissus. I do not fear him!" His voice was like steel, and it grated its way out through his gruesome visage with gifted articulation. "I will not disappoint you. Find someone else to play this game with Scratch. Surely you have a dozen other talented spirits who can facilitate that important function. I mean no disrespect, sire, but give me this opportunity and I will forthrightly remove Narcissus and these other Cherub pawns from the game with a serious vengeance."

As Abaddon studied Jinn, he was reminded of himself. An intelligent and sinister demon, Jinn was dreadful to look upon and impressively underhanded in his actions. One could say he was the monster of ghouls. Abaddon felt a special bond with

371

Jinn, sensing that the blend of ferocity and astuteness Jinn possessed had been passed down directly from him.

"Patience, Jinn. Do not be in such a hurry to drink, that you drown yourself. In time, I will see that your thirst is quenched, but we must wait until the opportune moment. As far as dealing with Narcissus, I may have to reserve that dance for myself. You will be given more than enough action to satisfy your appetite.

"Now listen," Abaddon said with authority, "though I have full confidence in you and your abilities to defeat our adversaries, there are sometimes larger forces at work. The call of destiny is greater than the desire for blood. Let me inform both of you now—it is destiny that calls *me* to conquer this unfallen angel. *I have already seen it!*

"But let me remind you, all men are *not* created equal, and neither are celestial beings. We are all created with gifts, some obviously more than others. I remember Narcissus well and I have seen his weakness, *and I understand it intimately!* His first failure was that he was too weak to follow his heart when he had the chance, and thus the ultimate humbling—he was removed from the game! His gifts were no match for me when we shared the same celestial space, and after all this time, while he has been idle, I have grown stronger. He may have bested Scratch and the rest of Gorguol's devils, but he will not be so lucky with me. No, I am not afraid of this angel! I pity him, but I will also crush him without a second thought, when the time is right."

"Your Majesty," Jinn bowed, "I only hope I will have the honor to be at your side on that glorious day."

30
Reorganize

Harry was back on the highway driving south towards Isles End. The window was down, as usual, and a cool fall breeze passed through the cab of his truck. He remembered a drive like this from over a year ago and was reminded how he felt back then. He became melancholy, imagining himself driving off without direction, just to feel the breeze flow through the open windows of the cab. But things were different now. He knew where he was going this time. He had a life up ahead and was stronger now, than he had been back then.

Harry thought about Beth and how badly he wanted to see her. The image of her with someone else caused him pain. There must be a way to know without asking her. And what had happened to Rachael was still a mystery. He could only hope she was alright. Maybe her disappearance would turn out to be something simple. But then, the strange man with the blood on his collar and . . . the burning door! He didn't want to guess at an explanation. Where was Narcissus when he needed him? The whole episode made him feel sick.

I kissed Rachael Sapphire!

He couldn't help recalling the warm desire he felt while he was with her in the suite . . . above the crescent bay and the city, when their mouths came together!

And . . . I wanted more!

Harry was disgusted with himself. He didn't want Rachael Sapphire. He wanted Beth! That's where his heart was. But what if she was seeing someone else? Please, no! He wanted to trust her.

But can she trust me?

And what about Narcissus there on the street, looking like a vagrant with his cardboard warning, and no explanation?

The drive back to Isles End was becoming more ominous than peaceful. How had he managed to relax at all under these circumstances? He credited his sister. Gwen always had a way of setting him at ease. But he didn't have her now, and he would have to deal with these issues on his own.

On the way home, Harry stopped by ABC to evaluate the developments there. His subs had made great progress over the weekend. Back in Isles End, he checked in with his crew at the Ivory Lane project. They had worked all weekend. The second story was framed, the trusses were up, and the roof was nearly sheeted. The windows were being delivered tomorrow, which meant the house would be dried in. In another three weeks, the place would be roofed, plumbed, heated and wired, ready for drywall.

After a quick talk with Ed, Harry was back on the road, headed for home. Once again, he'd visited the project without pounding a single nail. He pulled into his driveway and checked his phone. Maybe he'd missed a text or message from Beth. There was nothing. He grabbed the cardboard sign from his truck, retrieved his mail, and went inside. There was a message on his home phone. He pressed the button and listened:

> *Hi, Harry, it's Gwen. I sure enjoyed seeing you.*
> *Made me realize how much I missed my little brother!*
> *Hey, don't forget about your promise now. I'm expecting*
> *to get an invite soon . . . Love you! Bye.*

No more guilt, Harry thought. He was reconnected with Gwen in a new way. His trip to the city couldn't have worked out better—well, he could have spent the entire weekend with her, without any other plans. All things considered, that might have been a better experience all the way around.

Harry studied the chest at the foot of his bed. Opening it, he placed the cardboard sign inside, just over the package containing the fern. He stretched out on the bed and tried to relax. There was work to do—mainly phone calls to make—but the comfort of the bed suddenly took priority. The weekend had caught up with him. His hands and arms still bore the bruises inflicted upon him. He would try calling Rachael again, but wanted to talk with Beth even more. Narcissus could probably explain everything, but there was no way to reach him. Suddenly, he wasn't sure he wanted to concern himself with anything.

Things had been much simpler just a few weeks ago!

Simpler, maybe, but better? No, he answered himself.

The closer you get to people, the greater chance of being let down. The greater chance of being hurt.

Plane Goes Down—Three Perish in Tragedy . . .

That wasn't fair!

He couldn't let that philosophy rule his life or he would never get close to anyone. He could hardly go live in isolation— he was not a monk! He tried to rephrase his thinking.

The more you open up to people, the better chance you have of growing and learning and experiencing life, the greater your chance of loving and being loved. . .

That sounded better!

Better to have loved and lost, than never to have loved at all . . . words for the wounded, although maybe the saying did have some truth to it. Harry had a better one—

Better to have loved and won—!

Either way, Harry had some things to work through.

He pulled out his cell phone and scrolled down his saved list. When he reached Beth's name, he pushed a button and listened while it rang. Where would she be this afternoon? Where *could* she be? Home, waiting for him to call? Or taking care of her aunt? Or . . . Seemed like a long time since he'd seen her. It was nearly two weeks now since he'd left her on her front door with a kiss—just a peck, but still the sweetest kiss! Was he stupid for having allowed himself to become so infatuated with her? He just couldn't imagine that she would have been seeing anyone else after they met. Even if she had been occupied with someone before, there was no indication she was still involved. But Rachael wouldn't make up something like that, would she? It didn't make sense.

The phone continued ringing. He thought through the logistics of the scenario. Rachael had told him that Reese had said something to Abraham. What would Reese know about Beth? Maybe through his association with Bill Algren. If she *had* been seeing someone before they met—would that be so bad? He could understand why she might not want to mention it, especially if the prior relationship was over. Then again, she did seem suddenly busy all the time. If she really did want to see him, wouldn't she have made more of an effort? He had made several attempts to connect with her but she had not been available. For now, Harry did not want to think of Beth being with another man. Explaining her apparent lack of interest was too much as he worked the latest circumstances together. He was suddenly pulled back by the sound of her voice coming out of his phone.

Hi, you've reached Beth.
I could go on about beeps and things,
but I think you know what to do.
Talk to you soon.

The problem now was that Harry didn't know what to do. He heard the beep and he found himself at a complete loss. He formed a greeting in his mind, but then abruptly hung up.

Idiot!

Couldn't he have left her just a simple message? But then, did he really want to have his voice recorded right now? He didn't want to play games, but why not let her show some effort? Seems like she could have made some attempt to call him at least once this last week.

Frustrated, he arranged his pillows and threw his head back. It was getting late and he should make some calls but he had lost interest and his body still ached. He felt guilty now, not staying at the Ivory Lane project—he should have spent some time with the crew, or even just pounded some nails. The weekend had taken its toll and he felt the weight of his struggles coming down like a dark cloud. Once again, he was standing over that well of grief he had come to know so well, not so long ago. Closing his eyes, he pulled away and tried to imagine he was somewhere else, but here he was again—the sense of falling. How was it that this despair could come upon him so suddenly, as though the devastating feelings were always there just under the surface, waiting for the opportunity to rise up and swallow him?

The twilight coming in through the windows began to fade to darkness as Harry lay half under the blankets on his bed. He drifted off and found himself lingering between consciousness and sleep. With his new-found gift of strength, he managed to escape the dark hole he expected to fall into and imagined he was flying somewhere, drifting through the clouds. He could see the tree tops below with green fields and trails, and he could see the ocean too, but he could also still feel his body curled up on his bed. It was a peaceful feeling. He was reminded of when he was with Narcissus, moving through the supernatural, light as a feather and without a care. He let himself fly on as he entered into a deeper sleep. Now he remembered.

As he continued gliding along, the scenery began to change and he realized he was coming up on his old neighborhood. There was the hill above his house and the street below that wound down into town. His mother was standing on the front porch. Leaning forward, he began to glide down until he landed just up the street from his front yard.

The feeling of déjà vu came over him as he recognized the familiar scenario. He was eight years old and headed off to school. His mother ran over and handed him his lunch and kissed him good-bye. As usual, she warned him to be careful and gave him some encouraging words, his guardian angel would protect him. Laughing, he waved back and smiled. She looked so lovely!

He walked the familiar path and recognized all the details along the way. But once again, as he neared the bottom of the road, things began to change.

He approached the foreboding bridge. Why was it off limits? He couldn't remember, but he was required once again to move forward. Soon, he would have to cross. Far below, he could hear water rushing under the bridge. Just before he was forced onto the overpass, he jumped to the side and slid down into the ravine. The water rushed up until he met it with a splash. The current gripped him as he fought to balance himself. The water was only knee deep, but once again he was trapped. He strained in trepidation as the bridge came upon him. Anticipating the recurring scene, he tried to control his fear but the same feeling of terror began to envelop him.

Against his will, he moved like a target in a shooting gallery into the dark opening. Directly ahead, the beastly figure loomed, waiting for him just as before. The creature's skin glistened in the darkness and the glowing crimson eyes pulled Harry in like a fish on a line. The fierce expression on its face became strangely familiar as Harry found himself standing mutely before the being. The dark tailored suit Harry remembered from the last dream had been replaced. Now the hulking creature wore a dark, multi-colored robe that sparkled with various intensities as its skin lit up like a furnace. But there was something different here. He'd seen this face many times, but the violent countenance the creature wore didn't go with the features that Harry was used to. He stared up at the dark face in disbelief. It couldn't be! It didn't make sense . . .

Narcissus?

The figure smiled down at Harry with the same malicious expression he remembered from before and extended his hand.

"Come, Harry," he said invitingly. "Do you understand yet?"

The face was Narcissus but the voice was not. Harry tried to back away but could not. The heat from the spirit's body *glowed with an intensity that blinded him. Now he could only see the angelic face coming closer. "It is finally time for you to satisfy my ambitious appetite!"*

Harry strained to pull away with all his strength and tumbled out of his bed and onto the floor with a thud. He quit thrashing the moment he realized he was just having another nightmare. He went to the bathroom and washed the sweat off of his face. As he stared into the mirror, all he could see was Narcissus' face glaring down at him with burning eyes. But he didn't remember seeing his celestial friend in the other dreams! He'd never been close enough before to see the creature's face in detail. Could the figure in his dream have been his angelic friend all along? *No!* It didn't make sense.

But it was just a dream . . .

Harry was interrupted by his cell phone. He pulled himself off of the floor and hurried across the room where he had left his phone on the dresser.

"Hello?"

"Harry, it's Rachael—"

"Rachael—I've been worried about you!"

"Harry, I'm so sorry. . . I feel terrible! Am I calling too late?"

Harry heard the struggle in her voice—she sounded almost in tears. "Don't worry, Rachael. . . are you alright? What happened to you?"

"I'm fine. I truly did not mean to leave you stranded the

382

other night, and I meant to get back to you sooner than this. After I left your room, I went up to my apartment and was freshening up when I got a call from a friend regarding my father. Unfortunately, he had an accident and was in the hospital. I rushed off so fast that I left my phone behind. I wanted to call you while I was in route but without my phone I couldn't."

"It's okay, Rachael, I understand . . . things happen. Is your dad okay?"

"He's still in the hospital recovering. He's diabetic and apparently misjudged his dose of insulin, which caused him to go into insulin shock and have a seizure. To make matters worse, he was on the road when it happened. Someone reported him driving recklessly. He ended up on the side of the highway where someone tried to raise his blood sugar by pouring juice down his throat—they must have found his medical bracelet—but he was already unconscious and the juice went into his lungs. Finally the medics showed up and took him to the hospital. Somewhere during all this, he was robbed."

"I'm so sorry!" Harry exclaimed, recalling the day he received the news about Jennifer and his parents.

"Thank you—your understanding means a lot to me. I just felt horrible the whole time, imagining you waiting for me and not knowing what was going on. What did you end up doing?"

"Well," Harry began, wondering how much of his trouble he wanted to burden her with after she had gone through such an ordeal herself. He began to share the basics, the man with the bloody shirt and the burning door that held him in its grasp. Maybe she would be able to explain some of the mystery. "It was hard to see clearly in the darkness, and I don't know how to explain the door. I was burned or shocked when I placed my hands on the surface and I couldn't let go!"

"Harry, I know about the man you encountered on my floor. There is something wrong with him, trust me . . . he is not normal. And you are right—it is very dark up there! I've asked them several times to use brighter bulbs or something. I guess I've just gotten used to it. Regarding the penthouse floor, an eccentric gentleman owns the entire floor. I understand there is some kind of special security system in place there. I remember someone getting shocked once before when they tried to deliver a package. I wondered if they ever got it repaired!"

Harry was glad they were talking. He felt silly now, realizing there were normal and natural reasons for everything. Funny how the mind will come up with all kinds of crazy ideas, but when the truth is revealed, there is a simple explanation. He wondered if it might be the same with Beth.

"Rachael, I'm just happy you're okay and your dad too. When you didn't return, I had a feeling there was something wrong."

"I'm glad you didn't wait for me all night!"

"So," Harry changed the subject, "are you ready to continue our work on the waterfront project?"

"I was just going to ask you the same thing. I know you're

still working with Advanced Bio-Cell. Why don't you get back with me tomorrow and let me know when you'll have time to look at those plans again. Also, the drugstore—we want to start with that."

"Of course, Rachael, I'll call you tomorrow."

"Sounds good—oh, and Harry?"

"Yes?"

"I really did enjoy our time together. I thought about you while I sat at my dad's bedside. You're such a gentleman!"

"Yes," Harry answered. "I enjoyed our time together as well."

He said goodnight and fell back onto the bed. Why was he so tired? He remembered the dream and felt exhausted just thinking about it. He needed something to eat, that was it! Jumping up, he grabbed a potato and put it in the microwave. What a wonderful invention—so quick and easy! He gathered up the butter, sour cream, bacon bits, garlic, and salt and pepper. By that time, the microwave was sounding off. In five minutes he was eating like a king. The only thing lacking was meat. Even a fried hot dog would be tasty right now, but this would do until morning.

Back in bed, Harry was too tired to think about anything. Fortunately, though, some of his recent concerns had been laid to rest. As he stretched his limbs under the covers, he still couldn't help thinking about Beth and Narcissus. His friends would be okay until tomorrow, he assured himself as he faded away.

31
I Want You to Shine!

The Overseer looked down from high above the earth where things are not so easily described in earthly terms. There, from a position of indescribable beauty, entirely hidden from the small blue planet below, she anticipated the arrival of four celestial visitors.

She carefully observed all that surrounded her. This had been her domain to rule over since the beginning. Like clockwork, never missing a beat, she was acutely aware of every formation of time and space, always seeing that it was measured out in perfect increments.

But she did not do this on her own. There were a multitude of other celestial beings who all worked together in unison, seeing that all things continued to move in harmony around the great source of heat and light called the sun.

Now, amidst the continual display of splendor surrounding the Overseer, there appeared before her four figures: a Seraph and three Cherubim. With a voice like divinely inspired music, she addressed each of the beings by name.

"Greetings to you, Ranan, Psallo, and Agalliao!"

The three Cherubim bowed before her.

"And a special welcome to you, Narcissus!"

The Seraph also bowed in respect and acknowledgement of her position.

"I want to tell you first, my friends, the precision and integrity you have displayed in the execution of your assignments has been flawless! Well done!"

Narcissus noted that his three friends had allowed themselves to smile at these words, and he naturally did likewise. Then he spoke, "My Overseer, it is good to be fully reinstated in the service of Elohim. I am truly thriving and completely in awe of the magnificence to come!"

"Yes, as we all are, my dear friend! I knew it was just a matter of occasion before I would see you again . . . and I must say you look splendid." She spoke with delight and motioned for them to join her.

"Thank you, my Overseer," Narcissus answered as he stood in the midst of splendor. "I want to express my deepest gratitude and praise unto our magnificent Creative Designer! It is by His grace alone that I am standing with you all on this celebrated occasion. With all my heart, mind, strength and soul, I am His!"

"Yes, Narcissus, you do belong to Him. Now let us not postpone this gifting any longer," she said with authority as she drew in closer to her four guests. "It is time!"

Then, as if there had been a preordained announcement, other angels began to appear from all directions. There were Archangels, and both Seraphim and Cherubim in great numbers, whose extraordinary manifestations became like a symphony of brilliance and beauty all around the small group. If that wasn't enough of a sight, they began to unfold their many wings and move them in all different directions. The sound started out as a subtle humming, like many voices barely audible, reverberating with intertwining melodies. The other three Cherubs moved back and spread their own massive wings to join in the choir of harmony that continued to build and echo throughout the antechamber. Narcissus' friends formed a circle around him while the Overseer knelt down before the Seraph. Then, all became still.

"Narcissus," she exclaimed triumphantly so that all could hear, *"I WANT YOU TO SHINE!"*

With that, she stood, and joined in with the multitude of angels encircling the small group and they resumed their chorus of beating wings with a thundering shout.

Whatever healing and restoration Narcissus had felt up to this point was diminutive compared to what he experienced now. As the mass of observers cheered to witness this Seraph regain his full potential, he felt as though all the power they had to offer was being poured into his being. He stood tall as his body started to glow. Then, as though it were coming out from the depths of his soul, a sharp light poured out like a bolt of lightning. The applause became louder as he felt himself begin to shine with an intensity that was bursting out in every direction. Narcissus was a pillar of blinding radiance, and the celestial beings surrounding him were ecstatic as they watched the angel become fully transformed back into the great Seraph he had formerly been.

Finally, when the restoration was complete, the body of Narcissus could be seen clearly again, as the intense light engulfing his body began to retreat. He stood in his glorified state, which was largely altered by three pairs of enormous wings. One pair came out from his shoulders and folded around to hide his face. The second pair extended from his back and was fully expanded in both directions. The final pair grew out from behind his calves and were neatly tucked away. His physical characteristics had already been exquisite in every detail, but now he was chiseled, his countenance was fearful and more magnificent than before, with every feature fully enhanced. Narcissus parted his upper wings, revealing his face, and gazed with deep, knowing eyes at the throng of heavenly creatures who surrounded him. Then Narcissus uttered a phrase that could not be described in human words, but which every onlooker understood and received. The words were living, and they transferred a shared understanding of oneness. He had given them peace rather than just wishing it for them. As the Archangel was now fully complete and whole, the other angels in turn became fuller.

"Ranan," the Overseer spoke to the taller, fierce-looking Cherub, "take your friend now, along with Psallo and Agalliao, and go to the living gates!"

Narcissus heard this and recalled the last time he was outside those gates—living gates with a magnificent city within. This was where he had introduced the three Cherubim to his friend, Harry Turner.

"Once there, Narcissus," the Overseer proudly proclaimed, "YOU MAY ENTER!"

32
Meet the Family

The next morning Harry was up early and headed over to Ivory Lane to meet with his crew. When he arrived, everyone was hard at work.

Butch saw him first. "Hey, boss! What are you doing here?"

"I'm going to work here this morning! Can you believe it?"

Ed popped his head out from an upstairs window. "Hey, Harry, did I hear you say you're here to pound some nails?"

"Believe it or not," Harry answered, "I am, if I can remember how to hold a hammer!"

He counted four new guys scrambling around the upper floor. Making the rounds, he made acquaintance with the new help. They all watched as Harry sank a few nails, strictly for show. Ed and Butch cheered and applauded as Harry showed off his hammering skills. Just as he finished, his cell phone rang. It was Beth.

"Excuse me, I have to take this." Harry stepped away to a quieter place and tapped his phone with a greeting.

"Hello, Mr. Turner," he heard her say. "Do you have a minute?"

"Of course! How are you?"

"Exhausted! Mr. Algren has had me running all over the

place. It's been like a zoo around here this past week! I heard you were going to be by soon?"

"Yes, but I'm keeping my guys here at Ivory Lane. I was able to get some other subs up there and they've accomplished a great deal already."

There was a pause, then, "I've missed you, Harry—"

"Really?"

"Yes! It seems like a long time now since you left me on my doorstep . . . "

"I know—I guess things have been a little hectic for both of us. How's your aunt doing?"

"Not much has changed. Her back is getting worse and she's been having trouble breathing. She's afraid to go out by herself and she needs help with cleaning and running errands. I was thinking, Harry, it would be nice if you could meet her . . ."

"I'd love to—sometime soon?"

"Yes, but I should check with her first."

"Sure, just let me know."

"So how was *your* weekend?"

Harry was not prepared for this question, though he should have expected it. "It was okay—I ended up doing some work in the city and spent the night at my sister's."

"Oh yes, Gwen, right? That must have been nice!"

"Yeah, she's great!" He could be honest about that. "I'd like you to meet *her* sometime, too!"

"I'd love to! But listen, why don't I check in with my aunt

and I'll call you right back."

As soon as Harry hung up, Ed sounded off. "Sounds like things are getting serious there, Harry!"

Butch came to Harry's aid. "Hey, leave him alone, that's a good thing!"

Harry's phone rang again.

"Hello?"

"My aunt wants to meet you, Harry . . . tonight! Can you do it?"

"Of course—what time?"

"If you can pick me up at five, we can go visit her together—I'll bring dinner."

Harry was excited. Maybe Rachael had been wrong about Beth seeing someone else. Maybe Beth's aunt was the only one she'd been spending time with. But why would Bill Algren say anything different? "I'll see you at five," he confirmed and said good-bye.

Harry spent the rest of the day at Ivory Lane. There was something satisfying about using his own hands to accomplish something that was solid and recognizable. Being there was also an escape. Things had become complicated lately and focusing on work felt good.

As four o'clock neared, the guys were ready to finish up and began collecting their tools. With one hour to go, Harry thanked his team for their hard work, raced home, showered, dressed, and was on his way to Beth's place. He pulled into her driveway and there she was, waiting on her front porch with their dinner in a box.

"It's good to see you again," she said and hurried over to his truck before he could get out.

"It's good to see you too!" She looked divine and he wanted to stick his head through the open window and kiss her, but that would have to wait. Climbing out, he took the box and placed it on the seat of the truck. When he turned around, she stood close, ready to embrace him. He couldn't help but pull her into his arms and give her a squeeze. It felt natural. After a moment, he walked her around to the passenger door and opened it. "What's for dinner?" he asked.

"Home-made mushroom soup and Caesar salad," Beth answered. "Upon aunties request."

"Sounds good." He was so elated to be with her, he forgot all about what Rachael had told him.

Her aunt's home was only a short drive. Harry followed Beth's instructions while the fall air drifted through the open windows.

"There it is, on the right," she pointed to a small cottage surrounded by fir trees.

Harry pulled into the driveway. "Wait here," he said as he stepped out of the truck.

Beth looked at him curiously as he walked around to her side and opened the door for her.

"Well, thank you, sir," she said with gleeful surprise.

Harry helped her out of the cab, grabbed the meal, and followed her to the front door. The home was slightly rustic but well kept, not unlike most of the homes in the area—shingle siding and real shutters on the windows. The front door had a large knocker mounted below a small grated window but Beth unlocked the door with her own key and cracked it open. "Auntie, we're here," she announced, then turned back to Harry, "C'mon!"

He watched her disappear down the hall while he surveyed the front room. It was exactly what he would expect any elderly woman's parlor to look like. There were hutch-style display cases full of crystal glasses and porcelain tea cups and ornamental plates. In the middle of the room was a coffee table with a small couch in front of it and two stuffed chairs to each side. Beneath the table, a flowery rug covered the hardwood floor and in the corner sat a china calico cat.

"Harry, can you bring the dinner into the kitchen? I'll just be a minute."

He found the kitchen, set the box on the counter, and removed the plastic containers that held the soup and salad.

"Harry," he heard her lilting voice again, "could you put the soup on the stove and heat it up a bit?"

He figured he could handle that. He chose a pan from the cupboard, poured the soup in and set it on the stove. The soup heated quickly over the gas burner and filled the room with a wonderful aroma.

Every time he was with Beth, he felt a strong tugging in

his heart, and he felt it now. He wanted to tell that annoying voice inside that kept warning him to be cautious . . . to shut up! Narcissus had told him to trust his abilities. Well, that is what he was going to do.

Two days ago you kissed another woman!

That was a mistake, he countered his own accusation. Beth was the girl he wanted to spend time with. He had only been momentarily confused, that was all. He wasn't even sure Rachael Sapphire was really interested in him, but then, she had a funny way of being friendly.

Why was Beth taking so long?

Maybe Rachael Sapphire had been caught up in the moment, too. It had been a beautiful day and they had spent that afternoon together at a lovely waterfront park. Of course Rachael liked him, but surely it was nothing more than a friendly business relationship. But had she been the one who made a move on him? Or, was it possible that she was only following his leads? He was sure he'd been a perfect gentleman over the course of the entire afternoon. Stirring the soup, Harry began to review all that had transpired between them. He was sure he hadn't lead Miss Sapphire on in any way. What could he have possibly done differently?

Turned away from her sooner when she edged up to him so boldly . . . !

"Well, where is this young man of yours?" Harry heard an aging woman's voice from the hallway.

"He's in the kitchen, Auntie," he heard Beth answer, and then right behind him, "Harry, I'd like you to meet my aunt."

He swung around from the stove and there was Beth standing with a small gray-haired woman. Clearly she had a problem with her back, but as Harry focused on her, his stomach tightened into a hard knot.

"So, you're Harry Turner," the elderly woman said.

"Yes, pleased to meet you," he forced the words out as he extended his hand. Harry was shocked to see Beth's aunt was the same woman he'd seen in the vision. The woman at the bank with the ugly head growing on her back, speaking in her ear and telling her what to say! What was her name? He almost had it . . .

"My name is Emily Matson. The girls used to call me Auntie Em, you know, from the old Oz movie? But you can call me Auntie, if you like."

"Yes, of course," Harry said, "The Wizard of Oz—"

Beth stepped in, "We watched that movie every year when we were young, and we loved calling you Auntie Em, didn't we!"

"That's right, dear," her aunt said lovingly.

Harry stood there uneasily until Beth said, "Why don't we set the table, Harry?"

"Sure."

"Well, first let me get my Auntie comfortable."

"Yes," her aunt said, "I do need to sit. You see my back is not as straight as it used to be."

Harry could see a lump near the top of her hunched shoulders. Could that *thing* be hiding there, under her sweater? He couldn't tell if the deformity was large enough to conceal that beastly head. But he reminded himself that the first time he'd seen her, he had been looking through different eyes—*spiritual eyes*, Narcissus had explained.

Beth got her aunt seated, turned the stove off, and handed some plates and bowls to Harry. After a few minutes they were all seated together at the kitchen table.

"Beth dear, you are a darling to bring me dinner! And you too, Harry!"

"Auntie, it's our pleasure! Besides, I wanted you to meet Harry."

With a mouth full of salad, Harry nodded and smiled, but he was really wondering if that creature was whispering to the old woman even now. Strangely, he didn't have that sense. She seemed very nice . . . sweet even, and sincere. Hardly the coarse sounding woman he'd listened in on at the bank. He recalled his recent encounter with the bank clerk, Mr. Hauser—it was the same thing, friendly and kind, nothing like he'd witnessed during the vision.

The dinner went smoothly until the elderly woman burst out coughing in the middle of a sentence.

"Auntie, are you okay?" Beth cried out as her aunt seemed to be choking. Harry stopped eating and looked at Beth with concern.

"Harry, she's choking! Can you help her?"

"What should I do?" he responded jumping out of his chair.

"Not a thing," Beth's aunt interrupted. "I'm okay." But she was still choking a bit as she hacked and sputtered, her breathing irregular.

"Are you sure?" Beth was at her aunt's side now, holding her shoulders.

"Beth, darling, you know this is nothing new. I choke more than once at almost every meal." Then she regained her composure, wiped her mouth with her napkin, and went right back to finishing her soup.

Beth went back to her seat and studied her aunt. "You worry me, Auntie! Are you sure you're okay?"

"Don't fuss over me now! That's enough. Please, Harry, have a seat."

Beth looked at Harry and shrugged her shoulders as he sat back down. "Guess she's alright—"

Harry gazed at both the women waiting for a sign from either of them, but Beth had resumed her meal, and her aunt was sipping her tea.

Harry continued with his meal as well, still struggling inwardly, dealing with the uncomfortable feeling that there was some unseen thing, influencing the situation.

Still, for the most part, Harry was able to stay focused, but there were a few instances when his thoughts wandered. Did

Beth have any similarities to her aunt, and would he see them through "spiritual eyes?" Could there be a dark influence attached to her, or maybe she had a guardian of light at her side! That would seem more likely, he thought. Harry couldn't imagine her any other way. She was too kind and sweet, too pure and innocent. In fact, he'd never seen a side of Beth that reflected anything but goodness. Still, he hoped there was no 'family resemblance'.

Getting through the remainder of the evening was easier with Beth sitting across from him. She was especially supportive of him whenever her aunt inquired further, regarding Harry's past, his business, and his intentions. Still, his stomach didn't stop churning and he only ate a moderate portion of the meal.

Soon, Beth's aunt complained she was tired. Harry helped Beth clean up and they said goodnight to Auntie Em. The drive back to Beth's was quiet. When they arrived, they sat silently for a moment in the cab of Harry's truck until Beth turned to him. "Did you enjoy meeting my aunt, Harry?"

"Yes, she's very nice. I'm sorry about the trouble with her back. She looks very uncomfortable!"

"She is suffering," Beth agreed, "but she doesn't want to see a doctor. And her choking during meals has definitely gotten worse! I have tried to persuade her to go in, but she's gotten so stubborn."

Harry nodded, "It must be difficult."

"It is, but what can I do?"

There was silence again for a moment, then Beth leaned closer to Harry. "Can I ask you something?"

"Of course, what is it?"

"Well, you seemed unusually quiet tonight, like you had something weighing on your mind."

"What do you mean?" Harry feigned ignorance, unsure where this was going to go. Were his inner emotions that obvious?

"Harry, I had the feeling that you were withdrawn, or maybe just preoccupied. I'm wondering, is there something that's bothering you, or rather, is there something about me that you're concerned about?"

Harry wasn't sure what to say. He hadn't expected this question. It caught him off-guard and he just blurted out, "Beth, is there another man in your life that I don't know about?"

"What?" She looked startled.

"I'm just asking—" He looked down for a moment, avoiding eye contact.

"Harry, I realize we haven't known each other very long. I'm very fond of you and I wouldn't do anything to hurt you, especially by being involved with anyone behind your back! There is no one else I'm interested in, besides you. Where did you get such a silly idea?"

Now he did feel silly. There *had* been the question of another man, but that wasn't the only reason he was noticeably distant. But how could he tell her about the vision, seeing her aunt in the ugly condition he had witnessed? And he didn't want to bring up Rachael Sapphire's suggestion that Beth was involved with someone else. That could create all kinds of problems.

"I'm sorry, Beth, that was a dumb question. I guess I've been feeling a little insecure lately and since I haven't seen much of you the past couple of weeks—"

"Harry, it's okay, I understand. The timing has not been good for either of us. But I want you to know I am very interested in spending as much time with you as possible. Also, I believe that a good relationship is built on trust. Attraction may get the ball rolling, and commonalities will help bind things together, but trust is crucial. Without it, what do you have?"

Now Harry had to work hard to hide his disappointment—in himself! Trust? He felt trustworthy, but he just couldn't imagine himself talking to her about the afternoon with Rachael, especially regarding the incident in the suite.

And there was so much else he needed to keep from her— from everyone, really. This sort of dilemma was new to him. He wasn't used to keeping secrets. He hadn't been comfortable broaching the subject with his own sister. How do you tell someone that you've been in contact with a celestial being? An angel! A member of the Seraphim! How do you explain traveling through the supernatural, visiting places from the past, breathing under water with angels? The truth was, he might never be able to tell anyone.

"You're right, Beth. I feel the same way. Trust *is* essential.

I'm also very pleased you are interested in spending time with me," he added with half a smile.

"As much time as possible, is what I said!"

If he had to keep a few honest secrets to keep his world in order, then it would be worth it. Hopefully at some point, he would find a way to tell her all about his celestial friend. Maybe she would even have a chance to meet Narcissus someday.

Harry got out of his truck while Beth waited. He walked around to her side and opened her door.

"Thank you again, Harry."

He guided her to the front door but before he could say a word, she wrapped her arms around him and embraced him warmly.

I don't deserve this, he thought, but he couldn't help reciprocating the gesture. This felt nothing like the hug with Rachael Sapphire. It was not unwarranted or awkward. He thought of Jennifer suddenly, but not in a bad way. It confirmed something positive. If this woman could bring out such warmth and trust from a place that had been so shut down—that is, his heart—then there had to be something very special about her. He found himself wanting to thank his lost Jennifer for letting him know what love was supposed to feel like.

"That was nice. Thank you," he offered instead.

"You're welcome," she accepted, and then tilted her head up as he pressed his lips against hers.

Now, this kiss, well . . . it was real! As he lingered there, leaning against Beth's front door, every concern melted away. He realized at that moment that he truly loved this woman, though he wasn't sure he was ready to broadcast it to the world, or even to her just yet. But he was sending her the message right now, through this very simple and intimate act.

33
Talk of Cloning

Harry had plenty to think about with the Ivory Lane project, the Advanced Bio-Cell remodel, the renovation of the old drug store downtown, and now, the old warehouses on the waterfront. It seems he would be instrumental in refurbishing them into replicas of the "Old Towne" buildings he and Rachael had visited in the city. He even had the plans for the originals, thanks to her.

Rather than drive to the Ivory Lane project, he gave Ed a call. His foreman confirmed they had all the materials they needed and were making great progress. Harry would still need to see how the improvements were going at Advanced Bio-Cell. He called Rachael to schedule a meeting at the old drug store. She would be available later this afternoon but Harry hoped to speak directly with Abraham Dante to discuss the waterfront buildings. He called Abraham and left a message on his voice mail. That was fine—Abraham was sure to get back to him.

So, there it was! Having things neatly laid out felt good.

He hadn't seen Narcissus since he plowed him over outside Rachael's building. Why the angel had been there in the first place was still a mystery, and it seemed increasingly strange that his angelic friend had not made any effort to contact him with an explanation. Didn't he deserve at least that? If he trusted Narcissus, he would just have to be patient. In the meantime, he would keep moving forward and juggle things as best he could.

When Harry arrived at Advanced Bio-Cell, his subs were hard at work. The entire ABC group seemed to be present as well: Bill Algren, Beth and her colleague, Valerie, and of course, Preston Hart, and Dr. Shushi Yang. Even Reese Orchard made an appearance.

The new water feature grabbed Harry's attention as he stepped through the front door and into the large foyer. Bill sat under the impressive granite pillar, visiting with Beth and Valerie. They seemed to be enjoying themselves, watching the water spill from the ceiling and down the sides of the monolithic obelisk, spreading out into small pools of water and weaving through grassy streams, feeding large ferns, and blending in with overstuffed chairs and couches.

"Harry, come over here and join us," Bill called with a broad smile.

"Hello, Bill," Harry answered, remembering Bill's emphasis on calling him by his first name.

"Hi, Harry," added Beth with a warm look.

Valerie smiled and, lifting her jeweled hand, gave a small wave.

"Harry," Bill started, motioning for him to sit down, "we were just talking about how we will be greeting our guests and making them feel comfortable from the moment they enter this building."

"It's the most impressive lobby I've ever seen," Harry said, taking a seat next to Beth. "I think anyone who walks in

406

through that front door will be amazed!"

"Yes," Bill answered. "But of course, that's the whole idea, isn't it?"

"I think it's remarkable!" Beth added.

Bill leaned forward and his voice took on a serious tone. "Harry, you're probably anxious to check in with your subs. I don't want to keep you from your work, but tell me, how's it going? I mean, it looks like we're on track to finish up . . . ?"

"Yes," Harry stated. "In fact, we're ahead of schedule. I *do* want to make the rounds and see how things look this morning, but we've made fast progress."

"Preston!" Bill gave a shout as Preston Hart entered the reception room from one of the elevators. "Harry's here!" Preston hurried over to greet everyone.

"Good morning to you all," he said enthusiastically. "How are we all doing on this fine day?" He sat next to Valerie and shifted his glasses up to the top of his nose. "Harry, this place has been hopping since your first visit. We are all quite impressed with the progress you've made."

"Well, I guess I'm fortunate to have some great contacts," Harry beamed.

Beth looked at Harry admiringly as she watched him soak in the praise.

"Preston, have you seen Shushi?" Bill interrupted.

"Yes, he's around here somewhere," Preston answered, and then added, "He's another one who has been working

407

overtime. He just doesn't stop! I wonder how he ever finds time to sleep!"

"Speak of the devil," Bill said, looking up to see Dr. Yang coming in from the far end of the room.

"What a wonderful surprise. Everyone's here," Shushi exclaimed as he hurried over to the group.

"Shushi, have you tried one of these chairs yet?" Preston said standing. Then, "Anyone like some coffee?"

There were gestures of interest all around.

"It won't be long before we have an espresso bar right inside the front door," Preston added excitedly, "but until then, we do have some pretty good java in the other room."

"Tea for me, Preston," Shushi reminded his colleague.

Preston hurried off while Shushi walked over to where Harry and Beth were sitting and bowed before Harry. "Mr. Turner, you have exceeded my expectations," he said with a touch of a smile.

"Wow!" Bill exclaimed. "You have to understand, Harry, that gesture is a sign of great honor and respect."

"I'm the one who is honored," Harry said humbly.

"I just appreciate people," Shushi explained, "who do what they say they are going to do, *when* they say they will do it, and I understand that this doesn't happen regularly with building contractors."

"Well," Harry said, "in defense of my trade, I'll just say that scheduling can be the most challenging part of the job. A general contractor is only as good as the sub-contractors he hires. But, thank you, Doctor, I am thrilled that things have worked out so well."

Preston returned with a large tray and set it on a table in the center of the group. "Here we go—I'll let you all serve yourselves. There are cups, creamer, sugar, and the carafe is full and fresh."

There was a round of appreciation as everyone joined in the process of making up their drinks.

Shushi found the hot water and tea bag and began the steeping process while Preston made an apology for having to take care of some business and hurried off. That seemed to be a signal to the girls and they dismissed themselves and headed over to the reception counter to continue the organizing process. Harry was left with Bill and Shushi. The scientist seemed unusually relaxed, compared to what Harry had experienced so far. Until now, Dr. Yang had always been in a rush and seemed regularly preoccupied. Now he sat comfortably across from Bill and Harry and began a fresh conversation, surprising the other two men.

"Harry, I'm guessing you have some idea of the kind of project we are working on here?"

"I suppose I do," Harry answered, "but what little I know is pretty vague. Preston explained some, but I really don't have a clue, to be honest."

"Mr. Algren permitting, I'd be happy to enlighten you right now, since it seems you have become more than just a builder to us."

"Of course, Shushi," Bill responded. "Feel free! We don't have any secrets here—at least, not from Harry. Are you in a hurry to meet with your subs, or do you have some time to visit—maybe hear a little about our operation?"

"I'm in no hurry," Harry answered.

The doctor cleared his throat and began matter-of-factly.

"Last year we completed what is known as the human genome project. Since then we have continued working with recombinant DNA, gene splicing, and even more importantly, the real possibilities of reproducing vital organs and other body parts. I know, it's a very controversial subject with strong feelings from both sides. When you begin to discuss cloning in real terms, there are passionate concerns from both sides, with some referring to our work as divinely inspired and others comparing it to Dr. Frankenstein or even claiming we want to equate ourselves with the highest powers of creation. But here we find ourselves: the answers to creating life, so to speak, within our grasp. What do you think?"

Harry was caught off-guard. He wasn't sure how to answer such a question.

"Dr. Yang, to be honest, I don't know what I think. I'm sure there are reasons for opposing concerns on both sides. I like the idea of helping people who might otherwise not have a chance to continue living—or maybe those who are living, but are not able to experience a decent quality of life."

"That's it, Harry! Quality of life is what makes life worth living, don't you agree? But of course you do! What is life when one is not able to enjoy it as others do? Or rather, why allow some to live handicapped lives when there are viable alternatives?"

"I agree," Harry answered. "So why is there so much concern about the idea of cloning?"

"In 1997," Shushi leaned forward, "when Dolly the sheep was successfully cloned—and it was not us who did it—the whole idea of cloning took on a completely new dimension because it suddenly became a real possibility. In 2001 they banned human cloning here in the States, due to concerns over the vast opportunities for abuse."

"What kind of abuse do you mean?" Harry asked, not sure if he really wanted to know the gory details.

"There's a long list, Harry. I'm sure if you had the time to consider it even briefly, you would come up with many of the fears that have already been discussed at length by those involved in the field of cloning. But, just to name a few, there are those who have concerns that human cloning could present the problem of slave labor. I know that might sound farfetched, but it might easily become a problem, especially in countries lacking the ethics we promote here."

"Wow," Harry nodded.

"Yes, and imagine the ability to create a clone whose intelligence is purposefully low, but who is physically designed to be very strong, maybe for the purpose of labor.

"One must also accept that this is new territory for us holding many unknowns. There is no assurance of safety, especially for the clones. We have no idea about the quality of *their* lives or what their lifespan would be. Imagine we obtained the DNA of a very intelligent person, such as Albert Einstein; there would be the expectation that this cloned version would be just as intelligent as its original, but we don't know what the results would be until we actually achieve it."

"If left unchecked," Bill interjected, "body parts and even clones themselves could easily become *merchandise.* When you 'create' life, who owns it? Imagine farms that harvest organs, or worse."

"That does sound creepy," Harry responded, almost spilling his coffee.

"And possibly more disturbing," Shushi continued, "is the next level of thought. Questions would certainly arise regarding whether or not a clone has what one might call a 'soul.' In other words, are they equated as human, or are they created objects with human appearance? Life for a clone could certainly be very difficult. Creating body parts is one thing, but to create a replica of a human being!"

"Another consideration," Bill added, " if cloning becomes commonplace, how will the government deal with the reality of so many people with the same finger prints."

"Right," Shushi agreed, "and life for a clone might turn

out to be much more difficult than anyone has realized. It couldn't be easy—we don't know how they will adapt. They might be confused about emotional issues such as love and belonging. There is the potential of becoming emotionally crippled once they discover their unique beginnings. There is so much we don't know yet because this is undiscovered territory."

"And Shushi," Bill added, "remember our discussion regarding the potential for serious discrimination from the non-cloned population who might legitimately feel endangered by the clones' mere existence."

"Exactly," Shushi agreed. "And then there's the legal ramifications of clones. Do they have the same rights as naturally born humans? How can they, if they are considered to be a product or commodity?

"Or what if someone was mistaken for a clone, or vice versa? That would invite a whole new set of laws, wouldn't it? Clones might need to have labels or permanent identity markers, something to distinguish them from non-cloned humans.

"Harry, I mentioned the banning of human cloning here in the States due to concerns regarding abuse? Well, as you might imagine now, the implications for abuse are literally astronomical. What if you could 'grow' a replica of someone you know? They would be virtually identical in every way, that is, physically. Or, let's take it a step further. What if you could grow someone who was no longer living? Let's say, someone from the past who was very healthy, very handsome . . . or very smart?

Now, let's be really creative. Let's combine all three! Can you imagine the possibilities? It's mind boggling."

"You've obviously given this some thought," Harry observed.

Dr. Yang leaned in closer and spoke somberly. "Harry, no doubt! This is our business and we have given it a great deal of consideration. It's because we are on the brink of taking the next step to making this process a reality, and so we could not begin to take it lightly. We must study all the possible repercussions: Will cloning organs be cost effective? Will it make man just another man-made thing? Will it undermine the value of human life?"

"I see," Harry said, wincing at the doctor's words, "but the ideas of growing human organs, versus creating a cloned version of another human being, still seem far removed from each other."

"Harry, all we need is a cell from a human, or a sample of blood . . . that's it! The entire human genome—the complete unique and individual, one-of-a-kind DNA—can be read, if you will, through this sample of genetic make-up. It's an all-inclusive blueprint of the entire person!" Dr. Yang leaned back in his chair and sipped his lukewarm tea.

"How are you doing with all this, Harry?" Bill asked, sensing Harry's uneasy demeanor.

"I'm good," Harry said with a nervous smile. "This is fascinating, really. I could sit here for hours and listen to all the possibilities. It reminds me of a science fiction book I read years ago in high school."

"Except," Shushi interrupted, "this is no longer science fiction, but rather science *reality*. Over time, things like sci-fi books and movies have presented these ideas in so many ways, even comically, that the overall viewpoint of most people has softened from the original fear this topic originally produced. But now, here is the concern. When the U.S. came up with a hydrogen bomb, they were the only ones who had it. They were in control. Tell me, Harry, do you know how long it took for them to use the bomb, that is, from the time they finally had it ready to deliver?"

"I know the answer," Harry said. "Not very long."

"You are right! Just as soon as it was completed, it was delivered!"

"Yes, by a B-29 bomber called the 'Enola Gay.' And the potential death toll was greatly reduced because of that decision! My father told me the story when I was young," Harry remembered his dad telling him all the circumstances that led up to the delivery of that fatal bomb.

"Your dad was right. For the lives that were lost, many more were saved, in the long run. But this is different. I believe we can make incredible advancements for the betterment of mankind. Surely you can understand the great concern we have in being the first to share, or should I say, unleash our discovery. We may be able to maintain some control for a while, but undesired results are inevitable. What will the world do with such knowledge? You've heard the saying, 'Absolute power corrupts absolutely?'"

"Yes," answered Harry, "generally people are corrupted when they come into a position of too much power. It's human nature, right?"

"The bottom line is," Bill threw in, "whoever explores these ideas with the intention of bringing them to fruition must treat them responsibly and be aware of the temptations they may invite."

"Right," said Harry, "but if the cloning of human life has been banned in the United States, then how do you reconcile the act of pursuing it still?"

"Easy," Bill stated confidently. "That was back in 2001. We have new people in power now, with new ideas and belief systems. When we have something solid to offer people, those with influence will see things differently than they did back then. But still, we have not broken the law in any way. In our business, you have to be smart in more ways than one!"

"Yes," Shushi chimed in. "And when someone with wealth and power is grieving over the loss of a child, and then discover they can have that child back, essentially—the identical child they lost—then, do you think the laws will change?"

Bill sat silent while Shushi seemed to be considering what he had just said. The conversation was fascinating, Harry thought, the idea of returning a deceased child to someone. The whole notion just didn't seem real, but apparently it could soon be a reality.

Out of the corner of his eye, Harry could see Beth at the reception counter. She was looking his way and smiling. He was beginning to feel restless, and as intriguing as this topic was, he wanted to get on with his work.

"Wow, you guys really gave me something to think about. My head is whirling." Harry was sincere, but still looking for an exit strategy.

"Don't worry," Shushi responded. "We get that often. This topic always stirs up the thought process, especially when it's discussed in terms of being a real life possibility."

"We'll look forward to sharing more with you as we move forward," Bill added.

"Right now," Harry said, standing, "I'd better get back to work. In fact, my subs are probably wondering what happened to me."

Harry turned to see Abraham Dante marching in through the front door with Reese Orchard right behind him.

"Hey, this place is really shaping up," Reese announced loudly, hurrying over to the grassy oasis. "Hello, gentlemen! What—are you having a party and we weren't invited?" he laughed.

"Hello, Abraham." Bill stood and shook Dante's hand.

"Good to see you all," Abraham said with a nod, "and, Harry, I'm glad I caught you. I was wondering how you're handling all the new projects. It's got to be quite a juggling act."

"So far I've managed to keep up," Harry said confidently. "That is, with a little help from my friends."

"Glad to hear that. I understand you have some blueprints that will help us in our remodeling of the warehouses down on the waterfront?"

"Yes," Harry answered, unwittingly recalling the nightmare he encountered in Rachael's building. "Somehow, Rachael was able to find them. I'm sure they'll be invaluable in the restoration process."

"Yes, she already informed me. And how about our old drug store?" Abraham continued.

"We could start almost immediately," Harry explained, struggling to keep up with Dante.

Abraham continued. "Reese believes that restoring such a well-known landmark will be a great way to introduce the whole face lift idea to the rest of the town."

"Did I hear my name mentioned?" Reese interjected, cheerfully edging up to Harry and giving him a mild jab in the side.

"Yes, Reese," Abraham answered. "I was telling Harry your thoughts regarding the old drug store."

"Right," Reese agreed, "and Harry is the one to make it happen." He chuckled and turned to Harry. "So, how is the newest and most successful contractor in Isles End?"

Harry felt himself redden. He wasn't sure why, but he had

suddenly become uncomfortable with the conversation and the company. "I'm doing well, thanks, Reese, but you know, if I don't get to work, I may not be successful for very long."

With a couple of nods and understanding laughter, Harry excused himself and headed in the direction of the elevators. Beth watched him as he strode toward her. He paused long enough to smile at her and offer in a hushed voice, "I'll call you later." Then he hurried down to the basement where part of his team was still working. Confirming they were on track, he took the elevator up to the third floor where he found a second group of laborers finishing up.

What had recently been an expansive open floor had been transformed into a series of spacious cubicles and work stations. Harry remembered the first time he'd stepped into the huge open room where Beth had guided him up to meet with Reese and the other key figures of Advanced Bio-Cell. The meeting had not been that long ago. The room took on a different feel now but the reflective glass walls still let in plenty of light and the view was amazing. Feeling confident about the progress there, Harry took the elevator back down to the main floor. He had told Beth he would call her later but now hoped he might have a moment to visit. It would be especially nice if the crowd thinned out a bit.

The elevator doors opened and Harry stepped into the hallway and turned in Beth's direction. When he didn't see her at the counter, he continued into the foyer. The expansive room was still impressive. Up ahead he could make out Beth sitting near the fountain with another woman.

Rachael Sapphire.

He had no reason to feel anxious about seeing her there, but the fact that she was sitting and talking to Beth made him feel uncomfortable. Still, he had just spoken with her on the phone recently and she had a sincere and understandable explanation about her disappearance.

He was supposed to have called her yesterday!

As he moved in the direction of the two women, Rachael swung around as though she had ended her conversation with Beth, sensing he had just appeared behind her. She quickly stood and hurried in his direction.

"Rachael, I'm so sorry I didn't call you yesterday!" Harry blurted out as she approached. He could see Beth looking on with interest from where Rachael had just abandoned her. He couldn't help wondering about the content of their conversation.

"It's okay, Harry," Rachael offered as she came to a sudden stop before him. "No worries."

"How is your father doing?" he asked.

"Who?" Rachael responded, then, "Oh, my dad! Yes, of course! He's doing much better—thank you for asking. That was quite an ordeal, but he's already out of the hospital and back home."

She paused just inches away, and Harry was afraid she was going to brush up against him and embrace him like she had done before. As he gazed down at her, he was again struck by her remarkable beauty, even while he could see Beth was still showing interest in their direction. *There is nothing inappropriate going on here,* he reassured himself. But then as he shifted his attention from Beth back to Rachael, he realized there was something . . . wrong. Not in the fact that he was with her. There was something different about her.

It was her face!

What had happened to her? Not wanting to be obvious, he looked closer, studying her features. There—it was her mouth—it was crooked!

"Is there something wrong, Harry?" Rachael asked softly, gazing up at him.

"Of course not," Harry lied, taking a step back. He didn't know what to say, or what else he could have said . . . *Yes, your mouth is crooked?* He made an effort to focus on the issues at hand. "I was just remembering, Abraham wants us to get started right away on the old drug store, so I'm glad you're here. Maybe we can discuss that project now, over in the foyer—" Harry turned his gaze in the direction of the fountain. The area was deserted now and he could talk to her there about a starting date and simultaneously show any onlookers that there was nothing to hide—their relationship was strictly professional. Not that he really needed to make such an effort. In his heart, he recognized immediately that these trials were more for himself than for anyone else.

"Sure," Rachael agreed. "That would be fine."

"Great." He guided her that direction and then paused. "Go ahead, Rachael—why don't you find a comfortable seat and I'll catch up with you in a couple minutes."

"Okay, Harry," she answered with an awkward tone, "but—"

Before Rachael could voice any dissent, Harry jetted away toward the station where Beth had resumed with her responsibilities. With that, Rachael turned abruptly, marched directly over to the fern-laden sanctuary and plopped down under the pillar of stone.

"Busy morning," Harry commented as he approached Beth, who was crouched down behind the counter.

"I'll say!" she answered as she stood up with a bundle of documents in her arms.

Harry continued, "Rachael and I are going to spend a few minutes in the foyer discussing the downtown projects Abraham Dante has us working on."

"Alright, Harry," Beth responded, and then, "not that it's any of my business, but why here?"

Harry realized it did seem a bit odd that they would choose Advanced Bio- Cell to discuss a completely unrelated project that had nothing to do with this company. His thoughts were interrupted by Beth's voice.

"Harry, can I just ask, do you know what she's doing here? I mean, there's nothing wrong with Rachael being here, I suppose, but I'm just curious what business she has here."

Harry wondered about this too, but answered quickly, "Abraham Dante and Reese Orchard were here earlier; I would guess that maybe she was here looking for them? I saw you speaking with her. Did she explain herself to you?"

"She didn't talk about why she was here, but she did say a few things."

Harry waited patiently for Beth to continue.

"And I'm puzzled by what she asked me."

Harry glanced back to see Rachael sitting by the fountain waiting for him with an anxious expression on her face. "What did she say?" he asked in a hushed voice.

"Well, first she wanted to know if I was dating anyone," Beth said in an even quieter tone. "She already knows we've been seeing each other. She said she heard that I was seeing someone else, besides you—"

"Really. What did you tell her?"

"I told her that it wasn't true, of course!"

Harry already knew it wasn't true. Still, he felt relieved again as the words came out. "Anything else?"

"She told me that it didn't really matter either way since we are on the same team—"

"What does that mean?" Harry asked with a confused expression on his face.

"I really don't know! And that's what I said to her, but she just smiled a crooked smile at me. Then she turned away to see you across the lobby and quickly jumped up, excused herself, and raced towards you."

Harry had already forgotten Rachael's crooked smile and was wondering again why he hadn't noticed it before. He looked back over to the water feature where Rachael was still waiting.

"I better go finish up this business. I'm sorry, Beth, I don't know why she is here, but I may as well make the best of this opportunity. I'll call you soon and maybe we can make plans to get together."

"Okay, Harry—can't wait to see you again."

Harry smiled and then turned back to where Rachael was waiting. It didn't take him long to take a seat. The disturbing change in her facial features was more evident now, though she was still quite attractive.

"Is everything okay, Harry?"

"Of course, but I was going to ask you the same question—How are you?"

"Why would you ask me that?"

"Everything you've just been through—your dad! You seem a bit troubled."

"Yes, it's been a rough week, though my dad is doing much better. I haven't been sleeping well. I know Abraham wants to get started immediately on the drug store and I'm trying to stay on track. Can you meet me there in the morning? Afterwards, we can look at the buildings across the street." Rachael struggled to control her sagging mouth and wondered if Harry was beginning to see through her charade.

Harry studied her. She gazed back, covering her mouth now with her hand. Somewhere in her expression he could see an anxious concern making an effort to surface, like she was somehow pleading with him to do something. There was a vulnerability in her countenance he had never noticed before. He could see she was troubled, but why? He unexpectedly found himself wanting to console her, to set her at ease. He wanted to assure her, *Rachael, everything's going to be alright . . .*

"Harry, aside from being a business associate, are you my friend?"

This was a surprise. Were they friends? But here was an opportunity to give Rachael the comfort he sensed that she needed so badly.

"Rachael, of course. I think we need to understand each other's boundaries, though, you know? Healthy boundaries. But yes, I think I can say we are friends."

"I'm so glad to hear you say that, Harry. It just occurred to me," she lowered her head, "I don't think I have many friends."

Rachael Sapphire looked so sad sitting there and Harry found himself feeling sorry for her as she expressed such deep loneliness.

She turned to the fountain. "It's beautiful, isn't it, Harry?"

"Yes," he answered, following her gaze to the giant pinnacle of stone. "It looks like someone's artistic version of the fountain of youth."

Rachael turned her head up toward the ceiling. Just above

the top of the granite pillar, Abaddon floated comfortably.

With Gorguol missing in action, was this her new master?

The powerful devil hung there with a sly expression gleaming from his lustrous features. He was relaxed, hovering just above the obelisk, observing all that took place below. He winked at her, and she smiled a crooked smile back in response.

34
Ducks in a Row

Abaddon observed as Scratch played out the part of Rachael Sapphire. Clearly the podgy demon was slipping in his ability to perpetuate the role. Did the little waif not know about his crooked face? And what was this strategy about sharing the sob story that he, or rather, "she"—had no friends? How would gaining sympathy from Harry help their position? In Abaddon's opinion, this only made Scratch's character appear weaker. He preferred the Rachael Sapphire that was strong and independent. Also, if Rachael was vulnerable now, then how much more so was Scratch?

But the scarlet lord didn't have time for this waste of energy. Moving to a more private location he called for his right hand demons. He only needed to speak their names and they appeared.

"Yes, master!" Jinn stood in acquiescence.

"Lord?" Rull spoke almost simultaneously, standing in the shadow of the other spirit.

"Greetings, my most trusted," Abaddon began. "I must depart, only for a brief time. I want you to fill the gap until I return. I feel it necessary to visit the lair of Gorguol and see for myself what remains."

Abaddon laid out his instructions. The two devils took his commands easily, which reminded him how important it was to have such dependable comrades. Once he was sure his desires were understood, he dismissed the two ghouls and rose up high above his stronghold, hidden far beneath the Advanced Bio-Cell building. From this vantage point, he gazed south to see the edge of Isles End. He turned his visage north and could just make out the tops of the city buildings. Without further delay, he disengaged from the air he occupied and transported himself to the building that had so recently been the chamber of his master.

It didn't take long for the devil to see there had been trouble. The building that had recently been Gorguol's sanctuary was now crawling with a flood of local law enforcement, the entire structure roped off with yellow tape.

He glided down onto the roof top, still a lovely garden surrounded by stone gargoyles. The entryway he had required sanction before, seemed easy enough to access now. Once inside, Abaddon encountered the same foul aroma that had filled the upper room before. Now, however, the room was filled with more yellow tape, diagrams on the floor and furniture, and several uniformed men speaking somberly as they made observations and took notes. There were plastic bags on the table with collected items already sealed and tagged.

Abaddon moved forward through the room with the comfort of knowing he was undetected. He didn't need to wonder what had taken place here. He'd already heard a point-by-point description from Scratch, but now the facts were sinking in. Aside from having a decaying body in the room, it still hadn't been the best kept apartment by most standards, but now the penthouse was in complete disorder. He never had a great respect for his master, but he knew the devil was not foolish. How had this happened? Had Gorguol become complacent in his debauchery? The missing lord must have let his guard down. Now what?

Abaddon slipped down through the floor into the level below. More law enforcement! There was a man sitting, restrained, in the front room of his apartment. He looked awful. Clearly sleep deprived, the clothes he wore were dirty and disheveled, and he had blood stains on the front of his shirt. Abaddon remembered him.

"You have the right to remain silent," a uniformed officer began reciting to the man, but he didn't seem to be aware of his circumstances. He just sat there oblivious.

"There is no upper floor," he suddenly announced to no one in particular.

"You have the right to an attorney," the officer continued his mantra.

"I *am* an attorney!" the soiled man answered dully.

Abaddon moved back up through the floor to Gorguol's domain. He studied the rest of the penthouse suite. The entire floor was in ruins. There had been an unexpected attack here. It was clear that whatever had happened here had been a surprise, sudden and calculated. He used his unique abilities to envision the circumstances leading up to the conflict—the stronghold had not been guarded well. He could see the scenario unfolding and cursed under his breath. The weakness of his master's entourage was upsetting, and Gorguol himself, well, Abaddon would never have allowed this to happen.

The dark lord felt a surge of pleasure as he pieced together the events leading up to his master's demise. These reckless fiends had forgotten something about history. How many times had he seen one group caught off guard and then be overcome by their enemy due to an inflated assessment of their own skills and powers? Abaddon had studied the scenario and learned it many times over. But his pleasure was stained with disappointment. These had been his comrades. Not only that, but this was a defeat for his side.

Well, no matter. He would take up the reins. It was time to move his way up the ladder. In fact, he was surprised he hadn't heard from senior management already. He guessed he would hear from them soon, but until then, he had some serious decisions to make.

Abaddon sensed the approaching presence of a familiar spirit.

"Lord, forgive me for the sudden intrusion but we are in trouble!"

It was Jinn. Aside from his already monstrous features, he didn't look well at all, in fact, he had clearly taken a beating.

"Jinn!" Abaddon shouted. "What has happened to you?"

"Forgive me—" Jinn's suffering was obvious as he

struggled to speak. His cloak was shredded and his face was swollen, cuts dripping with yellow puss. He knew his wounds were apparent and he kept his head lowered out of humiliation.

"Jinn, I will not harm you. Tell me, what has happened?"

Jinn relaxed his composure—he was obviously distraught. "I strongly request that you return to our hold without delay. We have been compromised. Our enemies are at hand!"

"What do you mean?" Abaddon bellowed.

Jinn's response was filled with anger. "We were not idle and everything seemed to be under control," he answered in a low, desperate voice. "Then, with a sudden pounding, there was chaos!"

Abaddon studied Jinn's face. There was no deceit in his countenance, only a mixture of fear and shame.

"Jinn, be specific!"

"Lord," the gruesome looking devil snarled. "There were four of them, just as Scratch described. Their leader was the Seraph, Narcissus, the one whose name has become the subject of ridicule for so many centuries—and I must concur, he has become immensely powerful! And then I recognized Agalliao, the Cherub with the fool's grin. The other two I'm sure you remember, Ranan and Psallo. Their combined strength exuded so much light we were all blinded! They came out of nowhere and struck hard and effectively. I believe they could have crushed us entirely, but the Seraph, Narcissus, shouted that this was a warning and ordered us to vacate. 'Find somewhere else to abide', the grinning one commanded."

"Why do you believe they could have done *more* harm?" Abaddon questioned.

"When it seemed that we might be near defeat, they simply departed! I am truly regretful, but I must admit we were taken by surprise. Since when do the angels of Elohim attack like this?"

Abaddon nodded. "I have rarely seen it," he grated. "What is the status of your protégé, Scratch?"

Jinn grimaced at the mention of the name. "I am not his keeper! I do not know his whereabouts, but he was not with us when we were ambushed."

"Jinn, do you suspect that rascal could have had anything to do with the compromise of our stronghold?" Abaddon demanded with sudden concern.

"Surely not! He *is* cowardly, Sire, and has reason to fear this band of angelic marauders, but I can't imagine he would succumb to that kind of treachery."

"Yes, I agree," Abaddon said as his distrust was brought to rest. "But I do not understand this ability that these unfallen angels have—that they can just access our lair and overcome my most powerful guards. *I will not accept this!*"

Jinn was silent as Abaddon brooded, then, "Let us return immediately and secure our quarters."

Jinn formed a shrewd smirk on his trampled face, and the two devils sped off together in the direction of the Advanced Bio-

Cell buildings. Abaddon showed no fear when they arrived. He wore his anger like a mallet, ready to bludgeon anyone who got in his way.

"What is this trickery?" he snarled as they entered the stronghold.

"Yes," Jinn shielded his eyes. "They left this *light!*"

"*I will not have it!*" Abaddon growled under his breath.

They cautiously made their way through the dungeon-like halls to find a powerful luminescence filling the rooms.

"There is no source," Jinn exclaimed. "It's just here!"

As they moved deeper in the lower spaces, the light began to diminish until finally, as they neared the secret rooms below, they were able to see more clearly.

"There is someone ahead," Abaddon cautioned. "Wait!" They slid up against the wall, just before a larger room. "It's safe, Jinn, they are familiar spirits!"

Half a dozen demons charged forward, with Rull in the lead, his mannequin features scarred from the recent attack.

"HALT," Abaddon roared. "It is I, you fools!"

Rull nearly collapsed before his master but regained his footing and stood at attention. He spoke proudly through his inflamed features. "My Lord, we did not sense that you had arrived! There is this unearthly light! We moved deeper into the hidden quarters expecting to be followed. We were confident to have the upper hand down here, but our enemies vanished. They came on strong, but they have shown themselves to be cowards. I assure you, we did not relinquish our ground!"

"Yes, faithful one," Abaddon said with pride. He looked over the rest of the disheveled group. They all had the look of defeat in their faces but they stood before their master as though ready to fight at his slightest signal.

"Clean yourselves up and gather your wits," he spoke with authority. "We are going to vacate these premises temporarily until I figure out what is going on. You know where to go! I will meet up with you later. I shall not tolerate this or accept it as any kind of defeat. We will strike back, my friends, but first we must have all our ducks in a row. Jinn, I want you to locate our little friend, Scratch. Find out what the mischievous sprite is up to now."

With that, Abaddon moved guardedly as he made his way back through the celestial light that filled his domain. Above ground, the natural light was much more agreeable. He soared up above the ABC building and scanned the horizon. The early morning sun would soon be up. Down below, the building buzzed with personnel. He watched Shushi Yang hurrying in through a staff-only door on the side of the building where the doctor had his own private parking space. Preston Hart's car was already there along with William Algren's. Abaddon dropped down through the top of the building and carefully assessed his position. Had there been any angelic influence here lately? There didn't appear to be any recent disruptions, but he made his rounds with a measure of caution.

434

Everything looked to be in order. At least some things were still going according to plan. Human cloning was well on its way to becoming a reality, and with it, Abbadon's own fame and prestige would be established in the dark realm, once again. Satisfied, Abaddon located his minion and eased himself into the comfortable human space he had become so familiar with. His host responded with a noticeable degree of pleasure, and Abaddon realized he had interceded just in time. There was no room for error now and he quickly moved into position.

As Shushi entered his superior's office, he saw William Algren sitting in his new chair, obviously experiencing a high level of agitation. The doctor closed the door, nodded to Bill, and took a seat.

"What's going on, Shushi?" Bill asked.

"Good morning, Bill. Thank you for meeting with me on short notice. Where's Preston?"

No sooner had the words left Shushi's mouth than Preston Hart appeared in the doorway and walked over to Bill's desk. He sat down across from the other two men. "What's this all about?" he asked, pinching his nose to restrain a sneeze. He did not look happy.

"Well, gentlemen," Shushi began, leaning forward. "I called this meeting because I feel it is time to share some concerns I have with the direction that this company is headed. I have other news as well."

"I've been expecting this, Shushi," Bill responded, "and

435

I'm already prepared to set your mind at ease."

Preston sat silently and shifted his glasses higher onto his nose.

Bill continued, "I realize I shouldn't have been so secretive with you, Shushi, regarding the possible candidates for our first cloning operation."

"*What?* You have chosen candidates?" Preston exclaimed with surprise.

"Now, now, let's not jump to any conclusions just yet. Let's—"

"I don't mean to interrupt you, Bill, but I called this meeting for my own reasons," Shushi broke in. "Let me explain. While you both have been busy with all this moving, I have not remained idle. I've been conducting experiments of my own."

"Really!" Preston muttered. "What does that mean?"

"If you would remain silent for once, Preston, you might actually learn something! I have many resources, as you both know. I was not the one who was keen on this whole move in the first place. Quite honestly, I didn't need the extra space! Did you think I would just sit on my hands and do nothing when I was so close to completion, while you two spun your wheels with all *this*? New buildings, all this property development, streets bearing the names of artists, expensive water features! All this 'modern day Eden' doesn't impress me. Sorry, Bill—no offense, but you both should know me better than that!" He reached up and pushed back the thick white mop of hair that hung down over his forehead.

"Since you are both my friends, I want you to hear this from me first! I was already on the brink of several solutions to the very problems that held us back from completion. I have many other contacts who are more interested in results than all this *show*."

"Wait a minute!" Bill began to object but Shushi waved him off and continued.

"I am loyal to you, Bill. Please don't begin to assume anything just yet!

"Now, here it is! With some help from some trusted associates, I have been successful in sequencing and mapping the complete human genome. Furthermore, I have additional solutions we need for phase one in growing human organs. I know I led you to believe that we had hit a brick wall. The truth is, that simply wasn't the case. I apologize for that, but you left me no choice with all the mystery regarding our first human host. Keep in mind now, this is good news and I'm sharing it with you first."

Bill relaxed his scowl and leaned back in his chair. Preston looked agitated and jumped up like he was going to charge someone.

"Preston, sit down. There's more, and you don't want to interrupt me just yet!"

Preston obeyed, as Abaddon peered out through Preston Hart's eyes with a mixture of hostility and anticipation.

"With some help from two of my closest colleagues," Shushi continued, "we now, additionally, have all we require to safely begin the process of cloning the first human being! My data is complete and ready to be executed. Please . . . don't make the mistake of thinking we will rush into anything just yet."

"Why didn't you share this with us sooner?" Preston demanded, Abaddon's influence pushing him forward.

"Isn't it obvious?" Shushi responded. "You have not shown me, Preston, that you can be fully trusted. If we are going to share such powerful knowledge with the world, I will require that some very tight reins be put in place."

"Shushi," Bill broke in, "I am truly sorry. I did not show you the respect you deserve. I don't blame you for the decisions you've been forced to make. I'm actually quite pleased with this news."

As Abaddon gazed at Shushi through Preston's eyes, he began to see something he had not noticed before. There behind the white mop of thick white hair . . . what was that? A figure?

YES! The space behind Shushi began to reveal the form of . . . an unfallen angel!

Angelic interference! I should have known—!

Preston's mouth was moving but it was Abaddon who was formulating the thoughts into words. "Shushi, I'm sorry, my friend, but it appears *you* are the one in question of being trusted. I must admit, I'm a bit hurt and disappointed with you right now. What can I say? How long have we worked together? And this is

438

how you repay us?"

Abaddon studied the guardian. *Who is this angel who is so clearly watching over the white-haired scientist?* Finally, the features became clearer and he recognized the celestial being.

Ranan! OH . . . this one is bold!

And then, *Does he recognize me? Does he know I'm here?*

Abaddon had gone to great lengths to conceal himself within his ward. Even his own devils could not sense his presence when he occupied this chosen minion, but now he couldn't be sure. Preston's face twisted with Abaddon's frustration over the angelic intrusion.

"Please don't take it personally, Preston," he heard Shushi saying, "but I wasn't about to share such knowledge without taking responsibility for my personal involvement. I really couldn't live with myself if I allowed such powerful information to get into the wrong hands. Others may discover on their own what I now know, but it will not be anytime soon, trust me, and I shall not be reckless. As I mentioned earlier, I'll be setting up some very rigid guidelines. There will be more contracts, stringent boundaries, all the legalese, and of course, high security."

"You know, Shushi," Bill interjected, "the other morning when we were sharing our concerns regarding this operation with our contractor, Harry Turner, I was reminded by some of the things you shared, just how prudent we really do need to be. I

439

admit, I have allowed myself to become somewhat inflated. I'm sorry."

"I'm glad to hear you say that, Bill," Shushi said, relaxing his composure. "I honestly believed that you would see things clearly when faced with the reality of what we finally have in our grasp."

"I'm sorry, guys, but I feel like I've been left in the dark over here," Preston interrupted loudly. "You said something about some choices for a potential candidate earlier. What was that about, and why wasn't I informed? I know we've discussed certain possibilities but did you actually make some choices without me?"

"I did tell Shushi I had some firm blood samples available," Bill admitted. "Some of them rather expensive, I might add."

"Seriously now, Bill," Preston urged. "What specific candidate were you considering?"

"Alright, Preston, listen carefully," Bill let his frustration turn to anger. "I had nothing set in stone! There were several promising possibilities. I never reached the point where I had decided on one choice over any others."

"Bill!" Preston spoke the man's name with new fury in his voice.

"What do you want to hear, Preston?" Bill responded with heightened attitude. "Did we consider DaVinci? Yes! Hawking? Of course! Einstein? Seriously, Preston, what do you want to hear? Name any prominent artist, writer, philosopher, or leader. They are all candidates. We considered others as well who are not so well known. One of the most interesting acquisitions, however," Bill paused nervously and then let it spill out, "is the blood sample we purchased from the Shroud of Turin. Is that the information you are looking for, Mr. Hart?"

Preston's jaw dropped as though he'd been hit from behind with a baseball bat.

"If that is true," Shushi cut in, "then I was approached by the same gentleman. My research led me to believe that his organization may not have been the most reliable source."

"Oh, it's reliable, Shushi, you can trust me on that," Bill countered. "We would not have made the purchase otherwise. But, sharing this information would create a great deal of controversy, I've kept it under lock and key. I have to say though, it's still quite an alluring consideration."

Abaddon was furious now. He had gone through the process of securing that contact and had been instrumental in forming the relationship that made the connection possible to have that very special sample available. Now what . . . was it all in vain?

"That DNA sample from the Shroud of Turin is the perfect choice for the first cloned human being," Preston blurted out.

The doctor glared back at Preston with firm determination. "It won't be happening anytime soon, Preston, if

441

ever. I promise you that."

Now the angel Ranan focused his gaze as though he was looking through Preston Hart's eyes and staring directly at Abaddon. The dark lord was sure now he'd been detected. Preston's eyes darted around the room frantically and he began to moan. Abaddon decided he could not bear to listen to any more of this drivel. The position he held with Preston Hart quickly became worthless and it served no purpose to abide in this man any longer. It was time to end this charade and take leave.

The force of the dark spirit pulling out of his host so rapidly caused the body of Preston Hart to immediately slump to the floor. As Abaddon jetted away into the sky, he gazed back down to see the other two men jumping up to their friend's aid, but the angered demon had lost interest. There was nothing left for him in that building except failure. This particular breakdown could once again be directly attributed to the failure of his overseer, Gorguol. The humiliated devil spun around and turned his attention towards Isles End.

35
Romans 2:14

The familiar scene was back again. Harry was eight years old again and headed off to school. His mother handed him his lunch and kissed him good-bye. She gave him the usual warning: Be careful, Harry, and may your guardian angel protect you! He smiled and waved back. He walked the usual path, recognizing all the familiar details along the way. But once again, as he neared the bottom of the road, the landscape began to change.

Again, the foreboding bridge came into view. Don't go there! But he couldn't stop himself and continued to move ahead as usual. Soon, he would be forced to cross. Far below, he could hear water rushing under the bridge. Just before he reached the overpass he jumped to the side and slid down into the ravine. The water rushed up towards him until he met it with a splash and the current gripped him. He thought he might sink until he realized the water was only knee deep. Again, he was locked in place, moving toward the bridge. Harry held back his fear as the recurring scene unfolded, but the feeling of terror was hauntingly close.

Against his will, he moved forward into the murky opening. Directly ahead, the beastly figure loomed, waiting for him as always. Its skin glistened in the shadowy tunnel and the glowing eyes seemed to pull Harry in like a fish on a line. Now he remembered. This was a recurring dream! But that recognition didn't give him any relief, nor was he able to escape! The image became strangely familiar as Harry found himself standing mutely before the being. The last time it had been Narcissus. He had worn a sparkling multi-colored robe, but now it was a dark tailored suit—Harry remembered it from the prior dream. But this wasn't Narcissus . . . He'd seen this face before. The man smiled down at Harry with the same malevolent expression as before and extended his hand.

"Greetings, Harry," he said invitingly. "Do you enjoy these visits?"

The face was that of Abraham Dante. Harry tried to back away, but as usual, he could not move.

"What is it you fear, my friend? I'm only here to help you!"

The sudden ringing of Harry's alarm caused him to wake with a start. What was it with that dream? He climbed out of bed and went directly to the shower. The hot water helped him wake up and also relieved the feeling of dread still lingering from the dream. He let the water wash away his doubts as he thought again of the living water he had experienced in the pool with his angelic friends. The idea of this Mantle of Strength he'd received sounded great, but he had no idea how to use it, even though its power had risen to the surface more than once to become available to him. He recalled his ability to release himself from the grip of the door on the top floor of Rachael's building. Why hadn't he asked Narcissus more about it? The gift must have a very significant meaning or purpose, and he wanted to make better use of it. Out of the shower, he was almost dressed when his phone rang.

"Harry, it's Abraham."

"Yes, hello!"

"I understand you may have had an appointment with Miss Sapphire for sometime today?"

"Yes—in fact, I was supposed to meet her at the old drugstore sometime later this afternoon."

"Harry, I don't think she's going to make it. I haven't been able to contact her and I'm wondering if she was called away— maybe something to do with her father?"

"Oh yes," Harry confirmed. "She told me a little about her dad's troubles. I hope he's alright!"

"I don't know the details, Harry, but I believe we'll just have to wait until we hear from her. In the meantime, I'd like to fill in for her and keep the appointment with you myself."

Harry quickly considered the offer. Was he ready to blow off Rachael so quickly? Well, that wasn't really the case; Abraham *was* her boss.

"She was supposed to call me to confirm," Harry responded, "but I haven't heard from her yet."

"Change of plans, Harry! You will meet with me instead. We can have dinner at the cafe where we first met. Afterwards, we can look at the warehouses on the wharf and discuss the renovation process. If we have time, we can visit the drug store as

445

well. They are all so close. What do you say?"

"Sure, that'll be fine."

"Fantastic—looks like we have a date, then! I don't want to make it too late but I have a busy schedule today. Why don't we meet at six?"

Harry agreed and said goodbye. He sat there for a moment and considered Rachael Sapphire—her alluring features, his trip with her to the city . . . the semi-intimate encounter, and, her recently crooked mouth! It was too bad he couldn't meet with her, even though he had a curious feeling about her now. Something was amiss, but he couldn't quite pinpoint it.

He gazed across the room, and there at the foot of the bed, was the chest. He wished Narcissus was with him. Confusion began to surface. He didn't expect Narcissus to appear like a genie whenever he called, but he did wish he could see him on a more regular basis. Running into his angelic friend outside Rachael's apartment building still didn't make any sense. Had the angel been present knowing that he was there, or had he come for some other reason?

Having the chest there in his room was a physical reminder of the experiences he'd had since he freed the celestial being. Walking over to it, he opened the lid and let the leather straps hold it in place. Inside was the cardboard sign Narcissus had left with him in the city. Underneath was the fern branch from the garden, which the angel had carefully placed there for him. In addition, the intoxicating fragrance that had originally radiated from the strongbox was still as sweet as Harry remembered from the beginning. He leaned his head down into the cavity and inhaled deeply. Nothing short of wonderful! What could possibly be the real source of an aroma so exotic and breathtaking? He was reminded of the gate of living creatures. Maybe *that* place could be the origin of something so marvelous. He leaned forward again and breathed in the scent of the coffer a second time. Why hadn't he taken the opportunity to appreciate this treasure more often? The scent gave him strength! If he could only bottle this fragrance, he could be rich!

He dipped his head in again and noticed something down at the bottom. This was not here before! Harry reached down and lifted up a large envelope. He opened it and found a folded sheet of paper inside. Raising his head, Harry scanned the room nervously. He was alone. There didn't seem to be anything unusual, nothing rearranged or missing. Unfolding the page, he saw a handwritten message.

Harry, it began, *I'm going to tell you something about yourself that you have never heard before. It is this: There are those who have had no knowledge of Elohim or any of His ways. You are one of these. Yet, by instinct, you have confirmed living in the certainty of His ways just by your natural obedient nature and willingness to observe goodness. You are proof that Elohim's edicts are not unknown rules, imposed on anyone from without, but rather woven into the very fabric of your being. There is something deep within you that echoes His yes and no, and the understanding of what is right and wrong. Your response to His yes and no will become public knowledge someday. In the meantime, though, seek out that truth which has been planted in your heart. ~Narcissus*

When did the angel leave this in the chest? Harry read it again. The message caused him to feel lighthearted. Not only was the content itself encouraging, but it also showed Harry that Narcissus had not forgotten him. But the words themselves! Were they speaking about him? The angel said, *Yes!* He had a natural obedient nature! A willingness to observe goodness! The words were soothing and he read them a third time.

"Narcissus," Harry shouted aloud. "Thank you! If you can hear me, thank you, wherever you are!"

Harry finished his morning routine with renewed vigor and headed over to Ivory Lane. He felt like he had not been there for a while. Ed and Butch, along with four other workers, were busy cleaning up before they started on the finish framing. The roof was done, the windows installed, and the siding complete. The house looked great and he was sorry he'd missed out. Ed had a plumber there who was getting ready to begin.

"Hey, Harry!" Ed yelled out excitedly. "Glad you're here. We have the best plumber in the harbor here! I want you to meet him!"

"Okay," Harry answered. He climbed out of his truck and made his way to the front of the new building. Just inside was a man who could have been his older brother. *A little gray, equally as scruffy, and almost as good-looking*, Harry thought.

"Harry, I'd like you to meet Joe."

Harry extended his arm and shook the hand of the man inside the doorway.

"I'm pleased to meet you, Harry! You can call me Joe the Plumber."

Harry couldn't help smiling. "Okay, Joe the Plumber—glad to meet you, too!"

Ed explained to Harry how he and Joe had discussed the proper level of plumbing fixtures appropriate for this home. High-end biscuit colored toilets and sinks with oil-rubbed bronze faucets. Also, body sprays, ceiling heads, and hand-held slide bars in the tubs and showers.

"Are you sure we can afford this with our budget?" Harry asked Ed.

"I've already crunched the numbers, Harry. We're right in there, and Reese already approved the list!"

This was the exact reason Harry felt so comfortable with Ed as his foreman. The guy had talent.

"Hey there, Harry," came a voice from further inside the building.

"Butch!" Harry answered. "Good to see you! The place looks great!"

"Thanks! We like it."

"I expected you to say that it looks good from your house!"

"Oh no—I only say that on jobs where the finished product is not quite up to par," Butch laughed.

"That's right, I remember now," Harry said. "Well, this is really coming together nicely. You guys have exceeded my expectations!"

"Good to hear." Butch extended his tattooed arm with such grace that Harry couldn't help but embrace it with a hearty grip.

"We'll have the heating guys in next," Ed called out. "The electrician stopped by and marked everything out. We're looking at getting him over here next week."

"That sounds great, Ed," Harry said with a look of pride.

"If you're gonna stick around, " Ed added, "I've got an extra tool belt!"

"No, I've got some business to take care of. Besides, you guys are doing so well without me, I don't want to mess things up! I'm going to meet Mr. Dante downtown later for dinner to discuss the warehouses on the wharf."

"Okay, Boss," Ed said with a grin, "but you're missing all the fun!"

"I know, but listen, if this works out, we'll all be busy for quite some time!"

Harry drove back to his place to work on invoices, job material lists, and payroll. When he was finished, he couldn't help taking the letter out of the chest and reading it again.

Elohim's edicts are woven into the very fabric of your

450

being!

Edicts? Harry got online and looked it up. Proclamations, laws, decrees . . . *I have these woven into me?* He couldn't help feeling a sense of pride mixed with somber humility. What had he done to deserve any praise?

Harry realized it was almost six o'clock. Back in his truck, he drove to the cafe to meet with Abraham. As he pulled around to the back of the building, he remembered the first experience he'd had with the man. It was here where he had seen Abraham up the street, through the window, while he ate his pot roast dinner not so long ago. He had recognized Reese Orchard speaking with the man. Harry recalled how Abraham had been very cavalier until he realized Harry was the one Reese had spoken of so highly. Abraham's attitude had made a sudden adjustment, once he discovered who Harry was.

Inside, Harry saw that his usual seat by the front window was vacant. The waitress welcomed him and placed a menu on the table. Outside, the sun was dropping down on the water and a mixture of color splashed across the bay like a moving picture.

"You are prompt, as usual, Mr. Turner." Harry heard Abraham's voice call out from inside the front door. "Have you ordered yet?" Abraham asked as he hurried over and took a seat across from Harry.

"No, I was just looking at the specials."

"Do you like a good steak, Harry?"

"Of course!"

The waitress was just now approaching. Abraham opened the menu and said, "I don't see filet mignon on the menu—we'll both have the rib-eye, medium rare, with a calamari appetizer. I would like a Campari and soda if you have it."

"I have no idea what Campari is, sir. I'll check though, while I get the calamari started." She turned to Harry. "Something to drink?"

"I'll have a beer, whatever type of amber you have on draft."

She jotted down the remaining details of their orders and hurried away.

"Well, Harry, it seems we have quite a bit of work ahead of us. The drug store is ready to begin. There is some demo to take care of, but you can start any time. I believe you received a healthy check from my assistant?"

"Yes," Harry answered, suddenly uncomfortable. "I appreciate that. Thank you."

"I like to take care of my people, Harry. If we are going to work together, I want you to know you can depend on me to hold up my end of the bargain. Money always seems to help solidify these things, don't you agree?"

Before Harry had a chance to respond, the waitress returned with the calamari, a glass of beer for Harry, and Abraham's drink.

"Good news," she began, "The owner tried Campari at Belmar's recently, and he liked it so much he ordered a case for our inventory. I've just never had anyone ask for it!"

"Ah, wonderful," Abraham sighed. "A lovely color of red!" He held the drink up to the window and the last rays of the sun sparkled through the vermilion liquid and reflected the opaque crimson color onto the smooth features of his face. "A toast," he said, and Harry quickly raised his glass of beer. "To our mutual success—"

"Yes, to our success!" Harry repeated and tipped the glass to his lips.

They finished the calamari and then the rib-eye steaks with potatoes and salads, while Harry asked Abraham questions about how he wanted to approach the large amount of work he would be taking on. Harry liked the idea of recruiting all his people and focusing on the drug store and the warehouses at the same time. Abraham, however, seemed preoccupied and didn't show much interest in the subject of building. Rather, he was more interested in Harry's relationship with Beth Fairbanks and kept steering the conversation to personal topics.

But Harry didn't mind. In fact, he felt good about sharing his sincere interest in Beth. Abraham might share it with Rachael and help her to understand Harry's true feelings.

"Shall we take a walk down to the wharf?" Abraham suggested as they finished up their meals.

"Of course," Harry answered while the waitress cleared off their table and left the tab.

Abraham picked it up quickly. "Let me take care of this."

Harry thanked his host and they stepped outside into the cool evening air. They walked half a block to where the empty drug store was situated across the street from the water. Abraham suggested they skip the drug store for now and take a look at the view from where the old warehouses were lined up on the water side.

"I know you have the same vision for these buildings as I do," Abraham said as they walked up to the first structure. "You've seen firsthand, the type of architecture I'm looking for, not only in real life, but you've studied the actual plans as well. I believe we can reproduce here in Isles End what the buildings in Old Towne so beautifully portray. Can you imagine, Harry, how fitting they would be? This entire town would come to life!"

Harry was glad that Abraham was talking about work again. He remembered the speech Abraham had given that night at Belmar's and how excited the local merchants had been. Even Beth enjoyed it. The subject of Beth had caused him to feel a bit uncomfortable even though he welcomed the opportunity to clarify their relationship. He hoped that if the subject reached Rachael, she wouldn't be too concerned, but she had to know the truth!

"Can you see it, Harry?" Abraham interrupted his thoughts. "You walk up the street and see these large warm, welcoming shops with lots of affordable products: bath shops, garden supplies, boutiques. Then there are attractive high-end items for sale as well, along with art galleries filled with watercolor paintings reflecting Isles End themes, sculptures of fish and wildlife that are native to the area. All along the walkways there are giant containers filled with flowers. The parking is across the street with elevators and walkways over to the restaurants on the upper floors. On the waterside there are docks and piers where you can walk out toward the deeper parts of the bay to sit and enjoy the afternoon or maybe even do some fishing."

As Harry listened to Abraham describe his image of the waterfront, he began to visualize the scene for himself, just as it was being described.

"Yes, I see it," he exclaimed. As Abraham continued to put forth the details, they became alive in Harry's imagination. He and Abraham stepped aside as two young boys raced by with ice cream cones in their hands. "Look there, Harry!" Abraham pointed. Harry followed his gaze out over the water where there were kites flying with all the colors of the rainbow sailing across the sky. Now there was music flowing through the air. People were milling around with cotton candy and Italian sodas, wearing summer outfits, smiling and enjoying the weather and beauty of the wharf.

"Follow me," Abraham said and hurried away. Harry pursued him up a ramp to a flight of stairs where more music and chatter filled the air. There were people everywhere now, sitting at round tables under large umbrellas, being served lovely-looking lunches—Crab Louie, plates of sushi, club sandwiches, clam chowder, and every other dish that Harry would expect to find. From here, the deck revealed a view of the entire town, except now it seemed that Isles End had received a significant face lift.

From this vantage point, Harry found himself truly experiencing the full ramifications of the new Isles End. The sight was impressive! But then he realized it had been close to dusk when they had wandered down the street to the old warehouses. Had his imagination gone completely wild? He looked around in disbelief but it was all still there: the warm afternoon sun, the children playing on the shiny new wharf, young couples walking hand-in-hand in their summer clothes, and people bustling about, enjoying the lively atmosphere of the refurbished waterfront.

"Harry, would you like something to drink?" Abraham asked ecstatically.

"What has happened?" Harry forced himself to ask.

"What do you mean?" Abraham responded innocently.

"This!"

"What exactly are you talking about, Harry?"

"Abraham, I'm talking about this . . . *vision!*"

"It *is* nice, isn't it? Are you seeing it just as I am?"

"I have no idea!" Harry raised his voice out of frustration. "Help me out here! I'm totally turned around. How did we get here? How did *this* become *this*?" He waved his arms to include the entire area in view of the restaurant's deck. Finally, he walked over to Abraham who had just sat down at a table and was adjusting the umbrella to block the sun.

"Why don't you sit down and take a load off?" Abraham suggested.

Harry didn't want to sit down.

"Abraham, I really need to know what is happening to me—or to us—right now! This can't be real! It was almost evening when we arrived. There was no one around, and these buildings were still dilapidated. Suddenly, it's like a summer afternoon and there are people all around with restaurants and food and shops and . . . am I going crazy?"

"Harry, take my advice and sit down. Enjoy your vision, if that is what you are having. I'd call it your imaginative powers at work. Is this experience *really* new to you? I actually thought it was you who brought this about—wasn't it?"

"No!"

"You had nothing to do with this?"

"Abraham . . . NO!"

"Alright, remain calm. Let's try to figure this out together without losing our sense of reality."

"What can I get you, gentlemen?" a woman in a summery outfit asked as she sauntered up to the table.

"Two Campari and sodas please," Abraham responded.

"Very good, I'll be right back," she said and dashed away.

36
The Tempting

Harry sat down with Abraham, feeling very confused, and studied the view. It all seemed quite real. In fact, the more he looked across the expanse from this elevated position, the clearer and more refined the view became. The architecture itself looked as though *he* had been intimately involved with every detail.

"It's beautiful, isn't it, Harry?" Abraham pressed excitedly.

"It really is!" Harry had to agree.

He was fascinated, seeing his own creative genius at work even before it actually happened!

"What you see here, are your inventive ideas translated into reality. I know you have studied the plans to some degree and you've seen the actual finished product of the original buildings, so here we are now. This is the finished product with your signature on it! I must say, you exhibit amazing talent!"

Harry was dumbfounded. "Thank you," he responded with befuddled gratitude.

"No, my friend, thank you!" Abraham countered. "It's your hidden ability to express such understanding of design. I love it! I can see your autograph all over this place!"

Harry looked closely at the images in view. Abraham was right! Every detail had his imprint, and he couldn't help but feel proud as he recognized his impression infused into the structural artistry all around him. The idea this might be a vision escaped Harry's immediate thoughts as he soaked it all in.

"Abraham, I'm not sure how we came to be sitting here, experiencing this! It doesn't quite match the reality I'm used to, but I have to say, I like it!"

The waitress appeared with their drinks. "Here you go, gentlemen, two Campari and sodas," she set the two red drinks down on the table. "Can I bring you anything else?"

"For now, I think we're good," Abraham answered, sliding one of the drinks over to Harry. "Give this a try—I think you will find it quite enjoyable. The flavor is unique—actually, one of a kind!"

Harry lifted the red-colored drink and took a sip without waiting for any further toasts. The flavor was startling—slightly bitter, with a hint of citrus, orange, maybe berry, followed by a sweet aftertaste. It was . . . mysterious! He took a second drink. As the complex blend of flavors stimulated his taste buds, he experienced a sensation he'd never known before. It was quite intoxicating!

"Are you enjoying your Campari?" Abraham inquired.

"I've never tasted anything like it," Harry responded with passion.

"Yes, it is quite exquisite. One might say, divine!" Abraham added.

For a moment, they both sat quietly and relished the adult beverages. Time passed by at the normal pace as Harry watched

459

the day progress towards a second sunset. He almost forgot that this whole scenario could not be the reality he had entered into when he and Abraham had walked down the street from the cafe earlier, when the sun was already setting on the horizon.

"Abraham, I'm curious," Harry began, "how did we really arrive here in this imaginary depiction of the future Isles End?"

"How?"

"Yes, how . . . I think you know what I mean!" Harry countered with a measure of composure.

"I think it's time you get to know me better," Abraham answered with an equaled degree of calm.

"First, allow me to *really* introduce myself to you," Abraham began. "And let me apologize to you as well! Truly, I'm sorry, Harry, let me explain!" Abraham Dante lifted his glass and poured the remainder of his drink down his throat and then set the empty glass down hard on the wooden table.

"My real name is Abaddon."

"Pardon me?"

"Aba-ddon! I was once a close companion of your friend, Narcissus."

Harry almost choked on his drink. He coughed and spit and held a napkin up to his mouth, trying not to attract attention.

"I wish I could say we were still friends," Abraham continued with a hint of sorrow in his voice, "but unfortunately, he abandoned me long ago. In some ways, I'm still recovering from the rejection."

In an effort to clear his throat, Harry tipped his glass up high and let the remainder of his drink slide down. The red liqueur had a calming effect as it coated his throat. While the panic set in, the drink simultaneously gave him a feeling of relief as he fought to digest this disturbing revelation. Did Abraham just say what Harry thought he heard?

"Did you say, Narcissus?" Harry managed to sputter.

"Yes, Harry! We were once friends . . ."

Harry leaned forward and studied the man sitting across from him. *Who was this person?*

"Wait a minute—let me understand! You know Narcissus?"

Abaddon lifted his glass to his lips and sucked in a remaining ice cube. "Yes," he answered nonchalantly, "I knew him."

Harry couldn't believe what he was hearing. Neither could he believe what he was seeing and experiencing, but it was all there, as real as can be.

"Two more, please," Abraham called out firmly to the waitress as she passed by.

Harry pressed on. "How in the world do you know Narcissus . . . and how do you know that *I* know him?"

"Well, Harry, that could be a rather lengthy subject. You see, Narcissus and I go way back. For now, let's just say that I have many other friends and contacts. When someone is away for a very long time, as Narcissus has been, and then they suddenly appear out of nowhere, it doesn't take too much time for the word to get around."

Harry accepted the second round as the waitress handed him his drink. He sipped the fresh combination of soda and liqueur, and pondered as to why he'd not heard of this drink before. It was so tantalizing that he wanted to pour the entire glass down all at once and analyze every nuance and essence of the delightfully mystifying concoction.

"Alright," Harry began. "Now I'm beginning to understand. This is a game for you, isn't it? Maybe for both you and my friend, Narcissus. I'm looking around here and I'm having trouble putting things together but I'm not stupid. You *used* to be friends? *I don't believe you!* I know my friend, Narcissus. I don't believe he would do what you said—reject you!"

Just as he spoke the words, Harry realized that he had already felt rejected by the very same person more than once. Harry was angry, and it showed.

Abraham carefully observed his guest. "He has neglected you too, hasn't he? Yes . . . I see it!"

"What do you see?" Harry responded guardedly, sipping his drink.

"I see in you what I have seen in myself and others who have crossed paths with the one of whom we are speaking."

"Really? And what is that?"

"You have reason to trust, but then you struggle with mixed feelings of rejection. You don't know what to believe at times. When you are in his company, you feel comfortable, but then he disappears and you don't know when he will reappear. You have probably wondered what his real motives are. Am I right?"

Harry was silent. How did Abraham know these things, unless he had experienced them himself?

"No, you're wrong," Harry answered. "He has not rejected me!"

"Alright," Abraham surrendered. "I honestly don't know what kind of relationship you have had with Narcissus, but I am only going on my own personal experiences and those of many others whom I know quite intimately."

Harry knew he *had* felt rejected by his angelic friend. Well, maybe not rejected, not even abandoned . . . what was it? He stared at Abraham, trying to measure him up.

Who was this man, really?

"You are wondering about me," Abraham said as though reading Harry's mind. "You should wonder! I am no ordinary being. I have seen and learned a great deal over a very long time. I am a worthy adversary, equal to your friend, Narcissus. In fact, as long as we are on the subject, let me share this with you: Narcissus and I were brothers long ago. Do you understand what I'm saying?"

Harry remembered the details Narcissus had shared with him about the angel's own downfall, his moment of distraction when he had paused to gaze at his own reflection. At the time,

Harry had not fully understood the gravity of the story, but now he realized more clearly that Narcissus' hesitation to pause and admire his own beauty resulted in some serious consequences.

"We are wasting time, Harry," Abraham said, interrupting Harry's thoughts.

"Are you in a hurry?" Harry asked with annoyance.

"I want to show you something."

"What's that?"

"Are you willing to go somewhere with me?" Abraham ventured.

"I believe I've already gone somewhere with you, Abraham . . . or is it Aba—ddon?"

"It doesn't matter, Harry. You can call me Abraham Dante, or Abaddon, if you like. The fact is, I am here for you!"

"That sounds strangely familiar!"

"Really, did Narcissus use that line on you?"

Harry remembered the very first time he encountered Narcissus. The angel had used those very words.

"I'd like to show you something, Harry—that is, if you're willing?"

"Let me ask *you* something—are you a celestial being, like Narcissus?"

"One could say that!"

"Then you are a Seraph?"

"Well, I used to be—"

"So then," Harry chose his words carefully, "you are one

464

of the fallen?"

"That depends on one's perspective. But *I* am not the one who has been detained by being locked away for centuries. I have remained free! Narcissus probably didn't want to talk about *that*."

"Actually, he did explain it to me."

"I see, and what did he say?"

"He told me that when he saw his own reflection, he hesitated for only a moment. He wasn't cast out like many were, but he could not remain and abide in the presence of Elohim."

Abraham hid his distain at the mention of that name. "That is only partially true," he explained. "Listen, he *was* cast out, and even worse, he was held in seclusion for eons while I have been free."

Harry considered his words. "You wanted to show me something. Does it involve the supernatural?"

"Funny you should ask—"

"Well, it seems to me that we are already there. Why don't you just show me right now whatever it is you want me to see?"

Abraham smiled with glee as he redirected their vision to something that might entice his guest a little more than anything Harry had ever seen before.

As they sat there, the view transformed, but the changes were subtle. Harry was still sitting with Abraham Dante—or Abaddon—at a round table on a deck, but the view beyond was quickly altered. The restaurant had transformed into a large, luxurious home. There was a small pond below that Harry recognized, shaded by large weeping willows. There were terraced gardens and the same narrow stream winding down through the property, except now there were small waterfalls cascading over giant boulders. The wooden deck was a multi-colored stone with imprints of leaves and grapevines around the circumference. Again, everything he saw was a reflection of his own style and creativity.

"This looks exactly like something I would design!" Harry exclaimed, forgetting the distrust of his current company.

"That's because it is, Harry. This is your home . . . someday!"

Harry looked confused. "But how did you know?"

"I didn't. This is your creation. I am only the facilitator."

"So, I *did* design this?"

"Yes! See what one can do with the right connections?"

As grand as the property and home were, Harry began to sense an uncomfortable feeling in the pit of his stomach.

"There is a lot of opportunity out there," Abraham stated. "Anyone with the right associations could prosper here quite well. Do you see it, Harry?"

The idea of having a place like this was *very* alluring.

"Where are we, Abraham?"

"Let's take a short walk over here," Abraham stood from his chair and led Harry to a slate trail that wound past the pond to where the drive came up the hill. "See there," he pointed.

Far below the crest of the hill was Isles End proper, and the bay it rested on. The view felt familiar and suddenly Harry realized this was the property at the summit of Top of the Hill Road. He remembered how red the dirt was that day over a year ago when he first sat here and thought about a life in Isles End.

"I've been here before. Almost a year ago when I first discovered this property. I sat right here and imagined developing something like this!"

"Well," said Abraham, "maybe your dreams are finally becoming reality!"

"I'm wondering," Harry began, still confused, "are we actually in the supernatural, or is this . . . just some kind of vision?"

"Good question, Harry! You are right—we are not in the supernatural, as you understand. It is only an altered view of reality. If we were in the supernatural, your physical body would have been left behind, while your spiritual persona would have moved forward into the mystical."

"Abraham, what I really mean is—*is this me?*" he moved his hands over his face and shoulders.

"Yes, you are currently residing in your own physical body, rather than in what you might call the supernatural expression of your spiritual self."

Harry let himself relax just a bit, but he was still caught between the absurdity of knowing he was not really "here", but rather was more than likely still sitting on a curb in the dark, somewhere near the old warehouses down on the wharf.

"So, Abraham . . . I asked my friend, Narcissus, when I met him, what it was that he wanted from me. I'd like to ask you the same question."

Abraham looked back at Harry with a quizzical expression. After a moment he replied, "Harry, I want what every being wants—respect and power. What was your angelic friend's answer?"

"He told me he had no wants or desires that any human being could fulfill."

"Harry, do you not see—he was clearly lying to you? No one will ever come to you without a motive! The question is always, what is *this* creature's motive?"

Abaddon was having an internal struggle at this point to control the rage he was feeling. His master's lair had been compromised. Gorguol had fled and abandoned all his servants. The position Abaddon had gained with his minion, Preston Hart, had failed miserably, and the boundaries of his own domain had been breached and filled with an unearthly angelic light. He was becoming extremely agitated. What would it take to reel in this stubborn little fish?

Harry Turner should be in awe of what he has been shown and offered, but instead he only asks stupid questions!

"Have you ever known power, Harry?" Abraham asked, realizing full well that Harry had no clue what real power felt like. "You know, there are many who would do your bidding if you were in the position to persuade them. I believe you have that talent! The power to persuade—and whatever you are lacking, I am here with the ability and willingness to assist you in reaching your goals!"

The discomfort in Harry's stomach was mounting. It seemed he was being offered something that should be very enticing but, somehow, it held no attraction. The panic he had tried to ignore grew stronger. He thought about some of the things Narcissus had shared with him. As far as he could remember, the angel had never asked him for anything— and what he had offered him was more than any kind of worldly wealth. The angel had given him a deeper understanding of deception. Was this why he felt so wary in this position with Abraham?

Harry also wondered again about the strength he had received from Narcissus during his visit to the pool. Now he wanted to utilize it in a greater way and with more understanding. He wanted to wear that mantle now! Could he do it? He was gaining a new sense of confidence. Yes, he could feel the familiar presence of the gift rising up again, the ability to stand up for himself and not be afraid. The fear was still there, but there was a power growing in him and rising up to the surface to meet the oppression emanating from Abraham.

"Harry, I am offering you greatness! I understand that you want to know why . . . Here it is. In return for the riches and success you will surely accomplish, you will also serve me."

Harry looked at Abraham with an expression of disdain. "I will serve *you*? Don't you understand how repulsive that sounds to me?"

"Sometimes we must all do repulsive things to achieve our goals!"

Harry stared back at Abraham Dante. He felt a sense of strength he had not known before. The light in him began to course through his being and the words came out just as they were formulated.

"I'm just going to have to say NO to that!"

Abraham didn't like what he heard.

"Harry, you do not understand who I am! I can raise you up to greatness . . . or lay you low. Which is it that you desire? CHOOSE NOW!"

"Simple, I desire greatness . . . just not under *your* terms."

"Well then," Abraham jeered, "you shall have exactly what it is that you desire!"

37
Warfare

"*WHERE AM I?*" Harry screamed. "*ABRAHAM, WHAT HAVE YOU DONE?*"

Harry was completely bewildered until he realized he was back at the wharf, sitting beside the first of the old warehouses. It was dark now; the streets were empty and Abraham was nowhere to be seen. He couldn't believe what had just happened. Abraham knew Narcissus? Abraham and Narcissus were once brothers? This was too unreal.

Harry was more than shocked. Narcissus had never mentioned anything about Abraham Dante, or *Abaddon*. Getting some kind of warning from his angelic friend would have been helpful. But now, here he was, wondering what Abraham meant by his last comment, which actually sounded more like a threat. *A threat from a fallen Seraph . . .* It didn't sound good.

Harry suddenly remembered the twenty thousand dollar payment and wanted badly to give it back. But how would he do that now? The feeling of dread was growing worse. There were so many unknowns. What about all the work he had planned? Harry had an idea he would not be doing any contracting for Mr. Dante anytime soon. Had everything fallen apart through the course of one short meeting?

Abraham Dante . . . Aba—ddon!

How many others in his life were not who they appeared

to be? Could anyone be trusted?

Harry wanted to contact Gwen and tell her the whole story. He didn't care anymore about the repercussions, but changed his mind when he realized the late hour, and how far away she was. All things considered, going home and sleeping seemed like the best idea. Tomorrow he would try to sort things out. Maybe it was time to share everything with Beth. What would she make of all this?

The sound of a boat's motor pulled Harry's attention back to his current circumstance. Below the warehouses there were several old piers that had not been used for years. Some of them were covered by a roof, but still very worn. Curious, he made his way down an old stairway alongside the adjacent building and peered out at the bay to see what was going on. He heard a thud. It sounded like something heavy. He continued down onto the dock below. Darkness shrouded the waterfront, but the dim light from the boat made the small cuddy cabin visible at the end of the long pier. He could hear the motor sputtering louder as it gained strength.

"Get away from me!" he heard a woman's voice shouting frantically.

He tried to hurry across the wooden planks, but the deck was so slick that he immediately slipped and fell, sliding across the slimy surface. A piling caught him on the other side and he managed to scramble back to his feet. The boat was rocking now and he could see there was a struggle going on.

"Harry!" the garbled voice called out. Beth? Then he recognized the other person involved in the scuffle. Rachael Sapphire!

"What's going on out there?" he yelled.

Rachael pushed Beth aside and she tumbled backwards across the open rear of the boat. As he attempted to move forward without falling again, he watched Rachael hurrying to undo the ropes that held the boat to the dock. In the dim light, he could see that her whole face looked disfigured now, her crooked mouth distorted in an ugly grin.

Beth struggled to stand. Her shirt was torn and there was blood on her forehead.

"Harry, where have you been? They said I was supposed to meet you here," she cried and fell back with a jerk.

"That's not true," Harry shouted. "Who told you— Rachael! What are you doing?" Harry moved forward as swiftly as he dared.

"It was I who summoned you!" Rachael barked with the twisted face of a clown. "You two have caused us enough trouble—now we are finally going to put an end to it!"

Harry raced down the pier like it was a runway. Regardless of the slick surface, he was determined to get to the boat before Rachael got away. Again, his feet lost traction and he fell backwards and landed hard. Beth fought to move herself forward in an effort to jump out the back, but Rachael grabbed her and easily threw her back down. "You're coming with me!"

she snarled.

"Rachael, what's wrong with you?" Harry bellowed as he climbed back up and started forward again, but Rachael ignored him and began pulling the boat away.

Though the old dock was covered with algae, Harry moved forward now with steadfast determination, his back and legs covered with slime. He wasn't going to let that woman escape, especially with Beth in the boat, but as he neared the end of the pier, the boat was already moving away and making for open water.

There was no time to think. He just knew what he needed to do—save Beth! Pushing forward with all his strength, he lunged ahead and his feet left the surface of the dock. Suddenly he was in the air, still running, moving over the water and closer to the rear of the vessel. His feet came down and hit the water but he still moved forward, forcing himself not to sink. Rachael's distorted face glared back in disbelief as Harry continued to run along the surface of the water. How was this possible?

He couldn't take the time to try and comprehend what was happening. He kept moving until, extending his arms as far as he could reach, he was able to grip the edge of the boat. He threw himself over the side, tumbling into Beth who was already lying crumpled on the deck.

"What's the hurry, Scratch?" Harry heard a familiar voice address Rachael as Abraham Dante emerged from the cabin below. "If such an attractive woman as you, could not break up

474

this happy couple, it seems only fitting that they should remain together."

"Harry," Beth began, "Please tell me what's going on! Rachael called me explaining you had an emergency and needed to meet me down here right away."

"It's a lie," Harry assured her. "I had nothing to do with this." He turned to Abraham. "What are you doing—taking us hostage? You won't gain anything by this!"

"If I remember correctly, you were not invited onto this craft," Abraham replied. "In fact, I think it's very obvious you forced yourself aboard."

"Let Beth go," Harry demanded. "You have no reason to involve her. Whatever the problem is, we can work it out in a reasonable way!" Considering his previous conversation with Abraham, Harry knew this was not likely, but he wanted to buy time.

Harry turned to Beth. "I won't let anything happen to you. I'm really not sure anymore who these people are or why they are doing this, but—"

Before Harry could finish, Abraham took a long wooden club and swung it hard against the back of Harry's head and he toppled over onto Beth's lap.

"I'm just going to have to say no to that," Abraham mocked, but Harry didn't hear a word. He was already out cold.

The cuddy was moving at a slow pace now as Rachael turned the motor down to a slow purr. Beth sat sprawled on the floor of the deck, stunned. Harry lay slumped over her. She was crying as she carefully held his head up, but she was determined not to appear weak or beaten. She was more concerned about Harry's condition and the growing lump on his head.

"Where is your friend Agalliao now that you need him?" Abraham questioned Beth with sarcasm.

"I have no idea who you're talking about, Mr. Dante, but I assure you that when Reese Orchard hears about this, neither he, nor anyone at Advanced Bio-Cell, will want to have anything to do with you. If you have any sense of self-preservation, you'll take us back to the shore and let us go immediately."

Rachael Sapphire's crooked face looked puzzled. "Abaddon, I thought your servant, Rull, was in control of this woman. Now I'm confused!"

"Don't you see, Scratch? The Cherub known as Agalliao bested my favorite devil," Abaddon continued the lie he had started back in Gorguol's den. "She belonged to us until very recently when that Cherub gained power and interfered."

"How do you know this?" Rachael countered.

"I have many sources, my friend. One who was a member of Gorguol's entourage shared this information with me very recently. And, speaking of our great leader, things are quite a mess, thanks to him. He has deserted us. Now it's up to us to take control."

Abraham turned to Beth and wondered if she was playing dumb. *Did she really not know about the angelic guardian who had been watching over her?* In any case, she did not know enough to refute his stretch of the truth, exposing himself to Scratch as a liar.

"Maybe you do not recognize the name, Agalliao, my dear, but you might remember a man who has been known to loiter outside the Isles End market. I believe his name is Galileo, or more informally, Leo!"

Beth remembered the kind man who had helped her up and brought her water. What did he have to do with this?

Abraham saw the perplexity in Beth's face and realized that she was not aware of Agalliao or any of this revelation. Maybe she knew nothing at all. Well, it didn't matter now. He could not help it if the woman had inadvertently got in the way. He'd learned over the centuries, there was always a measure of collateral damage.

"Scratch, we're wasting time. Let's get out of here and take our nice friends with us. It's time they saw things from a different perspective."

The boat would not stay afloat for long as Abraham had pulled the plug in the hull. The Cuddy was filling with sea water and would soon sink to the bottom.

Scratch studied the scene. His new master, Abaddon, still held the persona of Abraham Dante. He himself still masqueraded as Rachael Sapphire, except his facade was failing rapidly. Things could be worse, he supposed.

Rachael turned her gaze to Beth. Though Beth was

making a noble effort to appear strong, she still looked quite vulnerable to the devil. The attempt at bravery in the face of defeat—it was an enticing sight! She had been such a thorn in his flesh, so to speak, and now, *she was his!*

Before Beth had a chance to understand what was about to happen, she saw Rachael's finely manicured hand flash towards her. In utter disbelief, Beth watched as Rachael's hand literally passed through her flesh and into her very being. Her body quaked and she felt a deep chill grip the essence of her soul.

Yanking hard, Rachael pulled Beth right out of her body. *Who needs permission?* Scratch thought triumphantly. Violating one of the most prime policies of adamite engagement filled Scratch with a power he had only fantasized about, until now. The imp felt his own evil strengthening by the second.

Unaware of what was actually occurring, Beth had a strong sense of weightlessness and simultaneously felt the excruciating pain of being ripped away from her flesh so abruptly. Caught up in the air in the grasp of something so powerful and evil created such a sweltering pain she could not contain the shriek rising in her throat. Beth peered through eyes that were swirling with visions she had never imagined before. Aware now of the grotesque creature that held her captive, a horrendous scream exploded from her throat. She felt herself fading as she looked down to the boat for Harry and watched as her own body fell limp over his.

"Good work, Scratch!" Abraham genuinely encouraged

his comrade. *This might work out after all,* he thought to himself as he considered his next move. He looked up to see Scratch, back to his old, mangled, podgy self, dangling his recent catch in the air beside him like a fresh caught fish. Beth, now only semi-conscious, still struggled weakly to escape his grasp.

"Hold still, Beth!" The smaller devil snarled. "You'll only make it worse on yourself!"

Below Abraham, the two bodies of his victims lay sprawled out on the floor of the sinking vessel. Beth's form rested there in a comatose state, while Harry began to groan underneath her.

"Come, my lord! What are we waiting for?" Scratch complained anxiously from the air above as he held Beth's essence tightly at his side.

"Forgive me," Abraham answered, "I was just enjoying the moment . . ."

Beth watched in horror, dangling from above in the clutches of her captor, as Abraham Dante reached down into Harry's body with a forceful grip and found the leverage he was looking for. He pulled up vigorously and extracted the spirit of Harry Turner in the same fashion as Scratch had done. The sudden awakening to consciousness that Harry experienced while being maliciously torn from his body, forced him into a severe state of panic as he recognized his own form lying motionless under the body of Beth Fairbanks. Out of sheer defense, he forced himself to focus, intent on overcoming any obstacle that got in his way.

"Come along, Harry. I'll give you an out of body experience you won't soon forget!" Abaddon gloated. "Welcome once again to the realm of the supernatural."

Harry understood quickly what had taken place. The separation he had just undergone was excruciatingly painful, nothing like the peaceful transition he'd experienced when Narcissus had taken him from his body. Down below, he could see the boat was already sinking. He wanted to shout out to his crumpled body, *Wake up, Harry! Grab Beth and get out of there!* But it was futile. Now he could only watch from above.

In the open rear of the vessel neither his nor Beth's body appeared to have any life left in them. To his side, there was a small ugly creature he did not identify immediately, but then suddenly recognized the crooked mouth. He understood with a piercing stab in his heart that it must be a spirit who had previously masqueraded as Rachael Sapphire. He felt the urge to vomit, realizing this was the true identity of the creature he had admired, been tantalized by . . . even kissed! Though bodiless now, he still lurched, choked and finally spat out the empty bile—there was nothing to expel. He was so repulsed by the revelation that the once lovely Rachael Sapphire was something so grotesque from what she once appeared to be.

In this repugnant demon's grip was Beth. *That* sight hurt Harry more than anything he could have imagined. Then he understood that he too, was being held against his will. The man he'd known as Abraham was no longer the human with whom he had been familiar. Abraham Dante had now taken on a far darker form! This was the genuine Abaddon, apparently no longer having the need to masquerade!

Harry studied the dark entity that held him against his will. He appeared repulsive, divisive, unscrupulous, and egotistical—a marked contrast from Narcissus. Even when he had first met his celestial friend, Narcissus had been radiant and beautiful. Nothing like this repellent figure!

"What's the matter, Harry? You don't look so well!"

"Why the sarcasm?" Harry retorted bravely. "You know what's wrong here."

"What I mean to say is, does the choice you made not suit you?"

"Any choice that does not include serving you is better than the alternative. But why are you doing this? Why are we so important that you would go to such extremes as you have? Every move you make is full of deception and lies. Not too long ago I might have made a different choice, but my eyes have been opened and I can see you for what you are. I will never be interested in the kind of power or greatness you might have to offer."

Harry paused, then continued, "Look, we're just ordinary people. Why do you bother with us? Shouldn't you be more concerned with world leaders, or people far more important?"

"You can blame your friend, Narcissus, for the position

you are in!" Abaddon accused.

"I don't know how he is to blame for your actions, but it seems your battle is with him, not us," Harry shot back. "Narcissus is greater than you will ever be. You would do better to just leave this place and go back from wherever you came."

"*This is our home, Harry!* We have been here far longer than you realize. The very air surrounding this world belongs to us. We were sent here long ago, and someday we will rule this place in its entirety. It's just a matter of time. But regarding Narcissus, you have obviously been under his supervision, though it seems that he is not doing a very good job right now. Unfortunately for you, he has chosen to take a stand against us, and you have rejected the opportunity for true greatness in return for whatever he has offered you. What might that be?"

"He offers truth," Harry stood his ground as his mantle of strength began to fit more comfortably. "Something you seem to know nothing about!"

"Right now, the *truth* is, this isn't the time to be questioning me, wouldn't you agree?" the scarlet lord scoffed arrogantly.

"Is that what you are used to? Not being questioned?"

"You won't question me much longer. I have suggested several times now that you would make a tasty morsel. Have you forgotten? Don't you recognize me, Harry? I've been waiting for you under the bridge! Now my waiting has come to an end. I will not waste any more time with this type of inquisition," Abaddon stated harshly.

Harry turned to Beth while he considered his recurring nightmares. Now it all made sense. It was this creature all along! Somehow, this understanding only gave Harry more resolve. He felt ready to take this devil on, but what about her?

Beth looked as beautiful as ever, though somewhat disheveled by her experience. She was clearly distraught, staring down at the cuddy cabin as the top of the vessel disappeared below the surface of the dark water.

"Harry, what kind of nightmare is this?" she pleaded.

"I don't know, Beth. These are some kind of spirits who have been masquerading as the people we knew as Rachael Sapphire and Abraham Dante."

"I don't understand," she cried with a panicked look on her face.

"We will find a way out of this, Beth. You must trust me," Harry tried to console her.

"I hope that *I* had nothing to do with this," she continued to weep.

"No, Beth, none of this is your fault, I promise you!"

They both looked down from their suspended positions and watched as the water swirled around on the surface of the sea while the boat, along with their bodies, came to rest on the bottom of the bay.

"What are you going to do with us now?" Harry questioned the two spirits boldly.

"There is only one thing we can do," Abaddon answered.

"You're right," Harry said. "You must return us."

"I can't do that, Harry."

"Why not?"

"Because you are both dead now. The ocean water has filled your lungs. This usually results in drowning. Your bodies are lying in the back of the boat on the ocean's floor, but I'm sure they will be found sometime soon. It will appear to be a terrible tragedy. You rented a boat and no sooner did you take it out, when the drain plug failed and the vessel sank while you were asleep. That being said, there's only one place left for you to go."

Harry carefully considered Abaddon's words. He studied Beth as she hung helplessly across from him. She looked fragile and dismayed. Summoning the strength he'd had earlier, he felt a force working its way up from deep within his being. It was still there! The same strength that had allowed him to reject Abraham's offers of greatness. As he hung there in the dark angel's grasp, he began to glow.

"What are you doing?" Scratch questioned Harry as the deformed ghoul recognized the unexpected hint of light that began to emanate from Harry's form. "Abaddon, why do we delay here?"

"Wait, Scratch, there is something—"

They all looked down at the water. There was a stirring from where the vessel had sunk. At the same time, Harry's spirit began to radiate more light and Scratch pulled away in surprise.

"Master," Scratch grated, "we must go!"

"SILENCE!" Abaddon growled. "Something is amiss—"

The water began to bubble and both demons reacted by rising up higher and away from the surface of the churning foam. At the same time, the light from Harry's spirit began to intensify. Abaddon became aware as the brightness began to burn him, but he still held Harry firmly in his grasp. Scratch cursed, and then as Beth saw it too, she lifted her head in wonder as Harry began to shine like a beacon.

"We are not dead," Harry shouted boldly, *"and you are a liar!"*

Before Abaddon could respond, the sea below erupted in an explosion of water and light. The force of it threw the two demons and their prey further away and Scratch nearly lost his grip on Beth. There was a blinding light before them with water surging everywhere. In the midst appeared the most fearful looking Seraph they had ever seen. Around him, two Cherubim wielded fiery swords that flashed like lightning bolts over the dark sea. A third Cherub held the bodies of Harry and Beth in his strong arms. He flashed a broad smile at Beth. The being was strangely familiar and a flicker of hope showed in her expression. She realized that somehow, it was Leo, the older gentleman from the store, except he was transformed into something, or someone, far beyond her imagination.

The three Cherubim were radiant, but they paled in comparison to the Seraph, who was enormous and incredibly brilliant. The faces of the dark spirits looked on in shock and disbelief as the Archangel rose up before them, its three sets of wings expanded and moving like fierce weaponry while its face was ablaze as the imposing figure studied the entire scene.

"You are correct, Harry! He *is* a liar . . . and his master is the father of lies!" The Seraph's voice boomed out into the air and Harry recognized it immediately.

NARCISSUS!

Abaddon was noticeably shaken by the turn of events. Now the light coming from his captive burned into his side while he assessed his position. Scratch was stunned. He'd already encountered this group before and feared he was about to be ripped up into the heavens and thrashed again.

"Master!" Scratch pleaded. "What is your bidding?"

Abaddon was not yet willing to relinquish his precious cargo. "Damn you, Narcissus!" he shouted violently as he pulled up further away from the group of angelic hosts.

"I'm sorry, Abaddon, but we both know you lack the authority to back up that kind of command," the Seraph responded fearlessly as he moved closer to the two devils and their captives.

"Lord, instruct me!" Scratch shrieked.

Abaddon looked over to his servant, panic filling his twisted face, then back to where the terrifying Seraph was approaching with his band of cherubim.

"Flee!" he roared.

38
The Archangel Narcissus

Harry felt himself being forced down through the water below. He had just become aware of the salty foam surrounding him when, without warning, both he and Beth were pulled further into the supernatural. Being out of body while still in the natural was one thing, but this turbulent transition was excruciating, and again, not at all like the experiences he'd had with Narcissus. He had the sense they were moving forward. Then they stopped. Wherever they had traveled to, was black and silent. To his side, he could make out Beth's form as the ugly demon he'd known as Rachael Sapphire held her limp body at his side.

"They will not find us here, I think," Abaddon said warily.

"I don't like it," Scratch groaned.

"Don't worry," the dark lord said as his eyes darted around. "We won't be here long."

Harry wanted to know where they had been taken. This place was dark but his eyes were adjusting to the gloomy landscape.

"Where are we?" Beth whimpered.

An ominous fear came over Harry as he realized where their captors had taken them. The demons lowered themselves down closer to where Harry could only make out an uneven horizon. Beth stared with a growing look of terror in her eyes as the small group hovered just above a sea of orb-like forms.

They were like giant eggs, gray and smooth, all bound together as though there were some magnetic force keeping them in place. Harry looked at Beth still hanging helplessly in the grip of their adversaries. The sea of stagnating spheres stretched out below them for miles in both directions.

"Welcome to your new home, you two love birds!" Abaddon said contemptuously as he loosened his grip and let Harry fall, landing on the surface of the objects below. Scratch followed suit and released Beth. She flopped down and landed next to Harry. The egg-shaped spheres absorbed the shock of their falls, bobbing around slightly as the two struggled to balance themselves. The sudden impact of their bodies did not affect the spheres and they maintained the positions they held with one another, all locked together.

"I know this place, Beth," Harry managed to groan. "It's called Gehenna."

"Not to worry, my dears," Abaddon said in a mocking tone. "I believe that in time you will both blend right in."

Scratch let out a chuckle of glee but it was short-lived as even he felt the desolation of Gehenna threatening to envelop him.

Beth lunged toward Harry and managed to grab a hold of his arm. They pulled themselves together as they both struggled to evaluate their condition.

"Sire," Scratch muttered. "We should leave this place!"

"That is exactly what I have in mind—"

Suddenly across the expanse a brilliant light appeared out of nowhere and quickly shot across the gap like a beam of lightening. In an instant, standing before them was a magnificent being of pure energy. Harry recognized him immediately. The same archangel he remembered from the last time Narcissus took him to this desolate place. The seraph looked more ominous this time, towering over them in his regal blue and violet robes.

"INTRUDERS!" he boomed so loudly that the ocean of orbs vibrated all around them as Harry and Beth fought to maintain their balance.

Abaddon expanded himself in an attempt to confront the powerful being, but his efforts were unsuccessful.

"YOU DO NOT BELONG HERE!" the archangel bellowed.

Both Abaddon and Scratch made an attempt to retreat but were frozen in the air-space where they hovered. The terrifying seraph opened his mouth and a fiery sword emerged and hung in the air before the demons. Harry and Beth felt themselves being lifted up until they were pressed up tight against their two captors.

"You will now be sent back from where you came!" The celestial being roared, and in an instant, both Harry, Beth, and the two devils were gone.

Harry felt himself jolted away. The scene of Gehenna disappeared. Where were they now? Beth appeared before him. He could see she was immersed in water. Of course! They were back in the ocean bay of Isles End.

He was being tugged again by Abaddon and experiencing the chilling sense of water rushing all around his being. Once more, he and Beth were moving quickly through water, and then suddenly, through earth. The light that still radiated from his spirit helped Harry see in every direction. Abaddon kept a firm grip on him while they sped through rock and dirt. The fact that they were spirit made them able to see the physical space they now occupied, while still moving easily through the rough material as though it were only air. Just behind Abaddon, Scratch followed, clutching Beth at his side. Large tree roots growing down from the surface became scorched by the dread which emanated from the two demons as they moved swiftly through the ground in an attempt to escape. Abaddon was sure that Narcissus and the other three angels would still be in pursuit now that they had been forced to return back to Isles End from Gehenna.

"Have you ever seen an Archangel so powerful?" Scratch panted fearfully as he fought to keep up with his master.

"Silence, fool!" Abaddon responded harshly. He wasn't sure if Scratch was referring to Narcissus or the Seraph they had just encountered in Gehenna, but he didn't need these humans hearing anything to suggest that he or Scratch were weaker than their opponents. He also wondered with some desperation how he could gain any kind of victory in this rapidly failing venture. There was a time not so long ago, Abaddon realized, when

Scratch would not have put up with the contempt Abaddon had just displayed. Thankfully, for now, Scratch seemed content to keep silent and follow his master's lead.

As the rock and stone sped around and through Harry's body, he twisted his head around until he could see part of Beth's form being held in Scratch's grip. Her essence appeared limp, and he could see her eyes were closed. Then, as the ugly devil that carried her changed his position, he lost sight of her. Harry guessed she was doing all she could to deal with the horrific situation they were in. He had to remind himself that the whole idea of dealing with angels and demons and the supernatural was all new to her. There must be some way to help or comfort her, but he wasn't close enough to get her attention. He could only wait for an opportunity.

Harry felt a tug as Abaddon changed direction. He wondered about their destination. The force of his captor's movements made him think they were traveling deeper now, down into the lower layers of the earth. There were no more tree roots and there was far more rock than soil. Why hadn't Narcissus rescued them right there in Isles End before they were dragged into Gehenna? He must have had a reason. Was he pursuing them now? Harry could only hope.

At least he was confident that both he and Beth were alive and their bodies were safely in the arms of the angels. Couldn't the Cherubim just wake them up and set them free from this nightmare? Either way, what could these evil creatures do to

491

them now, if they were still physically safe somewhere else? Harry was thankful that his friends had shown up when they did. They were so beautiful! Their appearance had changed dramatically since he'd first met the three Cherubim outside the celestial gates, but he still recognized each of them distinctly. The memory of the miraculous living water filled him with renewed courage. Swimming under the surface of the pool, the wide grin of Agalliao, and the mantle of strength he still possessed even now—all these things gave him a great feeling of peace. It was at that point he realized that he was still glowing. The more he considered the positive experiences he'd had, the more steadily the light flowed out from him. He hoped Beth could see it now and that his brightness might bring her some comfort.

For the first time since he'd discovered the chest, Harry believed there was a reason for all that had happened to him. The fact he had stumbled across Narcissus was no accident, but he already knew that! Every visitation had been calculated and everything the angel had shared with him was purposeful. Could it be that "Elohim" was responsible? It only made sense now, but how could an insignificant man such as he, possibly have any relevance to an omnipresent, omnipotent, omniscient being? Who was *he* that such a Creator would have any concern for him? All the things Narcissus had shared and taught him began to sink in. As his understanding increased, the lingering fear he had experienced so recently began to melt away. If this One, whom Narcissus called Elohim, was *for* him, then who could possibly be against him? The affairs of this evening were still no carnival ride, but Harry felt real strength flowing through his mind and spirit. He only hoped the same strength was also flowing through his physical body as well.

Suddenly the stone and earth which they had been passing through was gone and they were in the air again. How far they had traveled, Harry could not guess. He knew they could cover a lot of ground very quickly. He was disoriented now, not sure if they were deep into the supernatural again, or just out of body outside of Isles End somewhere deep in the earth. He and Beth were surely in an out of body experience, but he thought they had left the supernatural when they were forced out of Gehenna. They must be back on earth, but far below the surface. It really didn't matter either way; he prepared himself for anything.

Studying his surroundings, Harry could see they had entered an immense cavern, its walls sheer and jagged. A fissure on one end revealed a passageway that opened into an enormous crevasse and spread out to a walkway that circled the circumference of the massive chamber. In the center, a chasm dropped down steeply on all sides creating an opening so large that an army could be lost in moments. A dull smoldering glow rose up from the bottom and heated the vast space above.

"I remember this place!" Scratch snarled as he entered the enormous cavity.

"Yes, I know," Abaddon said.

They slowed down until they hovered over a large outcropping of stone, jetting out from where the tunnel opened up to the enormous room. There above the flat ledge, Abaddon lowered himself, slowly turning around until he had surveyed the entire expanse. Then he allowed his feet to come to rest on the warm stone. Scratch duplicated his master's every move.

"Where are our comrades, Jinn and Rull, and the rest?" Abaddon spoke guardedly in a hushed voice.

"It appears to be deserted, my lord!" Scratch said staring down into the abyss.

Abaddon nodded. "Here, Mr. Turner," he said, tossing Harry to the side. "There is nowhere for you to go, and this light you emanate has become extremely uncomfortable!"

Scratch relaxed his hold on Beth and she slumped down beside Harry onto the rough surface.

"May I go to her?" Harry didn't wait for permission as he moved in Beth's direction.

"Whatever you wish," Abaddon answered indifferently. His eyes darted around again with suspicion. "I expected to find a legion of ghouls here! Will anything go right for us?"

"Lord, I sense there has been activity here very recently!" Scratch stated.

"Yes, I feel it too!" Abaddon agreed. "Once again, something is terribly wrong!"

Harry crawled to Beth and knelt beside her. He lifted her onto his lap and brushed her hair away from her face with his hand. She opened her eyes and they quickly teared up. "What has happened, Harry? Where are we?"

"I don't know, but don't be afraid," he whispered in a comforting tone.

"Harry . . . you're glowing!"

"Yes," he answered with a smile.

"I noticed it earlier," she continued, "back there above the boat, and then again while we were moving. I felt stronger knowing the light was coming from you! What does it mean?"

"You two making plans?" Abaddon queried as he spun around and faced his victims. "Well, feel free! You are alone now and there is nothing left for you to do. You should have listened to reason when I offered you such an opportunity as most men can only dream of. I don't think your friends will find you down here, otherwise they would have arrived by now."

"I have already quit believing anything that comes out of your mouth!" Harry spat as he held Beth protectively.

"No matter," Abaddon said with a sardonic grin. "I am done with you both. You won't hear from me again." He stepped out of the way to make a clear path between Harry and Beth and the chasm below. Extending his arm out, he pointed his finger toward the abyss. "This is where your doom awaits you."

Harry rejected every word. He looked at Beth and managed a reassuring smile. All his fear had been replaced with a peace and strength he had never known before. He looked at Abaddon and spoke with authority.

"Narcissus said you are a liar and your master is the father of lies. I will choose to believe him. You want me to think you have power over us—that we are subject to your will. But this is only another lie! We will not submit or surrender to any of your wishes. You no longer hold any authority over us, *Abaddon!* You never did. It was all a ruse. Deception is your craft and I'm sure you have had many successes, but this time you have failed. That place down there," Harry extended *his* arm and pointed toward the gaping hole, "that's where *you* belong!"

"Master!" Scratch interrupted with a shriek.

Abaddon, Harry, and Beth all turned their focus to Scratch as he fearfully studied the fissure of the cave behind them. Simultaneously, they followed his stare to the dark opening. Standing there in the recesses was the likeness of a man.

"WHAT FOOL DARES TO COME HERE?" Abaddon howled as he swung around and expanded his stature while taking on a crimson glow. "Come out into the open where I can see you, or experience my wrath!"

They all stared as the figure moved gracefully forward into the dim light that radiated from Harry's form. At first, no one recognized the man. He was plain in appearance, wearing a basic robe of white, fastened with a wide sash. He stepped closer toward the small group and paused before Harry.

"Hello, my friend!"

"Narcissus?"

"Yes, it is I."

After so recently having seen the Archangel looking so frightening, winged and magnificent, none of them had recognized the celestial being in such a plain form as he held now.

"This is a dark place," Narcissus spoke with authority. "Well-hidden and containing a long history of evil."

"Where are your wings? Did you lose them again?" Abaddon braved his assault. "I see you are still weak, angel!"

"Maybe, but when I acknowledge my weakness, my master grows stronger within me!"

"That is nonsense!"

Narcissus stood quietly as though he had no concerns. Finally, Abaddon spoke again.

"I want to let you in on a little secret, Narcissus," the proud devil began with a laugh. "It was I who influenced a man, long ago, to write a story about one named Narcissus. Maybe you have heard the tale? It's about a young man who fell in love with his own reflection. He became entranced by his own beauty and enamored with his own image because of a curse, due to unrequited love. Does this sound familiar? Well, he lay by a pool and wasted away, staring down into the water. What was the attraction, you might ask? It was his own reflection in the water, of course! You see, he had fallen deeply in love with himself, and as he leaned closer and closer to his image, he eventually fell into the pond and drowned. Sad story, don't you agree? Did that chest of yours feel, at times, like a watery grave? But I digress. For ages now, the name Narcissus has stood for vanity, callousness, and insensitivity. Funny—as a result, there are few humans who will carry the name!"

Still, the angel stood humbly before the small group.

"What do you have to say for yourself?" Abaddon questioned the archangel as he began to feel strength growing in him. "Are you not even capable of a response? SPEAK!"

"You have not yet even imagined what the subjects of Elohim are capable of," Narcissus answered calmly. "And as for your story, the only funny thing about it is that it's true, except it's you who fits the description of the one who becomes vain!"

"*YOU WILL FIGHT ME!*" The fallen angel spat out as his flesh took on a darker scarlet hue.

"Abaddon, for someone who is so well- versed in deception, you have succeeded in only deceiving yourself. What made you believe you could find sanctuary in such a place as this?"

"You misjudge my power, angel! Do you think I am beaten? Come forward and I will gladly test your metal!"

"I will not admonish you," Narcissus answered graciously, "but I will let my Master do so according to His will."

"You will always be a coward, while I shall someday be reinstated to greatness!"

"I'm truly sorry, Abaddon. I have already been fully restored, but you missed that opportunity long ago."

"I will restore you now, *TO ASHES!*" Abaddon lunged

forward to strike, but Narcissus raised his hand and both the demons were immediately swept back towards the chasm.

"I'm grateful to see you, Narcissus," Harry ventured carefully as he climbed up from the stone and pulled Beth to his side.

"Do not fear, Harry. I am here for you, though you really do not need me," the celestial being stated warmly.

"What do you mean?" Harry was startled.

"It appears you are already learning that you do not need my help to combat these kinds of enemies!" Narcissus pointed to the two demons that stood so near.

"Yes, I'm beginning to understand that you are right, but you're so much more powerful. I saw you in your elevated state! You were magnificent, Narcissus! You were invincible!"

"We have our own way of dealing with our adversaries but you have the power in you now to rebuke them yourself, as I see you have begun to do quite well, Harry."

"Yes, thank you."

Abaddon and Scratch stood cringing near the edge of the abyss. The dark lord had been stunned by the hand of Narcissus but he still feigned in appearance that he was ready to fight back if given the opportunity. Scratch didn't seem to have the same resolve. He cowered next to his master, clinging to him like a lost dog.

"What will you do with them?" Harry asked his friend.

"They are yours to deal with, Harry," Narcissus

countered.

"Who are they, really?"

"Combined, they are selfishness, strife, envy, greed, sloth, pride and hate, just to name a few."

"I understand," Harry marveled with a questioning look. "How do I use my mantle to defeat them?"

Narcissus smiled at Harry. "Your mantle is your light! You have light, don't you?"

Harry nodded with quick understanding.

"Then, my friend, there is your weapon. Let it shine! They will succumb to your brightness, I promise!"

Harry turned to Beth and took her hand. Together they faced the demons who waited near the edge of the gaping hole. As Harry gripped Beth's hand, the light from his form began to grow and intensify. It flowed down his arm and moved up into Beth's hand, then into her arm. She willingly received the light as it continued to travel throughout her body until she began to glow as much as Harry. But it didn't end there . . .

Abaddon pulled himself forward to make a rush at the shining pair, pulling at Scratch to join him, but the smaller imp pulled away and retreated right up to the edge of the steep precipice behind them. Abaddon ignored the podgy devil and kept up his effort to move forward. Gaining only half a step, he was halted in his tracks and froze where he stood. The fury in his eyes turned into failure and retreat as the blinding light radiating from Harry and Beth was more than he could bear. The light grew to such intensity that it appeared as a beam of lightening, shooting out and rendering both demons powerless.

"How is this possible?" Scratch shrieked as his form began to dissipate.

Harry and Beth stepped forward. The two diminished devils were forced to move away until they wavered on the edge of the precipice. The light became so unbearable that finally Scratch stepped off the edge and fell into the chasm with a screech.

"What is it," Abaddon hurled in a rage at Narcissus, "that made these two so important?"

"Something you forfeited long ago," Narcissus answered. "The love of Elohim for all his creatures."

Abaddon clung to a jagged outcropping of stone, unwilling to accept he had been vanquished by mere mortals, but the light became so overwhelmingly bright that finally he too, could not withstand its brilliance and reluctantly hurled himself off the cliff with a horrible wail, down into the inferno.

Harry and Beth stood in silence for a moment and watched as a puff of smoke curled up from the massive pit.

"Where there is light," Beth said looking awestruck at Harry, "there can be no darkness!"

"You catch on quickly," he responded, his face beaming.

With that, their light began to fade until finally it was just a faint glimmer. They both turned back to Narcissus who watched them with a measure of pride.

"Will we see either of them again?" Harry asked the angel.

"No. They will be in exile for quite a long time."

"Narcissus, I didn't realize I held such authority over so powerful an enemy!"

"This is a common misconception. Your adversaries can appear to be unassailable. They may present themselves as bearers of light. They even deceive themselves into thinking they are invincible. The truth is, they are not so strong as they appear and are easily conquered by the light. Such was Abaddon. He had a highly inflated assessment of himself.

"But you should know this, Harry. Even when it seems you are being ripped from your very bodies, Elohim will never allow you to suffer more than He knows you can endure."

"Narcissus," Beth interjected, "what happened to the group that Abaddon was expecting to find here?"

"With the help of my friends, Ranan, Psallo and Agalliao, the four of us cleaned house here early this morning. It was a sight to see!"

"Awesome!" Harry exclaimed. "I would have loved to have seen that!"

"I may be able to arrange something," the angel responded lightheartedly. "Let me think about it."

"Narcissus," Harry asked. "I'm wondering . . . what happened to our bodies?"

"May I share something else with you first?"

Harry nodded.

"I think you have a good idea now, my dear friend, that your battle is not against flesh and blood, fighting against only physical opponents. The battle is really against shadows and spiritual forces of wickedness in this world's current darkness who reside in the supernatural sphere. Therefore, take advantage of all the gifts that are available to you! Then when difficulty comes, you will be able to stand your ground, whether in the natural or the supernatural. Do you understand?"

"I think so—but we will still remember your words and consider them carefully," Harry promised turning to Beth as she nodded in agreement.

"Then there is something more I'd like to do before I answer your question."

"What is it?"

"Will you come with me, to a place?"

"Where?"

"You remember the pool below the celestial city where you were immersed in the living water?"

"How could I forget? It was the most wondrous experience I've ever known! That is, aside from meeting you and Beth—"

Beth looked at Narcissus with wonder and then turned her gaze to Harry. "You never told me about a pool or a city!"

"I know. I was afraid you might think I was crazy."

"I want to go!" Beth affirmed. "Will you take me too?"

"Of course, Beth. Are you both ready?"

"Yes," they chimed, and before they could take a breath, they shot upward, leaving the grim cavern behind them, dark and empty.

39
A Heavenly Place

Before they knew it, Harry and Beth were hovering in the air with Narcissus, looking down on teal green pastures below the gates of a glorious city. The grass looked alive as it swayed and danced in the breeze that flowed down from the hills above. Narcissus guided them down to the pool where Harry had joined the angels during his first visit. The golden wall around the city stood high and mighty; the living creatures who formed the gate continued to guard the opening with their bright shields and armor.

The small group landed in the grass just a few yards from the water and Harry remembered the first time his toes felt the cool blades cushion his landing. Nothing had changed since his last visit here, except that Beth was with him. She gazed, wide-eyed, at the incredible views.

"You were here, Harry?" she exclaimed with amazement.

"Yes, isn't it wonderful?"

"There are no words!" she said, wiggling her toes in the blue green reeds. "Do you feel it?" She looked down at her feet.

Harry nodded and took in a breath of air. They stood there for a moment, delighted as the effects of the grass flowed up through the soles of their feet and spread into the rest of their limbs, bringing comfort and healing.

"Narcissus, can we take Beth to the pool?" he asked,

pointing. "See there," he showed her, "I stood on that rock that is rising up in the center!"

"I wish you had shared this with me sooner!"

"So do I. There just never seemed to be a good time . . . Besides, I wasn't sure you would have believed me."

"I understand, but I'm here with you now, aren't I," she giggled grabbing his hand, "and it's just incredible!"

"Yes, Harry," Narcissus cut in, "you may take her to the pool, but first it looks like you and Beth may have some company."

They followed his gaze up to the golden gate. It was slightly open now and two people, a young man and woman, had stepped through the opening. The pair were holding hands as they skipped out beyond the gate and walked toward them.

"Who—?" Harry asked, looking at Narcissus, but the angel remained quiet.

Then Beth gave out a small shout. "Oh my!"

Harry waited in silence as she studied the two.

"I can't believe it! Oh my! Excuse me—"

Before he could ask another question, Beth was off and running toward the young couple. He looked up at Narcissus, but kept still as he saw the smile on the angel's face and turned back to watch the scene unfold.

The two people stopped along the river and waded in just a bit. The cerulean water sprayed and bounced off of their bodies as they kicked their feet against the surface of the stream, splashing each other. When they turned and saw Beth approaching them, they paused and waited side by side for her advance. She reached them and stopped several yards away, then fell to her knees. They helped her up and the three of them embraced.

"Narcissus, who are they?" Harry finally asked.

"They are Beth's parents."

"But they are so young!"

"Yes!"

"I'm so happy for her," Harry exclaimed with growing emotion over the scene. "Narcissus, I love this place," Harry blurted out with tears in his eyes. "There is such beauty, and healing. If it's this wonderful out here, I can't imagine what it might be like inside those gates!"

"It's everything you can imagine, and more," the Archangel confirmed. Then he looked up to the city and smiled. "Let me rephrase that, Harry . . . It's nothing like you could ever imagine!"

"Tell me about it, Narcissus, would you? That is, unless we are expected to actually go inside—"

"Hmmm, we'll talk about that soon, Harry."

"Alright, can we just sit here for a while? Do we need to do anything right now? I don't want to hurry Beth, and I feel so content that I just want to sit here and take it all in!"

"Yes, my friend, we can do that!"

Narcissus bent down and stretched himself out on the

hillside. Harry stood there for a moment until he realized that the Seraph had really answered him by his actions and they were in no hurry. He flopped down beside the angel and rolled in the luxurious grass.

"I don't want to leave here, Narcissus!" Harry announced as he experienced the fullness of the air and water and the pasture and the city above.

"It's okay, Harry. You don't have to."

"Really?" he asked with surprise. He expected a response but the angel was silent. Finally he rolled over to study the angel's face. Narcissus looked back with fondness.

"Harry, it seems that you have company as well—"

"What?" Harry turned his head toward the gates and saw a figure stepping through onto the field. A lovely young woman walked alone in Harry's direction.

"Who is that?" he looked at Narcissus with a puzzled expression.

The Seraph just watched the woman as she glided away from the gates and down toward the pool behind them.

"Why don't you go and see for yourself, Harry?" the angel suggested.

Harry wasn't sure he wanted to do that. This was not what he expected and he looked back up at Beth and the company she was with. The three were sitting on the edge of the stream with their feet in the water. He could see the beads splashing up and dancing in the air around them. He was pleased. But who was coming down the hill in his direction?

"Go see," Narcissus suggested as though he knew Harry's thoughts.

Cautiously, Harry got up and walked a few steps to the side, away from Narcissus but not directly toward the young woman. He side-stepped his way in the direction of the pool with the idea that he would feel safer there. But why wouldn't he be safe anywhere here? The feelings growing in Harry's heart were suddenly very tender.

"Harry . . ." He heard the woman call.

Why am I backing away? He asked himself as his feet moved backwards toward the pond behind him.

I know her!

"Won't you stop walking away from me?" she spoke softly.

He stopped retreating and stood still with his feet planted firmly in the grass. The woman continued to advance until she was standing right before him. He didn't know what to say but it was as though he didn't need to speak. He just stood there and stared back at her with astonishment.

"Hello, Harry . . ." she offered, pausing before him.

"Jennifer!"

"Yes."

"Is it really you?"

"Don't you recognize me?"

"Yes, of course! How could I not? You look as beautiful

as the last time I saw you!"

"Oh Harry, come here."

He carefully stepped forward until he was just inches away. Her face was radiant and her smile was exactly as he remembered, as though it were designed just for him.

"This is breaking my heart," he whispered.

"No, Harry, your heart is not breaking, it's being restored," she answered, still smiling.

"Is this real?" he asked, his eyes filling with tears. "I can't believe I am standing in front of you! Oh, my Jenny!" he cried and fell to his knees.

"Harry, be at peace!" she spoke so gracefully. "You have suffered far more than I! You are the one who had to remain in life, with all the loss, while I moved quickly on into a new and eternal reality."

Harry held himself up, there on his knees before the woman he'd loved so deeply and couldn't believe he was seeing her again. So many things flooded his mind. He wasn't sure how to express them, but before he could speak another word, her voice interrupted his thoughts.

"Harry," she said, kneeling down to meet him, "I have so many things to tell you and I don't know how much time we have. Let me start with this. I have been given the privilege to oversee, so to speak, the process of your life since I was taken away. More than that, I was instrumental in the development, if you will, of your introduction to the very lovely Miss Beth

Fairbanks. Are you surprised? Don't worry, darling! I loved her from the moment I even considered her as someone you might be involved with! I am so happy for you, and it's my wish, my desire, that you find happiness. When she was brought to my attention, I thought, *She is wonderful! She is perfect for my Harry!*"

How could his Jenny be saying these things? But Harry knew before he posed the question to himself. She had always been that way. Pure, giving, generous, and selfless.

"Please tell me," he asked her directly, "how did you come to be here?"

"Harry, I'm thankful to have the chance to explain that to you. Let me take you back to that day. You remember when you could not make the trip as we had planned? So we went without you and we were up in the air and everything was fine. Your dad was always so confident!

"Anyway, I want you to know something. Just a few days before that trip, I was invited by a friend to a small group that was gathering to do some studying. There, I was exposed to some ideas I had never been introduced to before. I was excited about what I heard, but I kept it to myself since the ideas were so new. The discussion had to do with life after death and even the topic of prayer—that is, being able to talk with the Marvelous One who holds the universe in His hands.

"Well, the day of the accident when we were up in the air and the engines on the plane shut down, we began to fall. It happened so quickly! Suddenly I thought, *We need help!* As we plummeted down toward the ground, I suggested to your parents as much as to myself, that we pray. They agreed. Harry, it was so unexpected—so sudden! There was no time! I just blurted out, help *us . . . save us!* Your dad and mom shouted out in agreement. That is all I remember. The next thing I knew, I was here, outside the entrance," Jennifer paused turning her head up to the living gates.

"Since that day, I've had the opportunity to know how you are doing and to even look down on you, so to speak, on several occasions. Your parents and I have interceded more than once on your behalf, and do you know what, Harry? Our requests have not only been heard, but answered as well! We are so thrilled to see what has happened to you, though I understand it hasn't been easy."

"I'm amazed, Jen! I never imagined this could all be possible!"

Jennifer just smiled back with fondness and understanding.

"So my mom and dad are here, too?"

"Yes, of course!"

"I had a feeling they were! For a moment I actually thought I could feel their presence earlier! Are they well? I mean, of course they are—they're here!"

"Yes, Harry, they're wonderful . . . and they are *here*." She raised her arms up to embrace all that surrounded them.

512

"You know, it's possible that you *did* sense a moment of contact with them. That can happen in this place! But yes, Harry, they are young and whole and living to the fullest."

"And will I see them?"

"I don't know the answer to that question yet," she said with some uncertainty. "I suppose it will depend on whether you decide to stay. But they did want me to give you their love."

"What do you mean, if I decide to stay?" Harry was surprised by the possibility.

"Harry, you will need to talk to Narcissus about that."

"Alright."

The two knelt there in the grass and silently took in the moment. Harry wanted to express the thoughts and feelings that had built up inside him since the plane accident, but he wasn't sure how. Finally, he just let it all out, "Jennifer, losing you was the hardest thing I have ever had to face. Seeing you now, I can't help but wonder how things would have worked out if you hadn't been taken away. Many times, I have fantasized about how things might have been—our lives together, being married, having a family, you know? But those thoughts always turned into torture. For a while, I just wanted to die. I felt so cheated and I didn't understand how something so horrible could happen to someone so good. Just when life seemed to be bringing us both something so wonderful, it was all ripped away in a moment. I still wasn't over the pain of losing you when I met Beth, but she was a breath of fresh air, and in many ways, she reminded me of you, I suppose."

"Trust me, Harry, I know how hard it was for you, and I'm sorry too, that things turned out the way they did. You do not live in a perfect world, but one thing I do know; for every difficult challenge that life throws at you, there is always an opportunity to find goodness, even through the process of grieving."

"Wow! It's amazing that you should say that. Beth told me the same thing very recently. The first time we had dinner together at her home when she told me about the loss of her parents, she almost used the very same words you just spoke, expressing the same idea!"

"Yes, Harry, I remember."

"What do you mean?"

"Well, I was sort of a fly on the wall, that night. You don't mind, do you?"

Harry thought about it. It made sense that if his Jenny was instrumental, as she put it, in his meeting Beth, that she might have been able to witness a few details of his experiences with her.

"No, Jen, I don't mind. In fact, I'm pleased to know that you have been able to watch over me! But are you saying that you were actually in Beth's home that night?"

"No, no, I never left my home here. It may be hard to understand but I was allowed to see from here, some of the experiences you were going through, and I was allowed to hope for you as well."

"It must have been like looking through a window," Harry exclaimed, remembering his visions with Narcissus.

"Yes, you do understand," Jennifer smiled.

Harry smiled back, soaking it all in.

"Harry," Jennifer said after giving him time to consider all she had shared with him.

"Yes?"

"It's time for me to go."

"I understand."

"You're going to be okay," she smiled at him as they both stood. Harry felt comfortable putting his arm around Jennifer. They shared a long embrace. Then he watched her as she turned away and headed back up to the gates. She called this place her home! He couldn't help but feel a sense of loss, but he also felt a greater sense of completeness and renewed hope. What did she mean, if he decided to stay? He had a feeling he would soon find out, but in the meantime he also felt sure that if he did, he would see his parents again—something he had never considered before.

Turning back toward the river he saw Narcissus accompanying Beth as they walked in the direction of the pool.

"Hey, wait for me," he called and ran to meet them. They paused before the pool as Harry joined them. Beth reached out her hand and he took it. She still had tears in her eyes, but they were sparkling in a new way.

"You were given the chance to see your parents!" Harry

claimed excitedly.

"Yes, I'm so thankful, Harry! There have been times when I thought I felt their presence. It made me wonder if they might be in a better place, together. They told me that they think of me often and make every effort to intervene for all of my sisters and me. They explained that both of them had a real experience just before they passed on that caused them to receive something more than they had expected or even deserved."

Harry realized that what had happened to Beth's parents was similar in a way to what had happened to Jennifer. Somehow during the last minutes of their lives, they were allowed a measure of conviction that caused a sudden but graceful transformation.

"Why don't you two enjoy a swim?" Narcissus offered. "I'll return shortly."

Harry looked back toward the gates to see Narcissus' three angelic friends waiting there for the Seraph.

"We'll be fine, Narcissus," Beth said. "You go ahead, and will you please tell Leo I said thank you!"

Narcissus gave her a stately nod and turned away to meet his companions.

Now it was just Harry and Beth, alone together by the pool.

"Did you ever imagine," Beth began, "that we would be standing here together some day?"

"When we were in that cavern," he answered, "I wasn't

sure we would be standing anywhere together again!"

"Harry, I saw something in you down there that I hadn't seen before. I may not have survived without your strength and the bravery you displayed in the face of such darkness! The way you stood up to those . . . evil creatures! It gave me hope, and it caused me to really believe in you."

"This is where I gained that strength," Harry said gazing at the pool before them. "I only wish I had learned to rely on it sooner."

"I saw you with a woman," Beth said changing the subject. "I'm guessing you had another loss that you didn't share with me—"

"Yes."

"It's alright. I'm glad you got to see her, Harry. I can see that everything here is about healing and wholeness, so I know your reunion was a good thing."

"Yes, it was. And she told me that she had something to do with us meeting," he added.

"Really! Well, I guess I'm not surprised. There is so much we have to learn, isn't there?"

"I suppose so! Would you like to go for a swim now?"

Beth nodded and together they stepped into the pool.

"It's amazing how the water springs back into the pool, as though it's alive," she marveled.

"This water *is* alive," Harry confirmed. "Living water— that's what Narcissus calls it."

The pool was cool and inviting as they waded in deeper. Harry ducked his head under the surface and Beth followed. There, Beth watched as Harry opened his mouth and inhaled deeply. His eyes lit up as he let the water fill him, just as he'd learned to do before. The experience had the same effect as the first time—an indescribable feeling of wholeness. "Don't be afraid," he gurgled as the water and bubbles escaped through his nose and mouth.

"I'm not afraid, Harry," she answered and began to breathe in and let the water enter her lungs. Her smile indicated she was experiencing the same instant fullness as Harry.

"I have the feeling I will never be thirsty again!" Beth said as the water spread throughout her being. Harry smiled back, and with their hands clasped together, they floated under the surface until they were satisfied.

Beside them, in the center of the pool, the monolithic pinnacle of stone jetted upward to the surface. They turned to study the features of the rock: polished granite, smooth and colorful with veins of beautiful precious stones flowing through it. Harry remembered standing on the flat surface where the rock protruded just above the water. Then, as though it was planned, they floated upward until they were standing on the surface of the water. Harry gestured to Beth that she walk over and step onto the top of the pinnacle. She did so and immediately saw her reflection in the cascade of water that spilled down from the sea above like a clear sheet of glass. She sensed that she had been transformed somehow. She felt new and more alive than ever.

"How are you two doing?" Narcissus called from the bank.

They both responded with gleaming smiles.

"I'd like you to come over here, if you would."

Beth stepped off of the stone and onto the surface of the pool as though she was used to walking on water. Together they made their way across the water to the grass and sat down with the Archangel.

"There is something I wish to discuss with you," he said somberly.

"What is it?" Harry responded with concern.

"When we found your bodies in the boat, lying at the bottom of the bay, neither of you were breathing any longer. You were, in fact, deceased, so to speak. This does not mean however, that you were dead."

"What *does* it mean?" Harry asked with increased urgency.

"It means that we found you just in time to make a difference. That is to say, if you wish to go back, I have been given permission to grant you that opportunity."

"And what if we would choose not to return..." Beth asked.

"If you choose to stay, we can have that arranged as well."

Harry looked at Beth and she stared back at him with wide eyes.

519

"We could go back!" Beth exclaimed.

"Or we can stay . . . " Harry added.

"I love it here!" she stated. "What will we go back to that could compare to this?"

"I agree," Harry said. "But how do you feel about the lives we might have shared together back in Isles End?"

"I want that, too!"

"We can't have both, can we?" Harry questioned the angel.

"Of course you can, Harry. You can go back to Isles End and live out your lives, whatever course they take, and then someday return here. It's simple."

"So we *can* have both," Beth confirmed with a thoughtful expression on her face. "I kind of like that option, too. What do you think, Harry?"

"What do you have to say about it, Narcissus?" Harry turned to the angel. "Do you see anything in our future that would make a significant difference to us?"

"Well, yes . . . there is something, or rather . . . someone."

"Who?" they both asked together.

"I see," the angel said slowly, ". . . I see, a child."

"A child?" Harry asked with a confused expression on his face.

"A child!" Beth said with complete understanding.

"Yes," Narcissus interceded. "*Your* child, Harry."

"Oh!"

A warm feeling came over both Harry and Beth as they gazed at each other with wonder and delight.

"That sounds nice!" Harry exclaimed excitedly. "What do you think?" he said looking back at Beth.

"I like that!" she answered.

"Life on earth will still have its challenges, Harry," Narcissus added, "not like here."

"I think I have the strength to handle it, thanks to all that you have done!"

"Alright," the Seraph spoke, "if you are both in agreement, I will see about reviving your bodies so they are ready to receive you."

"Narcissus, there is something else . . . maybe, that you could take care of?"

"I know what you are about to ask, Harry. Consider it already done."

"Really?"

"Yes, Harry, it's been taken care of."

Beth listened with curiosity but kept silent.

"I want you both to walk back out and stand there on the surface of that solid rock at the center of the pool."

They both stood and faced the Archangel.

"Will we see you again?" Harry asked.

"Anything is possible, my friend, but either way, I will always be watching over you."

"Don't you mean, guarding over me?" Harry tried to joke.

"Yes, Harry, I will be your guardian angel, just as Agalliao will guard over Beth."

She grinned while they spoke; then Harry turned to her.

"Are you ready, Miss Fairbanks?"

"I am!"

"Well then, good bye, until next time, Narcissus!" Harry leaned forward and the angel embraced them both.

"Until we meet again," the angel smiled.

The two walked lightly across the surface of the water and stood side by side on the flat crest of the monolith.

"Oh, Harry," Narcissus put forth suddenly.

"Yes," Harry answered obediently.

"There was one more thing I wanted to share with you before you return."

"Okay . . ."

"It's about Elohim, the one who has made all of this possible—"

"Yes!"

"There is one more thing I want you to know about him," Narcissus proposed.

"What is it?" Harry asked, wondering at the hesitancy of the archangel.

"Well, Harry, I just wanted you to know . . . Elohim—"

Harry and Beth stood silent, anticipating the angel's words.

"He has a Son!"

Just as they heard the words, "He has a Son" proceed from the angel's mouth, both Harry and Beth felt themselves transported peacefully back through the supernatural and bound for home. The next thing Harry knew, he was stretching his arms and legs under the sheets and covers of his bed. The sun was coming up and he wondered how long he'd been sleeping. What day of the week was it, and had he been dreaming about something? He remembered going downtown for a meeting with Abraham Dante to discuss the remodeling projects . . .

Then it all came back to him!

Where was Beth?

His phone rang.

"Hello?"

"Harry, it's Beth!"

"Good morning—!"

"Harry, I had the most fantastic dream!"

40
Home Again

"Beth, where are you?"

"I'm home in my bed. Where are you?"

"I'm in my bed, too! I just woke up. I don't know if I actually slept, but I feel rested."

"Me, too! It was all real . . . wasn't it, Harry?"

Harry was tempted to play dumb, but this was too fresh and personal. "Yes, dear, it was all real and I was with you the entire time."

"I want to see you!"

"I can't wait."

"I don't know about you, but I'm starving. They do a nice breakfast at Belmar's on the weekends. Can we meet there?"

"Give me time to take a shower and I'll see you in half an hour!"

Everything that had transpired since Harry had met with Abraham the night before *did* seem like a dream, but the more he considered the horrible and wonderful details, the more real they became. It took a while to put all the pieces together, but by the time he was on the road, he remembered everything clearly.

Beth's Karmann Ghia was already in the parking lot when Harry pulled his truck into the nearest space. Inside, she was seated at the same table they had shared not so long ago. She waved him over and as he approached, she jumped out of her seat and embraced him. He responded with equal passion, and after a moment, she sat back down and he slid onto the bench across from her. She had already ordered their coffee and Harry eagerly sipped from the cup in front of him.

"Harry, my head is whirling!" she said reaching her hand across the table.

"Yes, what happened to us—it's extraordinary," he said taking her hand in his.

"I really would have believed it was a dream," she continued, "if you hadn't quickly confirmed that you were there with me. I spent the entire morning going over every detail."

"Yes," Harry said, "I imagine we will be doing that for quite some time!"

"I'm so glad it's Sunday!" Beth sighed, sipping her coffee. "As refreshed and vibrant as I feel, I think I'd still be quite useless if I had to be at work today. What I keep thinking, is . . . where do we go from here?"

Harry understood the feeling. It had already crossed his mind, too. "You mean, how does one go back to a normal life and business as usual after going through an experience so unbelievable?"

"Yes! I don't imagine our lives will ever be the same—"

"I think we can forget about living ordinary lives. After what we've been through, how can our future together be anything but extraordinary?" he said, smiling.

After Harry and Beth studied their menus, the waitress

took their orders and refilled their cups. The room began to fill with local patrons who came in to enjoy the weekend brunch.

"Hello there, you two!" a man's voice startled them both. Harry looked up to see Reese Orchard walking in from the lobby.

"And how are you two doing this fine morning?" He grinned as he approached their table. "Looks like we all had the same thing in mind. I almost went to the cafe down the street but they have such a great brunch here on the weekends!"

"We're doing fine," Harry answered. He was immediately wondering what Reese's involvement had been with Abraham regarding the warehouses on the waterfront.

"Reese, Mr. Dante was working with you on those old buildings down on the wharf—"

"Yes, I have a meeting with him here this morning to discuss the matter further. There are a few things I'm anxious about, but I'm sorry, that's not your concern. He did mention that you've been looking at some original plans from the buildings in Old Towne."

"That's right," Harry admitted uncomfortably, "I think incorporating the designs from those plans would work well with the buildings on the wharf." Except Harry knew that Mr. Dante wouldn't be showing up this morning, or ever. That, he was sure of, but he wasn't about to mention anything to Reese.

"Well, I think we all agree that Isles End could use a face lift!" Reese said. "You know, I'd better grab a table. Abraham should be here any minute. Good to see you both!"

Reese made his way to the other side of the room and found an empty booth.

Beth leaned toward Harry and spoke in a low voice. "Do you suppose that Reese knows anything about Abraham Dante or Rachael Sapphire?"

"I'm not positive, but somehow I don't think so. He's always seemed genuine to me. A bit peculiar, but he's never given me the feeling he has some dark design in his makeup. I wonder if Narcissus would have answered that question for us. I meant to ask him about a couple of different people."

Beth laughed. "You mean like, hey Narcissus, is there anyone in our immediate circle that are not who they appear to be?"

"I think that already goes without saying."

"Maybe we'll just have to figure a few things out for ourselves," Beth suggested as their breakfast arrived.

They both made quick work of their meals and sat drinking their third round of coffee. Harry looked over to see Reese still sitting alone with a newspaper. He wondered how it would affect Mr. Orchard when Abraham Dante never showed up again.

"Harry, there is something I wanted to do today," Beth began.

"What is that, my dear?"

"There are some canned goods in my back seat. I want to deliver them to my aunt. I wanted to check in on her anyway.

Would you like to come with me?"

"Of course!"

"We could go now if you don't have anything else to do."

"Alright, will you drive, and I can leave my truck here?"

"You've got a deal."

"Oh, Beth, there's something else—"

"Yes, Harry?"

"I thought of a question we should have asked Narcissus!"

"What's that?"

"Boy . . . or girl?"

"What?"

"Will we have a boy, or a girl?" Harry came out with it. "It would help to know so that we could narrow down the list of names to choose from!"

Beth was puzzled for a moment by Harry's teasing expression, then she leaned forward and stated, "I already know. If it's a boy, we will call him, Harry junior, but I should remind you, darling, we're not even married yet!"

"That was my next thought!" Harry grinned confidently. "We're going to have to do something about that, aren't we?"

"Are you proposing to me right here in the restaurant?"

"I would gladly, but I actually have something else in mind. I want to take you somewhere. Maybe after we visit your aunt, you'll come with me."

"We're burning daylight, darling!"

Without bothering Reese, they exited Belmar's and were

on their way to Beth's aunt's home. As they walked up to the front door, Harry wondered how the elderly woman would be doing since the last time he'd seen her. When Beth's aunt greeted them at the door, they could hardly believe their eyes.

"Why, hello, you two," she welcomed them cheerfully.

"Auntie, you look . . . great!"

"Thank you, Beth dear. Come in, come in, both of you."

Harry held the bag of canned goods while Beth embraced her aunt and then followed them inside.

"Yes, dear, I can't explain it, but I feel like a new woman. It's as though a heavy burden has been lifted—I just can't figure out why! I woke up this morning and had breakfast, and I didn't choke once! Then I walked to the bathroom and stood before the mirror, just like I do every morning, and I suddenly realized that I was standing up straight! You know how my back has been in such horrible shape? Well, that horrible lump is gone! Look at me!" she said gaily and spun around like a school girl.

"Oh, careful, Auntie!" Beth warned.

"It's like I'm twenty years younger. I want to go out. I want to see some of my old friends."

Harry gazed at Ms. Matson's back and shoulders, and sure enough the lump was gone. Her back was miraculously healed! Somehow, Narcissus had not only known what Harry's request was going to be, even before he asked it, but the angel had somehow found a way to see that the cruel specter that had attached itself to the poor woman's back was fully removed. He guessed that the woman was spiritually healed as well, and would probably be speaking for herself again.

"There's a dear friend of mine," she continued, "whom I always see at the bank. I feel as though I've neglected her, though I'm not sure why."

"It's never too late to connect with an old friend," Beth agreed.

"You are absolutely right, my dear. That's exactly what I'm going to do. Now, how are you two doing? You both make such a handsome couple. We must get together more often. I want to have you both over for dinner soon. I have a recipe for the most wonderful homemade noodles. I put them in chicken broth. You will just love it!"

"Did you hear that, Harry? Auntie wants to have us over for dinner."

"Yes, that will be fun!"

Beth's aunt walked over to Harry. "I'm glad you're going to be part of the family," she stated and gave him a warm hug. Harry responded likewise with a look of surprise at Beth. He didn't realize her aunt knew they were planning a lifetime commitment, but he was happy she had been freed of the evil oppression. How she had ever come under the influence of the ghoulish attachment was a mystery, but just the fact that Narcissus had been instrumental in the healing process of the poor woman was enough for him to accept her without reservations.

"See you soon, Auntie," Beth called as she and Harry walked back to her car. Beth's aunt waved back energetically as they sped off.

"What do you make of that?" Harry asked.

"I know exactly what happened," Beth answered. "Your angel friend helped my Auntie. I'm so happy!"

"So am I, Beth!" Harry said, feeling quite pleased.

"Now, where are we going?"

"Alright, go past the bridge and then turn right."

Beth followed Harry's directions as they wound up away from town. Soon they came to Top of the Hill Road.

"Turn here," he instructed her.

The fall colors of Isles End were almost in full bloom. The maple trees were bright yellow and orange, while the firs kept their rich dark green coats. Beth followed the windy road up through the wooded hillsides until they reached the top. The property wasn't quite like it had been the last time Harry had visited. There was no luxury home, stamped concrete, or landscaped yard, but it was beautiful just as it was. Beth parked and they got out.

"'So, what do you think?" he asked, presenting the property like it was a gift.

"It's very nice, Harry! What is it?"

"I'm going to buy this land and build a home here! Our home, if you approve."

She looked around and studied the landscape. Harry took

her hand and they walked past the pond and under the shade of the weeping willows.

"Is this another attempt at a proposal, Harry?"

"Well, I guess it does sound that way, but really I just wanted you to see this property—find out what you might think about living here . . ."

"I see!" she said gazing around. "Well, the answer is yes, it's a beautiful location!"

"I knew you would like it."

"Look at that," she pointed. "You can see all of Isles End from here, and the bay too!"

"Yes, isn't it wonderful?"

"I love it, Harry . . . I just love it."

"After Abraham showed me who he really was, he gave me a glimpse of what I might do with this property. He showed me a beautiful home right there," he pointed. "The grounds were completely landscaped, as though I did it all myself! He presented the finished product to me, expecting that I would accept his offer; the catch being that I would serve him in some way. I told him I'd rather do the work on my own. He didn't like that. I think he chose to hurt you, as a way to get even with me. I'm so sorry, Beth!"

"It wasn't your fault, Harry. I think he also knew something that even I didn't know—the fact that Agalliao, or Leo, was guarding over me."

"Yes, you're right. They had many reasons to try to harm

us, but I feel that we are safe now. We have some powerful friends in high places."

"Yes," Beth agreed as Harry wrapped his arms around her, "we do have someone looking out for us, don't we?"

"Beth," he whispered as he pulled her close. "I am so excited—everything we have to look forward to—our future!"

"So am I, Harry!"

"But I just want to say to you right now, I'm not in a hurry. I mean, I want to discover each and every moment with you, like it's a treasure hunt with lots of wonderful surprises hidden around every corner."

"Harry, that is the most wonderful thing anyone has ever said to me!"

Pulling Beth tightly against his chest, Harry let his lips brush gently against hers. It felt so right that he kissed her again. She responded with a yielding sigh. As the day began to move into late afternoon, the couple sat and watched the view change as a few wispy clouds drifted by and the setting sun created shadows and reflections of sparkling light across the silhouette of the town below. Rich colors emerged from the shaded areas and lights began to flicker in the windows of the homes.

While it was still light, Beth drove Harry back to his truck at Belmar's. They were tempted to go inside again, but feeling tired now, they agreed to call it a day. Harry promised he would see her the next morning at ABC. He needed to check in and see that his sub-contractors had finished up properly. He kissed Beth again and said goodnight, drove home, and went straight to bed.

Morning came quickly. Harry hadn't slept so soundly for a long time. Invigorated, he followed his usual routine: shower, potato in the microwave, cell phone and measuring tape on the belt, briefcase in hand. He drove directly to the Ivory Lane project. As usual, his guys were there on time and working hard. The plumber was already well into the installation of the drain system while Ed and Butch were busy doing pick-up work.

"How's it going, Boss?" Ed called out.

"Hey," Harry said walking carefully around nails and boards. "I feel kind of bad," he began.

"What's up?" Butch asked with concern.

"Well, I was having you guys work on Saturdays so that we could get started on the old drug store downtown and then the warehouses on the wharf, and now the whole deal has fallen through. I'm really sorry."

"Not to worry," Ed offered immediately.

"Yeah, no problem," Butch joined in.

"We don't mind putting in overtime," Ed continued.

"We like the extra money," Butch added with a grin.

"You guys are the best," Harry said, relieved. "I'll make it up to you. I just have to find some more work now!"

"So we have next Saturday off?" Ed asked.

"Yeah, let's do that," Harry answered, "and thanks for everything. I wasn't sure how you would feel about the news."

"No big deal, Harry. It's all good." Ed reassured him.

"Well, listen. I've got to go up to Advanced Bio-Cell and see how things look there. Then I may be back to put on my tool belt."

"That'll be something to see!" Butch shouted.

They all laughed as Harry climbed into his truck and drove away. In no time at all, he was pulling into the parking lot of Advanced Bio-Cell. He thought he might find Beth alone and steal a kiss, but she was busy with Valerie loading the last of the files onto the new computers that had arrived. He admired the water feature and oasis as he walked through the foyer toward the reception area.

"Hello, ladies! Wonderful morning, isn't it?" he offered with a smile.

Valerie nodded with a smirk. "'Tis," she answered while she kept her eyes on her work.

Beth looked up and grinned. "Hello, Mr. Turner," she said with a twinkle in her eye.

"I'm just going to take a look around," Harry explained, "see how things are shaping up."

"Alright, let me know if there's anything else you need," Beth offered.

He winked back and started down the hallway. He took the elevator to the basement first. The rooms were empty and everything looked finished. There was still equipment that had been ordered by ABC, but everything else was done, even down to the lighting, plumbing fixtures, and paint.

Back in the elevator, Harry went to the upper floor where the cubicles had been added in the large windowed room. It too, looked completed. He crossed the room admiring the finished product and was startled as two men appeared around a corner.

Bill Algren and Dr. Yang were walking toward him.

"Harry, good to see you," Bill stated.

"Greetings, Mr. Turner," Shushi said politely.

Before Harry could respond, Bill continued, "Harry, Shushi and I were just commenting on how great the place looks. Good job! I guess we're ready to really move in."

"Yes, Harry, you've provided excellent leadership here with all your subs. Thank you," Shushi extended his arm, smiling.

"You're welcome, both of you," Harry said taking the doctor's hand. Shushi gripped Harry's hand and squeezed extra hard just for a moment and winked. Harry wasn't sure what that meant exactly, as he didn't know the doctor very well. He decided that Shushi was just very pleased with the progress.

"Make sure you get a bill to us soon," Mr. Algren suggested. "We want to keep good guys like you in business. We may need you again, you know?"

"Yes, thanks, Bill, I'll be getting an invoice out to you just as soon as I receive the billings from my subs."

"Very good then, Harry. We hope to hear from you soon."

Bill and Shushi continued their walk along the bright side of the room where the full length windows lined the walls, while

Harry continued his inspection. Satisfied that everything had been accomplished according to plan, he started back toward the elevator and there was Shushi waiting for him.

"Harry, can I speak with you for a moment?"

"Of course, what is it?"

"I simply wished to inform you that we will not be seeing Preston Hart for a while."

"Is there something wrong?"

"He's going to be fine, but I believe the pressure of the move was too much for him. You understand—the deadlines, all that goes along with the kind of work we do; you remember our discussion recently. It can be daunting when you are dealing with such serious work and all the possible repercussions. The stress must have been building for some time, and now he seems to have suffered a nervous breakdown."

"Wow, I'm sorry to hear that. I hope he's going to be alright."

"I'm sure he'll recover, though it may take some time."

"Be sure to wish him my best. He seemed very nice."

"Oh yes, he's a very likable man, and a good person. I think he just got terribly confused and distracted for a time. In the meantime, we are pressing forward with our research and development on a more modified scale. It seems we are far more concerned with improving people's health right now than we are with reproducing human beings."

The elevator rang and the doors opened. Harry smiled

courteously and stepped inside. Preston Hart with a nervous breakdown! It seemed more likely that it would have been Dr. Yang. He was the one who had always seemed overly anxious. *You just never know,* Harry thought.

Back on the main floor, Harry stepped out of the elevator and into the lobby. There was no sign of Beth or Valerie, but at the far end of the room Reese Orchard was just entering the building.

He caught Harry's attention and hurried forward.

"Harry, so good to see you," he exclaimed. "I'm here to meet with Bill, but you were next on my list of contacts. Do you have a minute?"

"Of course. What can I do for you?"

"Here, let's sit down. This won't take long, but I want to keep it confidential."

"Okay," Harry responded as Reese found a chair next to the fountain.

"Well, it seems that Abraham Dante and his assistant, Rachael Sapphire, have vanished! Not only that, but the financial backing they were purported to have . . . well, the accounts were never valid. You received a check from them recently, isn't that right?"

"Yes!"

"Did you deposit it?"

Harry nodded.

"I believe it was a sizable sum—"

"Twenty thousand!"

"Have you heard anything about that deposit from your bank?"

"No, I've been so busy lately I haven't—"

"Don't worry about it," Reese interrupted quietly. "Here's the thing. I don't know what has happened to Mr. Dante and his lovely assistant, or if we will even see them again, but I have control over these properties and I'm not going to let something good escape my grasp!" Reese reached into his jacket and produced a check. "Here is another check for twenty thousand dollars, Harry. Take care of the bank fees, if there are any, and consider yourself assigned to both projects, that is, the warehouses on the wharf and the drug store. That money should be enough to get started, and we can work out the details and contracts later. I don't know what those two were up to, and I feel a bit silly having been played, if in fact, that is the case. But the good news is that I wasn't taken for anything. I guess we all make mistakes."

Harry accepted the money and stood up as Reese Orchard climbed out of his chair.

"Harry, please don't mention this to anyone, at least not yet. Let's see if those two resurface first and have any kind of legitimate excuses, though I am doubtful at this point. So far, I can find no sign that they were ever even here, and believe me, I have my sources. The whole thing is very irregular."

"I won't say a thing to anyone—you can count on that!"

"Thank you, Harry. So, you're just about done here, then?"

"Just finishing up the final details, yes."

"Great! Let's concentrate on the Ivory Lane project then, and in a couple of weeks we will start on the drug store."

"Sounds good."

"Harry . . ."

"Yes?"

"I'm glad to have you as my contractor, really!"

"Thanks, Reese, I appreciate that."

"Right," he said tapping Harry on the shoulder.

Harry scanned the room to see if Beth had returned to her post, but it seemed that he was alone. The building was just about finished now and he wondered what kind of clients would soon be visiting a place like this. People from all walks of life, he imagined, would be coming in through those doors, looking for hope and a way to improve their lives.

Harry decided to drive back to Isles End and try calling Beth later. Just as he walked through the front doors, he heard her voice.

"Harry!"

He turned to see her running in his direction.

"Wait for me," she shouted as she hurried toward him.

He held the door open for her as she fell into his arms. Together, they made their way to the parking lot.

"Mr. Algren told me to take the rest of the day off!" Beth

said as they stopped by her car.

"Nice," Harry commented. "Do you know why?"

"He mentioned all the overtime I've been putting in and suggested we might like to have some time together."

"Wow—that's the kind of boss to have!"

"Yes," she agreed. "So, what are your plans now?"

"Well, I was going to visit the project on Ivory Lane and let the guys know I would be working with them for a few days, but since Mr. Algren has so generously let you off work to spend time with me, I can hardly disappoint him now, can I?"

"You are so considerate," Beth giggled.

"So why don't you follow me. There's something I want to show you."

"What is it this time?"

"You'll see," he said. "Stay with me!"

Beth wondered at first where Harry might be leading her but she soon realized they were going to his house. He waited for her as she parked behind him and came over to open her door.

"Welcome to my home," he said with a wave of his arm. "Will you step into my parlor?"

"Said the spider to the fly," she finished the phrase for him, with a laugh.

"I don't know what I have to eat in this place," Harry said as he unlocked the door and let her in. "Potatoes for sure—are you hungry?"'

"Actually, I'm fine," she answered. "This is a cozy little

place—I like it."

"Yeah, for a single guy, it's perfect." He hung up his coat in the front closet, placing hers alongside it. "They look good together," he grinned.

"So is this what you wanted to show me?"

"Not exactly—come over here by the bed."

"What?" she responded with surprise. "You don't waste any time, do you Mr. Turner!"

Harry realized that it hadn't come out quite the way he had planned, and he laughed at himself. "Now I'm embarrassed. But seriously, come over here . . . it's this," he said pointing to something on the floor.

As Beth made her way closer, she realized there was a large stately-looking chest sitting at the foot of his bed.

"Why, it's beautiful, Harry."

"Yes, it is rather attractive, isn't it?"

Beth sat down on the edge of the bed and ran her hands over the leathery straps and the shiny brass. "Is it some kind of heirloom?"

"It wasn't, but I guess it is now. I haven't told you about how I originally met Narcissus."

Beth sat with silent expectation.

"You see, I was beginning the demo work at the Ivory Lane project and we found this chest in the basement. The home had burned down, but the chest was in pristine condition, just as you see it now. Later that evening after the guys left, I was so curious about the contents, I managed with a little effort, to open it. The course of events that led up to this occasion were slightly more complicated, but basically, after I opened it, Narcissus slowly appeared before me and informed me that he'd been held there for quite a long time!"

Beth listened with wonder, taking it all in.

Harry proceeded to tell her the rest of the story as best as he could, describing each time he'd had an encounter with the angel after the initial discovery. Beth admitted that his reluctance to share these experiences with anyone made complete sense.

"This all reminds me of that story where the old miser is visited by three ghosts during the night. Do you know the one I'm talking about?"

"Yes, I suppose there are some similarities," he mused.

"Or, that movie where the angel gets his wings."

"There are probably many stories like that. I haven't really thought about it."

"You've been pretty busy. I can't imagine that you've even had the time."

They sat there at the foot of Harry's bed with the chest resting below them like an object of mystery, silently containing its secrets.

"So, Harry, can I look inside?"

"That's exactly what I had in mind," he answered. "Come over to this side," he said as he got down on his knees and prepared to raise the lid. Beth complied, and as soon as she was situated beside the chest, he opened it.

"Lean forward," he encouraged her.

Beth shifted her position and tilted her head into the cavity. Immediately, she was overwhelmed with the most euphoric scent she had ever experienced. Harry watched while she breathed in the intoxicating fragrance. He could tell from her reaction, and from his close proximity, that the aroma had become even stronger since the last time he had raised the lid.

"Harry, I've never smelled anything so exotic!"

"It's really something, isn't it?"

"It's magical! What else is in here?" she asked as she lifted a section of cardboard.

"Oh yes, something I received from Narcissus while I was in the city doing some research. That is another story I will have to tell you sometime."

Beth studied the sign and then read aloud, "Will work for friends." She turned it over and on the other side she read, "Be careful, Harry."

"Interesting. I suppose you know what it means?"

"I'm still piecing it together . . ."

"Harry! I love you," Beth suddenly gushed affectionately, raising her hand to caress his face.

"You do?"

"Of course! Do you think I'd be here if I didn't?"

"No. I guess I just haven't heard those words spoken to me for some time."

"I love you, Harry! Can I tell you that?"

"Please do, darling!"

"I love you . . ." she whispered again softly.

Harry wanted to propose to Beth right there on the spot, but he held himself back. He was confident he knew what the answer would be, and as far as his feelings for her, they had been true since the beginning. Again, he wished he had asked Narcissus more about their future, but then he mildly scolded himself. Some things were not meant to be known. Why spoil all the wonderful surprises that lay ahead?

Beth reached into the chest again and pulled out a clear plastic zip-lock bag.

"What's this?" she asked, holding it up in the air.

"Oh, that is a branch from a fern."

"It's unusually magnificent! Where is it from?"

"You might not believe me if I told you."

"After everything we've been through? Try me!"

"Well, what if I told you it was from the oldest garden we know of . . . called Eden?"

Beth listened with amazement while Harry continued.

"That branch is from one of the ferns that a woman in the garden used to make a covering for herself."

"It's so delicate. So you really believe it's from the original Garden of Eden?"

"I don't know for sure. I'm just saying that when I watched her begin to cover herself with these fern branches, she suddenly called out the name, Adam."

"And Narcissus took you there?"

"Yes."

"Well, Harry, I would say there is no doubting it then. This fern branch is from Eden! Amazing."

She looked deeper into the chest and pulled out a sheet of paper that was folded in half.

"Shall I open this?"

"Please."

She unfolded the paper and studied it.

"Beth, will you read it aloud?"

"Yes, Harry," she answered, and held the form up and read aloud:

"Harry, I'm going to tell you something about yourself that you have never heard before. It is this: There are those who have had no knowledge of Elohim or any of His ways. You are one of these. Yet by instinct, you have confirmed living in the certainty of His ways just by your natural obedient nature and willingness to observe goodness. You are proof that Elohim's edicts are not unknown rules, imposed on anyone from without, but rather woven into the very fabric of your being. There is something deep within you that echoes His yes and no, and the understanding of what is right and wrong. Your response to His yes and no will become public knowledge someday. In the meantime, though, seek out that truth which has been planted in your heart. ~Narcissus."

Beth finished reading the letter and then smiled warmly. "That's a very deep and thought-provoking letter, don't you think?"

"No question! I'm still afraid to realize the full extent of its meaning, but I'm working on it."

Beth read the letter again in silence while Harry watched her. She was so lovely, he realized. He already knew this, but suddenly he saw her in a way he had not appreciated yet. As she sat there studying the message again on his behalf—a message he'd received from an angel, no less—Harry saw her in a new light. Knowing now that Jennifer loved her, too, he felt a deeper affection for this woman who had intrigued him from the moment he'd met her. And now, there she was, sitting across from him under the most unusual circumstances, and she seemed so comfortable there, so right at home. How could this be?

Beth leaned forward again to breathe in the perfumed scent of the chest. Harry watched as her nostrils flared and she inhaled the contents of all the chest had to offer. He himself was not only profoundly intoxicated by the aroma wafting from the strong box, but was almost equally as drunk from the scent this lovely woman radiated all around her. Was it her, or the chest? Now the two appeared to mix together in the air, causing Harry to want to sing. He refrained, however—but he was, nonetheless, singing in his inner being.

"And what is this?" Beth asked as she looked even further into the cavity of the chest.

Harry had no idea. Was there something else hidden in the recesses of the chest that he had overlooked? There couldn't be! Unless . . . well, what then?

"Harry," Beth squealed. "What is this? What kind of trick are you trying to play here?"

What was it? Harry was anxious to find out for himself.

Beth reached down and picked up whatever it was she had found.

"Oh, Harry! The answer is a deep, heartfelt, YES!"

"Yes?"

"Of course, yes . . . you handsome, wonderful, sensitive, thoughtful man!"

What . . .?

Whatever she had found inside the box, she lifted up into the air and Harry saw something sparkling so bright he wondered if she had found some kind of magical light hidden in the recesses.

"What did you find?" Harry asked with mild trepidation.

"Harry, you are too clever and wonderful," Beth answered as she slid the object onto her finger. "The answer is yes, Harry! Stop playing around. I'm saying *yes* to you, you clever fool!"

He watched as she held her left hand up proudly. On her ring finger was the largest diamond Harry had ever seen, not that he'd seen a lot of diamond rings in his time. But this stone, set in a solitary white gold band, had to be at least two carats, maybe more.

"Wow," he said with astonishment.

"Wow is right!" Beth responded. "This rock is huge! How did you do it? When did you have the time?"

"Well . . ."

"I don't even want to know," she squealed again reaching over and grabbing him. "I can't believe it. It's beautiful, Harry, just beautiful!"

He would have to tell her at some point, and he knew she would be thrilled regardless. A wedding gift from an angel? Who could complain about that? Besides, that's just the way she was, always finding the positive! But for now, he let them both enjoy the moment. It was wonderful. Narcissus was to blame either way, Harry laughed to himself, and so he decided to join with her in the experience.

"Darling, I do love you," Harry exclaimed as he watched her revel in her joy. "But I haven't yet asked you the question you have just answered!"

"You're right . . ."

"Well, I'm already kneeling! Beth, will you spend the rest of your life with me? Will you do me the honor of marrying me and becoming my wife?"

"I will, Harry!"

"YES!"

"Harry, I have never known such happiness! Thank you."

"And you don't think this might be too soon?" Harry ventured with a smile.

"Normally, maybe," Beth answered. "But when you have the preordained confirmation of an Archangel, it's kind of easy to accept fate, especially when there is already love and chemistry!"

What could he say to that? He had never had the opportunity to engage in this kind of closeness before either. Almost, that is . . . once upon a time … but that seemed long ago now. *Life is for the living, right?* Jennifer had set him free. Not only that, but she had given him her own personal blessing.

Thank you, Jenny!

Harry received Beth's embrace as she reached over to wrap her arms around him.

They held onto each other for a while, sharing caresses, and occasionally Beth would hold up her hand and admire the stone that shined so brightly on her finger. Harry almost felt as though he had entered the supernatural again. The flow of time seemed to have come to a halt as they knelt intimately at the foot of his bed, enjoying the scent of the Archangel's chest.

"This is nice, isn't it, Beth?"

"Yes, very nice."

"Are you uncomfortable?" he asked, realizing that they had been kneeling on the floor for a while.

"I'm okay," she answered.

"But would you be more comfortable on the bed?" he asked with purely altruistic motives.

"Yes, Harry, I would," she replied. "I know you're a gentleman, and I feel completely safe in your arms," she answered as she climbed up off the floor and onto the bed.

Harry joined her and they lay there side by side.

"Is this okay?" he asked her.

"You mean us, together in your bed?"

"Yes, that . . ."

"I think we just might get away with it, Harry. We are not committing any crime, are we?"

"No, dear, I suppose not."

They held hands and let the moments slip away as they drifted off. Harry didn't know how much time had passed but after a while, he tugged at her arm.

"Beth, do you remember the last words that Narcissus spoke to us?"

"Yes, my love," Beth sounded barely awake. "I've been puzzled by those words ever since." After a pause, she repeated the words aloud. "Elohim . . . He has a Son!"

Harry considered the implications of the words as he lay there beside her. "Yes, darling, those were the last words that Narcissus chose to share with us. They must have some real significance!"

"What do you suppose it means, Harry?"

"Elohim has a Son? I'm not entirely sure yet, but I have a feeling that we are going to find out. It's my guardian angel's wish—his last words to us. So I believe we will find out the truth of it . . . very soon!"

Beth sighed and managed to whisper, "Yes, I want that—"

before she finally drifted off to sleep.

"So do I," Harry answered while Beth dozed off. "We will find out who the Son is, and I have a feeling this will bring us into a new understanding of the very purpose of our lives."

"Yes," Beth surprised Harry with a sleepy response. "The very purpose of our lives . . . "

Epilogue of a Dream

Harry was a boy again and his mother was seeing him off to school. She handed him his lunch and kissed him good-bye. As he turned to begin the half-mile walk to school, she warned him to be careful and shouted a short prayer that his guardian angel would protect him. He laughed and waved. His mother looked so lovely as she smiled proudly and waved back.

He continued down the road. Everything was so familiar. He had walked this path many times; the stone wall that ran along the roadside, every cracked square of sidewalk, every twisted tree, the road signs, every bird, they all knew him well. They belonged to him!

As he neared the bottom of the road, he could see a small bridge ahead. He remembered now being told not to go near it, but as he continued forward, he couldn't remember why. To the side, he could see below where a stream ran under the structure. He realized now that he'd been through this scenario many times before. It had been a recurring nightmare! Each time, he had jumped over the side to avoid crossing, and landed in the creek below where a menacing figure waited for him.

There was no fear now as Harry ignored the impulse to jump. The bridge felt inviting as he advanced. It didn't matter anymore whether he was "supposed" to cross or not. He was free. Casually now, Harry simply walked forward onto the overpass. Ahead, there was a sign. It read: *Bome Biv Land.* What does that mean? He heard a voice faintly speaking to him. It was Narcissus.

"Hello, Harry. I'm glad to see that you are free now."

"Yes, thank you, again!"

"You are welcome, my friend."

"Narcissus, what is this place?"

"Bome Biv Land is a place where a child, such as you are at this moment, can play and be at peace. You are safe here. Safe to be a child, to laugh and find wonder in the beauty of the world around you. Safe to be innocent and to explore without fear. Safe to grow up and become who you are meant to be."

"But where do the words themselves come from?"

"That remains a mystery for now, but someday, this knowledge too, will come to you."

"Will you always be able to visit me?"

"I'm sorry, but I don't know the answer to that question just yet. You can be sure that I will drop by whenever I have the opportunity, but I'll always be guarding over you."

"My guardian angel!"

"Yes, of course, now be at peace . . . and, sweet dreams!"

Harry turned and looked ahead to see some small children playing in the stream on the other side. He crossed to see other children climbing fruit trees bearing ripe apples, peaches, and pears. Further on, there was a park with swings and slides, and beyond that were more children riding ponies and *walking dogs, and rolling down grassy hillsides. Harry continued down the trail taking in all the scenery. The view changed as he walked further up the grassy road. He suddenly took notice that his arms and legs were no longer the limbs of a boy, but of a grown man! There was hair on his chest and his cheeks were rough. He was no longer a ten-year-old. Up ahead there was a scene that looked very familiar.*

It was a beautiful spread of land with a home, surrounded by wonderfully sculpted landscaping. He stepped over a narrow stream that spilled into a small pond shaded by two large weeping willows. Above the well-manicured yard was a glorious estate. Standing by the front door was his lovely wife, Beth, and in her arms was a small child. The whole scene was extraordinary! They stood there waving as he began to hurry toward them. Could it really be? "Welcome home, Harry," she said. "I've missed you!"

Harry moved over the top of the covers on the bed as he shifted his position. How comfortable he felt as he stretched his arms and legs in all directions.

"Hmmm?" he heard the warm voice of Beth stirring next to him.

"Oh, darling . . . " he said with a deep, sleepy sigh, "I just had the most wonderful dream!"

Thank you for reading Isles End.

Hope you enjoyed it!

We invite you to join us on facebook.

http://www.facebook.com/IslesEndThriller

* Share your thoughts about Isles End
* See what other fans have shared
* Correspond with the author

Maybe you have a friend who would enjoy the book?

Purchase additional copies at amazon.com